# The Complete Rose Campbell Story

## Eight Cousins and Rose in Bloom

Louisa May Alcott

# TABLE OF CONTENTS

ROSE IN BLOOM

Preface

The Author is quite aware of the defects of this little story, many of which were unavoidable, as it first appeared serially. But, as Uncle Alec's experiment was intended to amuse the young folks, rather than suggest educational improvements for the consideration of the elders, she trusts that these shortcomings will be overlooked by the friends of the Eight Cousins, and she will try to make amends in a second volume, which shall attempt to show The Rose in Bloom.

L.M.A.

## Chapter 1—Two Girls

Rose sat all alone in the big best parlor, with her little handkerchief laid ready to catch the first tear, for she was thinking of her troubles, and a shower was expected. She had retired to this room as a good place in which to be miserable; for it was dark and still, full of ancient furniture, sombre curtains, and hung all around with portraits of solemn old gentlemen in wigs, severe-nosed ladies in top-heavy caps, and staring children in little bob-tailed coats or short-waisted frocks. It was an excellent place for woe; and the fitful spring rain that pattered on the window-pane seemed to sob, "Cry away: I'm with you."

Rose really did have some cause to be sad; for she had no mother, and had lately lost her father also, which left her no home but this with her great-aunts. She had been with them only a week, and, though the dear old ladies had tried their best to make her happy, they had not succeeded very well, for she was unlike any child they had ever seen, and they felt very much as if they had the care of a low-spirited butterfly.

They had given her the freedom of the house, and for a day or two she had amused herself roaming all over it, for it was a capital old mansion, and was full of all manner of odd nooks, charming rooms, and mysterious passages. Windows broke out in unexpected places, little balconies overhung the garden most romantically, and there was a long upper hall full of curiosities from all parts of the world; for the Campbells had been sea-captains for generations.

Aunt Plenty had even allowed Rose to rummage in her great china closet a spicy retreat, rich in all the "goodies" that children love; but Rose seemed to care little for these toothsome temptations; and when that hope failed, Aunt Plenty gave up in despair.

Gentle Aunt Peace had tried all sorts of pretty needle-work, and planned a doll's wardrobe that would have won the heart of even an older child. But Rose took little interest in pink satin hats and tiny hose, though she sewed dutifully till her aunt caught her wiping tears away with the train of a wedding-dress, and that discovery put an end to the sewing society.

Then both old ladies put their heads together and picked out the model child of the neighbourhood to come and play with their niece. But Ariadne Blish was the worst failure of all, for Rose could not bear the sight of her, and said she was so like a wax doll she longed to give her a pinch and see if she would squeak. So prim little Ariadne was sent home, and the exhausted aunties left Rose to her own devices for a day or two.

Bad weather and a cold kept her in-doors, and she spent most of her time in the library where her father's books were stored. Here she read a great deal, cried a little, and dreamed many of the innocent bright dreams in which imaginative children find such comfort and delight. This suited her better than anything else, but it was not good for her, and she grew pale, heavy-eyed and listless, though Aunt Plenty gave her iron enough to make a cooking-stove, and Aunt Peace petted her like a poodle.

Seeing this, the poor aunties racked their brains for a new amusement and determined to venture a bold stroke, though not very hopeful of its success. They said nothing to Rose about their plan for this Saturday afternoon, but let her alone till the time came for the grand surprise, little dreaming that the odd child would find pleasure for herself in a most unexpected quarter.

Before she had time to squeeze out a single tear a sound broke the stillness, making her prick up her ears. It was only the soft twitter of a bird, but it seemed to be a peculiarly gifted bird, for while she listened the soft twitter changed to a lively whistle, then a trill, a coo, a chirp, and ended in a musical mixture of all the notes, as if the bird burst out laughing. Rose laughed also, and, forgetting her woes, jumped up, saying eagerly,

1

"It is a mocking-bird. Where is it?"

Running down the long hall, she peeped out at both doors, but saw nothing feathered except a draggle-tailed chicken under a burdock leaf. She listened again, and the sound seemed to be in the house. Away she went, much excited by the chase, and following the changeful song, it led her to the china-closet door.

"In there? How funny!" she said. But when she entered, not a bird appeared except the everlastingly kissing swallows on the Canton china that lined the shelves. All of a sudden Rose's face brightened, and, softly opening the slide, she peered into the kitchen. But the music had stopped, and all she saw was a girl in a blue apron scrubbing the hearth. Rose stared about her for a minute, and then asked abruptly,

"Did you hear that mocking-bird?"

"I should call it a phebe-bird," answered the girl, looking up with a twinkle in her black eyes.

"Where did it go?"

"It is here still."

"Where?"

"In my throat. Do you want to hear it?"

"Oh, yes! I'll come in." And Rose crept through the slide to the wide shelf on the other side, being too hurried and puzzled to go round by the door.

The girl wiped her hands, crossed her feet on the little island of carpet where she was stranded in a sea of soap-suds, and then, sure enough, out of her slender throat came the swallow's twitter, the robin's whistle, the blue-jay's call, the thrush's song, the wood-dove's coo, and many another familiar note, all ending as before with the musical ecstacy of a bobolink singing and swinging among the meadow grass on a bright June day.

Rose was so astonished that she nearly fell off her perch, and when the little concert was over clapped her hands delightedly.

"Oh, it was lovely! Who taught you?"

"The birds," answered the girl, with a smile, as she fell to work again.

"It is very wonderful! I can sing, but nothing half so fine as that. What is your name, please?"

"Phebe Moore."

"I've heard of phebe-birds; but I don't believe the real ones could do that," laughed Rose, adding, as she watched with interest the scattering of dabs of soft soap over the bricks, "May I stay and see you work? It is very lonely in the parlor."

"Yes, indeed, if you want to," answered Phebe, wringing out her cloth in a capable sort of way that impressed Rose very much.

"It must be fun to swash the water round and dig out the soap. I'd love to do it, only aunt wouldn't like it, I suppose," said Rose, quite taken with the new employment.

"You'd soon get tired, so you'd better keep tidy and look on."

"I suppose you help your mother a good deal?"

"I haven't got any folks."

"Why, where do you live, then?"

"I'm going to live here, I hope. Debby wants some one to help round, and I've come to try for a week."

"I hope you will stay, for it is very dull," said Rose, who had taken a sudden fancy to this girl, who sung like a bird and worked like a woman.

"Hope I shall; for I'm fifteen now, and old enough to earn my own living. You have come to stay a spell, haven't you?" asked Phebe, looking up at her guest and wondering how life could be dull to a girl who wore a silk frock, a daintily frilled apron, a pretty locket, and had her hair tied up with a velvet snood.

"Yes, I shall stay till my uncle comes. He is my guardian now, and I don't know what he will do with me. Have you a guardian?"

"My sakes, no! I was left on the poor-house steps a little mite of a baby, and Miss Rogers took a liking to me, so I've been there ever since. But she is dead now, and I take care of myself."

"How interesting! It is like Arabella Montgomery in the 'Gypsy's Child.' Did you ever read that sweet story?" asked Rose, who was fond of tales of found-lings, and had read many.

"I don't have any books to read, and all the spare time I get I run off into the woods; that rests me better than stories," answered Phebe, as she finished one job and began on another.

Rose watched her as she got out a great pan of beans to look over, and wondered how it would seem to have life all work and no play. Presently Phebe seemed to think it was her turn to ask questions, and said, wistfully,

"You've had lots of schooling, I suppose?"

"Oh, dear me, yes! I've been at boarding school nearly a year, and I'm almost dead with lessons. The more I got, the more Miss Power gave me, and I was so miserable that I 'most cried my eyes out. Papa never gave me hard things to do, and he always taught me so pleasantly I loved to study. Oh, we were so happy and so fond of one another! But now he is gone, and I am left all alone."

The tear that would not come when Rose sat waiting for it came now of its own accord two of them in fact and rolled down her cheeks, telling the tale of love and sorrow better than any words could do it.

For a minute there was no sound in the kitchen but the little daughter's sobbing and the sympathetic patter of the rain. Phebe stopped rattling her beans from one pan to another, and her eyes were full of pity as they rested on the curly head bent down on Rose's knee, for she saw that the heart under the pretty locket ached with its loss, and the dainty apron was used to dry sadder tears than any she had ever shed.

3

Somehow, she felt more contented with her brown calico gown and blue-checked pinafore; envy changed to compassion; and if she had dared she would have gone and hugged her afflicted guest.

Fearing that might not be considered proper, she said, in her cheery voice,

"I'm sure you ain't all alone with such a lot of folks belonging to you, and all so rich and clever. You'll be petted to pieces, Debby says, because you are the only girl in the family."

Phebe's last words made Rose smile in spite of her tears, and she looked out from behind her apron with an April face, saying in a tone of comic distress,

"That's one of my troubles! I've got six aunts, and they all want me, and I don't know any of them very well. Papa named this place the Aunt-hill, and now I see why."

Phebe laughed with her as she said encouragingly,

"Everyone calls it so, and it's a real good name, for all the Mrs. Campbells live handy by, and keep coming up to see the old ladies."

"I could stand the aunts, but there are dozens of cousins, dreadful boys all of them, and I detest boys! Some of them came to see me last Wednesday, but I was lying down, and when auntie came to call me I went under the quilt and pretended to be asleep. I shall have to see them some time, but I do dread it so." And Rose gave a shudder, for, having lived alone with her invalid father, she knew nothing of boys, and considered them a species of wild animal.

"Oh! I guess you'll like 'em. I've seen 'em flying round when they come over from the Point, sometimes in their boats and sometimes on horseback. If you like boats and horses, you'll enjoy yourself first-rate."

"But I don't! I'm afraid of horses, and boats make me ill, and I hate boys!" And poor Rose wrung her hands at the awful prospect before her. One of these horrors alone she could have borne, but all together were too much for her, and she began to think of a speedy return to the detested school.

Phebe laughed at her woe till the beans danced in the pan, but tried to comfort her by suggesting a means of relief.

"Perhaps your uncle will take you away where there ain't any boys. Debby says he is a real kind man, and always bring heaps of nice things when he comes."

"Yes, but you see that is another trouble, for I don't know Uncle Alec at all. He hardly ever came to see us, though he sent me pretty things very often. Now I belong to him, and shall have to mind him, till I am eighteen. I may not like him a bit, and I fret about it all the time."

"Well, I wouldn't borrow trouble, but have a real good time. I'm sure I should think I was in clover if I had folks and money, and nothing to do but enjoy myself," began Phebe, but got no further, for a sudden rush and tumble outside made them both jump.

"It's thunder," said Phebe.

"It's a circus!" cried Rose, who from her elevated perch had caught glimpses of a gay cart of some sort and several ponies with flying manes and tails.

The sound died away, and the girls were about to continue their confidences when old Debby appeared, looking rather cross and sleepy after her nap.

"You are wanted in the parlor, Miss Rose."

"Has anybody come?"

"Little girls shouldn't ask questions, but do as they are bid," was all Debby would answer.

"I do hope it isn't Aunt Myra; she always scares me out of my wits asking how my cough is, and groaning over me as if I was going to die," said Rose, preparing to retire the way she came, for the slide, being cut for the admission of bouncing Christmas turkeys and puddings, was plenty large enough for a slender girl.

"Guess you'll wish it was Aunt Myra when you see who has come. Don't never let me catch you coming into my kitchen that way again, or I'll shut you up in the big b'iler," growled Debby, who thought it her duty to snub children on all occasions.

Chapter 2—The Clan

Rose scrambled into the china-closet as rapidly as possible, and there refreshed herself by making faces at Debby, while she settled her plumage and screwed up her courage. Then she crept softly down the hall and peeped into the parlor. No one appeared, and all was so still she felt sure the company was upstairs. So she skipped boldly through the half-open folding-doors, to behold on the other side a sight that nearly took her breath away.

Seven boys stood in a row all ages, all sizes, all yellow-haired and blue-eyed, all in full Scotch costume, and all smiling, nodding, and saying as with one voice, "How are you, cousin?"

Rose gave a little gasp, and looked wildly about her as if ready to fly, for fear magnified the seven and the room seemed full of boys. Before she could run, however, the tallest lad stepped out of the line, saying pleasantly,

"Don't be frightened. This is the Clan come to welcome you; and I'm the chief, Archie, at your service."

He held out his hand as he spoke, and Rose timidly put her own into a brown paw, which closed over the white morsel and held it as the chief continued his introductions.

"We came in full rig, for we always turn out in style on grand occasions. Hope you like it. Now I'll tell you who these chaps are, and then we shall be all right. This big one is Prince Charlie, Aunt Clara's boy. She has but one, so he is an extra good one. This old fellow is Mac, the bookworm, called Worm for short. This sweet creature is Steve the Dandy. Look at his gloves and top-knot, if you please. They are Aunt Jane's lads, and a precious pair you'd better believe. These are the Brats, my brothers, Geordie and Will, and Jamie the Baby. Now, my men, step out and show your manners."

At this command, to Rose's great dismay, six more hands were offered, and it was evident that she was expected to shake them all. It was a trying moment to the bashful child; but, remembering that they were her kinsmen come to welcome her, she tried her best to return the greeting cordially.

5

This impressive ceremony being over, the Clan broke ranks, and both rooms instantly appeared to be pervaded with boys. Rose hastily retired to the shelter of a big chair and sat there watching the invaders and wondering when her aunt would come and rescue her.

As if bound to do their duty manfully, yet rather oppressed by it, each lad paused beside her chair in his wanderings, made a brief remark, received a still briefer answer, and then sheered off with a relieved expression.

Archie came first, and, leaning over the chair-back, observed in a paternal tone,

"I'm glad you've come, cousin, and I hope you'll find the Aunt-hill pretty jolly."

"I think I shall."

Mac shook his hair out of his eyes, stumbled over a stool, and asked abruptly,

"Did you bring any books with you?"

"Four boxes full. They are in the library."

Mac vanished from the room, and Steve, striking an attitude which displayed his costume effectively, said with an affable smile,

"We were sorry not to see you last Wednesday. I hope your cold is better."

"Yes, thank you." And a smile began to dimple about Rose's mouth, as she remembered her retreat under the bed-cover.

Feeling that he had been received with distinguished marks of attention, Steve strolled away with his topknot higher than ever, and Prince Charlie pranced across the room, saying in a free and easy tone,

"Mamma sent her love and hopes you will be well enough to come over for a day next week. It must be desperately dull here for a little thing like you."

"I'm thirteen and a half, though I do look small," cried Rose, forgetting her shyness in indignation at this insult to her newly acquired teens.

"Beg pardon, ma'am; never should have guessed it." And Charlie went off with a laugh, glad to have struck a spark out of his meek cousin.

Geordie and Will came together, two sturdy eleven and twelve year olders, and, fixing their round blue eyes on Rose, fired off a question apiece, as if it was a shooting match and she the target.

"Did you bring your monkey?"

"No; he is dead."

"Are you going to have a boat?"

"I hope not."

Here the two, with a right-about-face movement, abruptly marched away, and little Jamie demanded with childish frankness,

"Did you bring me anything nice?"

"Yes, lots of candy," answered Rose, whereupon Jamie ascended into her lap with a sounding kiss and the announcement that he liked her very much.

This proceeding rather startled Rose, for the other lads looked and laughed, and in her confusion she said hastily to the young usurper,

"Did you see the circus go by?"

"When? Where?" cried all the boys in great excitement at once.

"Just before you came. At least I thought it was a circus, for I saw a red and black sort of cart and ever so many little ponies, and—"

She got no farther, for a general shout made her pause suddenly, as Archie explained the joke by saying in the middle of his laugh,

"It was our new dog-cart and the Shetland ponies. You'll never hear the last of your circus, cousin."

"But there were so many, and they went so fast, and the cart was so very red," began Rose, trying to explain her mistake.

"Come and see them all!" cried the Prince. And before she knew what was happening, she was borne away to the barn and tumultuously introduced to three shaggy ponies and the gay new dog-cart.

She had never visited these regions before, and had her doubts as to the propriety of her being there now, but when she suggested that "Auntie might not like it," there was a general cry of,

"She told us to amuse you, and we can do it ever so much better out here than poking round in the house."

"I'm afraid I shall get cold without my sacque," began Rose, who wanted to stay, but felt rather out of her element.

"No, you won't! We'll fix you," cried the lads, as one clapped his cap on her head, another tied a rough jacket round her neck by the sleeves, a third neatly smothered her in a carriage blanket, and a fourth threw open the door of the old barouche that stood there, saying with a flourish,

"Step in, ma'am, and make yourself comfortable while we show you some fun."

So Rose sat in state enjoying herself very much, for the lads proceeded to dance a Highland Fling with a spirit and skill that made her clap her hands and laugh as she had not done for weeks.

"How is that, my lassie?" asked the Prince, coming up all flushed and breathless when the ballet was over.

"It was splendid! I never went to the theatre but once, and the dancing was not half so pretty as this. What clever boys you must be!" said Rose, smiling upon her kinsmen like a little queen upon her subjects.

7

"Ah, we're a fine lot, and that is only the beginning of our larks. We haven't got the pipes here or we'd,

'Sing for you, play for you
A dulcy melody,'"

answered Charlie, looking much elated at her praise.

"I did not know we were Scotch; papa never said anything about it, or seemed to care about Scotland, except to have me sing the old ballads," said Rose, beginning to feel as if she had left America behind her somewhere.

"Neither did we till lately. We've been reading Scott's novels, and all of a sudden we remembered that our grandfather was a Scotchman. So we hunted up the old stories, got a bagpipe, put on our plaids, and went in, heart and soul, for the glory of the Clan. We've been at it some time now, and it's great fun. Our people like it, and I think we are a pretty canny set."

Archie said this from the other coach-step, where he had perched, while the rest climbed up before and behind to join in the chat as they rested.

"I'm Fitzjames and he's Roderick Dhu, and we'll give you the broadsword combat some day. It's a great thing, you'd better believe," added the Prince.

"Yes, and you should hear Steve play the pipes. He makes 'em skirl like a good one," cried Will from the box, eager to air the accomplishments of his race.

"Mac's the fellow to hunt up the old stories and tell us how to dress right, and pick out rousing bits for us to speak and sing," put in Geordie, saying a good word for the absent Worm.

"And what do you and Will do?" asked Rose of Jamie, who sat beside her as if bound to keep her in sight till the promised gift had been handed over.

"Oh, I'm the little foot-page, and do errands, and Will and Geordie are the troops when we march, and the stags when we hunt, and the traitors when we want to cut any heads off."

"They are very obliging, I'm sure," said Rose, whereat the "utility men" beamed with modest pride and resolved to enact Wallace and Montrose as soon as possible for their cousin's special benefit.

"Let's have a game of tag," cried the Prince, swinging himself up to a beam with a sounding slap on Stevie's shoulder.

Regardless of his gloves, Dandy tore after him, and the rest swarmed in every direction as if bent on breaking their necks and dislocating their joints as rapidly as possible.

It was a new and astonishing spectacle to Rose, fresh from a prim boarding-school, and she watched the active lads with breathless interest, thinking their antics far superior to those of Mops, the dear departed monkey.

Will had just covered himself with glory by pitching off a high loft head first and coming up all right, when Phebe appeared with a cloak, hood, and rubbers, also a message from Aunt Plenty that "Miss Rose was to come in directly."

"All right; we'll bring her!" answered Archie, issuing some mysterious order, which was so promptly obeyed that, before Rose could get out of the carriage, the boys had caught hold of the pole and rattled her out of the barn, round the oval and up to the front door with a cheer that brought two caps to an upper window, and caused Debby to cry aloud from the back porch,

"Them harum-scarum boys will certainly be the death of that delicate little creter!"

But the "delicate little creter" seemed all the better for her trip, and ran up the steps looking rosy, gay, and dishevelled, to be received with lamentation by Aunt Plenty, who begged her to go and lie down at once.

"Oh, please don't! We have come to tea with our cousin, and we'll be as good as gold if you'll let us stay, auntie," clamoured the boys, who not only approved of "our cousin" but had no mind to lose their tea, for Aunt Plenty's name but feebly expressed her bountiful nature.

"Well, dears, you can; only be quiet, and let Rose go and take her iron and be made tidy, and then we will see what we can find for supper," said the old lady as she trotted away, followed by a volley of directions for the approaching feast.

"Marmalade for me, auntie."

"Plenty of plum-cake, please."

"Tell Debby to trot out the baked pears."

"I'm your man for lemon-pie, ma'am."

"Do have fritters; Rose will like 'em."

"She'd rather have tarts, I know."

When Rose came down, fifteen minutes later, with every curl smoothed and her most beruffled apron on, she found the boys loafing about the long hall, and paused on the half-way landing to take an observation, for till now she had not really examined her new-found cousins.

There was a strong family resemblance among them, though some of the yellow heads were darker than others, some of the cheeks brown instead of rosy, and the ages varied all the way from sixteen-year-old Archie to Jamie, who was ten years younger. None of them were especially comely but the Prince, yet all were hearty, happy-looking lads, and Rose decided that boys were not as dreadful as she had expected to find them.

They were all so characteristically employed that she could not help smiling as she looked. Archie and Charlie, evidently great cronies, were pacing up and down, shoulder to shoulder, whistling "Bonnie Dundee"; Mac was reading in a corner, with his book close to his near-sighted eyes; Dandy was arranging his hair before the oval glass in the hat-stand; Geordie and Will investigating the internal economy of the moon-faced clock; and Jamie lay kicking up his heels on the mat at the foot of the stairs, bent on demanding his sweeties the instant Rose appeared.

She guessed his intention, and forestalled his demand by dropping a handful of sugar-plums down upon him.

At his cry of rapture the other lads looked up and smiled involuntarily, for the little kinswoman standing there above was a winsome sight with her shy, soft eyes, bright hair, and laughing face.

The black frock reminded them of her loss, and filled the boyish hearts with a kindly desire to be good to "our cousin," who had no longer any home but this.

"There she is, as fine as you please," cried Steve, kissing his hand to her.

"Come on, Missy; tea is ready," added the Prince encouragingly.

"I shall take her in." And Archie offered his arm with great dignity, an honour that made Rose turn as red as a cherry and long to run upstairs again.

It was a merry supper, and the two elder boys added much to the fun by tormenting the rest with dark hints of some interesting event which was about to occur. Something uncommonly fine, they declared it was, but enveloped in the deepest mystery for the present.

"Did I ever see it?" asked Jamie.

"Not to remember it; but Mac and Steve have, and liked it immensely," answered Archie, thereby causing the two mentioned to neglect Debby's delectable fritters for several minutes, while they cudgelled their brains.

"Who will have it first?" asked Will, with his mouth full of marmalade.

"Aunt Plenty, I guess."

"When will she have it?" demanded Geordie, bouncing in his seat with impatience.

"Sometime on Monday."

"Heart alive! what is the boy talking about?" cried the old lady from behind the tall urn, which left little to be seen but the topmost bow of her cap.

"Doesn't auntie know?" asked a chorus of voices.

"No; and that's the best of the joke, for she is desperately fond of it."

"What colour is it?" asked Rose, joining in the fun.

"Blue and brown."

"Is it good to eat?" asked Jamie.

"Some people think so, but I shouldn't like to try it," answered Charlie, laughing so he split his tea.

"Who does it belong to?" put in Steve.

Archie and the Prince stared at one another rather blankly for a minute, then Archie answered with a twinkle of the eye that made Charlie explode again,

"To Grandfather Campbell."

This was a poser, and they gave up the puzzle, though Jamie confided to Rose that he did not think he could live till Monday without knowing what this remarkable thing was.

Soon after tea the Clan departed, singing "All the blue bonnets are over the border," at the tops of their voices.

"Well, dear, how do you like your cousins?" asked Aunt Plenty, as the last pony frisked round the corner and the din died away.

"Pretty well, ma'am; but I like Phebe better." An answer which caused Aunt Plenty to hold up her hands in despair and trot away to tell sister Peace that she never should understand that child, and it was a mercy Alec was coming soon to take the responsibility off their hands.

Fatigued by the unusual exertions of the afternoon, Rose curled herself up in the sofa corner to rest and think about the great mystery, little guessing that she was to know it first of all.

Right in the middle of her meditations she fell asleep and dreamed she was at home again in her own little bed. She seemed to wake and see her father bending over her; to hear him say, "My little Rose"; to answer, "Yes, papa"; and then to feel him take her in his arms and kiss her tenderly. So sweet, so real was the dream, that she started up with a cry of joy to find herself in the arms of a brown, bearded man, who held her close, and whispered in a voice so like her father's that she clung to him involuntarily,

"This is my little girl, and I am Uncle Alec."

Chapter 3—Uncles
When Rose woke next morning, she was not sure whether she had dreamed what occurred the night before, or it had actually happened. So she hopped up and dressed, although it was an hour earlier than she usually rose, for she could not sleep any more, being possessed with a strong desire to slip down and see if the big portmanteau and packing cases were really in the hall. She seemed to remember tumbling over them when she went to bed, for the aunts had sent her off very punctually, because they wanted their pet nephew all to themselves.

The sun was shining, and Rose opened her window to let in the soft May air fresh from the sea. As she leaned over her little balcony, watching an early bird get the worm, and wondering how she should like Uncle Alec, she saw a man leap the garden wall and come whistling up the path. At first she thought it was some trespasser, but a second look showed her that it was her uncle returning from an early dip into the sea. She had hardly dared to look at him the night before, because whenever she tried to do so she always found a pair of keen blue eyes looking at her. Now she could take a good stare at him as he lingered along, looking about him as if glad to see the old place again.

A brown, breezy man, in a blue jacket, with no hat on the curly head, which he shook now and then like a water dog; broad-shouldered, alert in his motions, and with a general air of strength and stability about him which pleased Rose, though she could not explain the feeling of comfort it gave her. She had just said to herself, with a sense of relief, "I guess I shall like him, though he looks as if he made people mind," when he lifted his eyes to examine the budding horse-chestnut overhead, and saw the eager face peering down at him. He waved his hand to her, nodded, and called out in a bluff, cheery voice,

"You are on deck early, little niece."

"I got up to see if you had really come, uncle."

"Did you? Well, come down here and make sure of it."

"I'm not allowed to go out before breakfast, sir."

"Oh, indeed!" with a shrug. "Then I'll come aboard and salute," he added; and, to Rose's great amazement, Uncle Alec went up one of the pillars of the back piazza hand over hand, stepped across the roof, and swung himself into her balcony, saying, as he landed on the wide balustrade: "Have you any doubts about me now, ma'am?"

Rose was so taken aback, she could only answer with a smile as she went to meet him.

"How does my girl do this morning?" he asked, taking the little cold hand she gave him in both his big warm ones.

"Pretty well, thank you, sir."

"Ah, but it should be very well. Why isn't it?"

"I always wake up with a headache, and feel tired."

"Don't you sleep well?"

"I lie awake a long time, and then I dream, and my sleep does not seem to rest me much."

"What do you do all day?"

"Oh, I read, and sew a little, and take naps, and sit with auntie."

"No running about out of doors, or house-work, or riding, hey?"

"Aunt Plenty says I'm not strong enough for much exercise. I drive out with her sometimes, but I don't care for it."

"I'm not surprised at that," said Uncle Alec, half to himself, adding, in his quick way: "Who have you had to play with?"

"No one but Ariadne Blish, and she was such a goose I couldn't bear her. The boys came yesterday, and seemed rather nice; but, of course, I couldn't play with them."

"Why not?"

"I'm too old to play with boys."

"Not a bit of it; that's just what you need, for you've been molly-coddled too much. They are good lads, and you'll be mixed up with them more or less for years to come, so you may as well be friends and playmates at once. I will look you up some girls also, if I can find a sensible one who is not spoilt by her nonsensical education."

"Phebe is sensible, I'm sure, and I like her, though I only saw her yesterday," cried Rose, waking up suddenly.

"And who is Phebe, if you please?"

Rose eagerly told all she knew, and Uncle Alec listened, with an odd smile lurking about his mouth, though his eyes were quite sober as he watched the face before him.

"I'm glad to see that you are not aristocratic in your tastes, but I don't quite make out why you like this young lady from the poor-house."

"You may laugh at me, but I do. I can't tell why, only she seems so happy and busy, and sings so beautifully, and is strong enough to scrub and sweep, and hasn't any troubles to plague her," said Rose, making a funny jumble of reasons in her efforts to explain.

"How do you know that?"

"Oh, I was telling her about mine, and asked if she had any, and she said, 'No, only I'd like to go to school, and I mean to some day.'"

"So she doesn't call desertion, poverty, and hard work, troubles? She's a brave little girl, and I shall be proud to know her." And Uncle Alec gave an approving nod, that made Rose wish she had been the one to earn it.

"But what are these troubles of yours, child?" he asked, after a minute of silence.

"Please don't ask me, uncle."

"Can't you tell them to me as well as to Phebe?"

Something in his tone made Rose feel that it would be better to speak out and be done with it, so she answered, with sudden colour and averted eyes,

"The greatest one was losing dear papa."

As she said that, Uncle Alec's arm came gently round her, and he drew her to him, saying, in the voice so like papa's,

"That is a trouble which I cannot cure, my child; but I shall try to make you feel it less. What else, dear?"

"I am so tired and poorly all the time, I can't do anything I want to, and it makes me cross," sighed Rose, rubbing the aching head like a fretful child.

"That we can cure and we will," said her uncle, with a decided nod that made the curls bob on his head, to that Rose saw the gray ones underneath the brown.

"Aunt Myra says I have no constitution, and never shall be strong," observed Rose, in a pensive tone, as if it was rather a nice thing to be an invalid.

"Aunt Myra is a ahem! an excellent woman, but it is her hobby to believe that everyone is tottering on the brink of the grave; and, upon my life, I believe she is offended if people don't fall into it! We will show her how to make constitutions and turn pale-faced little ghosts into rosy, hearty girls. That's my business, you know," he added, more quietly, for his sudden outburst had rather startled Rose.

"I had forgotten you were a doctor. I'm glad of it, for I do want to be well, only I hope you won't give me much medicine, for I've taken quarts already, and it does me no good."

13

As she spoke, Rose pointed to a little table just inside the window, on which appeared a regiment of bottles.

"Ah, ha! Now we'll see what mischief these blessed women have been at." And, making a long arm, Dr. Alec set the bottles on the wide railing before him, examined each carefully, smiled over some, frowned over others, and said, as he put down the last: "Now I'll show you the best way to take these messes." And, as quick as a flash, he sent one after another smashing down into the posy-beds below.

"But Aunt Plenty won't like it; and Aunt Myra will be angry, for she sent most of them!" cried Rose, half frightened and half pleased at such energetic measures.

"You are my patient now, and I'll take the responsibility. My way of giving physic is evidently the best, for you look better already," he said, laughing so infectiously that Rose followed suit, saying saucily,

"If I don't like your medicines any better than those, I shall throw them into the garden, and then what will you do?"

"When I prescribe such rubbish, I'll give you leave to pitch it overboard as soon as you like. Now what is the next trouble?"

"I hoped you would forget to ask."

"But how can I help you if I don't know them? Come, let us have No. 3."

"It is very wrong, I suppose, but I do sometimes wish I had not quite so many aunts. They are all very good to me, and I want to please them; but they are so different, I feel sort of pulled to pieces among them," said Rose, trying to express the emotions of a stray chicken with six hens all clucking over it at once.

Uncle Alec threw back his head and laughed like a boy, for he could entirely understand how the good ladies had each put in her oar and tried to paddle her own way, to the great disturbance of the waters and the entire bewilderment of poor Rose.

"I intend to try a course of uncles now, and see how that suits your constitution. I'm going to have you all to myself, and no one is to give a word of advice unless I ask it. There is no other way to keep order aboard, and I am captain of this little craft, for a time at least. What comes next?"

But Rose stuck there, and grew so red, her uncle guessed what that trouble was.

"I don't think I can tell this one. It wouldn't be polite, and I feel pretty sure that it isn't going to be a trouble any more."

As she blushed and stammered over these words, Dr. Alec turned his eyes away to the distant sea, and said so seriously, so tenderly, that she felt every word and long remembered them,

"My child, I don't expect you to love and trust me all at once, but I do want you to believe that I shall give my whole heart to this new duty; and if I make mistakes, as I probably shall, no one will grieve over them more bitterly than I. It is my fault that I am a stranger to you, when I want to be your best friend. That is one of my mistakes, and I never repented it more deeply than I do now. Your father and I had a trouble once, and I thought I could never forgive him; so I kept away for years. Thank God, we made it all up the last time I saw him, and he told me then, that if he was forced to leave her he should bequeath his little girl to me as a token of his love. I can't fill his place, but I shall try to be a father to her; and if she learns to love me half as well as she did the good one she has lost, I shall be a proud and happy man. Will she believe this and try?"

Something in Uncle Alec's face touched Rose to the heart, and when he held out his hand with that anxious troubled look in his eyes, she was moved to put up her innocent lips and seal the contract with a confiding kiss. The strong arm held her close a minute, and she felt the broad chest heave once as if with a great sigh of relief; but not a word was spoken till a tap at the door made both start.

Rose popped her head through the window to say "come in," while Dr. Alec hastily rubbed the sleeve of his jacket across his eyes and began to whistle again.

Phebe appeared with a cup of coffee.

"Debby told me to bring this and help you get up," she said, opening her black eyes wide, as if she wondered how on earth "the sailor man" got there.

"I'm all dressed, so I don't need any help. I hope that is good and strong," added Rose, eyeing the steaming cup with an eager look.

But she did not get it, for a brown hand took possession of it as her uncle said quickly,

"Hold hard, my lass, and let me overhaul that dose before you take it. Do you drink all this strong coffee every morning, Rose?"

"Yes, sir, and I like it. Auntie says it 'tones' me up, and I always feel better after it."

"This accounts for the sleepless nights, the flutter your heart gets into at the least start, and this is why that cheek of yours is pale yellow instead of rosy red. No more coffee for you, my dear, and by and by you'll see that I am right. Any new milk downstairs, Phebe?"

"Yes, sir, plenty right in from the barn."

"That's the drink for my patient. Go bring me a pitcherful, and another cup; I want a draught myself. This won't hurt the honeysuckles, for they have no nerves to speak of." And, to Rose's great discomfort, the coffee went after the medicine.

Dr. Alec saw the injured look she put on, but took no notice, and presently banished it by saying pleasantly,

"I've got a capital little cup among my traps, and I'll give it to you to drink your milk in, as it is made of wood that is supposed to improve whatever is put into it something like a quassia cup. That reminds me; one of the boxes Phebe wanted to lug upstairs last night is for you. Knowing that I was coming home to find a ready-made daughter, I picked up all sorts of odd and pretty trifles along the way, hoping she would be able to find something she liked among them all. Early to-morrow we'll have a grand rummage. Here's our milk! I propose the health of Miss Rose Campbell and drink it with all my heart."

It was impossible for Rose to pout with the prospect of a delightful boxful of gifts dancing before her eyes; so, in spite of herself, she smiled as she drank her own health, and found that fresh milk was not a hard dose to take.

"Now I must be off, before I am caught again with my wig in a toss," said Dr. Alec, preparing to descend the way he came.

"Do you always go in and out like a cat, uncle?" asked Rose, much amused at his odd ways.

"I used to sneak out of my window when I was a boy, so I need not disturb the aunts, and now I rather like it, for it's the shortest road, and it keeps me limber when I have no rigging to climb. Good-bye till breakfast." And away he went down the water-spout, over the roof, and vanished among the budding honey-suckles below.

"Ain't he a funny guardeen?" exclaimed Phebe, as she went off with the cups.

"He is a very kind one, I think," answered Rose, following, to prowl round the big boxes and try to guess which was hers.

When her uncle appeared at sound of the bell, he found her surveying with an anxious face a new dish that smoked upon the table.

"Got a fresh trouble, Rosy?" he asked, stroking her smooth head.

"Uncle, are you going to make me eat oatmeal?" asked Rose, in a tragic tone.

"Don't you like it?"

"I de-test it!" answered Rose, with all the emphasis which a turned-up nose, a shudder, and a groan could give to the three words.

"You are not a true Scotchwoman, if you don't like the 'parritch.' It's a pity, for I made it myself, and thought we'd have such a good time with all that cream to float it in. Well, never mind." And he sat down with a disappointed air.

Rose had made up her mind to be obstinate about it, because she did heartily "detest" the dish; but as Uncle Alec did not attempt to make her obey, she suddenly changed her mind and thought she would.

"I'll try to eat it to please you, uncle; but people are always saying how wholesome it is, and that makes me hate it," she said, half-ashamed at her silly excuse.

"I do want you to like it, because I wish my girl to be as well and strong as Jessie's boys, who are brought up on this in the good old fashion. No hot bread and fried stuff for them, and they are the biggest and bonniest lads of the lot. Bless you, auntie, and good morning!"

Dr. Alec turned to greet the old lady, and, with a firm resolve to eat or die in the attempt, Rose sat down.

In five minutes she forgot what she was eating, so interested was she in the chat that went on. It amused her very much to hear Aunt Plenty call her forty-year-old nephew "my dear boy"; and Uncle Alec was so full of lively gossip about all creation in general, and the Aunt-hill in particular, that the detested porridge vanished without a murmur.

"You will go to church with us, I hope, Alec, if you are not too tired," said the old lady, when breakfast was over.

"I came all the way from Calcutta for that express purpose, ma'am. Only I must send the sisters word of my arrival, for they don't expect me till to-morrow, you know, and there will be a row in church if those boys see me without warning."

"I'll send Ben up the hill, and you can step over to Myra's yourself; it will please her, and you will have plenty of time."

Dr. Alec was off at once, and they saw no more of him till the old barouche was at the door, and Aunt Plenty just rustling downstairs in her Sunday best, with Rose like a little black shadow behind her.

Away they drove in state, and all the way Uncle Alec's hat was more off his head than on, for everyone they met smiled and bowed, and gave him as blithe a greeting as the day permitted.

It was evident that the warning had been a wise one, for, in spite of time and place, the lads were in such a ferment that their elders sat in momentary dread of an unseemly outbreak somewhere. It was simply impossible to keep those fourteen eyes off Uncle Alec, and the dreadful things that were done during sermon-time will hardly be believed.

Rose dared not look up after a while, for these bad boys vented their emotions upon her till she was ready to laugh and cry with mingled amusement and vexation. Charlie winked rapturously at her behind his mother's fan; Mac openly pointed to the tall figure beside her; Jamie stared fixedly over the back of his pew, till Rose thought his round eyes would drop out of his head; George fell over a stool and dropped three books in his excitement; Will drew sailors and Chinamen on his clean cuffs, and displayed them, to Rose's great tribulation; Steve nearly upset the whole party by burning his nose with salts, as he pretended to be overcome by his joy; even dignified Archie disgraced himself by writing in his hymn book, "Isn't he blue and brown?" and passing it politely to Rose.

Her only salvation was trying to fix her attention upon Uncle Mac a portly, placid gentleman, who seemed entirely unconscious of the iniquities of the Clan, and dozed peacefully in his pew corner. This was the only uncle Rose had met for years, for Uncle Jem and Uncle Steve, the husbands of Aunt Jessie and Aunt Clara, were at sea, and Aunt Myra was a widow. Uncle Mac was a merchant, very rich and busy, and as quiet as a mouse at home, for he was in such a minority among the women folk he dared not open his lips, and let his wife rule undisturbed.

Rose liked the big, kindly, silent man who came to her when papa died, was always sending her splendid boxes of goodies at school, and often invited her into his great warehouse, full of teas and spices, wines and all sorts of foreign fruits, there to eat and carry away whatever she liked. She had secretly regretted that he was not to be her guardian; but since she had seen Uncle Alec she felt better about it, for she did not particularly admire Aunt Jane.

When church was over, Dr. Alec got into the porch as quickly as possible, and there the young bears had a hug all round, while the sisters shook hands and welcomed him with bright faces and glad hearts. Rose was nearly crushed flat behind a door in that dangerous passage from pew to porch; but Uncle Mac rescued her, and put her into the carriage for safe keeping.

"Now, girls, I want you to come and dine with Alec; Mac also, of course. But I cannot ask the boys, for we did not expect this dear fellow till tomorrow, you know, so I made no preparations. Send the lads home, and let them wait till Monday, for really I was shocked at their behaviour in church," said Aunt Plenty, as she followed Rose.

In any other place the defrauded boys would have set up a howl; as it was, they growled and protested till Dr. Alec settled the matter by saying,

"Never mind, old chaps, I'll make it up to you to-morrow, if you sheer off quietly; if you don't, not a blessed thing shall you have out of my big boxes."

Chapter 4—Aunts

All dinner-time Rose felt that she was going to be talked about, and afterward she was sure of it, for Aunt Plenty whispered to her as they went into the parlour,

"Run up and sit awhile with Sister Peace, my dear. She likes to have you read while she rests, and we are going to be busy."

Rose obeyed, and the quiet rooms above were so like a church that she soon composed her ruffled feelings, and was unconsciously a little minister of happiness to the sweet old lady, who for years had sat there patiently waiting to be set free from pain.

Rose knew the sad romance of her life, and it gave a certain tender charm to this great-aunt of hers, whom she already loved. When Peace was twenty, she was about to be married; all was done, the wedding dress lay ready, the flowers were waiting to be put on, the happy hour at hand, when word came that the lover was dead. They thought that gentle Peace would die, too; but she bore it bravely, put away her bridal gear, took up her life afresh, and lived on a beautiful, meek woman, with hair as white as snow and cheeks that never bloomed again. She wore no black, but soft, pale colours, as if always ready for the marriage that had never come.

For thirty years she had lived on, fading slowly, but cheerful, busy, and full of interest in all that went on in the family; especially the joys and sorrows of the young girls growing up about her, and to them she was adviser, confidante, and friend in all their tender trials and delights. A truly beautiful old maiden, with her silvery hair, tranquil face, and an atmosphere of repose about her that soothed whoever came to her!

Aunt Plenty was utterly dissimilar, being a stout, brisk old lady, with a sharp eye, a lively tongue, and a face like a winter-apple. Always trotting, chatting, and bustling, she was a regular Martha, cumbered with the cares of this world and quite happy in them.

Rose was right; and while she softly read psalms to Aunt Peace, the other ladies were talking about her little self in the frankest manner.

"Well, Alec, how do you like your ward?" began Aunt Jane, as they all settled down, and Uncle Mac deposited himself in a corner to finish his doze.

"I should like her better if I could have begun at the beginning, and so got a fair start. Poor George led such a solitary life that the child has suffered in many ways, and since he died she has been going on worse than ever, judging from the state I find her in."

"My dear boy, we did what we thought best while waiting for you to wind up your affairs and get home. I always told George he was wrong to bring her up as he did; but he never took my advice, and now here we are with this poor dear child upon our hands. I, for one, freely confess that I don't know what to do with her any more than if she was one of those strange, outlandish birds you used to bring home from foreign parts." And Aunt Plenty gave a perplexed shake of the head which caused great commotion among the stiff loops of purple ribbon that bristled all over the cap like crocus buds.

"If my advice had been taken, she would have remained at the excellent school where I placed her. But our aunt thought best to remove her because she complained, and she has been dawdling about ever since she came. A most ruinous state of things for a morbid, spoilt girl like Rose," said Mrs. Jane, severely.

She had never forgiven the old ladies for yielding to Rose's pathetic petition that she might wait her guardian's arrival before beginning another term at the school, which was a regular Blimber hot-bed, and turned out many a feminine Toots.

"I never thought it the proper school for a child in good circumstances an heiress, in fact, as Rose is. It is all very well for girls who are to get their own living by teaching, and that sort of thing; but all she needs is a year or two at a fashionable finishing school, so that at eighteen she can come out with eclat," put in Aunt Clara, who had been a beauty and a belle, and was still a handsome woman.

"Dear, dear! how short-sighted you all are to be discussing education and plans for the future, when this unhappy child is so plainly marked for the tomb," sighed Aunt Myra, with a lugubrious sniff and a solemn wag of the funereal bonnet, which she refused to remove, being afflicted with a chronic catarrh.

"Now, it is my opinion that the dear thing only wants freedom, rest, and care. There is look in her eyes that goes to my heart, for it shows that she feels the need of what none of us can give her a mother," said Aunt Jessie, with tears in her own bright eyes at the thought of her boys being left, as Rose was, to the care of others.

Uncle Alec, who had listened silently as each spoke, turned quickly towards the last sister, and said, with a decided nod of approval,

"You've got it, Jessie; and, with you to help me, I hope to make the child feel that she is not quite fatherless and motherless."

"I'll do my best, Alec; and I think you will need me, for, wise as you are, you cannot understand a tender, timid little creature like Rose as a woman can," said Mrs. Jessie, smiling back at him with a heart full of motherly goodwill.

"I cannot help feeling that I, who have had a daughter of my own, can best bring up a girl; and I am very much surprised that George did not entrust her to me," observed Aunt Myra, with an air of melancholy importance, for she was the only one who had given a daughter to the family, and she felt that she had distinguished herself, though ill-natured people said that she had dosed her darling to death.

"I never blamed him in the least, when I remember the perilous experiments you tried with poor Carrie," began Mrs. Jane, in her hard voice.

"Jane Campbell, I will not hear a word! My sainted Caroline is a sacred object," cried Aunt Myra, rising as if to leave the room.

Dr. Alec detained her, feeling that he must define his position at once, and maintain it manfully if he hoped to have any success in his new undertaking.

"Now, my dear souls, don't let us quarrel and make Rose a bone of contention though, upon my word, she is almost a bone, poor little lass! You have had her among you for a year, and done what you liked. I cannot say that your success is great, but that is owing to too many fingers in the pie. Now, I intend to try my way for a year, and if at the end of it she is not in better trim than now, I'll give up the case, and hand her over to someone else. That's fair, I think."

"She will not be here a year hence, poor darling, so no one need dread future responsibility," said Aunt Myra, folding her black gloves as if all ready for the funeral.

"By Jupiter! Myra, you are enough to damp the ardour of a saint!" cried Dr. Alec, with a sudden spark in his eyes. "Your croaking will worry that child out of her wits, for she is an imaginative puss, and will fret and fancy untold horrors. You have put it into her head that she has no constitution, and she rather likes the idea. If she had not had a pretty good one, she would have been 'marked for the tomb' by this time, at the rate you have been going on with her. I will not have any interference please understand that; so just wash your hands of her, and let me manage till I want help, then I'll ask for it."

"Hear, hear!" came from the corner where Uncle Mac was apparently wrapt in slumber.

"You were appointed guardian, so we can do nothing. But I predict that the girl will be spoilt, utterly spoilt," answered Mrs. Jane, grimly.

"Thank you, sister. I have an idea that if a woman can bring up two boys as perfectly as you do yours, a man, if he devotes his whole mind to it, may at least attempt as much with one girl," replied Dr. Alec, with a humorous look that tickled the others immensely, for it was a well-known fact in the family that Jane's boys were more indulged than all the other lads put together.

"I am quite easy, for I really do think that Alec will improve the child's health; and by the time his year is out, it will be quite soon enough for her to go to Madame Roccabella's and be finished off," said Aunt Clara, settling her rings, and thinking, with languid satisfaction, of the time when she could bring out a pretty and accomplished niece.

"I suppose you will stay here in the old place, unless you think of marrying, and it's high time you did," put in Mrs. Jane, much nettled at her brother's last hit.

"No, thank you. Come and have a cigar, Mac," said Dr. Alec, abruptly.

"Don't marry; women enough in the family already," muttered Uncle Mac; and then the gentlemen hastily fled.

"Aunt Peace would like to see you all, she says," was the message Rose brought before the ladies could begin again.

"Hectic, hectic! dear me, dear me!" murmured Aunt Myra, as the shadow of her gloomy bonnet fell upon Rose, and the stiff tips of a black glove touched the cheek where the colour deepened under so many eyes.

"I am glad these pretty curls are natural; they will be invaluable by and by," said Aunt Clara, taking an observation with her head on one side.

"Now that your uncle has come, I no longer expect you to review the studies of the past year. I trust your time will not be entirely wasted in frivolous sports, however," added Aunt Jane, sailing out of the room with the air of a martyr.

Aunt Jessie said not a word, but kissed her little niece, with a look of tender sympathy that made Rose cling to her a minute, and follow her with grateful eyes as the door closed behind her.

After everybody had gone home, Dr. Alec paced up and down the lower hall in the twilight for an hour, thinking so intently that sometimes he frowned, sometimes he smiled, and more than once he stood still in a brown study. All of a sudden he said, half aloud, as if he had made up his mind,

"I might as well begin at once, and give the child something new to think about, for Myra's dismals and Jane's lectures have made her as blue as a little indigo bag."

Diving into one of the trunks that stood in a corner, he brought up, after a brisk rummage, a silken cushion, prettily embroidered, and a quaint cup of dark carved wood.

"This will do for a start," he said, as he plumped up the cushion and dusted the cup. "It won't do to begin too energetically, or Rose will be frightened. I must beguile her gently and pleasantly along till I've won her confidence, and then she will be ready for anything."

Just then Phebe came out of the dining-room with a plate of brown bread, for Rose had been allowed no hot biscuit for tea.

"I'll relieve you of some of that," said Dr. Alec, and, helping himself to a generous slice, he retired to the study, leaving Phebe to wonder at his appetite.

She would have wondered still more if she had seen him making that brown bread into neat little pills, which he packed into an attractive ivory box, out of which he emptied his own bits of lovage.

"There! if they insist on medicine, I'll order these, and no harm will be done. I will have my own way, but I'll keep the peace, if possible, and confess the joke when my experiment has succeeded," he said to himself, looking very much like a mischievous boy, as he went on with his innocent prescriptions.

Rose was playing softly on the small organ that stood in the upper hall, so that Aunt Peace could enjoy it; and all the while he talked with the old ladies, Uncle Alec was listening to the fitful music of the child, and thinking of another Rose who used to play for him.

As the clock struck eight, he called out,

"Time for my girl to be abed, else she won't be up early, and I'm full of jolly plans for to-morrow. Come and see what I've found for you to begin upon."

Rose ran in and listened with bright attentive face, while Dr. Alec said impressively,

"In my wanderings over the face of the earth, I have picked up some excellent remedies, and, as they are rather agreeable ones, I think you and I will try them. This is a herb-pillow, given to me by a wise old woman when I was ill in India. It is filled with saffron, poppies, and other soothing plants; so lay your little head on it to-night, sleep sweetly without a dream, and wake to-morrow without a pain."

"Shall I really? How nice it smells." And Rose willingly received the pretty pillow, and stood enjoying its faint, sweet odour, as she listened to the doctor's next remedy.

"This is the cup I told you of. Its virtue depends, they say, on the drinker filling it himself; so you must learn to milk. I'll teach you."

"I'm afraid I never can," said Rose; but she surveyed the cup with favour, for a funny little imp danced on the handle, as if all ready to take a header into the white sea below.

"Don't you think she ought to have something more strengthening than milk, Alec? I really shall feel anxious if she does not have a tonic of some sort," said Aunt Plenty, eyeing the new remedies suspiciously, for she had more faith in her old-fashioned doses than all the magic cups and poppy pillows of the East.

"Well, ma'am, I'm willing to give her a pill, if you think best. It is a very simple one, and very large quantities may be taken without harm. You know hasheesh is the extract of hemp? Well, this is a preparation of corn and rye, much used in old times, and I hope it will be again."

"Dear me, how singular!" said Aunt Plenty, bringing her spectacles to bear upon the pills, with a face so full of respectful interest that it was almost too much for Dr. Alec's gravity.

"Take one in the morning, and a good-night to you, my dear," he said, dismissing his patient with a hearty kiss.

Then, as she vanished, he put both hands into his hair, exclaiming, with a comical mixture of anxiety and amusement,

"When I think what I have undertaken, I declare to you, aunt, I feel like running away and not coming back till Rose is eighteen!"

Chapter 5—A Belt and a Box
When Rose came out of her chamber, cup in hand, next morning, the first person she saw was Uncle Alec standing on the threshold of the room opposite, which he appeared to be examining with care. When he heard her step, he turned about and began to sing,

"Where are you going, my pretty maid?"

"I'm going a-milking, sir, she said," answered Rose, waving the cup; and then they finished the verse together in fine style.

Before either spoke, a head, in a nightcap so large and beruffled that it looked like a cabbage, popped out of a room farther down the hall, and an astonished voice exclaimed,

"What in the world are you doing about so early?"

"Clearing our pipes for the day, ma'am. Look here, auntie, can I have this room?" said Dr. Alec, making her a sailor's bow.

"Any room you like, except sister's."

"Thanks. And may I go rummaging round in the garrets and glory-holes to furnish it as I like?"

"My dear boy, you may turn the house upside down if you will only stay in it."

"That's a handsome offer, I'm sure. I'll stay, ma'am; here's my little anchor, so you will get more than you want of me this time."

"That's impossible! Put on your jacket, Rose. Don't tire her out with antics, Alec. Yes, sister, I'm coming!" and the cabbage vanished suddenly.

The first milking lesson was a droll one; but after several scares and many vain attempts, Rose at last managed to fill her cup, while Ben held Clover's tail so that it could not flap, and Dr. Alec kept her from turning to stare at the new milkmaid, who objected to both these proceedings very much.

"You look chilly in spite of all this laughing. Take a smart run round the garden and get up a glow," said the doctor, as they left the barn.

"I'm too old for running, uncle; Miss Power said it was not lady-like for girls in their teens," answered Rose, primly.

"I take the liberty of differing from Madame Prunes and Prisms, and, as your physician, I order you to run. Off with you!" said Uncle Alec, with a look and a gesture that made Rose scurry away as fast as she could go.

Anxious to please him, she raced round the beds till she came back to the porch where he stood, and, dropping down upon the steps, she sat panting, with cheeks as rosy as the rigolette on her shoulders.

"Very well done, child; I see you have not lost the use of your limbs though you are in your teens. That belt is too tight; unfasten it, then you can take a long breath without panting so."

"It isn't tight, sir; I can breathe perfectly well," began Rose, trying to compose herself.

Her uncle's only answer was to lift her up and unhook the new belt of which she was so proud. The moment the clasp was open the belt flew apart several inches, for it was impossible to restrain the involuntary sigh of relief that flatly contradicted her words.

"Why, I didn't know it was tight! it didn't feel so a bit. Of course it would open if I puff like this, but I never do, because I hardly ever run," explained Rose, rather discomfited by this discovery.

"I see you don't half fill your lungs, and so you can wear this absurd thing without feeling it. The idea of cramping a tender little waist in a stiff band of leather and steel just when it ought to be growing," said Dr. Alec, surveying the belt with great disfavour as he put the clasp forward several holes, to Rose's secret dismay, for she was proud of her slender figure, and daily rejoiced that she wasn't as stout as Luly Miller, a former schoolmate, who vainly tried to repress her plumpness.

"It will fall off if it is so loose," she said anxiously, as she stood watching him pull her precious belt about.

"Not if you keep taking long breaths to hold it on. That is what I want you to do, and when you have filled this out we will go on enlarging it till your waist is more like that of Hebe, goddess of health, and less like that of a fashion-plate the ugliest thing imaginable."

"How it does look!" and Rose gave a glance of scorn at the loose belt hanging round her trim little waist. "It will be lost, and then I shall feel badly, for it cost ever so much, and is real steel and Russia leather. Just smell how nice."

"If it is lost I'll give you a better one. A soft silken sash is much fitter for a pretty child like you than a plated harness like this; and I've got no end of Italian scarfs and Turkish sashes among my traps. Ah! that makes you feel better, doesn't it?" and he pinched the cheek that had suddenly dimpled with a smile.

"It is very silly of me, but I can't help liking to know that" here she stopped and blushed and held down her head, ashamed to add, "you think I am pretty."

Dr. Alec's eyed twinkled, but he said very soberly,

"Rose, are you vain?"

"I'm afraid I am," answered a very meek voice from behind the veil of hair that hid the red face.

"That is a sad fault." And he sighed as if grieved at the confession.

"I know it is, and I try not to be; but people praise me, and I can't help liking it, for I really don't think I am repulsive."

The last word and the funny tone in which it was uttered were too much for Dr. Alec, and he laughed in spite of himself, to Rose's great relief.

"I quite agree with you; and in order that you may be still less repulsive, I want you to grow as fine a girl as Phebe."

"Phebe!" and Rose looked so amazed that her uncle nearly went off again.

"Yes, Phebe; for she has what you need health. If you dear little girls would only learn what real beauty is, and not pinch and starve and bleach yourselves out so, you'd save an immense deal of time and money and pain. A happy soul in a healthy body makes the best sort of beauty for man or woman. Do you understand that, my dear?"

"Yes, sir," answered Rose, much taken down by this comparison with the girl from the poorhouse. It nettled her sadly, and she showed that it did by saying quickly,

"I suppose you would like to have me sweep and scrub, and wear an old brown dress, and go round with my sleeves rolled up, as Phebe does?"

"I should very much, if you could work as well as she does, and show as strong a pair of arms as she can. I haven't seen a prettier picture for some time than she made of herself this morning, up to the elbows in suds, singing like a blackbird whilst she scrubbed on the back stoop."

"Well, I do think you are the queerest man that ever lived!" was all Rose could find to say after this display of bad taste.

"I haven't begun to show you my oddities yet, so you must make up your mind to worse shocks than this," he said, with such a whimsical look that she was glad the sound of a bell prevented her showing more plainly what a blow her little vanities had already received.

"You will find your box all open up in auntie's parlor, and there you can amuse her and yourself by rummaging to your heart's content; I've got to be cruising round all the morning getting my room to rights," said Dr. Alec, as they rose from breakfast.

"Can't I help you, uncle?" asked Rose, quite burning to be useful.

24

"No, thank you, I'm going to borrow Phebe for a while, if Aunt Plenty can spare her."

"Anybody anything, Alec. You will want me, I know, so I'll give orders about dinner and be all ready to lend a hand"; and the old lady bustled away full of interest and good-will.

"Uncle will find that I can do some things that Phebe can't, so now!" thought Rose, with a toss of the head as she flew to Aunt Peace and the long-desired box.

Every little girl can easily imagine what an extra good time she had diving into a sea of treasures and fishing up one pretty thing after another, till the air was full of the mingled odours of musk and sandalwood, the room gay with bright colours, and Rose in a rapture of delight. She began to forgive Dr. Alec for the oatmeal diet when she saw a lovely ivory workbox; became resigned to the state of her belt when she found a pile of rainbow-coloured sashes; and when she came to some distractingly pretty bottles of attar of rose, she felt that they almost atoned for the great sin of thinking Phebe the finer girl of the two.

Dr. Alec meanwhile had apparently taken Aunt Plenty at her word, and was turning the house upside down. A general revolution was evidently going on in the green-room, for the dark damask curtains were seen bundling away in Phebe's arms; the air-tight stove retiring to the cellar on Ben's shoulder; and the great bedstead going up garret in a fragmentary state, escorted by three bearers. Aunt Plenty was constantly on the trot among her store-rooms, camphor-chests, and linen-closets, looking as if the new order of things both amazed and amused her.

Half the peculiar performances of Dr. Alec cannot be revealed; but as Rose glanced up from her box now and then she caught glimpses of him striding by, bearing a bamboo chair, a pair of ancient andirons, a queer Japanese screen, a rug or two, and finally a large bathing-pan upon his head.

"What a curious room it will be," she said, as she sat resting and refreshing herself with "Lumps of Delight," all the way from Cairo.

"I fancy you will like it, deary," answered Aunt Peace, looking up with a smile from some pretty trifle she was making with blue silk and white muslin.

Rose did not see the smile, for just at that moment her uncle paused at the door, and she sprang up to dance before him, saying, with a face full of childish happiness,

"Look at me! look at me! I'm splendid I don't know myself. I haven't put these things on right, I dare say, but I do like them so much!"

"You look as gay as a parrot in your fez and cabaja, and it does my heart good to see the little black shadow turned into a rainbow," said Uncle Alec, surveying the bright figure before him with great approbation.

He did not say it, but he thought she made a much prettier picture than Phebe at the wash-tub, for she had stuck a purple fez on her blonde head, tied several brilliant scarfs about her waist, and put on a truly gorgeous scarlet jacket with a golden sun embroidered on the back, a silver moon on the front, and stars of all sizes on the sleeves. A pair of Turkish slippers adorned her feet, and necklaces of amber, coral, and filigree hung about her neck, while one hand held a smelling-bottle, and the other the spicy box of oriental sweetmeats.

"I feel like a girl in the 'Arabian Nights,' and expect to find a magic carpet or a wonderful talisman somewhere. Only I don't see how I ever can thank you for all these lovely things," she said, stopping her dance, as if suddenly oppressed with gratitude.

"I'll tell you how by leaving off the black clothes, that never should have been kept so long on such a child, and wearing the gay ones I've brought. It will do your spirits good, and cheer up this sober old house. Won't it, auntie?"

"I think you are right, Alec, and it is fortunate that we have not begun on her spring clothes yet, for Myra thought she ought not to wear anything brighter than violet, and she is too pale for that."

"You just let me direct Miss Hemming how to make some of these things. You will be surprised to see how much I know about piping hems and gathering arm-holes and shirring biases," began Dr. Alec, patting a pile of muslin, cloth and silk with a knowing air.

Aunt Peace and Rose laughed so that he could not display his knowledge any farther, till they stopped, when he said good-naturedly,

"That will go a great way toward filling out the belt, so laugh away, Morgiana, and I'll go back to my work, or I never shall be done."

"I couldn't help it, 'shirred biases' were so very funny!" Rose said, as she turned to her box after the splendid laugh. "But really, auntie," she added soberly, "I feel as if I ought not to have so many nice things. I suppose it wouldn't do to give Phebe some of them? Uncle might not like it."

"He would not mind; but they are not suitable for Phebe. Some of the dresses you are done with would be more useful, if they can be made over to fit her," answered Aunt Peace in the prudent, moderate tone which is so trying to our feelings when we indulge in little fits of charitable enthusiasm.

"I'd rather give her new ones, for I think she is a little bit proud and might not like old things. If she was my sister it would do, because sisters don't mind, but she isn't, and that makes it bad, you see. I know how I can manage beautifully; I'll adopt her!" and Rose looked quite radiant with this new idea.

"I'm afraid you could not do it legally till you are older, but you might see if she likes the plan, and at any rate you can be very kind to her, for in one sense we are all sisters, and should help one another."

The sweet old face looked at her so kindly that Rose was fired with a desire to settle the matter at once, and rushed away to the kitchen, just as she was. Phebe was there, polishing up the antique andirons so busily that she started when a voice cried out: "Smell that, taste this, and look at me!"

Phebe sniffed attar of rose, crunched the "Lump of Delight" tucked into her mouth, and stared with all her eyes at little Morgiana prancing about the room like a brilliant paroquet.

"My stars, ain't you splendid!" was all she could say, holding up two dusty hands.

"I've got heaps of lovely things upstairs, and I'll show them all to you, and I'd go halves, only auntie thinks they wouldn't be useful, so I shall give you something else; and you won't mind, will you? because I want to adopt you as Arabella was in the story. Won't that be nice?"

"Why, Miss Rose, have you lost your wits?"

No wonder Phebe asked, for Rose talked very fast, and looked so odd in her new costume, and was so eager she could not stop to explain. Seeing Phebe's bewilderment, she quieted down and said, with a pretty air of earnestness,

"It isn't fair that I should have so much and you so little, and I want to be as good to you as if you were my sister, for Aunt Peace says we are all sisters really. I thought if I adopted you as much as I can now, it would be nicer. Will you let me, please?"

To Rose's great surprise, Phebe sat down on the floor and hid her face in her apron for a minute without answering a word.

"Oh, dear, now she's offended, and I don't know what to do," thought Rose, much discouraged by this reception of her offer.

"Please, forgive me; I didn't mean to hurt your feelings, and hope you won't think—" she faltered presently, feeling that she must undo the mischief, if possible.

But Phebe gave her another surprise, by dropping the apron and showing a face all smiles, in spite of tears in the eyes, as she put both arms round Rose and said, with a laugh and sob,

"I think you are the dearest girl in the world, and I'll let you do anything you like with me."

"Then you do like the plan? You didn't cry because I seemed to be kind of patronising? I truly didn't mean to be," cried Rose, delighted.

"I guess I do like it! and cried because no one was ever so good to me before, and I couldn't help it. As for patronising, you may walk on me if you want to, and I won't mind," said Phebe, in a burst of gratitude, for the words, "we are sisters" went straight to her lonely heart and nestled there.

"Well, now, we can play I'm a good sprite out of the box, or, what is better, a fairy godmother come down the chimney, and you are Cinderella, and must say what you want," said Rose, trying to put the question delicately.

Phebe understood that, for she had a good deal of natural refinement, though she did come from the poor-house.

"I don't feel as if I wanted anything now, Miss Rose, but to find some way of thanking you for all you've done," she said, rubbing off a tear that went rolling down the bridge of her nose in the most unromantic way.

"Why, I haven't done anything but given you a bit of candy! Here, have some more, and eat 'em while you work, and think what I can do. I must go and clear up, so good-bye, and don't forget I've adopted you."

"You've given me sweeter things than candy, and I'm not likely to forget it." And carefully wiping off the brick-dust, Phebe pressed the little hand Rose offered warmly in both her hard ones, while the black eyes followed the departing visitor with a grateful look that made them very soft and bright.

Chapter 6—Uncle Alec's Room

Soon after dinner, and before she had got acquainted with half her new possessions, Dr. Alec proposed a drive, to carry round the first instalment of gifts to the aunts and cousins. Rose was quite ready to go, being anxious to try a certain soft burnous from the box, which not only possessed a most engaging little hood, but had funny tassels bobbing in all directions.

The big carriage was full of parcels, and even Ben's seat was loaded with Indian war clubs, a Chinese kite of immense size, and a pair of polished ox-horns from Africa. Uncle Alec, very blue as to his clothes, and very brown as to his face, sat bolt upright, surveying well known places with interest, while Rose, feeling unusually elegant and comfortable, leaned back folded in her soft mantle, and played she was an Eastern princess making a royal progress among her subjects.

At three of the places their calls were brief, for Aunt Myra's catarrh was unusually bad; Aunt Clara had a room full of company; and Aunt Jane showed such a tendency to discuss the population, productions, and politics of Europe, Asia and Africa, that even Dr. Alec was dismayed, and got away as soon as possible.

"Now we will have a good time! I do hope the boys will be at home," said Rose, with a sigh of relief, as they wound yet higher up the hill to Aunt Jessie's.

"I left this for the last call, so that we might find the lads just in from school. Yes, there is Jamie on the gate watching for us; now you'll see the Clan gather; they are always swarming about together."

The instant Jamie saw the approaching guests he gave a shrill whistle, which was answered by echoes from meadow, house and barn, as the cousins came running from all directions, shouting, "Hooray for Uncle Alec!" They went at the carriage like highwaymen, robbed it of every parcel, took the occupants prisoners, and marched them into the house with great exultation.

"Little Mum! little Mum! here they are with lots of goodies! Come down and see the fun right away! Quick!" bawled Will and Geordie amidst a general ripping off of papers and a reckless cutting of strings that soon turned the tidy room into a chaos.

Down came Aunt Jessie with her pretty cap half on, but such a beaming face below it that one rather thought the fly-away head-gear an improvement than otherwise. She had hardly time to greet Rose and the doctor before the boys were about her, each clamouring for her to see his gift and rejoice over it with him, for "little Mum" went halves in everything. The great horns skirmished about her as if to toss her to the ceiling; the war clubs hurtled over her head as if to annihilate her; an amazing medley from the four quarters of the globe filled her lap, and seven excited boys all talked to her at once.

But she liked it; oh dear, yes! and sat smiling, admiring, and explaining, quite untroubled by the din, which made Rose cover up her ears and Dr. Alec threaten instant flight if the riot was not quelled. That threat produced a lull, and while the uncle received thanks in one corner, the aunt had some little confidences made to her in the other.

"Well, dear, and how are things going with you now? Better, I hope, than they were a week ago."

"Aunt Jessie, I think I'm going to be very happy, now uncle has come. He does the queerest things, but he is so good to me I can't help loving him"; and, nestling closer to little Mum, Rose told all that had happened, ending with a rapturous account of the splendid box.

"I am very glad, dear. But, Rose, I must warn you of one thing; don't let uncle spoil you."

"But I like to be spoilt, auntie."

"I don't doubt it; but if you turn out badly when the year is over he will be blamed, and his experiment prove a failure. That would be a pity, wouldn't it? when he wants to do so much for you, and can do it if his kind heart does not get in the way of his good judgment."

"I never thought of that, and I'll try not to be spoilt. But how can I help it?" asked Rose anxiously.

"By not complaining of the wholesome things he wants you to do; by giving him cheerful obedience as well as love; and even making some small sacrifices for his sake."

"I will, I truly will! and when I get in a worry about things may I come to you? Uncle told me to, and I feel as if I shouldn't be afraid."

"You may, darling; this is the place where little troubles are best cured, and this is what mothers are for, I fancy"; and Aunt Jessie drew the curly head to her shoulder with a tender look that proved how well she knew what medicine the child most needed.

It was so sweet and comfortable that Rose sat still enjoying it till a little voice said,

"Mamma, don't you think Pokey would like some of my shells? Rose gave Phebe some of her nice things, and it was very good of her. Can I?"

"Who is Pokey?" asked Rose, popping up her head, attracted by the odd name.

"My dolly; do you want to see her?" asked Jamie, who had been much impressed by the tale of adoption he had overheard.

"Yes; I'm fond of dollies, only don't tell the boys, or they will laugh at me."

"They don't laugh at me, and they play with my dolly a great deal; but she likes me best"; and Jamie ran away to produce his pet.

"I brought my old doll, but I keep her hidden because I am too big to play with her, and yet I can't bear to throw her away, I'm so fond of her," said Rose, continuing her confidences in a whisper.

"You can come and play with Jamie's whenever you like, for we believe in dollies up here," began Aunt Jessie, smiling to herself as if something amused her.

Just then Jamie came back, and Rose understood the smile, for his dolly proved to be a pretty four-year-old little girl, who trotted in as fast as her fat legs would carry her, and making straight for the shells, scrambled up an armful, saying, with a laugh that showed her little white teeth,

"All for Dimmy and me, for Dimmy and me!"

"That's my dolly; isn't she a nice one?" asked Jamie, proudly surveying his pet with his hands behind him and his short legs rather far apart a manly attitude copied from his brothers.

"She is a dear dolly. But why call her Pokey?" asked Rose, charmed with the new plaything.

"She is such an inquisitive little body she is always poking that mite of a nose into everything; and as Paul Pry did not suit, the boys fell to calling her Pokey. Not a pretty name, but very expressive."

It certainly was, for, having examined the shells, the busy tot laid hold of everything she could find, and continued her researches till Archie caught her sucking his carved ivory chessmen to see if they were not barley sugar. Rice paper pictures were also discovered crumpled up in her tiny pocket, and she nearly smashed Will's ostrich egg by trying to sit upon it.

"Here, Jim, take her away; she's worse than the puppies, and we can't have her round," commanded the elder brother, picking her up and handing her over to the little fellow, who received her with open arms and the warning remark,

"You'd better mind what you do, for I'm going to 'dopt Pokey like Rose did Phebe, and then you'll have to be very good to her, you big fellows."

"'Dopt away, baby, and I'll give you a cage to keep her in, or you won't have her long, for she is getting worse than a monkey"; and Archie went back to his mates, while Aunt Jessie, foreseeing a crisis, proposed that Jamie should take his dolly home, as she was borrowed, and it was time her visit ended.

"My dolly is better than yours, isn't she? 'cause she can walk and talk and sing and dance, and yours can't do anything, can she?" asked Jamie with pride, as he regarded his Pokey, who just then had been moved to execute a funny little jig and warble the well-known couplet,

"'Puss-tat, puss-tat, where you been?'
'I been Lunnin, to saw a Tween.'"
After which superb display she retired, escorted by Jamie, both making a fearful din blowing on conch shells.

"We must tear ourselves away, Rose, because I want to get you home before sunset. Will you come for a drive, Jessie?" said Dr. Alec, as the music died away in the distance.

"No, thank you; but I see the boys want a scamper, so, if you don't mind, they may escort you home, but not go in. That is only allowed on holidays."

The words were hardly out of Aunt Jessie's mouth when Archie said, in a tone of command,

"Pass the word, lads. Boot and saddle, and be quick about it."

"All right!" And in a moment not a vestige of boy remained but the litter on the floor.

The cavalcade went down the hill at a pace that made Rose cling to her uncle's arm, for the fat old horses got excited by the antics of the ponies careering all about them, and went as fast as they could pelt, with the gay dog-cart rattling in front, for Archie and Charlie scorned shelties since this magnificent equipage had been set up. Ben enjoyed the fun, and the lads cut up capers till Rose declared that "circus" was the proper name for them after all.

When they reached the house they dismounted, and stood, three on each side the steps, in martial attitudes, while her ladyship was handed out with great elegance by Uncle Alec. Then the Clan saluted, mounted at word of command, and with a wild whoop tore down the avenue in what they considered the true Arab style.

"That was splendid, now it is safely ended," said Rose, skipping up the steps with her head over her shoulder to watch the dear tassels bob about.

"I shall get you a pony as soon as you are a little stronger," said Dr. Alec, watching her with a smile.

"Oh, I couldn't ride one of those horrid, frisky little beasts! They roll their eyes and bounce about so, I should die of fright," cried Rose, clasping her hands tragically.

"Are you a coward?"

"About horses I am."

"Never mind, then; come and see my new room"; and he led the way upstairs without another word.

As Rose followed she remembered her promise to Aunt Jessie, and was sorry she had objected so decidedly. She was a great deal more sorry five minutes later, and well she might be.

"Now, take a good look, and tell me what you think of it," said Dr. Alec, opening the door and letting her enter before him, while Phebe was seen whisking down the backstairs with a dust-pan.

Rose walked to the middle of the room, stood still, and gazed about her with eyes that brightened as they looked, for all was changed.

This chamber had been built out over the library to suit some fancy, and had been unused for years, except at Christmas times, when the old house overflowed. It had three windows one to the east, that overlooked the bay; one to the south, where the horse-chestnuts waved their green fans; and one to the west, towards the hill and the evening sky. A ruddy sunset burned there now, filling the room with an enchanted glow; the soft murmur of the sea was heard, and a robin chirped "Good-night!" among the budding trees.

Rose saw and heard these things first, and felt their beauty with a child's quick instinct; then her eye took in the altered aspect of the room, once so shrouded, still and solitary, now so full of light and warmth and simple luxury.

India matting covered the floor, with a gay rug here and there; the antique andirons shone on the wide hearth, where a cheery blaze dispelled the dampness of the long-closed room. Bamboo lounges and chairs stood about, and quaint little tables in cosy corners; one bearing a pretty basket, one a desk, and on a third lay several familiar-looking books. In a recess stood a narrow white bed, with a lovely Madonna hanging over it. The Japanese screen half-folded back showed a delicate toilet service of blue and white set forth on a marble slab, and near by was the great bath-pan, with Turkish towels and a sponge as big as Rose's head.

"Uncle must love cold water like a duck," she thought, with a shiver.

Then her eye went on to the tall cabinet, where a half-open door revealed a tempting array of the drawers, shelves and "cubby holes," which so delight the hearts of children.

"What a grand place for my new things," she thought, wondering what her uncle kept in that cedar retreat.

"Oh me, what a sweet toilet table!" was her next mental exclamation, as she approached this inviting spot.

A round old-fashioned mirror hung over it, with a gilt eagle a-top, holding in his beak the knot of blue ribbon that tied up a curtain of muslin falling on either side of the table, where appeared little ivory-handled brushes, two slender silver candle-sticks, a porcelain match-box, several pretty trays for small matters, and, most imposing of all, a plump blue silk cushion, coquettishly trimmed with lace, and pink rose-buds at the corners.

That cushion rather astonished Rose; in fact, the whole table did, and she was just thinking, with a sly smile,

"Uncle is a dandy, but I never should have guessed it," when he opened the door of a large closet, saying, with a careless wave of the hand,

"Men like plenty of room for their rattle-traps; don't you think that ought to satisfy me?"

Rose peeped in and gave a start, though all she saw was what one usually finds in closets clothes and boots, boxes and bags. Ah! but you see these clothes were small black and white frocks; the row of little boots that stood below had never been on Dr. Alec's feet; the green bandbox had a gray veil straying out of it, and yes! the bag hanging on the door was certainly her own piece-bag, with a hole in one corner. She gave a quick look round the room and understood now why it had seemed too dainty for a man, why her Testament and Prayer Book were on the table by the bed, and what those rose-buds meant on the blue cushion. It came upon her in one delicious burst that this little paradise was all for her, and, not knowing how else to express her gratitude, she caught Dr. Alec round the neck, saying impetuously,

"O uncle, you are too good to me! I'll do anything you ask me; ride wild horses and take freezing baths and eat bad-tasting messes, and let my clothes hang on me, to show how much I thank you for this dear, sweet, lovely room!"

"You like it, then? But why do you think it is yours, my lass?" asked Dr. Alec, as he sat down looking well pleased, and drew his excited little niece to his knee.

"I don't think, I know it is for me; I see it in your face, and I feel as if I didn't half deserve it. Aunt Jessie said you would spoil me, and I must not let you. I'm afraid this looks like it, and perhaps oh me! perhaps I ought not to have this beautiful room after all!" and Rose tried to look as if she could be heroic enough to give it up if it was best.

"I owe Mrs. Jessie one for that," said Dr. Alec, trying to frown, though in his secret soul he felt that she was quite right. Then he smiled that cordial smile, which was like sunshine on his brown face, as he said,

"This is part of the cure, Rose, and I put you here that you might take my three great remedies in the best and easiest way. Plenty of sun, fresh air, and cold water; also cheerful surroundings, and some work; for Phebe is to show you how to take care of this room, and be your little maid as well as friend and teacher. Does that sound hard and disagreeable to you, dear?"

"No, sir; very, very pleasant, and I'll do my best to be a good patient. But I really don't think anyone could be sick in this delightful room," she said, with a long sigh of happiness as her eye went from one pleasant object to another.

"Then you like my sort of medicine better than Aunt Myra's, and don't want to throw it out of the window, hey?"

Chapter 7—A Trip to China

"Come, little girl, I've got another dose for you. I fancy you won't take it as well as you did the last, but you will like it better after a while," said Dr. Alec, about a week after the grand surprise.

Rose was sitting in her pretty room, where she would gladly have spent all her time if it had been allowed; but she looked up with a smile, for she had ceased to fear her uncle's remedies, and was always ready to try a new one. The last had been a set of light gardening tools, with which she had helped him put the flower-beds in order, learning all sorts of new and pleasant things about the plants as she worked, for, though she had studied botany at school, it seemed very dry stuff compared with Uncle Alec's lively lesson.

"What is it now?" she asked, shutting her work-box without a murmur.

"Salt-water."

"How must I take it?"

"Put on the new suit Miss Hemming sent home yesterday, and come down to the beach; then I'll show you."

"Yes, sir," answered Rose obediently, adding to herself, with a shiver, as he went off: "It is too early for bathing, so I know it is something to do with a dreadful boat."

Putting on the new suit of blue flannel, prettily trimmed with white, and the little sailor-hat with long streamers, diverted her mind from the approaching trial, till a shrill whistle reminded her that her uncle was waiting. Away she ran through the garden, down the sandy path, out upon the strip of beach that belonged to the house, and here she found Dr. Alec busy with a slender red and white boat that lay rocking on the rising tide.

"That is a dear little boat; and 'Bonnie Belle' is a pretty name," she said, trying not to show how nervous she felt.

"It is for you; so sit in the stern and learn to steer, till you are ready to learn to row."

"Do all boats wiggle about in that way?" she asked, lingering as if to tie her hat more firmly.

"Oh, yes, pitch about like nutshells when the sea is a bit rough," answered her sailor uncle, never guessing her secret woe.

"Is it rough to-day?"

"Not very; it looks a trifle squally to the eastward, but we are all right till the wind changes. Come."

"Can you swim, uncle?" asked Rose, clutching at his arm as he took her hand.

"Like a fish. Now then."

"Oh, please hold me very tight till I get there! Why do you have the stern so far away?" and, stifling several squeaks of alarm in her passage, Rose crept to the distant seat, and sat there holding on with both hands and looking as if she expected every wave to bring a sudden shipwreck.

Uncle Alec took no notice of her fear, but patiently instructed her in the art of steering, till she was so absorbed in remembering which was starboard and which larboard, that she forgot to say "OW!" every time a big wave slapped against the boat.

"Now where shall we go?" she asked, as the wind blew freshly in her face, and a few, long swift strokes sent them half across the little bay.

"Suppose we go to China?"

"Isn't that rather a long voyage?"

"Not as I go. Steer round the Point into the harbour, and I'll give you a glimpse of China in twenty minutes or so."

"I should like that!" and Rose sat wondering what he meant, while she enjoyed the new sights all about her.

Behind them the green Aunt-hill sloped gently upward to the grove at the top, and all along the seaward side stood familiar houses, stately, cosy, or picturesque. As they rounded the Point, the great bay opened before them full of shipping, and the city lay beyond, its spires rising above the tall masts with their gay streamers.

"Are we going there?" she asked, for she had never seen this aspect of the rich and busy old city before.

"Yes. Uncle Mac has a ship just in from Hong Kong, and I thought you would like to go and see it."

"Oh, I should. I love dearly to go poking about in the warehouses with Uncle Mac; everything is so curious and new to me; and I'm specially interested in China because you have been there."

"I'll show you two genuine Chinamen who have just arrived. You will like to welcome Whang Lo and Fun See, I'm sure."

"Don't ask me to speak to them, uncle; I shall be sure to laugh at the odd names and the pig-tails and the slanting eyes. Please let me just trot round after you; I like that best."

"Very well; now steer toward the wharf where the big ship with the queer flag is. That's the 'Rajah,' and we will go aboard if we can."

In among the ships they went, by the wharves where the water was green and still, and queer barnacles grew on the slippery piles. Odd smells saluted her nose, and odd sights met her eyes, but Rose liked it all, and played she was really landing in Hong Kong when they glided up to the steps in the shadow of the tall "Rajah." Boxes and bales were rising out of the hold and being carried into the warehouse by stout porters, who tugged and bawled and clattered about with small trucks, or worked cranes with iron claws that came down and clutched heavy weights, whisking them aloft to where wide doors like mouths swallowed them up.

Dr. Alec took her aboard the ship, and she had the satisfaction of poking her inquisitive little nose into every available corner, at the risk of being crushed, lost, or drowned.

"Well, child, how would you like to take a voyage round the world with me in a jolly old craft like this?" asked her uncle, as they rested a minute in the captain's cabin.

"I should like to see the world, but not in such a small, untidy, smelly place as this. We would go in a yacht all clean and comfortable; Charlie says that is the proper way," answered Rose, surveying the close quarters with little favour.

"You are not a true Campbell if you don't like the smell of tar and salt-water, nor Charlie either, with his luxurious yacht. Now come ashore and chin-chin with the Celestials."

After a delightful progress through the great warehouse, peeping and picking as they went, they found Uncle Mac and the yellow gentlemen in his private room, where samples, gifts, curiosities, and newly arrived treasures of all sorts were piled up in pleasing pro-fusion and con-fusion.

As soon as possible Rose retired to a corner, with a porcelain god on one side, a green dragon on the other, and, what was still more embarrassing, Fun See sat on a tea-chest in front, and stared at her with his beady black eyes till she did not know where to look.

Mr. Whang Lo was an elderly gentleman in American costume, with his pig-tail neatly wound round his head. He spoke English, and was talking busily with Uncle Mac in the most commonplace way so Rose considered him a failure. But Fun See was delightfully Chinese from his junk-like shoes to the button on his pagoda hat; for he had got himself up in style, and was a mass of silk jackets and slouchy trousers. He was short and fat, and waddled comically; his eyes were very "slanting," as Rose said; his queue was long, so were his nails; his yellow face was plump and shiny, and he was altogether a highly satisfactory Chinaman.

Uncle Alec told her that Fun See had come out to be educated and could only speak a little pigeon English; so she must be kind to the poor fellow, for he was only a lad, though he looked nearly as old as Mr. Whang Lo. Rose said she would be kind; but had not the least idea how to entertain the queer guest, who looked as if he had walked out of one of the rice-paper landscapes on the wall, and sat nodding at her so like a toy Mandarin that she could hardly keep sober.

In the midst of her polite perplexity, Uncle Mac saw the two young people gazing wistfully at one another, and seemed to enjoy the joke of this making acquaintance under difficulties. Taking a box from his table, he gave it to Fun See, with an order that seemed to please him very much.

Descending from his perch, he fell to unpacking it with great neatness and despatch, while Rose watched him, wondering what was going to happen. Presently, out from the wrappings came a teapot, which caused her to clasp her hands with delight, for it was made in the likeness of a plump little Chinaman. His hat was the cover, his queue the handle, and his pipe the nose. It stood upon feet in shoes turned up at the toes, and the smile on the fat, sleepy face was so like that on Fun's when he displayed the teapot, that Rose couldn't help laughing, which pleased him much.

Two pretty cups with covers, and a fine scarlet tray completed the set, and made one long to have a "dish of tea," even in Chinese style, without cream or sugar.

When he had arranged them on a little table before her, Fun signified in pantomime that they were hers, from her uncle. She returned her thanks in the same way, whereupon he returned to his tea-chest, and, having no other means of communication, they sat smiling and nodding at one another in an absurd sort of way till a new idea seemed to strike Fun. Tumbling off his seat, he waddled away as fast as his petticoats permitted, leaving Rose hoping that he had not gone to get a roasted rat, a stewed puppy, or any other foreign mess which civility would oblige her to eat.

While she waited for her funny new friend, she improved her mind in a way that would have charmed Aunt Jane. The gentlemen were talking over all sorts of things, and she listened attentively, storing up much of what she heard, for she had an excellent memory, and longed to distinguish herself by being able to produce some useful information when reproached with her ignorance.

She was just trying to impress upon her mind that Amoy was two hundred and eighty miles from Hong Kong, when Fun came scuffling back, bearing what she thought was a small sword, till he unfurled an immense fan, and presented it with a string of Chinese compliments, the meaning of which would have amused her even more than the sound, if she could have understood it.

She had never seen such an astonishing fan, and at once became absorbed in examining it. Of course, there was no perspective whatever, which only gave it a peculiar charm to Rose, for in one place a lovely lady, with blue knitting-needles in her hair, sat directly upon the spire of a stately pagoda. In another charming view a brook appeared to flow in at the front door of a stout gentleman's house, and out at his chimney. In a third a zig-zag wall went up into the sky like a flash of lightning, and a bird with two tails was apparently brooding over a fisherman whose boat was just going aground upon the moon.

It was altogether a fascinating thing, and she would have sat wafting it to and fro all the afternoon, to Fun's great satisfaction, if Dr. Alec's attention had not suddenly been called to her by a breeze from the big fan that blew his hair into his eyes, and reminded him that they must go. So the pretty china was repacked, Rose furled her fan, and with several parcels of choice teas for the old ladies stowed away in Dr. Alec's pockets, they took their leave, after Fun had saluted them with "the three bendings and the nine knockings," as they salute the Emperor, or "Son of Heaven," at home.

"I feel as if I had really been to China, and I'm sure I look so," said Rose, as they glided out of the shadow of the "Rajah."

She certainly did, for Mr. Whang Lo had given her a Chinese umbrella; Uncle Alec had got some lanterns to light up her balcony; the great fan lay in her lap, and the tea-set reposed at her feet.

"This is not a bad way to study geography, is it?" asked her uncle, who had observed her attention to the talk.

"It is a very pleasant way, and I really think I have learned more about China to-day than in all the lessons I had at school, though I used to rattle off the answers as fast as I could go. No one explained anything to us, so all I remember is that tea and silk come from there, and the women have little bits of feet. I saw Fun looking at mine, and he must have thought them perfectly immense," answered Rose, surveying her stout boots with sudden contempt.

"We will have out the maps and the globe, and I'll show you some of my journeys, telling stories as we go. That will be next best to doing it actually."

"You are so fond of travelling, I should think it would be very dull for you here, uncle. Do you know, Aunt Plenty says she is sure you will be off in a year or two."

"Very likely."

"Oh, me! what shall I do then?" sighed Rose, in a tone of despair that made Uncle Alec's face brighten with a look of genuine pleasure as he said significantly,

"Next time I go I shall take my little anchor with me. How will that suit?"

"Really, uncle?"

"Really, niece."

Rose gave a little bounce of rapture which caused the boat to "wiggle" in a way that speedily quieted her down. But she sat beaming joyfully and trying to think which of some hundred questions she would ask first, when Dr. Alec said, pointing to a boat that was coming up behind them in great style,

"How well those fellows row! Look at them, and take notes for your own use by and by."

The "Stormy Petrel" was manned by half a dozen jaunty looking sailors, who made a fine display of blue shirts and shiny hats, with stars and anchors in every direction.

"How beautifully they go, and they are only boys. Why, I do believe they are our boys! Yes, I see Charlie laughing over his shoulder. Row, uncle, row! Oh, please do, and not let them catch up with us!" cried Rose, in such a state of excitement that the new umbrella nearly went overboard.

"All right, here we go!" and away they did go with a long steady sweep of the oars that carried the "Bonnie Belle" through the water with a rush.

The lads pulled their prettiest, but Dr. Alec would have reached the Point first, if Rose, in her flurry, had not retarded him by jerking the rudder ropes in a most unseamanlike way, and just as she got right again her hat blew off. That put an end to the race, and while they were still fishing for the hat the other boat came alongside, with all the oars in the air, and the jolly young tars ready for a frolic.

"Did you catch a crab, uncle?"

"No, a blue-fish," he answered, as the dripping hat was landed on a seat to dry.

"What have you been doing?"

"Seeing Fun."

"Good for you, Rose! I know what you mean. We are going to have him up to show us how to fly the big kite, for we can't get the hang of it. Isn't he great fun, though?"

"No, little Fun."

"Come, stop joking, and show us what you've got."

"You'd better hoist that fan for a sail."

"Lend Dandy your umbrella; he hates to burn his pretty nose."

"I say, uncle, are you going to have a Feast of Lanterns?"

"No, I'm going to have a feast of bread and butter, for it's tea-time. If that black cloud doesn't lie, we shall have a gust before long, so you had better get home as soon as you can, or your mother will be anxious, Archie."

"Ay, ay, skipper. Good-night, Rose; come out often, and we'll teach you all there is to know about rowing," was Charlie's modest invitation.

Then the boats parted company, and across the water from the "Petrel's" crew came a verse from one of the Nonsense songs in which the boys delighted.

"Oh, Timballoo! how happy we are,
We live in a sieve and a crockery jar!
And all night long, in the starlight pale,
We sail away, with a pea-green sail,

37

And whistle and warble a moony song
To the echoing sound of a coppery gong.
Far and few, far and few
Are the lands where the Jumblies live;
Their heads are green, and their hands are blue,
And they went to sea in a sieve."


Chapter 8—And what came of it

"Uncle, could you lend me a ninepence? I'll return it as soon as I get my pocket-money," said Rose, coming into the library in a great hurry that evening.

"I think I could, and I won't charge any interest for it, so you need not be in any hurry to repay me. Come back here and help me settle these books if you have nothing pleasanter to do," answered Dr. Alec, handing out the money with that readiness which is so delightful when we ask small loans.

"I'll come in a minute; I've been longing to fix my books, but didn't dare to touch them, because you always shake your head when I read."

"I shall shake my head when you write, if you don't do it better than you did in making out this catalogue."

"I know it's bad, but I was in a hurry when I did it, and I am in one now." And away went Rose, glad to escape a lecture.

But she got it when she came back, for Uncle Alec was still knitting his brows over the list of books, and sternly demanded, pointing to a tipsy-looking title staggering down the page,

"Is that meant for 'Pulverized Bones,' ma'am?"

"No, sir; it's 'Paradise Lost.'"

"Well, I'm glad to know it, for I began to think you were planning to study surgery or farming. And what is this, if you please? 'Babies' Aprons' is all I can make of it."

Rose looked hard at the scrawl, and presently announced, with an air of superior wisdom,

"Oh, that's 'Bacon's Essays.'"

"Miss Power did not teach anything so old-fashioned as writing, I see. Now look at this memorandum Aunt Plenty gave me, and see what a handsome plain hand that is. She went to a dame-school and learnt a few useful things well; that is better than a smattering of half a dozen so-called higher branches, I take the liberty of thinking."

"Well, I'm sure I was considered a bright girl at school, and learned everything I was taught. Luly and me were the first in all our classes, and 'specially praised for our French and music and those sort of things," said Rose, rather offended at Uncle Alec's criticism.

"I dare say; but if your French grammar was no better than your English, I think the praise was not deserved, my dear."

"Why, uncle, we did study English grammar, and I could parse beautifully. Miss Power used to have us up to show off when people came. I don't see but I talk as right as most girls."

"I dare say you do, but we are all too careless about our English. Now, think a minute, and tell me if these expressions are correct 'Luly and me,' 'those sort of things,' and 'as right as most girls.'"

Rose pulled her pet curl and put up her lip, but had to own that she was wrong, and said meekly, after a pause which threatened to be sulky,

"I suppose I should have said 'Luly and I,' in that case, and 'that sort of things' and 'rightly,' though 'correctly' would have been a better word, I guess."

"Thank you; and if you will kindly drop 'I guess,' I shall like my little Yankee all the better. Now, see here, Rosy, I don't pretend to set myself up for a model in anything, and you may come down on my grammar, manners or morals as often as you think I'm wrong, and I'll thank you. I've been knocking about the world for years, and have got careless, but I want my girl to be what I call well-educated, even if she studies nothing but the three 'Rs' for a year to come. Let us be thorough, no matter how slowly we go."

He spoke so earnestly and looked so sorry to have ruffled her that Rose went and sat on the arm of his chair, saying, with a pretty air of penitence,

"I'm sorry I was cross, uncle, when I ought to thank you for taking so much interest in me. I guess no, I think you are right about being thorough, for I used to understand a great deal better when papa taught me a few lessons than when Miss Power hurried me through so many. I declare my head used to be such a jumble of French and German, history and arithmetic, grammar and music, I used to feel sometimes as if it would split. I'm sure I don't wonder it ached." And she held on to it as if the mere memory of the "jumble" made it swim.

"Yet that is considered an excellent school, I find, and I dare say it would be if the benighted lady did not think it necessary to cram her pupils like Thanks-giving turkeys, instead of feeding them in a natural and wholesome way. It is the fault with most American schools, and the poor little heads will go on aching till we learn better."

This was one of Dr. Alec's hobbies, and Rose was afraid he was off for a gallop, but he reined himself in and gave her thoughts a new turn by saying suddenly, as he pulled out a fat pocket-book,

"Uncle Mac has put all your affairs into my hands now, and here is your month's pocket money. You keep your own little accounts, I suppose?"

"Thank you. Yes, Uncle Mac gave me an account book when I went to school, and I used to put down my expenses, but I couldn't make them go very well, for figures are the one thing I am not at all clever about," said Rose, rummaging in her desk for a dilapidated little book, which she was ashamed to show when she found it.

"Well, as figures are rather important things to most of us, and you may have a good many accounts to keep some day, wouldn't it be wise to begin at once and learn to manage your pennies before the pounds come to perplex you?"

"I thought you would do all that fussy part and take care of the pounds, as you call them. Need I worry about it? I do hate sums, so!"

"I shall take care of things till you are of age, but I mean that you shall know how your property is managed, and do as much of it as you can by and by; then you won't be dependent on the honesty of other people."

"Gracious me! as if I wouldn't trust you with millions of billions if I had them," cried Rose, scandalised at the mere suggestion.

"Ah, but I might be tempted; guardians are sometimes; so you'd better keep your eye on me, and in order to do that you must learn all about these affairs," answered Dr. Alec, as he made an entry in his own very neat account-book.

Rose peeped over his shoulder at it, and then turned to the arithmetical puzzle in her hand with a sigh of despair.

"Uncle, when you add up your expenses do you ever find you have got more money than you had in the beginning?"

"No; I usually find that I have a good deal less than I had in the beginning. Are you troubled in the peculiar way you mention?"

"Yes; it is very curious, but I never can make things come out square."

"Perhaps I can help you," began Uncle Alec, in the most respectful tone.

"I think you had better, for if I have got to keep accounts I may as well begin in the right way. But please don't laugh! I know I'm very stupid, and my book is a disgrace, but I never could get it straight." And with great trepidation, Rose gave up her funny little accounts.

It really was good in Dr. Alec not to laugh, and Rose felt deeply grateful when he said in a mildly suggestive tone,

"The dollars and cents seem to be rather mixed, perhaps if I just straightened them out a bit we should find things all right."

"Please do, and then show me on a fresh leaf how to make mine look nice and ship-shape as yours do."

As Rose stood by him watching the ease with which he quickly brought order out of chaos, she privately resolved to hunt up her old arithmetic and perfect herself in the four first rules, with a good tug at fractions, before she read any more fairy tales.

"Am I a rich girl, uncle?" she asked suddenly, as he was copying a column of figures.

"Rather a poor one, I should say, since you had to borrow a ninepence."

"That was your fault, because you forgot my pocket-money. But, really, shall I be rich by and by?"

"I am afraid you will."

"Why afraid, uncle?"

"Too much money is a bad thing."

"But I can give it away, you know; that is always the pleasantest part of having it I think."

"I'm glad you feel so, for you can do much good with your fortune if you know how to use it well."

"You shall teach me, and when I am a woman we will set up a school where nothing but the three R's shall be taught, and all the children live on oatmeal, and the girls have waists a yard round," said Rose, with a sudden saucy smile dimpling her cheeks.

"You are an impertinent little baggage, to turn on me in that way right in the midst of my first attempt at teaching. Never mind, I'll have an extra bitter dose for you next time, miss."

"I knew you wanted to laugh, so I gave you a chance. Now, I will be good, master, and do my lesson nicely."

So Dr. Alec had his laugh, and then Rose sat down and took a lesson in accounts which she never forgot.

"Now come and read aloud to me; my eyes are tired, and it is pleasant to sit here by the fire while the rain pours outside and Aunt Jane lectures upstairs," said Uncle Alec, when last month's accounts had been put in good order and a fresh page neatly begun.

Rose liked to read aloud, and gladly gave him the chapter in "Nicholas Nickleby" where the Miss Kenwigses take their French lesson. She did her very best, feeling that she was being criticised, and hoping that she might not be found wanting in this as in other things.

"Shall I go on, sir?" she asked very meekly, when the chapter ended.

"If you are not tired, dear. It is a pleasure to hear you, for you read remarkably well," was the answer that filled her heart with pride and pleasure.

"Do you really think so, uncle? I'm so glad! Papa taught me, and I read for hours to him, but I thought perhaps, he liked it because he was fond of me."

"So am I; but you really do read unusually well, and I'm very glad of it, for it is a rare accomplishment, and one I value highly. Come here in this cosy, low chair; the light is better, and I can pull these curls if you go too fast. I see you are going to be a great comfort as well as a great credit to your old uncle, Rosy." And Dr. Alec drew her close beside him with such a fatherly look and tone that she felt it would be very easy to love and obey him, since he knew how to mix praise and blame so pleasantly together.

Another chapter was just finished, when the sound of a carriage warned them that Aunt Jane was about to depart. Before they could go to meet her, however, she appeared in the doorway looking like an unusually tall mummy in her waterproof, with her glasses shining like cat's eyes from the depths of the hood.

"Just as I thought! petting that child to death and letting her sit up late reading trash. I do hope you feel the weight of the responsibility you have taken upon yourself, Alec," she said, with a certain grim sort of satisfaction at seeing things go wrong.

"I think I have a very realising sense of it, sister Jane," answered Dr. Alec, with a comical shrug of the shoulders and a glance at Rose's bright face.

"It is sad to see a great girl wasting these precious hours so. Now, my boys have studied all day, and Mac is still at his books, I've no doubt, while you have not had a lesson since you came, I suspect."

"I've had five to-day, ma'am," was Rose's very unexpected answer.

"I'm glad to hear it; and what were they, pray?" Rose looked very demure as she replied,

"Navigation, geography, grammar, arithmetic, and keeping my temper."

"Queer lessons, I fancy; and what have you learned from this remarkable mixture, I should like to know?"

A naughty sparkle came into Rose's eyes as she answered, with a droll look at her uncle,

"I can't tell you all, ma'am, but I have collected some useful information about China, which you may like, especially the teas. The best are Lapsing Souchong, Assam Pekoe, rare Ankoe, Flowery Pekoe, Howqua's mixture, Scented Caper, Padral tea, black Congou, and green Twankey. Shanghai is on the Woosung River. Hong Kong means 'Island of Sweet waters.' Singapore is 'Lion's Town.' 'Chops' are the boats they live in; and they drink tea out of little saucers. Principal productions are porcelain, tea, cinnamon, shawls, tin, tamarinds and opium. They have beautiful temples and queer gods; and in Canton is the Dwelling of the Holy Pigs, fourteen of them, very big, and all blind."

The effect of this remarkable burst was immense, especially the fact last mentioned. It entirely took the wind out of Aunt Jane's sails; it was so sudden, so varied and unexpected, that she had not a word to say. The glasses remained fixed full upon Rose for a moment, and then, with a hasty "Oh, indeed!" the excellent lady bundled into her carriage and drove away, somewhat bewildered and very much disturbed.

She would have been more so if she had seen her reprehensible brother-in-law dancing a triumphal polka down the hall with Rose in honour of having silenced the enemy's battery for once.

Chapter 9—Phebe's Secret
"Why do you keep smiling to yourself, Phebe?" asked Rose, as they were working together one morning, for Dr. Alec considered house-work the best sort of gymnastics for girls; so Rose took lessons of Phebe in sweeping, dusting and bed-making.

"I was thinking about a nice little secret I know, and couldn't help smiling."

"Shall I know it, sometime?"

"Guess you will."

"Shall I like it?"

"Oh, won't you, though!"

"Will it happen soon?"

"Sometime this week."

"I know what it is! The boys are going to have fireworks on the fourth, and have got some surprise for me. Haven't they?"

"That's telling."

"Well, I can wait; only tell me one thing is uncle in it?"

"Of course he is; there's never any fun without him."

"Then it's all right, and sure to be nice."

Rose went out on the balcony to shake the rugs, and, having given them a vigorous beating, hung them on the balustrade to air, while she took a look at her plants. Several tall vases and jars stood there, and a month of June sun and rain had worked wonders with the seeds and slips she had planted. Morning-glories and nasturtiums ran all over the bars, making haste to bloom. Scarlet beans and honeysuckles were climbing up from below to meet their pretty neighbours, and the woodbine was hanging its green festoons wherever it could cling.

The waters of the bay were dancing in the sunshine, a fresh wind stirred the chestnut-trees with a pleasant sound, and the garden below was full of roses, butterflies and bees. A great chirping and twittering went on among the birds, busy with their summer house-keeping, and, far away, the white-winged gulls were dipping and diving in the sea, where ships, like larger birds, went sailing to and fro.

"Oh, Phebe, it's such a lovely day, I do wish your fine secret was going to happen right away! I feel just like having a good time; don't you?" said Rose, waving her arms as if she was going to fly.

"I often feel that way, but I have to wait for my good times, and don't stop working to wish for 'em. There, now you can finish as soon as the dust settles; I must go do my stairs," and Phebe trudged away with the broom, singing as she went.

Rose leaned where she was, and fell to thinking how many good times she had had lately, for the gardening had prospered finely, and she was learning to swim and row, and there were drives and walks, and quiet hours of reading and talk with Uncle Alec, and, best of all, the old pain and ennui seldom troubled her now. She could work and play all day, sleep sweetly all night, and enjoy life with the zest of a healthy, happy child. She was far from being as strong and hearty as Phebe, but she was getting on; the once pale cheeks had colour in them now, the hands were growing plump and brown, and the belt was not much too loose. No one talked to her about her health, and she forgot that she had "no constitution." She took no medicine but Dr. Alec's three great remedies, and they seemed to suit her excellently. Aunt Plenty said it was the pills; but, as no second batch had ever followed the first, I think the old lady was mistaken.

Rose looked worthy of her name as she stood smiling to herself over a happier secret than any Phebe had a secret which she did not know herself till she found out, some years later, the magic of good health.

> "'Look only,' said the brownie,
> 'At the pretty gown of blue,
> At the kerchief pinned about her head,
> And at her little shoe,'"

said a voice from below, as a great cabbage-rose came flying against her cheek.

"What is the princess dreaming about up there in her hanging-garden?" added Dr. Alec as she flung back a morning-glory.

"I was wishing I could do something pleasant this fine day; something very new and interesting, for the wind makes me feel frisky and gay."

"Suppose we take a pull over to the Island? I intended to go this afternoon; but if you feel more like it now, we can be off at once."

"I do! I do! I'll come in fifteen minutes, uncle. I must just scrabble my room to rights, for Phebe has got a great deal to do."

Rose caught up the rugs and vanished as she spoke, while Dr. Alec went in, saying to himself, with an indulgent smile,

"It may upset things a trifle, but half a child's pleasure consists in having their fun when they want it."

Never did duster flap more briskly than the one Rose used that day, and never was a room "scrabbled" to rights in such haste as hers. Tables and chairs flew into their places as if alive; curtains shook as if a gale was blowing; china rattled and small articles tumbled about as if a young earthquake was playing with them. The boating suit went on in a twinkling, and Rose was off with a hop and a skip, little dreaming how many hours it would be before she saw her pretty room again.

Uncle Alec was putting a large basket into the boat when she arrived, and before they were off Phebe came running down with a queer, knobby bundle done up in a water-proof.

"We can't eat half that luncheon, and I know we shall not need so many wraps. I wouldn't lumber the boat up so," said Rose, who still had secret scares when on the water.

"Couldn't you make a smaller parcel, Phebe?" asked Dr. Alec, eyeing the bundle suspiciously.

"No, sir, not in such a hurry," and Phebe laughed as she gave a particularly large knob a good poke.

"Well, it will do for ballast. Don't forget the note to Mrs. Jessie, I beg of you."

"No, sir. I'll send it right off," and Phebe ran up the bank as if she had wings to her feet.

"We'll take a look at the lighthouse first, for you have not been there yet, and it is worth seeing. By the time we have done that it will be pretty warm, and we will have lunch under the trees on the Island."

Rose was ready for anything, and enjoyed her visit to the lighthouse on the Point very much, especially climbing up the narrow stairs and going inside the great lantern. They made a long stay, for Dr. Alec seemed in no hurry to go, and kept looking through his spy-glass as if he expected to discover something remarkable on sea or land. It was past twelve before they reached the Island, and Rose was ready for her lunch long before she got it.

"Now this is lovely! I do wish the boys were here. Won't it be nice to have them with us all their vacation? Why, it begins to-day, doesn't it? Oh, I wish I'd remembered it sooner, and perhaps they would have come with us," she said, as they lay luxuriously eating sandwiches under the old apple-tree.

"So we might. Next time we won't be in such a hurry. I expect the lads will take our heads off when they find us out," answered Dr. Alec, placidly drinking cold tea.

"Uncle, I smell a frying sort of a smell," Rose said, pausing suddenly as she was putting away the remains of the lunch half an hour later.

"So do I; it is fish, I think."

For a moment they both sat with their noses in the air, sniffing like hounds; then Dr. Alec sprang up, saying with great decision,

"Now, this won't do! No one is permitted on this island without asking leave. I must see who dares to fry fish on my private property."

Taking the basket on one arm and the bundle on the other, he strode away towards the traitorous smell, looking as fierce as a lion, while Rose marched behind under her umbrella.

"We are Robinson Crusoe and his man Friday going to see if the savages have come," she said presently, for her fancy was full of the dear old stories that all children love so well.

"And there they are! Two tents and two boats, as I live! These rascals mean to enjoy themselves, that's evident."

"There ought to be more boats and no tents. I wonder where the prisoners are?"

"There are traces of them," and Dr. Alec pointed to the heads and tails of fishes strewn on the grass.

"And there are more," said Rose, laughing, as she pointed to a scarlet heap of what looked like lobsters.

"The savages are probably eating their victims now; don't you hear the knives rattle in that tent?"

"We ought to creep up and peep; Crusoe was cautious, you know, and Friday scared out of his wits," added Rose, still keeping up the joke.

"But this Crusoe is going to pounce upon them, regardless of consequences. If I am killed and eaten, you seize the basket and run for the boat; there are provisions enough for your voyage home."

With that Uncle Alec slipped round to the front of the tent and, casting in the big bundle like a bomb-shell, roared out, in a voice of thunder,

"Pirates, surrender!"

A crash, a shout, a laugh, and out came the savages, brandishing knives and forks, chicken bones, and tin mugs, and all fell upon the intruder, pommelling him unmercifully as they cried,

"You came too soon! We are not half ready! You've spoilt it all! Where is Rose?"

"Here I am," answered a half-stifled voice, and Rose was discovered sitting on the pile of red flannel bathing clothes, which she had mistaken for lobsters, and where she had fallen in a fit of merriment when she discovered that the cannibals were her merry cousins.

"You good-for-nothing boys! You are always bursting out upon me in some ridiculous way, and I always get taken in because I'm not used to such pranks. Uncle is as bad as the rest, and it's great fun," she said, as the lads came round her, half scolding, half welcoming, and wholly enjoying the double surprise.

"You were not to come till afternoon, and mamma was to be here to receive you. Everything is in a mess now, except your tent; we got that in order the first thing, and you can sit there and see us work," said Archie, doing the honours as usual.

"Rose felt it in her bones, as Dolly says, that something was in the wind, and wanted to be off at once. So I let her come, and should have kept her away an hour longer if your fish had not betrayed you," explained Uncle Alec, subsiding from a ferocious Crusoe into his good-natured self again.

"As this seat is rather damp, I think I'll rise," said Rose, as the excitement lessened a little.

Several fishy hands helped her up, and Charlie said, as he scattered the scarlet garments over the grass with an oar,

"We had a jolly good swim before dinner, and I told the Brats to spread these to dry. Hope you brought your things, Rose, for you belong to the Lobsters, you know, and we can have no end of fun teaching you to dive and float and tread water."

"I didn't bring anything—" began Rose, but was interrupted by the Brats (otherwise Will and Geordie), who appeared bearing the big bundle, so much demoralised by its fall that a red flannel tunic trailed out at one end and a little blue dressing-gown at the other, while the knobs proved to be a toilet-case, rubbers, and a silver mug.

"Oh, that sly Phebe! This was the secret, and she bundled up those things after I went down to the boat," cried Rose, with sparkling eyes.

"Guess something is smashed inside, for a bit of glass fell out," observed Will, as they deposited the bundle at her feet.

"Catch a girl going anywhere without a looking-glass. We haven't got one among the whole lot of us," added Mac, with masculine scorn.

"Dandy has; I caught him touching up his wig behind the trees after our swim," cut in Geordie, wagging a derisive finger at Steve, who promptly silenced him by a smart rap on the head with the drum-stick he had just polished off.

"Come, come, you lazy lubbers, fall to work, or we shall not be ready for mamma. Take Rose's things to her tent, and tell her all about it, Prince. Mac and Steve, you cut away and bring up the rest of the straw; and you small chaps, clear off the table, if you have stuffed all you can. Please, uncle, I'd like your advice about the boundary lines and the best place for the kitchen."

Everyone obeyed the chief, and Rose was escorted to her tent by Charlie, who devoted himself to her service. She was charmed with her quarters, and still more so with the programme which he unfolded before her as they worked.

"We always camp out somewhere in vacation, and this year we thought we'd try the Island. It is handy, and our fireworks will show off well from here."

"Shall we stay over the Fourth? Three whole days! Oh, me! what a frolic it will be!"

"Bless your heart, we often camp for a week, we big fellows; but this year the small chaps wanted to come, so we let them. We have great larks, as you'll see; for we have a cave and play Captain Kidd, and have shipwrecks, and races, and all sorts of games. Arch and I are rather past that kind of thing now, but we do it to please the children," added Charlie, with a sudden recollection of his sixteen years.

"I had no idea boys had such good times. Their plays never seemed a bit interesting before. But I suppose that was because I never knew any boys very well, or perhaps you are unusually nice ones," observed Rose, with an artless air of appreciation that was very flattering.

"We are a pretty clever set, I fancy; but we have a good many advantages, you see. There are a tribe of us, to begin with; then our family has been here for ages, and we have plenty of 'spondulics,' so we can rather lord it over the other fellows, and do as we like. There, ma'am, you can hang your smashed glass on that nail and do up your back hair as fine as you please. You can have a blue blanket or a red one, and a straw pillow or an air cushion for your head, whichever you like. You can trim up to any extent, and be as free and easy as squaws in a wigwam, for this corner is set apart for you ladies and we never cross the line uncle is drawing until we ask leave. Anything more I can do for you, cousin?"

"No, thank you. I think I'll leave the rest till auntie comes, and go and help you somewhere else, if I may."

"Yes, indeed, come on and see to the kitchen. Can you cook?" asked Charlie, as he led the way to the rocky nook where Archie was putting up a sail-cloth awning.

"I can make tea and toast bread."

"Well, we'll shew you how to fry fish, and make chowder. Now you just set these pots and pans round tastefully, and sort of tidy up a bit, for Aunt Jessie insists on doing some of the work, and I want it to be decent here."

By four o'clock the camp was in order, and the weary workers settled down on Lookout Rock to watch for Mrs. Jessie and Jamie, who was never far from mamma's apron string. They looked like a flock of blue-birds, all being in sailor rig, with blue ribbon enough flying from the seven hats to have set up a milliner. Very tuneful blue-birds they were, too, for all the lads sang, and the echo of their happy voices reached Mrs. Jessie long before she saw them.

The moment the boat hove in sight up went the Island flag, and the blue-jackets cheered lustily, as they did on every possible occasion, like true young Americans. This welcome was answered by the flapping of a handkerchief and the shrill "Rah! Rah! Rah!" of the one small tar who stood in the stern waving his hat manfully, while a maternal hand clutched him firmly in the rear.

Cleopatra landing from her golden galley never received a heartier greeting than "Little Mum" as she was borne to her tent by the young folk, for love of whom she smilingly resigned herself to three days of discomfort; while Jamie immediately attached himself to Rose, assuring her of his protection from the manifold perils which might assail them.

Taught by long experience that boys are always hungry, Aunt Jessie soon proposed supper, and proceeded to get it, enveloped in an immense apron, with an old hat of Archie's stuck atop of her cap. Rose helped, and tried to be as handy as Phebe, though the peculiar style of table she had to set made it no easy task. It was accomplished at last, and a very happy party lay about under the trees, eating and drinking out of anyone's plate and cup, and quite untroubled by the frequent appearance of ants and spiders in places which these interesting insects are not expected to adorn.

"I never thought I should like to wash dishes, but I do," said Rose, as she sat in a boat after supper lazily rinsing plates in the sea, and rocking luxuriously as she wiped them.

"Mum is mighty particular; we just give 'em a scrub with sand, and dust 'em off with a bit of paper. It's much the best way, I think," replied Geordie, who reposed in another boat alongside.

"How Phebe would like this! I wonder uncle did not have her come."

"I believe he tried to, but Dolly was as cross as two sticks, and said she couldn't spare her. I'm sorry, for we all like the Phebe bird, and she'd chirp like a good one out here, wouldn't she?"

"She ought to have a holiday like the rest of us. It's too bad to leave her out."

This thought came back to Rose several times that evening, for Phebe would have added much to the little concert they had in the moonlight, would have enjoyed the stories told, been quick at guessing the conundrums, and laughed with all her heart at the fun. The merry going to bed would have been the best of all, for Rose wanted someone to cuddle under the blue blanket with her, there to whisper and giggle and tell secrets, as girls delight to do.

Long after the rest were asleep, Rose lay wide awake, excited by the novelty of all about her, and a thought that had come into her mind. Far away she heard a city clock strike twelve; a large star like a mild eye peeped in at the opening of the tent, and the soft plash of the waves seemed calling her to come out. Aunt Jessie lay fast asleep, with Jamie rolled up like a kitten at her feet, and neither stirred as Rose in her wrapper crept out to see how the world looked at midnight.

She found it very lovely, and sat down on a cracker keg to enjoy it with a heart full of the innocent sentiment of her years. Fortunately, Dr. Alec saw her before she had time to catch cold, for coming out to tie back the door-flap of his tent for more air, he beheld the small figure perched in the moonlight. Having no fear of ghosts, he quietly approached, and, seeing that she was wide awake, said, with a hand on her shining hair,

"What is my girl doing here?"

"Having a good time," answered Rose, not at all startled.

"I wonder what she was thinking about with such a sober look."

"The story you told of the brave sailor who gave up his place on the raft to the woman, and the last drop of water to the poor baby. People who make sacrifices are very much loved and admired, aren't they?" she asked, earnestly.

"If the sacrifice is a true one. But many of the bravest never are known, and get no praise. That does not lessen their beauty, though perhaps it makes them harder, for we all like sympathy," and Dr. Alec sighed a patient sort of sigh.

"I suppose you have made a great many? Would you mind telling me one of them?" asked Rose, arrested by the sigh.

"My last was to give up smoking," was the very unromantic answer to her pensive question.

"Why did you?"

"Bad example for the boys."

"That was very good of you, uncle! Was it hard?"

"I'm ashamed to say it was. But as a wise old fellow once said, 'It is necessary to do right; it is not necessary to be happy.'"

Rose pondered over the saying as if it pleased her, and then said, with a clear, bright look,

"A real sacrifice is giving up something you want or enjoy very much, isn't it?"

"Yes."

"Doing it one's own self because one loves another person very much and wants her to be happy?"

"Yes."

"And doing it pleasantly, and being glad about it, and not minding the praise if it doesn't come?"

"Yes, dear, that is the true spirit of self-sacrifice; you seem to understand it, and I dare say you will have many chances in your life to try the real thing. I hope they won't be very hard ones."

"I think they will," began Rose, and there stopped short.

"Well, make one now, and go to sleep, or my girl will be ill to-morrow, and then the aunts will say camping out was bad for her."

"I'll go good night!" and throwing him a kiss, the little ghost vanished, leaving Uncle Alec to pace the shore and think about some of the unsuspected sacrifices that had made him what he was.

Chapter 10—Rose's Sacrifice

There certainly were "larks" on Campbell's Island next day, as Charlie had foretold, and Rose took her part in them like one intent on enjoying every minute to the utmost. There was a merry breakfast, a successful fishing expedition, and then the lobsters came out in full force, for even Aunt Jessie appeared in red flannel. There was nothing Uncle Alec could not do in the water, and the boys tried their best to equal him in strength and skill, so there was a great diving and ducking, for every one was bent on distinguishing himself.

Rose swam out far beyond her depth, with uncle to float her back; Aunt Jessie splashed placidly in the shallow pools, with Jamie paddling near by like a little whale beside its mother; while the lads careered about, looking like a flock of distracted flamingoes, and acting like the famous dancing party in "Alice's Adventures in Wonderland."

Nothing but chowder would have lured them from their gambols in the briny deep; that time-honoured dish demanded the concentrated action of several mighty minds; so the "Water Babies" came ashore and fell to cooking.

It is unnecessary to say that, when done, it was the most remarkable chowder ever cooked, and the quantity eaten would have amazed the world if the secret had been divulged. After this exertion a siesta was considered the thing, and people lay about in tents or out as they pleased, the boys looking like warriors slumbering where they fell.

The elders had just settled to a comfortable nap when the youngsters rose, refreshed and ready for further exploits. A hint sent them all off to the cave, and there were discovered bows and arrows, battle clubs, old swords, and various relics of an interesting nature. Perched upon a commanding rock, with Jamie to "splain" things to her, Rose beheld a series of stirring scenes enacted with great vigour and historical accuracy by her gifted relatives.

Captain Cook was murdered by the natives of Owhyhee in the most thrilling manner. Captain Kidd buried untold wealth in the chowder kettle at the dead of night, and shot both the trusting villains who shared the secret of the hiding place. Sinbad came ashore there and had manifold adventures, and numberless wrecks bestrewed the sands.

Rose considered them by far the most exciting dramas she had ever witnessed; and when the performance closed with a grand ballet of Feejee Islanders, whose barbaric yells alarmed the gulls, she had no words in which to express her gratification.

Another swim at sunset, another merry evening on the rocks watching the lighted steamers pass seaward and the pleasure-boats come into port, ended the second day of the camping out, and sent everyone to bed early that they might be ready for the festivities of the morrow.

"Archie, didn't I hear uncle ask you to row home in the morning for fresh milk and things?"

"Yes, why?"

"Please, may I go too? I have something of great importance to arrange; you know I was carried off in a hurry," Rose said in a confidential whisper as she was bidding her cousins good night.

"I'm willing, and I guess Charlie won't mind."

"Thank you; be sure you stand by me when I ask leave in the morning, and don't say anything till then, except to Charlie. Promise," urged Rose, so eagerly, that Archie struck an attitude and cried dramatically,

"By yonder moon I swear!"

"Hush! it's all right, go along"; and Rose departed as if satisfied.

"She's a queer little thing, isn't she, Prince?"

"Rather a nice little thing, I think. I'm quite fond of her."

Rose's quick ears caught both remarks, and she retired to her tent, saying to herself with sleepy dignity,

"Little thing, indeed! Those boys talk as if I was a baby. They will treat me with more respect after to-morrow, I guess."

Archie did stand by her in the morning, and her request was readily granted, as the lads were coming directly back. Off they went, and Rose waved her hand to the islanders with a somewhat pensive air, for an heroic purpose glowed within her, and the spirit of self-sacrifice was about to be illustrated in a new and touching manner.

While the boys got the milk Rose ran to Phebe, ordered her to leave her dishes, to put on her hat, and take a note back to Uncle Alec, which would explain this somewhat mysterious performance. Phebe obeyed, and when she went to the boat Rose accompanied her, telling the boys she was not ready to go yet, but they could, some of them, come for her when she hung a white signal on her balcony.

"But why not come now? What are you about, miss? Uncle won't like it," protested Charlie, in great amazement.

"Just do as I tell you, little boy; uncle will understand and explain. Obey, as Phebe does, and ask no questions. I can have secrets as well as other people"; and Rose walked off with an air of lofty independence that impressed her friends immensely.

"It's some plot between uncle and herself, so we won't meddle. All right, Phebe? Pull away, Prince"; and off they went to be received with much surprise by the islanders.

This was the note Phebe bore:

"Dear Uncle, I am going to take Phebe's place to-day, and let her have all the fun she can. Please don't mind what she says, but keep her, and tell the boys to be very good to her for my sake. Don't think it is easy to do this; it is very hard to give up the best day of all, but I feel so selfish to have all the pleasure and Phebe none, that I wish to make this sacrifice. Do let me, and don't laugh at it; I truly do not wish to be praised, and I truly want to do it. Love to all from,

"Rose."

"Bless the little dear, what a generous heart she has! Shall we go after her, Jessie, or let her have her way?" said Dr. Alec, after the first mingled amusement and astonishment had subsided.

"Let her alone, and don't spoil her little sacrifice. She means it, I know, and the best way in which we can show our respect for her effort is to give Phebe a pleasant day. I'm sure she has earned it"; and Mrs. Jessie made a sign to the boys to suppress their disappointment and exert themselves to please Rose's guest.

Phebe was with difficulty kept from going straight home, and declared that she should not enjoy herself one bit without Miss Rose.

"She won't hold out all day, and we shall see her paddling back before noon, I'll wager anything," said Charlie; and the rest so strongly inclined to his opinion that they resigned themselves to the loss of the little queen of the revels, sure that it would be only a temporary one.

But hour after hour passed, and no signal appeared on the balcony, though Phebe watched it hopefully. No passing boat brought the truant back, though more than one pair of eyes looked out for the bright hair under the round hat; and sunset came, bringing no Rose but the lovely colour in the western sky.

"I really did not think the child had it in her. I fancied it was a bit of sentiment, but I see she was in earnest, and means that her sacrifice shall be a true one. Dear little soul! I'll make it up to her a thousand times over, and beg her pardon for thinking it might be done for effect," Dr. Alec said remorsefully, as he strained his eyes through the dusk, fancying he saw a small figure sitting in the garden as it had sat on the keg the night before, laying the generous little plot that had cost more than he could guess.

"Well, she can't help seeing the fireworks, any way, unless she is goose enough to think she must hide in a dark closet and not look," said Archie, who was rather disgusted at Rose's seeming ingratitude.

"She will see ours capitally, but miss the big ones on the hill, unless papa has forgotten all about them," added Steve, cutting short the harangue Mac had begun upon the festivals of the ancients.

"I'm sure the sight of her will be better than the finest fireworks that ever went off," said Phebe, meditating an elopement with one of the boats if she could get a chance.

"Let things work; if she resists a brilliant invitation we give her she will be a heroine," added Uncle Alec, secretly hoping that she would not.

Meanwhile Rose had spent a quiet, busy day helping Dolly, waiting on Aunt Peace, and steadily resisting Aunt Plenty's attempts to send her back to the happy island. It had been hard in the morning to come in from the bright world outside, with flags flying, cannon booming, crackers popping, and everyone making ready for a holiday, and go to washing cups, while Dolly grumbled and the aunts lamented. It was very hard to see the day go by, knowing how gay each hour must have been across the water, and how a word from her would take her where she longed to be with all her heart. But it was hardest of all when evening came and Aunt Peace was asleep, Aunt Plenty seeing a gossip in the parlor, Dolly established in the porch to enjoy the show, and nothing left for the little maid to do but sit alone in her balcony and watch the gay rockets whizz up from island, hill, and city, while bands played and boats laden with happy people went to and fro in the fitful light.

Then it must be confessed that a tear or two dimmed the blue eyes, and once, when a very brilliant display illuminated the island for a moment, and she fancied she saw the tents, the curly head went down on the railing, and a wide-awake nasturtium heard a little whisper,

"I hope someone wishes I was there!"

The tears were all gone, however, and she was watching the hill and island answer each other with what Jamie called "whizzers, whirligigs and busters," and smiling as she thought how hard the boys must be working to keep up such a steady fire, when Uncle Mac came walking in upon her, saying hurriedly,

"Come, child, put on your tippet, pelisse, or whatever you call it, and run off with me. I came to get Phebe, but aunt says she is gone, so I want you. I've got Fun down in the boat, and I want you to go with us and see my fireworks. Got them up for you, and you mustn't miss them, or I shall be disappointed."

"But, uncle," began Rose, feeling as if she ought to refuse even a glimpse of bliss, "perhaps—"

"I know, my dear, I know; aunt told me; but no one needs you now so much as I do, and I insist on your coming," said Uncle Mac, who seemed in a great hurry to be off, yet was unusually kind.

So Rose went and found the little Chinaman with a funny lantern waiting to help her in and convulse her with laughter trying to express his emotions in pigeon English. The city clocks were striking nine as they got out into the bay, and the island fireworks seemed to be over, for no rocket answered the last Roman candle that shone on the Aunt-hill.

"Ours are done, I see, but they are going up all round the city, and how pretty they are," said Rose, folding her mantle about her, and surveying the scene with pensive interest.

"Hope my fellows have not got into trouble up there," muttered Uncle Mac, adding with a satisfied chuckle, as a spark shone out, "No; there it goes! Look, Rosy, and see how you like this one; it was ordered especially in honour of your coming."

Rose looked with all her eyes, and saw the spark grow into the likeness of a golden vase, then green leaves came out, and then a crimson flower glowing on the darkness with a splendid lustre.

"Is it a rose, uncle?" she asked, clasping her hands with delight as she recognised the handsome flower.

"Of course it is! Look again, and guess what those are," answered Uncle Mac, chuckling and enjoying it all like a boy.

A wreath of what looked at first like purple brooms appeared below the vase, but Rose guessed what they were meant for, and stood straight up, holding by his shoulder, and crying excitedly,

"Thistles, uncle, Scotch thistles! There are seven of them one for each boy! Oh, what a joke!" and she laughed so that she plumped into the bottom of the boat and stayed there till the brilliant spectacle was quite gone.

"That was rather a neat thing, I flatter myself," said Uncle Mac, in high glee at the success of his illumination. "Now, shall I leave you on the Island or take you home again, my good little girl?" he added, lifting her up with such a tone of approbation in his voice that Rose kissed him on the spot.

"Home, please uncle; and I thank you very very much for the beautiful firework you got up for me. I'm so glad I saw it; and I know I shall dream about it," answered Rose steadily, though a wistful glance went toward the Island, now so near that she could smell powder and see shadowy figures flitting about.

Home they went; and Rose fell asleep saying to herself, "It was harder than I thought, but I'm glad I did it, and I truly don't want any reward but Phebe's pleasure."

Chapter 11—Poor Mac

Rose's sacrifice was a failure in one respect, for, though the elders loved her the better for it, and showed that they did, the boys were not inspired with the sudden respect which she had hoped for. In fact, her feelings were much hurt by overhearing Archie say that he couldn't see any sense in it; and the Prince added another blow by pronouncing her "the queerest chicken ever seen."

It is apt to be so, and it is hard to bear; for, though we do not want trumpets blown, we do like to have our little virtues appreciated, and cannot help feeling disappointed if they are not.

A time soon came, however, when Rose, quite unconsciously, won not only the respect of her cousins, but their gratitude and affection likewise.

Soon after the Island episode, Mac had a sunstroke, and was very ill for some time. It was so sudden that everyone was startled, and for some days the boy's life was in danger. He pulled through, however; and then, just as the family were rejoicing, a new trouble appeared which cast a gloom over them all.

Poor Mac's eyes gave out; and well they might, for he had abused them, and never being very strong, they suffered doubly now.

No one dared to tell him the dark predictions of the great oculist who came to look at them, and the boy tried to be patient, thinking that a few weeks of rest would repair the overwork of several years.

He was forbidden to look at a book, and as that was the one thing he most delighted in, it was a terrible affliction to the Worm. Everyone was very ready to read to him, and at first the lads contended for this honour. But as week after week went by, and Mac was still condemned to idleness and a darkened room, their zeal abated, and one after the other fell off. It was hard for the active fellows, right in the midst of their vacation; and nobody blamed them when they contented themselves with brief calls, running of errands, and warm expressions of sympathy.

The elders did their best, but Uncle Mac was a busy man, Aunt Jane's reading was of a funereal sort, impossible to listen to long, and the other aunties were all absorbed in their own cares, though they supplied the boy with every delicacy they could invent.

Uncle Alec was a host in himself, but he could not give all his time to the invalid; and if it had not been for Rose, the afflicted Worm would have fared ill. Her pleasant voice suited him, her patience was unfailing, her time of no apparent value, and her eager good-will was very comforting.

The womanly power of self-devotion was strong in the child, and she remained faithfully at her post when all the rest dropped away. Hour after hour she sat in the dusky room, with one ray of light on her book, reading to the boy, who lay with shaded eyes silently enjoying the only pleasure that lightened the weary days. Sometimes he was peevish and hard to please, sometimes he growled because his reader could not manage the dry books he wished to hear, and sometimes he was so despondent that her heart ached to see him. Through all these trials Rose persevered, using all her little arts to please him. When he fretted, she was patient; when he growled, she ploughed bravely through the hard pages not dry to her in one sense, for quiet tears dropped on them now and then; and when Mac fell into a despairing mood, she comforted him with every hopeful word she dared to offer.

He said little, but she knew he was grateful, for she suited him better than anyone else. If she was late, he was impatient; when she had to go, he seemed forlorn; and when the tired head ached worst, she could always soothe him to sleep, crooning the old songs her father used to love.

"I don't know what I should do without that child," Aunt Jane often said.

"She's worth all those racketing fellows put together," Mac would add, fumbling about to discover if the little chair was ready for her coming.

That was the sort of reward Rose liked, the thanks that cheered her; and whenever she grew very tired, one look at the green shade, the curly head so restless on the pillow, and the poor groping hands, touched her tender heart and put new spirit into the weary voice.

She did not know how much she was learning, both from the books she read and the daily sacrifices she made. Stories and poetry were her delight, but Mac did not care for them; and since his favourite Greeks and Romans were forbidden, he satisfied himself with travels, biographies, and the history of great inventions or discoveries. Rose despised this taste at first, but soon got interested in Livingstone's adventures, Hobson's stirring life in India, and the brave trials and triumphs of Watt and Arkwright, Fulton, and "Palissy, the Potter." The true, strong books helped the dreamy girl; her faithful service and sweet patience touched and won the boy; and long afterward both learned to see how useful those seemingly hard and weary hours had been to them.

One bright morning, as Rose sat down to begin a fat volume entitled "History of the French Revolution," expecting to come to great grief over the long names, Mac, who was lumbering about the room like a blind bear, stopped her by asking abruptly,

"What day of the month is it?"

"The seventh of August, I believe."

"More than half my vacation gone, and I've only had a week of it! I call that hard," and he groaned dismally.

"So it is; but there is more to come, and you may be able to enjoy that."

"May be able! I will be able! Does that old noodle think I'm going to stay stived up here much longer?"

"I guess he does, unless your eyes get on faster than they have yet."

"Has he said anything more lately?"

"I haven't seen him, you know. Shall I begin? this looks rather nice."

"Read away; it's all one to me." And Mac cast himself down upon the old lounge, where his heavy head felt easiest.

Rose began with great spirit, and kept on gallantly for a couple of chapters, getting over the unpronounceable names with unexpected success, she thought, for her listener did not correct her once, and lay so still she fancied he was deeply interested. All of a sudden she was arrested in the middle of a fine paragraph by Mac, who sat bolt upright, brought both feet down with a thump, and said, in a rough, excited tone,

"Stop! I don't hear a word, and you may as well save your breath to answer my question."

"What is it?" asked Rose, looking uneasy, for she had something on her mind, and feared that he suspected what it was. His next words proved that she was right.

"Now, look here, I want to know something, and you've got to tell me."

"Please, don't—" began Rose, beseechingly.

"You must, or I'll pull off this shade and stare at the sun as hard as ever I can stare. Come now!" and he half rose, as if ready to execute the threat.

"I will! oh, I will tell, if I know! But don't be reckless and do anything so crazy as that," cried Rose, in great distress.

"Very well; then listen, and don't dodge, as everyone else does. Didn't the doctor think my eyes worse the last time he came? Mother won't say, but you shall."

"I believe he did," faltered Rose.

"I thought so! Did he say I should be able to go to school when it begins?"

"No, Mac," very low.

"Ah!"

That was all, but Rose saw her cousin set his lips together and take a long breath, as if she had hit him hard. He bore the disappointment bravely, however, and asked quite steadily in a minute,

"How soon does he think I can study again?"

It was so hard to answer that! Yet Rose knew she must, for Aunt Jane had declared she could not do it, and Uncle Mac had begged her to break the truth to the poor lad.

"Not for a good many months."

"How many?" he asked with a pathetic sort of gruffness.

"A year, perhaps."

"A whole year! Why, I expected to be ready for college by that time." And, pushing up the shade, Mac stared at her with startled eyes, that soon blinked and fell before the one ray of light.

"Plenty of time for that; you must be patient now, and get them thoroughly well, or they will trouble you again when it will be harder to spare them," she said, with tears in her own eyes.

"I won't do it! I will study and get through somehow. It's all humbug about taking care so long. These doctors like to keep hold of a fellow if they can. But I won't stand it I vow I won't!" and he banged his fist down on the unoffending pillow as if he were pommelling the hard-hearted doctor.

"Now, Mac, listen to me," Rose said very earnestly, though her voice shook a little and her heart ached. "You know you have hurt your eyes reading by fire-light and in the dusk, and sitting up late, and now you'll have to pay for it; the doctor said so. You must be careful, and do as he tells you, or you will be blind."

"No!"

"Yes, it is true, and he wanted us to tell you that nothing but entire rest would cure you. I know it's dreadfully hard, but we'll all help you; I'll read all day long, and lead you, and wait upon you, and try to make it easier."

She stopped there, for it was evident that he did not hear a sound; the word "blind" seemed to have knocked him down, for he had buried his face in the pillow, and lay so still that Rose was frightened. She sat motionless for many minutes, longing to comfort him, but not knowing how, and wishing Uncle Alec would come, for he had promised to tell Mac.

Presently, a sort of choking sound came out of the pillow, and went straight to her heart the most pathetic sob she ever heard, for, though it was the most natural means of relief, the poor fellow must not indulge in it because of the afflicted eyes. The "French Revolution" tumbled out of her lap, and, running to the sofa, she knelt down by it, saying, with the motherly sort of tenderness girls feel for any sorrowing creature,

56

"Oh, my dear, you mustn't cry! It is so bad for your poor eyes. Take your head out of that hot pillow, and let me cool it. I don't wonder you feel so, but please don't cry. I'll cry for you; it won't hurt me."

As she spoke she pulled away the cushion with gentle force, and saw the green shade all crushed and stained with the few hot tears that told how bitter the disappointment had been. Mac felt her sympathy, but, being a boy, did not thank her for it; only sat up with a jerk, saying, as he tried to rub away the tell-tale drops with the sleeve of his jacket, "Don't bother; weak eyes always water. I'm all right."

But Rose cried out, and caught his arm, "Don't touch them with that rough woollen stuff! Lie down and let me bathe them, there's a dear boy; then there will be no harm done."

"They do smart confoundedly. I say, don't you tell the other fellows that I made a baby of myself, will you?" he added, yielding with a sigh to the orders of his nurse, who had flown for the eye-wash and linen cambric handkerchief.

"Of course I won't; but anyone would be upset at the idea of being well troubled in this way. I'm sure you bear it splendidly, and you know it isn't half so bad when you get used to it. Besides, it is only for a time, and you can do lots of pleasant things if you can't study. You'll have to wear blue goggles, perhaps; won't that be funny?"

And while she was pouring out all the comfortable words she could think of, Rose was softly bathing the eyes and dabbing the hot forehead with lavender-water, as her patient lay quiet with a look on his face that grieved her sadly.

"Homer was blind, and so was Milton, and they did something to be remembered by, in spite of it," he said, as if to himself, in a solemn tone, for even the blue goggles did not bring a smile.

"Papa had a picture of Milton and his daughters writing for him. It was a very sweet picture, I thought," observed Rose in a serious voice, trying to meet the sufferer on his own ground.

"Perhaps I could study if someone read and did the eye part. Do you suppose I could, by and by?" he asked, with a sudden ray of hope.

"I dare say, if your head is strong enough. This sunstroke, you know, is what upset you, and your brain needs rest, the doctor says."

"I'll have a talk with the old fellow next time he comes, and find out just what I may do; then I shall know where I am. What a fool I was that day to be stewing my brains and letting the sun glare on my book till the letters danced before me! I see 'em now when I shut my eyes; black balls bobbing round, and stars and all sorts of queer things. Wonder if all blind people do?"

"Don't think about them; I'll go on reading, shall I? We shall come to the exciting part soon, and then you'll forget all this," suggested Rose.

"No, I never shall forget. Hang the old 'Revolution'! I don't want to hear another word of it. My head aches, and I'm hot. Oh, wouldn't I like to go for a pull in the 'Stormy Petrel!'" and poor Mac tossed about as if he did not know what to do with himself.

"Let me sing, and perhaps you'll drop off; then the day will seem shorter," said Rose, taking up a fan and sitting down beside him.

"Perhaps I shall; I didn't sleep much last night, and when I did I dreamed like fun. See here, you tell the people that I know, and it's all right, and I don't want them to talk about it or howl over me. That's all; now drone away, and I'll try to sleep. Wish I could for a year, and wake up cured."

"Oh, I wish, I wish you could!"

Rose said it so fervently that Mac was moved to grope for her apron and hold on to a corner of it, as if it was comfortable to feel her near him. But all he said was,

"You are a good little soul, Rosy. Give us 'The Birks'; that is a drowsy one that always sends me off."

Quite contented with this small return for all her sympathy, Rose waved her fan and sang, in a dreamy tone, the pretty Scotch air, the burden of which is,

> "Bonny lassie, will ye gang, will ye gang
> To the Birks of Aberfeldie?"

Whether the lassie went or not I cannot say, but the laddie was off to the land of Nod, in about ten minutes, quite worn out with hearing the bad tidings and the effort to bear them manfully.

Chapter 12—"The Other Fellows"

Rose did tell "the people" what had passed, and no one "howled" over Mac, or said a word to trouble him. He had his talk with the doctor, and got very little comfort out of it, for he found that "just what he might do" was nothing at all; though the prospect of some study by and by, if all went well, gave him courage to bear the woes of the present. Having made up his mind to this, he behaved so well that everyone was astonished, never having suspected so much manliness in the quiet Worm.

The boys were much impressed, both by the greatness of the affliction which hung over him and by his way of bearing it. They were very good to him, but not always particularly wise in their attempts to cheer and amuse; and Rose often found him much downcast after a visit of condolence from the Clan. She still kept her place as head-nurse and chief-reader, though the boys did their best in an irregular sort of way. They were rather taken aback sometimes at finding Rose's services preferred to their's, and privately confided to one another that "Old Mac was getting fond of being molly-coddled." But they could not help seeing how useful she was, and owning that she alone had remained faithful a fact which caused some of them much secret compunction now and then.

Rose felt that she ruled in that room, if nowhere else, for Aunt Jane left a great deal to her, finding that her experience with her invalid father fitted her for a nurse, and in a case like this, her youth was an advantage rather than a drawback. Mac soon came to think that no one could take care of him so well as Rose, and Rose soon grew fond of her patient, though at first she had considered this cousin the least attractive of the seven. He was not polite and sensible like Archie, nor gay and handsome like Prince Charlie, nor neat and obliging like Steve, nor amusing like the "Brats," nor confiding and affectionate like little Jamie. He was rough, absent-minded, careless, and awkward, rather priggish, and not at all agreeable to a dainty, beauty-loving girl like Rose.

But when his trouble came upon him, she discovered many good things in this cousin of hers, and learned not only to pity but to respect and love the poor Worm, who tried to be patient, brave, and cheerful, and found it a harder task than anyone guessed, except the little nurse, who saw him in his gloomiest moods. She soon came to think that his friends did not appreciate him, and upon one occasion was moved to free her mind in a way that made a deep impression on the boys.

Vacation was almost over, and the time drawing near when Mac would be left outside the happy school-world which he so much enjoyed. This made him rather low in his mind, and his cousins exerted themselves to cheer him up, especially one afternoon when a spasm of devotion seemed to seize them all. Jamie trudged down the hill with a basket of blackberries which he had "picked all his ownself," as his scratched fingers and stained lips plainly testified. Will and Geordie brought their puppies to beguile the weary hours, and the three elder lads called to discuss baseball, cricket, and kindred subjects, eminently fitted to remind the invalid of his privations.

Rose had gone to drive with Uncle Alec, who declared she was getting as pale as a potato sprout, living so much in a dark room. But her thoughts were with her boy all the while, and she ran up to him the moment she returned, to find things in a fine state of confusion.

With the best intentions in life, the lads had done more harm than good, and the spectacle that met Nurse Rose's eye was a trying one. The puppies were yelping, the small boys romping, and the big boys all talking at once; the curtains were up, the room close, berries scattered freely about, Mac's shade half off, his cheeks flushed, his temper ruffled, and his voice loudest of all as he disputed hotly with Steve about lending certain treasured books which he could no longer use.

Now Rose considered this her special kingdom, and came down upon the invaders with an energy which amazed them and quelled the riot at once. They had never seen her roused before, and the effect was tremendous; also comical, for she drove the whole flock of boys out of the room like an indignant little hen defending her brood. They all went as meekly as sheep; the small lads fled from the house precipitately, but the three elder ones only retired to the next room, and remained there hoping for a chance to explain and apologise, and so appease the irate young lady, who had suddenly turned the tables and clattered them about their ears.

As they waited, they observed her proceedings through the half-open door, and commented upon them briefly but expressively, feeling quite bowed down with remorse at the harm they had innocently done.

"She's put the room to rights in a jiffey. What jacks we were to let those dogs in and kick up such a row," observed Steve, after a prolonged peep.

"The poor old Worm turns as if she was treading on him instead of cuddling him like a pussy cat. Isn't he cross, though?" added Charlie, as Mac was heard growling about his "confounded head."

"She will manage him; but it's mean in us to rumple him up and then leave her to smooth him down. I'd go and help, but I don't know how," said Archie, looking much depressed, for he was a conscientious fellow, and blamed himself for his want of thought.

"No, more do I. Odd, isn't it, what a knack women have for taking care of sick folks?" and Charlie fell a-musing over this undeniable fact.

"She has been ever so good to Mac," began Steve, in a self-reproachful tone.

"Better than his own brother, hey?" cut in Archie, finding relief for his own regret in the delinquencies of another.

"Well, you needn't preach; you didn't any of you do any more, and you might have, for Mac likes you better than he does me. I always fret him, he says, and it isn't my fault if I am a quiddle," protested Steve, in self-defence.

"We have all been selfish and neglected him, so we won't fight about it, but try and do better," said Archie, generously taking more than his share of blame, for he had been less inattentive than either of the others.

"Rose has stood by him like a good one, and it's no wonder he likes to have her round best. I should myself if I was down on my luck as he is," put in Charlie, feeling that he really had not done "the little thing" justice.

"I'll tell you what it is, boys we haven't been half good enough to Rose, and we've got to make it up to her somehow," said Archie, who had a very manly sense of honour about paying his debts, even to a girl.

"I'm awfully sorry I made fun of her doll when Jamie lugged it out; and I called her 'baby bunting' when she cried over the dead kitten. Girls are such geese sometimes, I can't help it," said Steve, confessing his transgressions handsomely, and feeling quite ready to atone for them if he only knew how.

"I'll go down on my knees and beg her pardon for treating her as if she was a child. Don't it make her mad, though? Come to think of it, she's only two years or so younger than I am. But she is so small and pretty, she always seems like a dolly to me," and the Prince looked down from his lofty height of five feet five as if Rose was indeed a pygmy beside him.

"That dolly has got a real good little heart, and a bright mind of her own, you'd better believe. Mac says she understands some things quicker than he can, and mother thinks she is an uncommonly nice girl, though she don't know all creation. You needn't put on airs, Charlie, though you are a tall one, for Rose likes Archie better than you; she said she did because he treated her respectfully."

"Steve looks as fierce as a game-cock; but don't you get excited, my son, for it won't do a bit of good. Of course, everybody likes the Chief best; they ought to, and I'll punch their heads if they don't. So calm yourself, Dandy, and mend your own manners before you come down on other people's."

Thus the Prince with great dignity and perfect good nature, while Archie looked modestly gratified with the flattering opinions of his kinsfolk, and Steve subsided, feeling he had done his duty as a cousin and a brother. A pause ensued, during which Aunt Jane appeared in the other room, accompanied by a tea-tray sumptuously spread, and prepared to feed her big nestling, as that was a task she allowed no one to share with her.

"If you have a minute to spare before you go, child, I wish you'd just make Mac a fresh shade; this has got a berry stain on it, and he must be tidy, for he is to go out to-morrow if it is a cloudy day," said Mrs. Jane, spreading toast in a stately manner, while Mac slopped his tea about without receiving a word of reproof.

"Yes, aunt," answered Rose, so meekly that the boys could hardly believe it could be the same voice which had issued the stern command, "Out of this room, every one of you!" not very long ago.

They had not time to retire, without unseemly haste, before she walked into the parlour and sat down at the work-table without a word. It was funny to see the look the three tall lads cast at the little person sedately threading a needle with green silk. They all wanted to say something expressive of repentance, but no one knew how to begin, and it was evident, from the prim expression of Rose's face, that she intended to stand upon her dignity till they had properly abased themselves. The pause was becoming very awkward, when Charlie, who possessed all the persuasive arts of a born scapegrace, went slowly down upon his knees before her, beat his breast, and said, in a heart-broken tone,

"Please forgive me this time, and I'll never do so any more."

It was very hard to keep sober, but Rose managed it and answered gravely,

"It is Mac's pardon you should ask, not mine, for you haven't hurt me, and I shouldn't wonder if you had him a great deal, with all that light and racket, and talk about things that only worry him."

"Do you really think we've hurt him, cousin?" asked Archie, with a troubled look, while Charlie settled down in a remorseful heap among the table legs.

"Yes, I do, for he has got a raging headache, and his eyes are as red as as this emery bag," answered Rose, solemnly plunging her needle into a fat flannel strawberry.

Steve tore his hair, metaphorically speaking, for he clutched his cherished top-knot, and wildly dishevelled it, as if that was the heaviest penance he could inflict upon himself at such short notice. Charlie laid himself out flat, melodramatically begging someone to take him away and hang him; but Archie, who felt worst of all, said nothing except to vow within himself that he would read to Mac till his own eyes were as red as a dozen emery bags combined.

Seeing the wholesome effects of her treatment upon these culprits, Rose felt that she might relent and allow them a gleam of hope. She found it impossible to help trampling upon the prostrate Prince a little, in words at least, for he had hurt her feelings oftener than he knew; so she gave him a thimble-pie on the top of his head, and said, with an air of an infinitely superior being,

"Don't be silly, but get up, and I'll tell you something much better to do than sprawling on the floor and getting all over lint."

Charlie obediently sat himself upon a hassock at her feet; the other sinners drew near to catch the words of wisdom about to fall from her lips, and Rose, softened by this gratifying humility, addressed them in her most maternal tone.

"Now, boys, if you really want to be good to Mac, you can do it in this way. Don't keep talking about things he can't do, or go and tell what fun you have had batting your ridiculous balls about. Get some nice book and read quietly; cheer him up about school, and offer to help him study by and by; you can do that better than I, because I'm only a girl, and don't learn Greek and Latin and all sorts of headachy stuff."

"Yes, but you can do heaps of things better than we can; you've proved that," said Archie, with an approving look that delighted Rose, though she could not resist giving Charlie one more rebuke, by saying, with a little bridling of the head, and a curl of the lip that wanted to smile instead,

"I'm glad you think so, though I am a 'queer chicken.'"

This scathing remark caused the Prince to hide his face for shame, and Steve to erect his head in the proud consciousness that this shot was not meant for him. Archie laughed, and Rose, seeing a merry blue eye winking at her from behind two brown hands, gave Charlie's ear a friendly tweak, and extended the olive-branch of peace.

"Now we'll all be good, and plan nice things for poor Mac," she said, smiling so graciously that the boys felt as if the sun had suddenly burst out from behind a heavy cloud and was shining with great brilliancy.

The storm had cleared the air, and quite a heavenly calm succeeded, during which plans of a most varied and surprising sort were laid, for everyone burned to make noble sacrifices upon the shrine of "poor Mac," and Rose was the guiding star to whom the others looked with most gratifying submission. Of course, this elevated state of things could not endure long, but it was very nice while it lasted, and left an excellent effect upon the minds of all when the first ardour had subsided.

"There, that's ready for to-morrow, and I do hope it will be cloudy," said Rose, as she finished off the new shade, the progress of which the boys had watched with interest.

"I'd bespoken an extra sunny day, but I'll tell the clerk of the weather to change it. He's an obliging fellow, and he'll attend to it, so make yourself easy," said Charlie, who had become quite perky again.

"It is very easy for you to joke, but how would you like to wear a blinder like that for weeks and weeks, sir?" and Rose quenched his rising spirits by slipping the shade over his eyes, as he still sat on the cushion at her feet.

"It's horrid! Take it off, take it off! I don't wonder the poor old boy has the blues with a thing like that on"; and Charlie sat looking at what seemed to him an instrument of torture, with such a sober face that Rose took it gently away, and went in to bid Mac good-night.

"I shall go home with her, for it is getting darkish, and she is rather timid," said Archie, forgetting that he had often laughed at this very timidity.

"I think I might, for she's taking care of my brother," put in Steve, asserting his rights.

"Let's all go, that will please her"; proposed Charlie, with a burst of gallantry which electrified his mates.

"We will!" they said with one voice, and they did, to Rose's great surprise and secret contentment; though Archie had all the care of her, for the other two were leaping fences, running races, and having wrestling matches all the way down.

They composed themselves on reaching the door, however; shook hands cordially all round, made their best bows, and retired with great elegance and dignity, leaving Rose to say to herself, with girlish satisfaction, as she went in,

"Now, that is the way I like to be treated."

Chapter 13—Cosey Corner

Vacation was over, the boys went back to school, and poor Mac was left lamenting. He was out of the darkened room now, and promoted to blue goggles, through which he took a gloomy view of life, as might have been expected; for there was nothing he could do but wander about, and try to amuse himself without using his eyes. Anyone who has ever been condemned to that sort of idleness knows how irksome it is, and can understand the state of mind which caused Mac to say to Rose in a desperate tone one day,

"Look here, if you don't invent some new employment or amusement for me, I shall knock myself on the head as sure as you live."

Rose flew to Uncle Alec for advice, and he ordered both patient and nurse to the mountains for a month, with Aunt Jessie and Jamie as escort. Pokey and her mother joined the party, and one bright September morning six very happy-looking people were aboard the express train for Portland two smiling mammas, laden with luncheon baskets and wraps; a pretty young girl with a bag of books on her arm; a tall thin lad with his hat over his eyes; and two small children, who sat with their short legs straight out before them, and their chubby faces beaming with the first speechless delight of "truly travelling."

An especially splendid sunset seemed to have been prepared to welcome them when, after a long day's journey, they drove into a wide, green door-yard, where a white colt, a red cow, two cats, four kittens, many hens, and a dozen people, old and young, were gaily disporting themselves. Everyone nodded and smiled in the friendliest manner, and a lively old lady kissed the new-comers all round, as she said heartily,

"Well, now, I'm proper glad to see you! Come right in and rest, and we'll have tea in less than no time, for you must be tired. Lizzie, you show the folks upstairs; Kitty, you fly round and help father in with the trunks; and Jenny and I will have the table all ready by the time you come down. Bless the dears, they want to go see the pussies, and so they shall!"

The three pretty daughters did "fly round," and everyone felt at home at once, all were so hospitable and kind. Aunt Jessie had raptures over the home-made carpets, quilts and quaint furniture; Rose could not keep away from the windows, for each framed a lovely picture; and the little folks made friends at once with the other children, who filled their arms with chickens and kittens, and did the honours handsomely.

The toot of a horn called all to supper, and a goodly party, including six children besides the Campbells, assembled in the long dining-room, armed with mountain appetites and the gayest spirits. It was impossible for anyone to be shy or sober, for such gales of merriment arose they blew the starch out of the stiffest, and made the saddest jolly. Mother Atkinson, as all called their hostess, was the merriest there, and the busiest; for she kept flying up to wait on the children, to bring out some new dish, or to banish the live stock, who were of such a social turn that the colt came into the entry and demanded sugar; the cats sat about in people's laps, winking suggestively at the food; and speckled hens cleared the kitchen floor of crumbs, as they joined in the chat with a cheerful clucking.

Everybody turned out after tea to watch the sunset till all the lovely red was gone, and mosquitoes wound their shrill horns to sound the retreat. The music of an organ surprised the new-comers, and in the parlor they found Father Atkinson playing sweetly on the little instrument made by himself. All the children gathered about him, and, led by the tuneful sisters, sang prettily till Pokey fell asleep behind the door, and Jamie gaped audibly right in the middle of his favourite,

"Coo," said the little doves: "Coo," said she,
"All in the top of the old pine-tree."

The older travellers, being tired, went to "bye low" at the same time, and slept like tops in home-spun sheets, on husk mattresses made by Mother Atkinson, who seemed to have put some soothing powder among them, so deep and sweet was the slumber that came.

Next day began the wholesome out-of-door life, which works such wonders with tired minds and feeble bodies. The weather was perfect, and the mountain air made the children as frisky as young lambs; while the elders went about smiling at one another, and saying, "Isn't it splendid?" Even Mac, the "slow coach," was seen to leap over a fence as if he really could not help it; and when Rose ran after him with his broad-brimmed hat, he made the spirited proposal to go into the woods and hunt for a catamount.

Jamie and Pokey were at once enrolled in the Cosey Corner Light Infantry a truly superb company, composed entirely of officers, all wearing cocked hats, carrying flags, waving swords, or beating drums. It was a spectacle to stir the dullest soul when this gallant band marched out of the yard in full regimentals, with Captain Dove a solemn, big-headed boy of eleven issuing his orders with the gravity of a general, and his Falstaffian regiment obeying them with more docility than skill. The little Snow children did very well, and Lieutenant Jack Dove was fine to see; so was Drummer Frank, the errand-boy of the house, as he rub-a-dub-dubbed with all his heart and drumsticks. Jamie had "trained" before, and was made a colonel at once; but Pokey was the best of all, and called forth a spontaneous burst of applause from the spectators as she brought up the rear, her cocked hat all over one eye, her flag trailing over her shoulder, and her wooden sword straight up in the air; her face beaming and every curl bobbing with delight as her fat legs tottered in the vain attempt to keep step manfully.

Mac and Rose were picking blackberries in the bushes beside the road when the soldiers passed without seeing them, and they witnessed a sight that was both pretty and comical. A little farther on was one of the family burial spots so common in those parts, and just this side of it Captain Fred Dove ordered his company to halt, explaining his reason for so doing in the following words,

"That's a graveyard, and it's proper to muffle the drums and lower the flags as we go by, and we'd better take off our hats, too; it's more respectable, I think."

"Isn't that cunning of the dears?" whispered Rose, as the little troop marched slowly by to the muffled roll of the drums, every flag and sword held low, all the little heads uncovered, and the childish faces very sober as the leafy shadows flickered over them.

"Let's follow and see what they are after," proposed Mac, who found sitting on the wall and being fed with blackberries luxurious but tiresome.

So they followed and heard the music grow lively, saw the banners wave in the breeze again when the graveyard was passed, and watched the company file into the dilapidated old church that stood at the corner of three woodland roads. Presently the sound of singing made the outsiders quicken their steps, and, stealing up, they peeped in at one of the broken windows.

Captain Dove was up in the old wooden pulpit, gazing solemnly down upon his company, who, having stacked their arms in the porch, now sat in the bare pews singing a Sunday-school hymn with great vigour and relish.

"Let us pray," said Captain Dove, with as much reverence as an army chaplain; and, folding his hands, he repeated a prayer which he thought all would know an excellent little prayer, but not exactly appropriate to the morning, for it was,

"Now I lay me down to sleep."

Everyone joined in saying it, and it was a pretty sight to see the little creatures bowing their curly heads and lisping out the words they knew so well. Tears came into Rose's eyes as she looked; Mac took his hat off involuntarily, and then clapped it on again as if ashamed of showing any feeling.

"Now I shall preach you a short sermon, and my text is, 'Little children, love one another.' I asked mamma to give me one, and she thought that would be good; so you all sit still and I'll preach it. You mustn't whisper, Marion, but hear me. It means that we should be good to each other, and play fair, and not quarrel as we did this very day about the wagon. Jack can't always drive, and needn't be mad because I like to go with Frank. Annette ought to be horse sometimes and not always driver; and Willie may as well make up his mind to let Marion build her house by his, for she will do it, and he needn't fuss about it. Jamie seems to be a good boy, but I shall preach to him if he isn't. No, Pokey, people don't kiss in church or put their hats on. Now you must all remember what I tell you, because I am the captain, and you should mind me."

Here Lieutenant Jack spoke right out in meeting with the rebellious remark,

"Don't care if you are; you'd better mind yourself, and tell how you took away my strap, and kept the biggest doughnut, and didn't draw fair when we had the truck."

"Yes, and you slapped Frank; I saw you!" bawled Willie Snow, bobbing up in his pew.

"And you took my book away and hid it 'cause I wouldn't go and swing when you wanted me to," added Annette, the oldest of the Snow trio.

"I shan't build my house by Willie's if he don't want me to, so now!" put in little Marion, joining the mutiny.

"I will tiss Dimmy! and I tored up my hat 'tause a pin picked me," shouted Pokey, regardless of Jamie's efforts to restrain her.

Captain Dove looked rather taken aback at this outbreak in the ranks; but, being a dignified and calm personage, he quelled the rising rebellion with great tact and skill, by saying, briefly,

"We'll sing the last hymn; 'Sweet, sweet good-by' you all know that, so do it nicely, and then we will go and have luncheon."

Peace was instantly restored, and a burst of melody drowned the suppressed giggles of Rose and Mac, who found it impossible to keep sober during the latter part of this somewhat remarkable service. Fifteen minutes of repose rendered it a physical impossibility for the company to march out as quietly as they had marched in. I grieve to state that the entire troop raced home as hard as they could pelt, and were soon skirmishing briskly over their lunch, utterly oblivious of what Jamie (who had been much impressed by the sermon) called "the captain's beautiful teck."

It was astonishing how much they all found to do at Cosey Corner; and Mac, instead of lying in a hammock and being read to, as he had expected, was busiest of all. He was invited to survey and lay out Skeeterville, a town which the children were getting up in a huckleberry pasture; and he found much amusement in planning little roads, staking off house-lots, attending to the water-works, and consulting with the "selectmen" about the best sites for public buildings; for Mac was a boy still, in spite of his fifteen years and his love of books.

Then he went fishing with a certain jovial gentleman from the West; and though they seldom caught anything but colds, they had great fun and exercise chasing the phantom trout they were bound to have. Mac also developed a geological mania, and went tapping about at rocks and stones, discoursing wisely of "strata, periods, and fossil remains"; while Rose picked up leaves and lichens, and gave him lessons in botany in return for his lectures on geology.

They led a very merry life; for the Atkinson girls kept up a sort of perpetual picnic; and did it so capitally, that one was never tired of it. So their visitors throve finely, and long before the month was out it was evident that Dr. Alec had prescribed the right medicine for his patients.

Chapter 14—A Happy Birthday

The twelfth of October was Rose's birthday, but no one seemed to remember that interesting fact, and she felt delicate about mentioning it, so fell asleep the night before wondering if she would have any presents. That question was settled early the next morning, for she was awakened by a soft tap on her face, and opening her eyes she beheld a little black and white figure sitting on her pillow, staring at her with a pair of round eyes very like blueberries, while one downy paw patted her nose to attract her notice. It was Kitty Comet, the prettiest of all the pussies, and Comet evidently had a mission to perform, for a pink bow adorned her neck, and a bit of paper was pinned to it bearing the words, "For Miss Rose, from Frank."

That pleased her extremely, and that was only the beginning of the fun, for surprises and presents kept popping out in the most delightful manner all through the day, the Atkinson girls being famous jokers and Rose a favourite. But the best gift of all came on the way to Mount Windy-Top, where it was decided to picnic in honour of the great occasion. Three jolly loads set off soon after breakfast, for everybody went, and everybody seemed bound to have an extra good time, especially Mother Atkinson, who wore a hat as broad-brimmed as an umbrella, and took the dinner-horn to keep her flock from straying away.

"I'm going to drive auntie and a lot of the babies, so you must ride the pony. And please stay behind us a good bit when we go to the station, for a parcel is coming, and you are not to see it till dinner-time. You won't mind, will you?" said Mac, in a confidential aside during the wild flurry of the start.

"Not a bit," answered Rose. "It hurts my feelings very much to be told to keep out of the way at any other time, but birthdays and Christmas it is part of the fun to be blind and stupid, and poked into corners. I'll be ready as soon as you are, Giglamps."

"Stop under the big maple till I call then you can't possibly see anything," added Mac, as he mounted her on the pony his father had sent up for his use. "Barkis" was so gentle and so "willin'," however, that Rose was ashamed to be afraid to ride him; so she had learned, that she might surprise Dr. Alec when she got home; meantime she had many a fine canter "over the hills and far away" with Mac, who preferred Mr. Atkinson's old Sorrel.

Away they went, and, coming to the red maple, Rose obediently paused; but could not help stealing a glance in the forbidden direction before the call came. Yes, there was a hamper going under the seat, and then she caught sight of a tall man whom Mac seemed to be hustling into the carriage in a great hurry. One look was enough, and with a cry of delight, Rose was off down the road as fast as Barkis could go.

"Now I'll astonish uncle," she thought. "I'll dash up in grand style, and show him that I am not a coward, after all."

Fired by this ambition, she startled Barkis by a sharp cut, and still more bewildered him by leaving him to his own guidance down the steep, stony road. The approach would have been a fine success if, just as Rose was about to pull up and salute, two or three distracted hens had not scuttled across

66

the road with a great squawking, which caused Barkis to shy and stop so suddenly that his careless rider landed in an ignominious heap just under old Sorrel's astonished nose.

Rose was up again before Dr. Alec was out of the carryall, and threw two dusty arms about his neck crying with a breathless voice,

"O uncle, I'm so glad to see you! It is better than a cart-load of goodies, and so dear of you to come!"

"But aren't you hurt, child! That was a rough tumble, and I'm afraid you must be damaged somewhere," answered the Doctor, full of fond anxiety, as he surveyed his girl with pride.

"My feelings are hurt, but my bones are all safe. It's too bad! I was going to do it so nicely, and those stupid hens spoilt it all," said Rose, quite crestfallen, as well as much shaken.

"I couldn't believe my eyes when I asked 'Where is Rose?' and Mac pointed to the little Amazon pelting down the hill at such a rate. You couldn't have done anything that would please me more, and I'm delighted to see how well you ride. Now, will you mount again, or shall we turn Mac out and take you in?" asked Dr. Alec, as Aunt Jessie proposed a start, for the others were beckoning them to follow.

"Pride goeth before a fall better not try to show off again, ma'am," said Mac, who would have been more than mortal if he had refrained from teasing when so good a chance offered.

"Pride does go before a fall, but I wonder if a sprained ankle always comes after it?" thought Rose, bravely concealing her pain, as she answered, with great dignity,

"I prefer to ride. Come on, and see who will catch up first."

She was up and away as she spoke, doing her best to efface the memory of her downfall by sitting very erect, elbows down, head well up, and taking the motion of the pony as Barkis cantered along as easily as a rocking-chair.

"You ought to see her go over a fence and race when we ride together. She can scud, too, like a deer when we play 'Follow the leader,' and skip stones and bat balls almost as well as I can," said Mac, in reply to his uncle's praise of his pupil.

"I'm afraid you will think her a sad tomboy, Alec; but really she seems so well and happy, I have not the heart to check her. She has broken out in the most unexpected way, and frisks like a colt; for she says she feels so full of spirits she must run and shout whether it is proper or not," added Mrs. Jessie, who had been a pretty hoyden years ago herself.

"Good good! that's the best news you could tell me," and Dr. Alec rubbed his hands heartily. "Let the girl run and shout as much as she will it is a sure sign of health, and as natural to a happy child as frisking is to any young animal full of life. Tomboys make strong women usually, and I had far rather find Rose playing football with Mac than puttering over bead-work like that affected midget, Ariadne Blish."

"But she cannot go on playing football very long, and we must not forget that she has a woman's work to do by and by," began Mrs. Jessie.

"Neither will Mac play football much longer, but he will be all the better fitted for business, because of the health it gives him. Polish is easily added, if the foundations are strong; but no amount of gilding will be of use if your timber is not sound. I'm sure I'm right, Jessie; and if I can do as well by my girl during the next six months as I have the last, my experiment will succeed."

"It certainly will; for when I contrast that bright, blooming face with the pale, listless one that made my heart ache a while ago, I can believe in almost any miracle," said Mrs. Jessie, as Rose looked round to point out a lovely view, with cheeks like the ruddy apples in the orchard near by, eyes clear as the autumn sky overhead, and vigour in every line of her girlish figure.

A general scramble among the rocks was followed by a regular gypsy lunch, which the young folks had the rapture of helping to prepare. Mother Atkinson put on her apron, turned up her sleeves, and fell to work as gaily as if in her own kitchen, boiling the kettle slung on three sticks, over a fire of cones and fir boughs; while the girls spread the mossy table with a feast of country goodies, and the children tumbled about in everyone's way till the toot of the horn made them settle down like a flock of hungry birds.

As soon as the merry meal and a brief interval of repose were over, it was unanimously voted to have some charades. A smooth, green spot between two stately pines was chosen for the stage; shawls hung up, properties collected, audience and actors separated, and a word quickly chosen.

The first scene discovered Mac in a despondent attitude and shabby dress, evidently much troubled in mind. To him entered a remarkable creature with a brown paper bag over its head. A little pink nose peeped through one hole in the middle, white teeth through another, and above two eyes glared fiercely. Spires of grass stuck in each side of the mouth seemed meant to represent whiskers; the upper corners of the bag were twisted like ears, and no one could doubt for a moment that the black scarf pinned on behind was a tail.

This singular animal seemed in pantomime to be comforting his master and offering advice, which was finally acted upon, for Mac pulled off his boots, helped the little beast into them, and gave him a bag; then, kissing his paw, with a hopeful gesture, the creature retired, purring so successfully that there was a general cry of "Cat, puss, boots!"

"Cat is the word," replied a voice, and the curtain fell.

The next scene was a puzzler, for in came another animal, on all-fours this time, with a new sort of tail and long ears. A gray shawl concealed its face, but an inquisitive sunbeam betrayed the glitter as of goggles under the fringe. On its back rode a small gentleman in Eastern costume, who appeared to find some difficulty in keeping his seat as his steed jogged along. Suddenly a spirit appeared, all in white, with long newspaper wings upon its back and golden locks about its face. Singularly enough, the beast beheld this apparition and backed instantly, but the rider evidently saw nothing and whipped up unmercifully, also unsuccessfully, for the spirit stood directly in the path, and the amiable beast would not budge a foot. A lively skirmish followed, which ended in the Eastern gentleman being upset into a sweet-fern bush, while the better bred animal abased itself before the shining one.

The children were all in the dark till Mother Atkinson said, in an inquiring tone,

"If that isn't Balaam and the ass, I'd like to know what it is. Rose makes a sweet angel, doesn't she?"

"Ass" was evidently the word, and the angel retired, smiling with mundane satisfaction over the compliment that reached her ears.

The next was a pretty little scene from the immortal story of "Babes in the Wood." Jamie and Pokey came trotting in, hand in hand, and, having been through the parts many times before, acted with great ease and much fluency, audibly directing each other from time to time as they went along. The berries were picked, the way lost, tears shed, baby consolation administered, and then the little pair lay down among the brakes and died with their eyes wide open and the toes of their four little boots turned up to the daisies in the most pathetic manner.

"Now the wobins tum. You be twite dead, Dimmy, and I'll peep in and see 'em," one defunct innocent was heard to say.

"I hope they'll be quick, for I'm lying on a stone, and ants are walking up my leg like fury," murmured the other.

Here the robins came flapping in with red scarves over their breasts and leaves in their mouths, which they carefully laid upon the babes wherever they would show best. A prickly blackberry leaf placed directly over Pokey's nose caused her to sneeze so violently that her little legs flew into the air; Jamie gave a startled "Ow!" and the pitying fowls fled giggling.

After some discussion it was decided that the syllable must be "strew or strow" and then they waited to see if it was a good guess.

This scene discovered Annette Snow in bed, evidently very ill; Miss Jenny was her anxious mamma, and her merry conversation amused the audience till Mac came in as a physician, and made great fun with his big watch, pompous manner, and absurd questions. He prescribed one pellet with an unpronounceable name, and left after demanding twenty dollars for his brief visit.

The pellet was administered, and such awful agonies immediately set in that the distracted mamma bade a sympathetic neighbour run for Mother Know-all. The neighbour ran, and in came a brisk little old lady in cap and specs, with a bundle of herbs under her arm, which she at once applied in all sorts of funny ways, explaining their virtues as she clapped a plantain poultice here, put a pounded catnip plaster there, or tied a couple of mullein leaves round the sufferer's throat. Instant relief ensued, the dying child sat up and demanded baked beans. The grateful parent offered fifty dollars; but Mother Know-all indignantly refused it and went smiling away, declaring that a neighbourly turn needed no reward, and a doctor's fee was all a humbug.

The audience were in fits of laughter over this scene, for Rose imitated Mrs. Atkinson capitally, and the herb cure was a good hit at the excellent lady's belief that "yarbs" would save mankind if properly applied. No one enjoyed it more than herself, and the saucy children prepared for the grand finale in high feather.

This closing scene was brief but striking, for two trains of cars whizzed in from opposite sides, met with a terrible collision in the middle of the stage, and a general smash-up completed the word catastrophe.

"Now let us act a proverb. I've got one all ready," said Rose, who was dying to distinguish herself in some way before Uncle Alec.

So everyone but Mac, the gay Westerner, and Rose, took their places on the rocky seats and discussed the late beautiful and varied charade, in which Pokey frankly pronounced her own scene the "bestest of all."

In five minutes the curtain was lifted; nothing appeared but a very large sheet of brown paper pinned to a tree, and on it was drawn a clock-face, the hands pointing to four. A small note below informed the public that 4 A.M. was the time. Hardly had the audience grasped this important fact when a long waterproof serpent was seen uncoiling itself from behind a stump. An inch-worm, perhaps, would be a better description, for it travelled in the same humpy way as that pleasing reptile. Suddenly a very wide-awake and active fowl advanced, pecking, chirping, and scratching vigorously. A tuft of green leaves waved upon his crest, a larger tuft of brakes made an umbrageous tail, and a shawl of many colours formed his flapping wings. A truly noble bird, whose legs had the genuine strut, whose eyes shone watchfully, and whose voice had a ring that evidently struck terror into the catterpillar's soul, if it was a catterpillar. He squirmed, he wriggled, he humped as fast as he could, trying to escape; but all in vain. The tufted bird espied him, gave one warbling sort of crow, pounced upon him, and flapped triumphantly away.

"That early bird got such a big worm he could hardly carry him off," laughed Aunt Jessie, as the children shouted over the joke suggested by Mac's nickname.

"That is one of uncle's favourite proverbs, so I got it up for his especial benefit," said Rose, coming up with the two-legged worm beside her.

"Very clever; what next?" asked Dr. Alec as she sat down beside him.

"The Dove boys are going to give us an 'Incident in the Life of Napoleon,' as they call it; the children think it very splendid, and the little fellows do it rather nicely," answered Mac with condescension.

A tent appeared, and pacing to and fro before it was a little sentinel, who, in a brief soliloquy, informed the observers that the elements were in a great state of confusion, that he had marched some hundred miles or so that day, and that he was dying for want of sleep. Then he paused, leaned upon his gun, and seemed to doze; dropped slowly down, overpowered with slumber, and finally lay flat, with his gun beside him, a faithless little sentinel. Enter Napoleon, cocked hat, gray coat, high boots, folded arms, grim mouth, and a melodramatic stride. Freddy Dove always covered himself with glory in this part, and "took the stage" with a Napoleonic attitude that brought down the house; for the big-headed boy, with solemn, dark eyes and square brow, was "the very moral of that rascal, Boneyparty," Mother Atkinson said.

Some great scheme was evidently brewing in his mighty mind a trip across the Alps, a bonfire at Moscow, or a little skirmish at Waterloo perhaps, for he marched in silent majesty till suddenly a gentle snore disturbed the imperial reverie. He saw the sleeping soldier and glared upon him, saying in an awful tone,

"Ha! asleep at his post! Death is the penalty he must die!"

Picking up the musket, he is about to execute summary justice, as emperors are in the habit of doing, when something in the face of the weary sentinel appears to touch him. And well it might, for a most engaging little warrior was Jack as he lay with his shako half off, his childish face trying to keep sober, and a great black moustache over his rosy mouth. It would have softened the heart of any Napoleon, and the Little Corporal proved himself a man by relenting, and saying, with a lofty gesture of forgiveness,

"Brave fellow, he is worn out; I will let him sleep, and mount guard in his place."

Then, shouldering the gun, this noble being strode to and fro with a dignity which thrilled the younger spectators. The sentinel awakes, sees what has happened, and gives himself up for lost. But the Emperor restores his weapon, and, with that smile which won all hearts, says, pointing to a high rock whereon a crow happens to be sitting, "Be brave, be vigilant, and remember that from yonder Pyramid generations are beholding you," and with these memorable words he vanishes, leaving the grateful soldier bolt upright, with his hand at his temple and deathless devotion stamped upon his youthful countenance.

The applause which followed this superb piece had hardly subsided, when a sudden splash and a shrill cry caused a general rush toward the waterfall that went gambolling down the rocks, singing sweetly as it ran. Pokey had tried to gambol also, and had tumbled into a shallow pool, whither Jamie had gallantly followed, in a vain attempt to fish her out, and both were paddling about half frightened, half pleased with the unexpected bath.

This mishap made it necessary to get the dripping infants home as soon as possible; so the wagons were loaded up, and away they went, as merry as if the mountain air had really been "Oxygenated Sweets not Bitters," as Dr. Alec suggested when Mac said he felt as jolly as if he had been drinking champagne instead of the current wine that came with a great frosted cake wreathed with sugar roses in Aunt Plenty's hamper of goodies.

Rose took part in all the fun, and never betrayed by look or word the twinges of pain she suffered in her ankle. She excused herself from the games in the evening, however, and sat talking to Uncle Alec in a lively way, that both amazed and delighted him; for she confided to him that she played horse with the children, drilled with the light infantry, climbed trees, and did other dreadful things that would have caused the aunts to cry aloud if they knew of them.

"I don't care a pin what they say if you don't mind, uncle," she answered, when he pictured the dismay of the good ladies.

"Ah, it's all very well to defy them, but you are getting so rampant, I'm afraid you will defy me next, and then where are we?"

"No, I won't! I shouldn't dare; because you are my guardian, and can put me in a strait-jacket if you like;" and Rose laughed in his face, even while she nestled closer with a confiding gesture pleasant to see.

"Upon my word, Rosy, I begin to feel like the man who bought an elephant, and then didn't know what to do with him. I thought I had got a pet and plaything for years to come; but here you are growing up like a bean-stalk, and I shall find I've got a strong-minded little woman on my hands before I can turn round. There's predicament for a man and an uncle!"

Dr. Alec's comic distress was mercifully relieved for the time being by a dance of goblins on the lawn, where the children, with pumpkin lanterns on their heads, frisked about like will-o'-the-wisps, as a parting surprise.

When Rose went to bed, she found that Uncle Alec had not forgotten her; for on the table stood a delicate little easel, holding two miniatures set in velvet. She knew them both, and stood looking at them till her eyes brimmed over with tears that were both sweet and sad; for they were the faces of her father and mother, beautifully copied from portraits fast fading away.

Presently, she knelt down, and, putting her arms round the little shrine, kissed one after the other, saying with an earnest voice, "I'll truly try to make them glad to see me by and by."

And that was Rose's little prayer on the night of her fourteenth birthday.

Two days later the Campbells went home, a larger party than when they came; for Dr. Alec was escort and Kitty Comet was borne in state in a basket, with a bottle of milk, some tiny sandwiches, and a doll's dish to drink out of, as well as a bit of carpet to lie on in her palace car, out of which she kept popping her head in the most fascinating manner.

There was a great kissing and cuddling, waving of handkerchiefs, and last good-byes, as they went; and when they had started, Mother Atkinson came running after them, to tuck in some little pies, hot from the oven, "for the dears, who might get tired of bread and butter during that long day's travel."

Another start, and another halt; for the Snow children came shrieking up to demand the three kittens that Pokey was cooly carrying off in a travelling bag. The unhappy kits were rescued, half smothered, and restored to their lawful owners, amid dire lamentation from the little kidnapper, who declared that she only "tooked um 'cause they'd want to go wid their sister Tomit."

Start number three and stoppage number three, as Frank hailed them with the luncheon basket, which had been forgotten, after everyone had protested that it was safely in.

All went well after that, and the long journey was pleasantly beguiled by Pokey and Pussy, who played together so prettily that they were considered public benefactors.

"Rose doesn't want to go home, for she knows the aunts won't let her rampage as she did up at Cosey Corner," said Mac, as they approached the old house.

"I can't rampage if I want to for a time, at least; and I'll tell you why. I sprained my ankle when I tumbled off of Barkis, and it gets worse and worse; though I've done all I know to cure it and hide it, so it shouldn't trouble anyone," whispered Rose, knitting her brows with pain, as she prepared to descend, wishing her uncle would take her instead of her bundles.

How he did it, she never knew; but Mac had her up the steps and on the parlour sofa before she could put her foot to the ground.

"There you are right side up with care; and mind, now, if your ankle bothers you, and you are laid up with it, I am to be your footman. It's only fair, you know; for I don't forget how good you have been to me." And Mac went to call Phebe, so full of gratitude and good-will that his very goggles shone.

Chapter 15—Ear-Rings

Rose's sprain proved to be a serious one, owing to neglect, and Dr. Alec ordered her to lie on the sofa for a fortnight at least; whereat she groaned dismally, but dared not openly complain, lest the boys turn upon her with some of the wise little sermons on patience which she had delivered for their benefit.

It was Mac's turn now, and honourably did he repay his debt; for, as school was still forbidden, he had plenty of leisure, and devoted most of it to Rose. He took many steps for her, and even allowed her to teach him to knit, after assuring himself that many a brave Scotchman knew how to "click the pricks." She was obliged to take a solemn vow of secrecy, however, before he would consent; for, though he did not mind being called "Giglamps," "Granny" was more than his boyish soul could bear, and at the approach of any of the Clan his knitting vanished as if by magic, which frequent "chucking" out of sight did not improve the stripe he was doing for Rose's new afghan.

She was busy with this pretty work one bright October afternoon, all nicely established on her sofa in the upper hall, while Jamie and Pokey (lent for her amusement) were keeping house in a corner, with Comet and Rose's old doll for their "childerns."

Presently, Phebe appeared with a card. Rose read it, made a grimace, then laughed and said,

"I'll see Miss Blish," and immediately put on her company face, pulled out her locket, and settled her curls.

"You dear thing, how do you do? I've been trying to call every day since you got back, but I have so many engagements, I really couldn't manage it till to-day. So glad you are alone, for mamma said I could sit awhile, and I brought my lace-work to show you, for it's perfectly lovely." cried Miss Blish, greeting Rose with a kiss, which was not very warmly returned, though Rose politely thanked her for coming, and bid Phebe roll up the easy chair.

"How nice to have a maid!" said Ariadne, as she settled herself with much commotion. "Still, dear, you must be very lonely, and feel the need of a bosom friend."

"I have my cousins," began Rose, with dignity, for her visitor's patronising manner ruffled her temper.

"Gracious, child! you don't make friends of those great boys, do you? Mamma says she really doesn't think it's proper for you to be with them so much."

"They are like brothers, and my aunts do think it's proper," replied Rose, rather sharply, for it struck her that this was none of Miss Blish's business.

"I was merely going to say I should be glad to have you for my bosom friend, for Hatty Mason and I have had an awful quarrel, and don't speak. She is too mean to live, so I gave her up. Just think, she never paid back one of the caramels I've given her, and never invited me to her party. I could have forgiven the caramels, but to be left out in that rude way was more than I could bear, and I told her never to look at me again as long as she lived."

"You are very kind, but I don't think I want a bosom friend, thank you," said Rose, as Ariadne stopped to bridle and shake her flaxen head over the delinquent Hatty Mason.

Now, in her heart Miss Blish thought Rose "a stuck-up puss," but the other girls wanted to know her and couldn't, the old house was a charming place to visit, the lads were considered fine fellows, and the Campbells "are one of our first families," mamma said. So Ariadne concealed her vexation at Rose's coolness, and changed the subject as fast as possible.

"Studying French, I see; who is your teacher?" she asked, flitting over the leaves of "Paul and Virginia," that lay on the table.

"I don't study it, for I read French as well as English, and uncle and I often speak it for hours. He talks like a native, and says I have a remarkably good accent."

Rose really could not help this small display of superiority, for French was one of her strong points, and she was vain of it, though she usually managed to hide this weakness. She felt that Ariadne would be the better for a little crushing, and could not resist the temptation to patronise in her turn.

"Oh, indeed!" said Miss Blish, rather blankly, for French was not her strong point by any means.

"I am to go abroad with uncle in a year or two, and he knows how important it is to understand the languages. Half the girls who leave school can't speak decent French, and when they go abroad they are so mortified. I shall be very glad to help you, if you like, for, of course, you have no one to talk with at home."

73

Now Ariadne, though she looked like a wax doll, had feelings within her instead of sawdust, and these feelings were hurt by Rose's lofty tone. She thought her more "stuck up" than ever, but did not know how to bring her down, yet longed to do it, for she felt as if she had received a box on the ear, and involuntarily put her hand up to it. The touch of an ear-ring consoled her, and suggested a way of returning tit for tat in a telling manner.

"Thank you, dear; I don't need any help, for our teacher is from Paris, and of course he speaks better French than your uncle." Then she added, with a gesture of her head that set the little bells on her ears to tingling: "How do you like my new ear-rings? Papa gave them to me last week, and everyone says they are lovely."

Rose came down from her high horse with a rapidity that was comical, for Ariadne had the upper hand now. Rose adored pretty things, longed to wear them, and the desire of her girlish soul was to have her ears bored, only Dr. Alec thought it foolish, so she never had done it. She would gladly have given all the French she could jabber for a pair of golden bells with pearl-tipped tongues, like those Ariadne wore; and, clasping her hands, she answered, in a tone that went to the hearer's heart,

"They are too sweet for anything! If uncle would only let me wear some, I should be perfectly happy."

"I wouldn't mind what he says. Papa laughed at me at first, but he likes them now, and says I shall have diamond solitaires when I am eighteen," said Ariadne, quite satisfied with her shot.

"I've got a pair now that were mamma's, and a beautiful little pair of pearl and turquoise ones, that I am dying to wear," sighed Rose.

"Then do it. I'll pierce your ears, and you must wear a bit of silk in them till they are well; your curls will hide them nicely; then, some day, slip in your smallest ear-rings, and see if your uncle don't like them."

"I asked him if it wouldn't do my eyes good once when they were red, and he only laughed. People do cure weak eyes that way, don't they?"

"Yes, indeed, and yours are sort of red. Let me see. Yes, I really think you ought to do it before they get worse," said Ariadne, peering into the large clear eye offered for inspection.

"Does it hurt much?" asked Rose, wavering.

"Oh dear, no; just a prick and a pull, and it's all over. I've done lots of ears, and know just how. Come, push up your hair and get a big needle."

"I don't quite like to do it without asking uncle's leave," faltered Rose, when all was ready for the operation.

"Did he ever forbid it?" demanded Ariadne, hovering over her prey like a vampire.

"No, never!"

"Then do it, unless you are afraid," cried Miss Blish, bent on accomplishing the deed.

That last word settled the matter, and, closing her eyes, Rose said "Punch!" in the tone of one giving the fatal order "Fire!"

Ariadne punched, and the victim bore it in heroic silence, though she turned pale and her eyes were full of tears of anguish.

"There! Now pull the bits of silk often, and cold-cream your ears every night, and you'll soon be ready for the rings," said Ariadne, well pleased with her job, for the girl who spoke French with "a fine accent" lay flat upon the sofa, looking as exhausted as if she had had both ears cut off.

"It does hurt dreadfully, and I know uncle won't like it," sighed Rose, as remorse began to gnaw. "Promise not to tell, or I shall be teased to death," she added, anxiously, entirely forgetting the two little pitchers gifted with eyes as well as ears, who had been watching the whole performance from afar.

"Never. Mercy me, what's that?" and Ariadne started as a sudden sound of steps and voices came up from below.

"It's the boys! Hide the needle. Do my ears show? Don't breathe a word!" whispered Rose, scrambling about to conceal all traces of their iniquity from the sharp eyes of the Clan.

Up they came, all in good order, laden with the proceeds of a nutting expedition, for they always reported to Rose and paid tribute to their queen in the handsomest manner.

"How many, and how big! We'll have a grand roasting frolic after tea, won't we?" said Rose, plunging both hands into a bag of glossy brown nuts, while the Clan "stood at ease" and nodded to Ariadne.

"That lot was picked especially for you, Rosy. I got every one myself, and they are extra whackers," said Mac, presenting a bushel or so.

"You should have seen Giglamps when he was after them. He pitched out of the tree, and would have broken his blessed old neck if Arch had not caught him," observed Steve, as he lounged gracefully in the window seat.

"You needn't talk, Dandy, when you didn't know a chestnut from a beech, and kept on thrashing till I told you of it," retorted Mac, festooning himself over the back of the sofa, being a privileged boy.

"I don't make mistakes when I thrash you, old Worm, so you'd better mind what you are about," answered Steve, without a ray of proper respect for his elder brother.

"It is getting dark, and I must go, or mamma will be alarmed," said Ariadne, rising in sudden haste, though she hoped to be asked to remain to the nut-party.

No one invited her; and all the while she was putting on her things and chatting to Rose the boys were telegraphing to one another the sad fact that someone ought to escort the young lady home. Not a boy felt heroic enough to cast himself into the breach, however; even polite Archie shirked the duty, saying to Charlie, as they quietly slipped into an adjoining room,

"I'm not going to do all the gallivanting. Let Steve take that chit home and show his manners."

"I'll be hanged if I do!" answered Prince, who disliked Miss Blish because she tried to be coquettish with him.

"Then I will," and, to the dismay of both recreant lads, Dr. Alec walked out of the room to offer his services to the "chit."

He was too late, however, for Mac, obeying a look from Rose, had already made a victim of himself, and trudged meekly away, wishing the gentle Ariadne at the bottom of the Red Sea.

"Then I will take this lady down to tea, as the other one has found a gentleman to go home with her. I see the lamps are lighted below, and I smell a smell which tells me that auntie has something extra nice for us to-night."

As he spoke, Dr. Alec was preparing to carry Rose downstairs as usual; but Archie and Prince rushed forward, begging with penitent eagerness for the honour of carrying her in an arm-chair. Rose consented, fearing that her uncle's keen eye would discover the fatal bits of silk; so the boys crossed hands, and, taking a good grip of each curly pate, she was borne down in state, while the others followed by way of the banisters.

Tea was ordered earlier than usual, so that Jamie and his dolly could have a taste, at least, of the holiday fun, for they were to stay till seven, and be allowed twelve roasted chestnuts apiece, which they were under bonds not to eat till next day.

Tea was despatched rapidly, therefore, and the party gathered round the wide hearth in the dining-room, where the nuts were soon dancing gaily on hot shovels or bouncing out among the company, thereby causing delightful panics among the little ones.

"Come, Rosy, tell us a story while we work, for you can't help much, and must amuse us as your share," proposed Mac, who sat in the shade pricking nuts, and who knew by experience what a capital little Scheherazade his cousin was.

"Yes, we poor monkeys can't burn our paws for nothing, so tell away, Pussy," added Charlie, as he threw several hot nuts into her lap and shook his fingers afterwards.

"Well, I happen to have a little story with a moral to it in my mind, and I will tell it, though it is intended for younger children than you," answered Rose, who was rather fond of telling instructive tales.

"Fire away," said Geordie, and she obeyed, little thinking what a disastrous story it would prove to herself.

"Well, once upon a time, a little girl went to see a young lady who was very fond of her. Now, the young lady happened to be lame, and had to have her foot bandaged up every day; so she kept a basketful of bandages, all nicely rolled and ready. The little girl liked to play with this basket, and one day, when she thought no one saw her, she took one of the rolls without asking leave, and put it in her pocket."

Here Pokey, who had been peering lovingly down at the five warm nuts that lay at the bottom of her tiny pocket, suddenly looked up and said, "Oh!" in a startled tone, as if the moral tale had become intensely interesting all at once.

Rose heard and saw the innocent betrayal of the small sinner, and went on in a most impressive manner, while the boys nudged one another and winked as they caught the joke.

"But an eye did see this naughty little girl, and whose eye do you think it was?"

"Eye of Dod," murmured conscience-stricken Pokey, spreading two chubby little hands before the round face, which they were not half big enough to hide.

Rose was rather taken aback by this reply, but, feeling that she was producing a good effect, she added seriously,

"Yes, God saw her, and so did the young lady, but she did not say anything; she waited to see what the little girl would do about it. She had been very happy before she took the bandage, but when it was in her pocket she seemed troubled, and pretty soon stopped playing, and sat down in a corner looking very sober. She thought a few minutes, and then went and put back the roll very softly, and her face cleared up, and she was a happy child again. The young lady was glad to see that, and wondered what made the little girl put it back."

"Tonscience p'icked her," murmured a contrite voice from behind the small hands pressed tightly over Pokey's red face.

"And why did she take it, do you suppose?" asked Rose, in a school-marmish tone, feeling that all the listeners were interested in her tale and its unexpected application.

"It was so nice and wound, and she wanted it deffly," answered the little voice.

"Well, I'm glad she had such a good conscience. The moral is that people who steal don't enjoy what they take, and are not happy till they put it back. What makes that little girl hide her face?" asked Rose, as she concluded.

"Me's so 'shamed of Pokey," sobbed the small culprit, quite overcome by remorse and confusion at this awful disclosure.

"Come, Rose, it's too bad to tell her little tricks before everyone, and preach at her in that way; you wouldn't like it yourself," began Dr. Alec, taking the weeper on his knee and administering consolation in the shape of kisses and nuts.

Before Rose could express her regret, Jamie, who had been reddening and ruffling like a little turkey-cock for several minutes, burst out indignantly, bent on avenging the wound given to his beloved dolly.

"I know something bad that you did, and I'm going to tell right out. You thought we didn't see you, but we did, and you said uncle wouldn't like it, and the boys would tease, and you made Ariadne promise not to tell, and she punched holes in your ears to put ear-rings in. So now! and that's much badder than to take an old piece of rag; and I hate you for making my Pokey cry."

Jamie's somewhat incoherent explosion produced such an effect that Pokey's small sin was instantly forgotten, and Rose felt that her hour had come.

"What! what! what!" cried the boys in a chorus, dropping their shovels and knives to gather round Rose, for a guilty clutching at her ears betrayed her, and with a feeble cry of "Ariadne made me!" she hid her head among the pillows like an absurd little ostrich.

"Now she'll go prancing round with bird cages and baskets and carts and pigs, for all I know, in her ears, as the other girls do, and won't she look like a goose?" asked one tormentor, tweaking a curl that strayed out from the cushions.

"I didn't think she'd be so silly," said Mac, in a tone of disappointment that told Rose she had sunk in the esteem of her wise cousin.

"That Blish girl is a nuisance, and ought not to be allowed to come here with her nonsensical notions," said the Prince, feeling a strong desire to shake that young person as an angry dog might shake a mischievous kitten.

"How do you like it, uncle?" asked Archie, who, being the head of a family himself, believed in preserving discipline at all costs.

"I am very much surprised; but I see she is a girl, after all, and must have her vanities like all the rest of them," answered Dr. Alec, with a sigh, as if he had expected to find Rose a sort of angel, above all earthly temptations.

"What shall you do about it, sir?" inquired Geordie, wondering what punishment would be inflicted on a feminine culprit.

"As she is fond of ornaments, perhaps we had better give her a nose-ring also. I have one somewhere that a Fiji belle once wore; I'll look it up," and, leaving Pokey to Jamie's care, Dr. Alec rose as if to carry out his suggestion in earnest.

"Good! good! We'll do it right away! Here's a gimlet, so you hold her, boys, while I get her dear little nose all ready," cried Charlie, whisking away the pillow as the other boys danced about the sofa in true Fiji style.

It was a dreadful moment, for Rose could not run away she could only grasp her precious nose with one hand and extend the other, crying distractedly,

"O uncle, save me, save me!"

Of course he saved her; and when she was securely barricaded by his strong arm, she confessed her folly in such humiliation of spirit, that the lads, after a good laugh at her, decided to forgive her and lay all the blame on the tempter, Ariadne. Even Dr. Alec relented so far as to propose two gold rings for the ears instead of one copper one for the nose; a proceeding which proved that if Rose had all the weakness of her sex for jewellery, he had all the inconsistency of his in giving a pretty penitent exactly what she wanted, spite of his better judgment.


Chapter 16—Bread and Button-Holes
"What in the world is my girl thinking about all alone here, with such a solemn face?" asked Dr. Alec, coming into the study, one November day, to find Rose sitting there with folded hands and a very thoughtful aspect.

"Uncle, I want to have some serious conversation with you, if you have time," she said, coming out of a brown study, as if she had not heard his question.

"I'm entirely at your service, and most happy to listen," he answered, in his politest manner, for when Rose put on her womanly little airs he always treated her with a playful sort of respect that pleased her very much.

Now, as he sat down beside her, she said, very soberly,

"I've been trying to decide what trade I would learn, and I want you to advise me."

"Trade, my dear?" and Dr. Alec looked so astonished that she hastened to explain.

"I forgot that you didn't hear the talk about it up at Cosey Corner. You see we used to sit under the pines and sew, and talk a great deal all the ladies, I mean and I liked it very much. Mother Atkinson thought that everyone should have a trade, or something to make a living out of, for rich people may grow poor, you know, and poor people have to work. Her girls were very clever, and could do ever so many things, and Aunt Jessie thought the old lady was right; so when I saw how happy and independent those young ladies were, I wanted to have a trade, and then it wouldn't matter about money, though I like to have it well enough."

Dr. Alec listened to this explanation with a curious mixture of surprise, pleasure, and amusement in his face, and looked at his little niece as if she had suddenly changed into a young woman. She had grown a good deal in the last six months, and an amount of thinking had gone on in that young head which would have astonished him greatly could he have known it all, for Rose was one of the children who observe and meditate much, and now and then nonplus their friends by a wise or curious remark.

"I quite agree with the ladies, and shall be glad to help you decide on something if I can," said the Doctor seriously. "What do you incline to? A natural taste or talent is a great help in choosing, you know."

"I haven't any talent, or any especial taste that I can see, and that is why I can't decide, uncle. So, I think it would be a good plan to pick out some very useful business and learn it, because I don't do it for pleasure, you see, but as a part of my education, and to be ready in case I'm ever poor," answered Rose, looking as if she rather longed for a little poverty so that her useful gift might be exercised.

"Well, now, there is one very excellent, necessary, and womanly accomplishment that no girl should be without, for it is a help to rich and poor, and the comfort of families depends upon it. This fine talent is neglected nowadays, and considered old-fashioned, which is a sad mistake, and one that I don't mean to make in bringing up my girl. It should be a part of every girl's education, and I know of a most accomplished lady who will teach you in the best and pleasantest manner."

"Oh, what is it?" cried Rose eagerly, charmed to be met in this helpful and cordial way.

"Housekeeping!" answered Dr. Alec.

"Is that an accomplishment?" asked Rose, while her face fell, for she had indulged in all sorts of vague, delightful dreams.

"Yes; it is one of the most beautiful as well as useful of all the arts a woman can learn. Not so romantic, perhaps, as singing, painting, writing, or teaching, even; but one that makes many happy and comfortable, and home the sweetest place in the world. Yes, you may open your big eyes; but it is a fact that I had rather see you a good housekeeper than the greatest belle in the city. It need not interfere with any talent you may possess, but it is a necessary part of your training, and I hope that you will set about it at once, now that you are well and strong."

"Who is the lady?" asked Rose, rather impressed by her uncle's earnest speech.

"Aunt Plenty."

"Is she accomplished?" began Rose in a wondering tone, for this great-aunt of hers had seemed the least cultivated of them all.

"In the good old-fashioned way she is very accomplished, and has made this house a happy home to us all, ever since we can remember. She is not elegant, but genuinely good, and so beloved and respected that there will be universal mourning for her when her place is empty. No one can fill it, for the solid, homely virtues of the dear soul have gone out of fashion, as I say, and nothing new can be half so satisfactory, to me at least."

"I should like to have people feel so about me. Can she teach me to do what she does, and to grow as good?" asked Rose, with a little prick of remorse for even thinking that Aunt Plenty was a commonplace old lady.

"Yes, if you don't despise such simple lessons as she can give. I know it would fill her dear old heart with pride and pleasure to feel that anyone cared to learn of her, for she fancies her day gone by. Let her teach you how to be what she has been a skilful, frugal, cheerful housewife; the maker and the keeper of a happy home, and by and by you will see what a valuable lesson it is."

"I will, uncle. But how shall I begin?"

"I'll speak to her about it, and she will make it all right with Dolly, for cooking is one of the main things, you know."

"So it is! I don't mind that a bit, for I like to mess, and used to try at home; but I had no one to tell me, so I never did much but spoil my aprons. Pies are great fun, only Dolly is so cross, I don't believe she will ever let me do a thing in the kitchen."

"Then we'll cook in the parlour. I fancy Aunt Plenty will manage her, so don't be troubled. Only mind this, I'd rather you learned how to make good bread than the best pies ever baked. When you bring me a handsome, wholesome loaf, entirely made by yourself, I shall be more pleased than if you offered me a pair of slippers embroidered in the very latest style. I don't wish to bribe you, but I'll give you my heartiest kiss, and promise to eat every crumb of the loaf myself."

"It's a bargain! it's a bargain! Come and tell aunty all about it, for I'm in a hurry to begin," cried Rose, dancing before him toward the parlor, where Miss Plenty sat alone knitting contentedly, yet ready to run at the first call for help of any sort, from any quarter.

No need to tell how surprised and gratified she was at the invitation she received to teach the child the domestic arts which were her only accomplishments, nor to relate how energetically she set about her pleasant task. Dolly dared not grumble, for Miss Plenty was the one person whom she obeyed, and Phebe openly rejoiced, for these new lessons brought Rose nearer to her, and glorified the kitchen in the good girl's eyes.

To tell the truth, the elder aunts had sometimes felt that they did not have quite their share of the little niece who had won their hearts long ago, and was the sunshine of the house. They talked it over together sometimes, but always ended by saying that as Alec had all the responsibility, he should have the larger share of the dear girl's love and time, and they would be contented with such crumbs of comfort as they could get.

Dr. Alec had found out this little secret, and, after reproaching himself for being blind and selfish, was trying to devise some way of mending matters without troubling anyone, when Rose's new whim suggested an excellent method of weaning her a little from himself. He did not know how fond he was of her till he gave her up to the new teacher, and often could not resist peeping in at the door to see how she got on, or stealing sly looks through the slide when she was deep in dough, or listening intently to some impressive lecture from Aunt Plenty. They caught him at it now and then, and ordered him off the premises at the point of the rolling-pin; or, if unusually successful, and, therefore, in a milder mood, they lured him away with bribes of ginger-bread, a stray pickle, or a tart that was not quite symmetrical enough to suit their critical eyes.

Of course he made a point of partaking copiously of all the delectable messes that now appeared at table, for both the cooks were on their mettle, and he fared sumptuously every day. But an especial relish was given to any dish when, in reply to his honest praise of it, Rose coloured up with innocent pride, and said modestly,

"I made that, uncle, and I'm glad you like it."

It was some time before the perfect loaf appeared, for bread-making is an art not easily learned, and Aunt Plenty was very thorough in her teaching; so Rose studied yeast first, and through various stages of cake and biscuit came at last to the crowning glory of the "handsome, wholesome loaf." It appeared at tea-time, on a silver salver, proudly borne in by Phebe, who could not refrain from whispering, with a beaming face, as she set it down before Dr. Alec,

"Ain't it just lovely, sir?"

"It is a regularly splendid loaf! Did my girl make it all herself?" he asked, surveying the shapely, sweet-smelling object with real interest and pleasure.

"Every particle herself, and never asked a bit of help or advice from anyone," answered Aunt Plenty, folding her hands with an air of unmitigated satisfaction, for her pupil certainly did her great credit.

"I've had so many failures and troubles that I really thought I never should be able to do it alone. Dolly let one splendid batch burn up because I forgot it. She was there and smelt it, but never did a thing, for she said, when I undertook to bake bread I must give my whole mind to it. Wasn't it hard? She might have called me at least," said Rose, recollecting, with a sigh, the anguish of that moment.

"She meant you should learn by experience, as Rosamond did in that little affair of the purple jar, you remember."

"I always thought it very unfair in her mother not to warn the poor thing a little bit; and she was regularly mean when Rosamond asked for a bowl to put the purple stuff in, and she said, in such a provoking way, 'I did not agree to lend you a bowl, but I will, my dear.' Ugh! I always want to shake that hateful woman, though she was a moral mamma."

"Never mind her now, but tell me all about my loaf," said Dr. Alec, much amused at Rose's burst of indignation.

"There's nothing to tell, uncle, except that I did my best, gave my mind to it, and sat watching over it all the while it was in the oven till I was quite baked myself. Everything went right this time, and it came out a nice, round, crusty loaf, as you see. Now taste it, and tell me if it is good as well as handsome."

"Must I cut it? Can't I put it under a glass cover and keep it in the parlor as they do wax flowers and fine works of that sort?"

"What an idea, uncle! It would mould and be spoilt. Besides, people would laugh at us, and make fun of my old-fashioned accomplishment. You promised to eat it, and you must; not all at once, but as soon as you can, so I can make you some more."

81

Dr. Alec solemnly cut off his favourite crusty slice, and solemnly ate it; then wiped his lips, and brushing back Rose's hair, solemnly kissed her on the forehead, saying, heartily,

"My dear, it is perfect bread, and you are an honour to your teacher. When we have our model school I shall offer a prize for the best bread, and you will get it."

"I've got it already, and I'm quite satisfied," said Rose, slipping into her seat, and trying to hide her right hand which had a burn on it.

But Dr. Alec saw it, guessed how it came there, and after tea insisted on easing the pain which she would hardly confess.

"Aunt Clara says I am spoiling my hands, but I don't care, for I've had such good times with Aunt Plenty, and I think she has enjoyed it as much as I have. Only one thing troubles me, uncle, and I want to ask you about it," said Rose, as they paced up and down the hall in the twilight, the bandaged hand very carefully laid on Dr. Alec's arm.

"More little confidences? I like them immensely, so tell away, my dear."

"Well, you see I feel as if Aunt Peace would like to do something for me, and I've found out what it can be. You know she can't go about like Aunty Plen, and we are so busy nowadays that she is rather lonely, I'm afraid. So I want to take lessons in sewing of her. She works so beautifully, and it is a useful thing, you know, and I ought to be a good needlewoman as well as housekeeper, oughtn't I?"

"Bless your kind little heart, that is what I was thinking of the other day when Aunt Peace said she saw you very seldom now, you were so busy I wanted to speak of it, but fancied you had as much on your hands as you could manage. It would delight the dear woman to teach you all her delicate handicraft, especially button-holes, for I believe that is where young ladies fail; at least, I've heard them say so. So, do you devote your mind to button-holes; make 'em all over my clothes if you want something to practice on. I'll wear any quantity."

Rose laughed at this reckless offer, but promised to attend to that important branch, though she confessed that darning was her weak point. Whereupon Uncle Alec engaged to supply her with socks in all stages of dilapidation, and to have a new set at once, so that she could run the heels for him as a pleasant beginning.

Then they went up to make their request in due form, to the great delight of gentle Aunt Peace, who got quite excited with the fun that went on while they would yarn, looked up darning needles, and fitted out a nice little mending basket for her pupil.

Very busy and very happy were Rose's days now, for in the morning she went about the house with Aunt Plenty attending to linen-closets and store-rooms, pickling and preserving, exploring garret and cellar to see that all was right, and learning, in the good old-fashioned manner, to look well after the ways of the household.

In the afternoon, after her walk or drive, she sat with Aunt Peace plying her needle, while Aunt Plenty, whose eyes were failing, knitted and chatted briskly, telling many a pleasant story of old times, till the three were moved to laugh and cry together, for the busy needles were embroidering all sorts of bright patterns on the lives of the workers, though they seemed to be only stitching cotton and darning hose.

It was a pretty sight to see the rosy-faced little maid sitting between the two old ladies, listening dutifully to their instructions, and cheering the lessons with her lively chatter and blithe laugh. If the kitchen had proved attractive to Dr. Alec when Rose was there at work, the sewing-room was quite irresistible, and he made himself so agreeable that no one had the heart to drive him away, especially when he read aloud or spun yarns.

"There! I've made you a new set of warm night-gowns with four button-holes in each. See if they are not neatly done," said Rose, one day, some weeks after the new lessons began.

"Even to a thread, and nice little bars across the end so I can't tear them when I twitch the buttons out. Most superior work, ma'am, and I'm deeply grateful; so much so, that I'll sew on these buttons myself, and save those tired fingers from another prick."

"You sew them on?" cried Rose, with her eyes wide open in amazement.

"Wait a bit till I get my sewing tackle, and then you shall see what I can do."

"Can he, really?" asked Rose of Aunt Peace, as Uncle Alec marched off with a comical air of importance.

"Oh, yes, I taught him years ago, before he went to sea; and I suppose he has had to do things for himself, more or less, ever since; so he has kept his hand in."

He evidently had, for he was soon back with a funny little work-bag, out of which he produced a thimble without a top; and, having threaded his needle, he proceeded to sew on the buttons so handily that Rose was much impressed and amused.

"I wonder if there is anything in the world that you cannot do," she said, in a tone of respectful admiration.

"There are one or two things that I am not up to yet," he answered, with a laugh in the corner of his eye, as he waxed his thread with a flourish.

"I should like to know what?"

"Bread and button-holes, ma'am."

Chapter 17—Good Bargains
It was a rainy Sunday afternoon, and four boys were trying to spend it quietly in the "liberry," as Jamie called the room devoted to books and boys, at Aunt Jessie's. Will and Geordie were sprawling on the sofa, deep in the adventures of the scapegraces and ragamuffins whose histories are now the fashion. Archie lounged in the easy chair, surrounded by newspapers; Charlie stood upon the rug, in an Englishman's favourite attitude, and, I regret to say, both were smoking cigars.

"It is my opinion that this day will never come to an end," said Prince, with a yawn that nearly rent him asunder.

"Read and improve your mind, my son," answered Archie, peering solemnly over the paper behind which he had been dozing.

"Don't you preach, parson, but put on your boots and come out for a tramp, instead of mulling over the fire like a granny."

"No, thank you, tramps in an easterly storm don't strike me as amusing." There Archie stopped and held up his hand, for a pleasant voice was heard saying outside,

"Are the boys in the library, auntie?"

"Yes, dear, and longing for sunshine; so run in and make it for them," answered Mrs. Jessie.

"It's Rose," and Archie threw his cigar into the fire.

"What's that for?" asked Charlie.

"Gentlemen don't smoke before ladies."

"True; but I'm not going to waste my weed," and Prince poked his into the empty inkstand that served them for an ash tray.

A gentle tap at the door was answered by a chorus of "Come in," and Rose appeared, looking blooming and breezy with the chilly air.

"If I disturb you, say so, and I'll go away," she began, pausing on the threshold with modest hesitation, for something in the elder boys' faces excited her curiosity.

"You never disturb us, cousin," said the smokers, while the readers tore themselves from the heroes of the bar-room and gutter long enough to nod affably to their guest.

As Rose bent to warm her hands, one end of Archie's cigar stuck out of the ashes, smoking furiously and smelling strongly.

"Oh, you bad boys, how could you do it, to-day of all days?" she said reproachfully.

"Where's the harm?" asked Archie.

"You know as well as I do; your mother doesn't like it, and it's a bad habit, for it wastes money and does you no good."

"Fiddlesticks! every man smokes, even Uncle Alec, whom you think so perfect," began Charlie, in his teasing way.

"No, he doesn't! He has given it up, and I know why," cried Rose eagerly.

"Now I think of it, I haven't seen the old meerschaum since he came home. Did he stop it on our account?" asked Archie.

"Yes," and Rose told the little scene on the seashore in the camping-out time.

Archie seemed much impressed, and said manfully, "He won't have done that in vain so far as I'm concerned. I don't care a pin about smoking, so can give it up as easy as not, and I promise you I will. I only do it now and then for fun."

"You too?" and Rose looked up at the bonny Prince, who never looked less bonny than at that moment, for he had resumed his cigar just to torment her.

Now Charlie cared as little as Archie about smoking, but it would not do to yield too soon: so he shook his head, gave a great puff, and said loftily,

"You women are always asking us to give up harmless little things just because you don't approve of them. How would you like it if we did the same by you, miss?"

"If I did harmful or silly things, I'd thank you for telling me of them, and I'd try to mend my ways," answered Rose heartily.

"Well, now, we'll see if you mean what you say. I'll give up smoking to please you, if you will give up something to please me," said Prince, seeing a good chance to lord it over the weaker vessel at small cost to himself.

"I'll agree if it is as foolish as cigars."

"Oh, it's ever so much sillier."

"Then I promise; what is it?" and Rose quite trembled with anxiety to know which of her pet habits or possessions she must lose.

"Give up your ear-rings," and Charlie laughed wickedly, sure that she would never hold to that bargain.

Rose uttered a cry and clapped both hands to her ears where the gold rings hung.

"Oh, Charlie, wouldn't anything else do as well? I've been through so much teasing and trouble, I do want to enjoy my pretty ear-rings, for I can wear them now."

"Wear as many as you like, and I'll smoke in peace," returned this bad boy.

"Will nothing else satisfy you?" imploringly.

"Nothing," sternly.

Rose stood silent for a minute, thinking of something Aunt Jessie once said "You have more influence over the boys than you know; use it for their good, and I shall thank you all my life." Here was a chance to do some good by sacrificing a little vanity of her own. She felt it was right to do it, yet found it very hard, and asked wistfully,

"Do you mean never wear them, Charlie?"

"Never, unless you want me to smoke."

"I never do."

"Then clinch the bargain."

He had no idea she would do it, and was much surprised when she took the dear rings from her ears, with a quick gesture, and held them out to him, saying, in a tone that made the colour come up to his brown cheek, it was so full of sweet good will,

"I care more for my cousins than for my ear-rings, so I promise, and I'll keep my word."

"For shame, Prince! let her wear her little danglers if she likes, and don't bargain about doing what you know is right," cried Archie, coming out of his grove of newspapers with an indignant bounce.

But Rose was bent on showing her aunt that she could use her influence for the boys' good, and said steadily,

"It is fair, and I want it to be so, then you will believe I'm in earnest. Here, each of you wear one of these on your watch-guard to remind you. I shall not forget, because very soon I cannot wear ear-rings if I want to."

As she spoke, Rose offered a little ring to each cousin, and the boys, seeing how sincere she was, obeyed her. When the pledges were safe, Rose stretched a hand to each, and the lads gave hers a hearty grip, half pleased and half ashamed of their part in the compact.

Just at that moment Dr. Alec and Mrs. Jessie came in.

"What's this? Dancing Ladies' Triumph on Sunday?" exclaimed Uncle Alec, surveying the trio with surprise.

"No, sir, it is the Anti-Tobacco League. Will you join?" said Charlie, while Rose slipped away to her aunt, and Archie buried both cigars behind the back log.

When the mystery was explained, the elders were well pleased, and Rose received a vote of thanks, which made her feel as if she had done a service to her country, as she had, for every boy who grows up free from bad habits bids fair to make a good citizen.

"I wish Rose would drive a bargain with Will and Geordie also, for I think these books are as bad for the small boys as cigars for the large ones," said Mrs. Jessie, sitting down on the sofa between the readers, who politely curled up their legs to make room for her.

"I thought they were all the fashion," answered Dr. Alec, settling in the big chair with Rose.

"So is smoking, but it is harmful. The writers of these popular stories intend to do good, I have no doubt, but it seems to me they fail because their motto is, 'Be smart, and you will be rich,' instead of 'Be honest, and you will be happy.' I do not judge hastily, Alec, for I have read a dozen, at least, of these stories, and, with much that is attractive to boys, I find a great deal to condemn in them, and other parents say the same when I ask them."

"Now, Mum, that's too bad! I like 'em tip-top. This one is a regular screamer," cried Will.

"They're bully books, and I'd like to know where's the harm," added Geordie.

"You have just shown us one of the chief evils, and that is slang," answered their mother quickly.

"Must have it, ma'am. If these chaps talked all right, there'd be no fun in 'em," protested Will.

"A boot-black mustn't use good grammar, and a newsboy must swear a little, or he wouldn't be natural," explained Geordie, both boys ready to fight gallantly for their favourites.

"But my sons are neither boot-blacks nor newsboys, and I object to hearing them use such words as 'screamer,' 'bully,' and 'buster.' In fact, I fail to see the advantage of writing books about such people unless it is done in a very different way. I cannot think they will help to refine the ragamuffins if they read them, and I'm sure they can do no good to the better class of boys, who

86

through these books are introduced to police courts, counterfeiters' dens, gambling houses, drinking saloons, and all sorts of low life."

"Some of them are about first-rate boys, mother; and they go to sea and study, and sail round the world, having great larks all the way."

"I have read about them, Geordie, and though they are better than the others, I am not satisfied with these optical delusions, as I call them. Now, I put it to you, boys, is it natural for lads from fifteen to eighteen to command ships, defeat pirates, outwit smugglers, and so cover themselves with glory, that Admiral Farragut invites them to dinner, saying, 'Noble boy, you are an honour to your country!' Or, if the hero is in the army, he has hair-breadth escapes and adventures enough in one small volume to turn his hair white, and in the end he goes to Washington at the express desire of the President or Commander-in-chief to be promoted to no end of stars and bars. Even if the hero is merely an honest boy trying to get his living, he is not permitted to do so in a natural way, by hard work and years of patient effort, but is suddenly adopted by a millionaire whose pocket-book he has returned; or a rich uncle appears from sea just in the nick of time; or the remarkable boy earns a few dollars, speculates in pea-nuts or neckties, and grows rich so rapidly that Sinbad in the diamond valley is a pauper compared to him. Isn't it so, boys?"

"Well, the fellows in these books are mighty lucky, and very smart, I must say," answered Will, surveying an illustration on the open page before him, where a small but virtuous youth is upsetting a tipsy giant in a bar-room, and under it the elegant inscription, "Dick Dauntless punches the head of Sam Soaker."

"It gives boys such wrong ideas of life and business; shows them so much evil and vulgarity that they need not know about, and makes the one success worth having a fortune, a lord's daughter, or some worldly honour, often not worth the time it takes to win. It does seem to me that some one might write stories that should be lively, natural and helpful tales in which the English should be good, the morals pure, and the characters such as we can love in spite of the faults that all may have. I can't bear to see such crowds of eager little fellows at the libraries reading such trash; weak, when it is not wicked, and totally unfit to feed the hungry minds that feast on it for want of something better. There! my lecture is done; now I should like to hear what you gentlemen have to say," and Aunt Jessie subsided with a pretty flush on the face that was full of motherly anxiety for her boys.

"Tom Brown just suits mother, and me too, so I wish Mr. Hughes would write another story as good," said Archie.

"You don't find things of this sort in Tom Brown; yet these books are all in the Sunday-school libraries" and Mrs. Jessie read the following paragraph from the book she had taken from Will's hand,

"'In this place we saw a tooth of John the Baptist. Ben said he could see locust and wild honey sticking to it. I couldn't. Perhaps John used a piece of the true cross for a tooth-pick.'"

"A larky sort of a boy says that, Mum, and we skip the parts where they describe what they saw in the different countries," cried Will.

"And those descriptions, taken mostly from guidebooks, I fancy, are the only parts of any real worth. The scrapes of the bad boys make up the rest of the story, and it is for those you read these books, I think," answered his mother, stroking back the hair off the honest little face that looked rather abashed at this true statement of the case.

"Anyway, mother, the ship part is useful, for we learn how to sail her, and by and by that will all come handy when we go to sea," put in Geordie.

"Indeed, then you can explain this manoeuvre to me, of course," and Mrs. Jessie read from another page the following nautical paragraph,

"The wind is south-south-west, and we can have her up four points closer to the wind, and still be six points off the wind. As she luffs up we shall man the fore and main sheets, slack on the weather, and haul on the lee braces."

"I guess I could, if I wasn't afraid of uncle. He knows so much more than I do, he'd laugh," began Geordie, evidently puzzled by the question.

"Ho, you know you can't, so why make believe? We don't understand half of the sea lingo, Mum, and I dare say it's all wrong," cried Will, suddenly going over to the enemy, to Geordie's great disgust.

"I do wish the boys wouldn't talk to me as if I was a ship," said Rose, bringing forward a private grievance. "Coming home from church this morning, the wind blew me about, and Will called out, right in the street, 'Brail up the foresail, and take in the flying-jib, that will ease her.'"

The boys shouted at the plaintive tone in which Rose repeated the words that offended her, and Will vainly endeavoured to explain that he only meant to tell her to wrap her cloak closer, and tie a veil over the tempest-tossed feathers in her hat.

"To tell the truth, if the boys must have slang, I can bear the 'sea lingo,' as Will calls it, better than the other. It afflicts me less to hear my sons talk about 'brailing up the foresail' than doing as they 'darn please,' and 'cut your cable' is decidedly preferable to 'let her rip.' I once made a rule that I would have no slang in the house. I give it up now, for I cannot keep it; but I will not have rubbishy books; so, Archie, please send these two after your cigars."

Mrs. Jessie held both the small boys fast with an arm round each neck, and when she took this base advantage of them they could only squirm with dismay. "Yes, right behind the back log," she continued, energetically. "There, my hearties (you like sea slang, so I'll give you a bit) now, I want you to promise not to read any more stuff for a month, and I'll agree to supply you with wholesome fare."

"Oh, mother, not a single one?" cried Will.

"Couldn't we just finish those?" pleaded Geordie.

"The boys threw away half-smoked cigars; and your books must go after them. Surely you would not be outdone by the 'old fellows,' as you call them, or be less obedient to little Mum than they were to Rose."

"Course not! Come on, Geordie," and Will took the vow like a hero. His brother sighed and obeyed, but privately resolved to finish his story the minute the month was over.

"You have laid out a hard task for yourself, Jessie, in trying to provide good reading for boys who have been living on sensation stories. It will be like going from raspberry tarts to plain bread and butter; but you will probably save them from a bilious fever," said Dr. Alec, much amused at the proceedings.

"I remember hearing grandpa say that a love for good books was one of the best safeguards a man could have," began Archie, staring thoughtfully at the fine library before him.

"Yes, but there's no time to read nowadays; a fellow has to keep scratching round to make money or he's nobody," cut in Charlie, trying to look worldly-wise.

"This love of money is the curse of America, and for the sake of it men will sell honour and honesty, till we don't know whom to trust, and it is only a genius like Agassiz who dares to say, 'I cannot waste my time in getting rich,'" said Mrs. Jessie sadly.

"Do you want us to be poor, mother?" asked Archie, wondering.

"No, dear, and you never need be, while you can use your hands; but I am afraid of this thirst for wealth, and the temptations it brings. O, my boys! I tremble for the time when I must let you go, because I think it would break my heart to have you fail as so many fail. It would be far easier to see you dead if it could be said of you as of Sumner 'No man dared offer him a bribe.'"

Mrs. Jessie was so earnest in her motherly anxiety that her voice faltered over the last words, and she hugged the yellow heads closer in her arms, as if she feared to let them leave that safe harbour for the great sea where so many little boats go down. The younger lads nestled closer to her, and Archie said, in his quiet, resolute way,

"I cannot promise to be an Agassiz or a Sumner, mother; but I do promise to be an honest man, please God."

"Then I'm satisfied!" and holding fast the hand he gave her, she sealed his promise with a kiss that had all a mother's hope and faith in it.

"I don't see how they ever can be bad, she is so fond and proud of them," whispered Rose, quite touched by the little scene.

"You must help her make them what they should be. You have begun already, and when I see those rings where they are, my girl is prettier in my sight than if the biggest diamonds that ever twinkled shone in her ears," answered Dr. Alec, looking at her with approving eyes.

"I'm so glad you think I can do anything, for I perfectly ache to be useful; everyone is so good to me, especially Aunt Jessie."

"I think you are in a fair way to pay your debts, Rosy, for when girls give up their little vanities, and boys their small vices, and try to strengthen each other in well-doing, matters are going as they ought. Work away, my dear, and help their mother keep these sons fit friends for an innocent creature like yourself; they will be the manlier men for it, I can assure you."

Chapter 18—Fashion and Physiology
"Please, sir, I guess you'd better step up right away, or it will be too late, for I heard Miss Rose say she knew you wouldn't like it, and she'd never dare to let you see her."

Phebe said this as she popped her head into the study, where Dr. Alec sat reading a new book.

"They are at it, are they?" he said, looking up quickly, and giving himself a shake, as if ready for a battle of some sort.

"Yes, sir, as hard as they can talk, and Miss Rose don't seem to know what to do, for the things are ever so stylish, and she looks elegant in 'em; though I like her best in the old ones," answered Phebe.

"You are a girl of sense. I'll settle matters for Rosy, and you'll lend a hand. Is everything ready in her room, and are you sure you understand how they go?"

"Oh, yes, sir; but they are so funny! I know Miss Rose will think it's a joke," and Phebe laughed as if something tickled her immensely.

"Never mind what she thinks so long as she obeys. Tell her to do it for my sake, and she will find it the best joke she ever saw. I expect to have a tough time of it, but we'll win yet," said the Doctor, as he marched upstairs with the book in his hand, and an odd smile on his face.

There was such a clatter of tongues in the sewing-room that no one heard his tap at the door, so he pushed it open and took an observation. Aunt Plenty, Aunt Clara, and Aunt Jessie were all absorbed in gazing at Rose, who slowly revolved between them and the great mirror, in a full winter costume of the latest fashion.

"Bless my heart! worse even than I expected," thought the Doctor, with an inward groan, for, to his benighted eyes, the girl looked like a trussed fowl, and the fine new dress had neither grace, beauty, nor fitness to recommend it.

The suit was of two peculiar shades of blue, so arranged that patches of light and dark distracted the eye. The upper skirt was tied so lightly back that it was impossible to take a long step, and the under one was so loaded with plaited frills that it "wobbled" no other word will express it ungracefully, both fore and aft. A bunch of folds was gathered up just below the waist behind, and a great bow rode a-top. A small jacket of the same material was adorned with a high ruff at the back, and laid well open over the breast, to display some lace and a locket. Heavy fringes, bows, puffs, ruffles, and revers finished off the dress, making one's head ache to think of the amount of work wasted, for not a single graceful line struck the eye, and the beauty of the material was quite lost in the profusion of ornament.

A high velvet hat, audaciously turned up in front, with a bunch of pink roses and a sweeping plume, was cocked over one ear, and, with her curls braided into a club at the back of her neck, Rose's head looked more like that of a dashing young cavalier than a modest little girl's. High-heeled boots tilted her well forward, a tiny muff pinioned her arms, and a spotted veil, tied so closely over her face that her eyelashes were rumpled by it, gave the last touch of absurdity to her appearance.

"Now she looks like other girls, and as I like to see her," Mrs. Clara was saying, with an air of great satisfaction.

"She does look like a fashionable young lady, but somehow I miss my little Rose, for children dressed like children in my day," answered Aunt Plenty, peering through her glasses with a troubled look, for she could not imagine the creature before her ever sitting in her lap, running to wait upon her, or making the house gay with a child's blithe presence.

"Things have changed since your day, Aunt, and it takes time to get used to new ways. But you, Jessie, surely like this costume better than the dowdy things Rose has been wearing all summer. Now, be honest, and own you do," said Mrs. Clara, bent on being praised for her work.

"Well, dear to be quite honest, then, I think it is frightful," answered Mrs. Jessie, with a candour that caused revolving Rose to stop in dismay.

"Hear, hear," cried a deep voice, and with a general start the ladies became aware that the enemy was among them.

Rose blushed up to her hat brim, and stood, looking, as she felt, like a fool, while Mrs. Clara hastened to explain.

"Of course, I don't expect you to like it, Alec, but I don't consider you a judge of what is proper and becoming for a young lady. Therefore, I have taken the liberty of providing a pretty street suit for Rose. She need not wear it if you object, for I know we promised to let you do what you liked with the poor dear for a year."

"It is a street costume, is it?" asked the Doctor, mildly. "Do you know, I never should have guessed that it was meant for winter weather and brisk locomotion. Take a turn, Rosy, and let me see all its beauties and advantages."

Rose tried to walk off with her usual free tread, but the under-skirt got in her way, the over-skirt was so tight she could not take a long step, and her boots made it impossible to carry herself perfectly erect.

"I haven't got used to it yet," she said, petulantly, kicking at her train, as she turned to toddle back again.

"Suppose a mad dog or a runaway horse was after you, could you get out of the way without upsetting, Colonel," asked the Doctor, with a twinkle in the eyes that were fixed on the rakish hat.

"Don't think I could, but I'll try," and Rose made a rush across the room. Her boot-heels caught on a rug, several strings broke, her hat tipped over her eyes, and she plunged promiscuously into a chair, where she sat laughing so infectiously that all but Mrs. Clara joined in her mirth.

"I should say that a walking suit in which one could not walk, and a winter suit which exposes the throat, head, and feet to cold and damp, was rather a failure, Clara, especially as it has no beauty to reconcile one to its utter unfitness," said Dr. Alec, as he helped Rose undo her veil, adding, in a low tone, "Nice thing for the eyes; you'll soon see spots when it's off as well as when it's on, and, by and by, be a case for an oculist."

"No beauty!" cried Mrs. Clara, warmly, "Now, that is just a man's blindness. This is the best of silk and camel's hair, real ostrich feathers, and an expensive ermine muff. What could be in better taste, or more proper for a young girl?"

"I'll shew you, if Rose will go to her room and oblige me by putting on what she finds there," answered the Doctor, with unexpected readiness.

"Alec, if it is a Bloomer, I shall protest. I've been expecting it, but I know I cannot bear to see that pretty child sacrificed to your wild ideas of health. Tell me it isn't a Bloomer!" and Mrs. Clara clasped her hands imploringly.

"It is not."

"Thank Heaven!" and she resigned herself with a sigh of relief, adding plaintively, "I did hope you'd accept my suit, for poor Rose has been afflicted with frightful clothes long enough to spoil the taste of any girl."

"You talk of my afflicting the child, and then make a helpless guy like that of her!" answered the Doctor, pointing to the little fashion plate that was scuttling out of sight as fast as it could go.

He closed the door with a shrug, but before anyone could speak, his quick eye fell upon an object which caused him to frown, and demand in an indignant tone,

"After all I have said, were you really going to tempt my girl with those abominable things?"

"I thought we put them away when she wouldn't wear them," murmured Mrs. Clara, whisking a little pair of corsets out of sight with guilty haste. "I only brought them to try, for Rose is growing stout, and will have no figure if it is not attended to soon," she added, with an air of calm conviction that roused the Doctor still more, for this was one of his especial abominations.

"Growing stout! Yes, thank Heaven, she is, and shall continue to do it, for Nature knows how to mould a woman better than any corset-maker, and I won't have her interfered with. My dear Clara, have you lost your senses that you can for a moment dream of putting a growing girl into an instrument of torture like this?" and with a sudden gesture he plucked forth the offending corsets from under the sofa cushion, and held them out with the expression one would wear on beholding the thumbscrews or the rack of ancient times.

"Don't be absurd, Alec. There is no torture about it, for tight lacing is out of fashion, and we have nice, sensible things nowadays. Everyone wears them; even babies have stiffened waists to support their weak little backs," began Mrs. Clara, rushing to the defence of the pet delusion of most women.

"I know it, and so the poor little souls have weak backs all their days, as their mothers had before them. It is vain to argue the matter, and I won't try, but I wish to state, once for all, that if I ever see a pair of corsets near Rose, I'll put them in the fire, and you may send the bill to me."

As he spoke the corsets were on their way to destruction, but Mrs. Jessie caught his arm, exclaiming merrily, "Don't burn them, for mercy sake, Alec; they are full of whalebones, and will make a dreadful odour. Give them to me. I'll see that they do no harm."

"Whalebones, indeed! A regular fence of them, and metal gate-posts in front. As if our own bones were not enough, if we'd give them a chance to do their duty," growled the Doctor, yielding up the bone of contention with a last shake of contempt. Then his face cleared suddenly, and he held up his finger, saying, with a smile, "Hear those girls laugh; cramped lungs could not make hearty music like that."

Peals of laughter issued from Rose's room, and smiles involuntarily touched the lips of those who listened to the happy sound.

"Some new prank of yours, Alec?" asked Aunt Plenty, indulgently, for she had come to believe in most of her nephew's odd notions, because they seemed to work so well.

"Yes, ma'am, my last, and I hope you will like it. I discovered what Clara was at, and got my rival suit ready for to-day. I'm not going to 'afflict' Rose, but let her choose, and if I'm not entirely mistaken, she will like my rig best. While we wait I'll explain, and then you will appreciate the general effect better. I got hold of this little book, and was struck with its good sense and good taste, for it suggests a way to clothe women both healthfully and handsomely, and that is a great point. It begins at the foundations, as you will see if you will look at these pictures, and I should think women would rejoice at this lightening of their burdens."

As he spoke, the Doctor laid the book before Aunt Plenty, who obediently brought her spectacles to bear upon the illustrations, and after a long look exclaimed, with a scandalised face,

"Mercy on us, these things are like the night-drawers Jamie wears! You don't mean to say you want Rose to come out in this costume? It's not proper, and I won't consent to it!"

"I do mean it, and I'm sure my sensible aunt will consent when she understands that these well I'll call them by an Indian name, and say pajamas are for underwear, and Rose can have as pretty frocks as she likes outside. These two suits of flannel, each in one piece from head to foot, with a skirt or so hung on this easily-fitting waist, will keep the child warm without burdening her with belts, and gathers, and buckles, and bunches round the waist, and leave free the muscles that need plenty of room to work in. She shall never have the back-ache if I can help it, nor the long list of ills you dear women think you cannot escape."

"I don't consider it modest, and I'm sure Rose will be shocked at it," began Mrs. Clara, but stopped suddenly, as Rose appeared in the doorway, not looking shocked a bit.

"Come on, my hygienic model, and let us see you," said her uncle, with an approving glance, as she walked in, looking so mischievously merry, that it was evident she enjoyed the joke.

"Well, I don't see anything remarkable. That is a neat, plain suit; the materials are good, and it's not unbecoming, if you want her to look like a little school-girl; but it has not a particle of style, and no one would ever give it a second glance," said Mrs. Clara, feeling that her last remark condemned the whole thing.

"Exactly what I want," answered the provoking Doctor, rubbing his hands with a satisfied air. "Rosy looks now like what she is, a modest little girl, who does not want to be stared at. I think she would get a glance of approval, though, from people who like sense and simplicity rather than fuss and feathers. Revolve, my Hebe, and let me refresh my eyes by the sight of you."

There was very little to see, however, only a pretty Gabrielle dress, of a soft warm shade of brown, coming to the tops of a trim pair of boots with low heels. A seal-skin sack, cap, and mittens, with a glimpse of scarlet at the throat, and the pretty curls tied up with a bright velvet of the same colour, completed the external adornment, making her look like a robin redbreast wintry, yet warm.

"How do you like it, Rosy?" asked the Doctor, feeling that her opinion was more important to the success of his new idea than that of all the aunts on the hill.

"I feel very odd and light, but I'm warm as a toast, and nothing seems to be in my way," answered Rose, with a skip which displayed shapely gaiters on legs that now might be as free and active as a boy's under the modest skirts of the girl.

"You can run away from the mad dogs, and walk off at a smart pace without tumbling on your nose, now, I fancy?"

"Yes, uncle! suppose the dog coming, I just hop over a wall so and when I walk of a cold day, I go like this."

Entering fully into the spirit of the thing, Rose swung herself over the high back of the sofa as easily as one of her cousins, and then went down the long hall as if her stout boots were related to the famous seven-leaguers.

"There! you see how it will be; dress her in that boyish way and she will act like a boy. I do hate all these inventions of strong-minded women!" exclaimed Mrs. Clara, as Rose came back at a run.

"Ah, but you see some of these sensible inventions come from the brain of a fashionable modiste, who will make you more lovely, or what you value more 'stylish' outside and comfortable within. Mrs. Van Tassel has been to Madame Stone, and is wearing a full suit of this sort. Van himself told me, when I asked how she was, that she had given up lying on the sofa, and was going about in a most astonishing way, considering her feeble health."

"You don't say so! Let me see that book a moment," and Aunt Clara examined the new patterns with a more respectful air, for if the elegant Mrs. Van Tassel wore these "dreadful things" it would never do to be left behind, in spite of her prejudices.

Dr. Alec looked at Mrs. Jessie, and both smiled, for "little Mum" had been in the secret, and enjoyed it mightily.

"I thought that would settle it," he said with a nod.

"I didn't wait for Mrs. Van to lead the way, and for once in my life I have adopted a new fashion before Clara. My freedom suit is ordered, and you may see me playing tag with Rose and the boys before long," answered Mrs. Jessie, nodding back at him.

Meantime Aunt Plenty was examining Rose's costume, for the hat and sack were off, and the girl was eagerly explaining the new under-garments.

"See, auntie, all nice scarlet flannel, and a gay little petticoat, and long stockings, oh, so warm! Phebe and I nearly died laughing when I put this rig on, but I like it ever so much. The dress is so comfortable, and doesn't need any belt or sash, and I can sit without rumpling any trimming, that's such a comfort! I like to be tidy, and so, when I wear fussed-up things, I'm thinking of my clothes all the time, and that's tiresome. Do say you like it. I resolved I would, just to please uncle, for he does know more about health than anyone else, I'm sure, and I'd wear a bag if he asked me to do it."

"I don't ask that, Rose, but I wish you'd weigh and compare the two suits, and then choose which seems best. I leave it to your own commonsense," answered Dr. Alec, feeling pretty sure he had won.

"Why, I take this one, of course, uncle. The other is fashionable, and yes I must say I think it's pretty but it's very heavy, and I should have to go round like a walking doll if I wore it. I'm much obliged to auntie, but I'll keep this, please."

Rose spoke gently but decidedly, though there was a look of regret when her eye fell on the other suit which Phebe had brought in; and it was very natural to like to look as other girls did. Aunt Clara sighed; Uncle Alec smiled, and said heartily,

"Thank you, dear; now read this book and you will understand why I ask it of you. Then, if you like, I'll give you a new lesson; you asked for one yesterday, and this is more necessary than French or housekeeping."

"Oh, what?" and Rose caught up the book which Mrs. Clara had thrown down with a disgusted look.

Though Dr. Alec was forty, the boyish love of teasing was not yet dead in him, and, being much elated at his victory, he could not resist the temptation of shocking Mrs. Clara by suggesting dreadful possibilities, so he answered, half in earnest, half in jest, "Physiology, Rose. Wouldn't you like to be a little medical student, with Uncle Doctor for teacher, and be ready to take up his practice when he has to stop? If you agree, I'll hunt up my old skeleton to-morrow."

That was too much for Aunt Clara, and she hastily departed, with her mind in a sad state of perturbation about Mrs. Van Tassel's new costume and Rose's new study.

Chapter 19—Brother Bones

Rose accepted her uncle's offer, as Aunt Myra discovered two or three days later. Coming in for an early call, and hearing voices in the study, she opened the door, gave a cry and shut it quickly, looking a good deal startled. The Doctor appeared in a moment, and begged to know what the matter was.

"How can you ask when that long box looks so like a coffin I thought it was one, and that dreadful thing stared me in the face as I opened the door," answered Mrs. Myra, pointing to the skeleton that hung from the chandelier cheerfully grinning at all beholders.

"This is a medical college where women are freely admitted, so walk in, madam, and join the class if you'll do me the honour," said the Doctor, waving her forward with his politest bow.

"Do, auntie, it's perfectly splendid," cried Rose's voice, and Rose's blooming face was seen behind the ribs of the skeleton, smiling and nodding in the gayest possible manner.

"What are you doing, child?" demanded Aunt Myra, dropping into a chair and staring about her.

"Oh, I'm learning bones to-day, and I like it so much. There are twelve ribs, you know, and the two lower ones are called floating ribs, because they are not fastened to the breastbone. That's why they go in so easily if you lace tight and squeeze the lungs and heart in the let me see, what was that big word oh, I know thoracic cavity," and Rose beamed with pride as she aired her little bit of knowledge.

"Do you think that is a good sort of thing for her to be poking over? She is a nervous child, and I'm afraid it will be bad for her," said Aunt Myra, watching Rose as she counted vertebrae, and waggled a hip-joint in its socket with an inquiring expression.

"An excellent study, for she enjoys it, and I mean to teach her how to manage her nerves so that they won't be a curse to her, as many a woman's become through ignorance or want of thought. To make a mystery or terror of these things is a mistake, and I mean Rose shall understand and respect her body so well that she won't dare to trifle with it as most women do."

"And she really likes it?"

"Very much, auntie! It's all so wonderful, and so nicely planned, you can hardly believe what you see. Just think, there are 600,000,000 air cells in one pair of lungs, and 2,000 pores to a square inch

95

of surface; so you see what quantities of air we must have, and what care we should take of our skin so all the little doors will open and shut right. And brains, auntie, you've no idea how curious they are; I haven't got to them yet, but I long to, and uncle is going to show me a manikin that you can take to pieces. Just think how nice it will be to see all the organs in their places; I only wish they could be made to work as ours do."

It was funny to see Aunt Myra's face as Rose stood before her talking rapidly with one hand laid in the friendliest manner on the skeleton's shoulder. Every word both the Doctor and Rose uttered hit the good lady in her weakest spot, and as she looked and listened a long array of bottles and pill-boxes rose up before her, reproaching her with the "ignorance and want of thought" that made her what she was, a nervous, dyspeptic, unhappy old woman.

"Well, I don't know but you may be right, Alec, only I wouldn't carry it too far. Women don't need much of this sort of knowledge, and are not fit for it. I couldn't bear to touch that ugly thing, and it gives me the creeps to hear about 'organs,'" said Aunt Myra, with a sigh and her hand on her side.

"Wouldn't it be a comfort to know that your liver was on the right side, auntie, and not on the left!" asked Rose with a naughty laugh in her eyes, for she had lately learnt that Aunt Myra's liver complaint was not in the proper place.

"It's a dying world, child, and it don't much matter where the pain is, for sooner or later we all drop off and are seen no more," was Aunt Myra's cheerful reply.

"Well, I intend to know what kills me if I can, and meantime, I'm going to enjoy myself in spite of a dying world. I wish you'd do so too, and come and study with uncle, it would do you good, I'm sure," and Rose went back to counting vertebrae with such a happy face, that Aunt Myra had not the heart to say a word to dampen her ardour.

"Perhaps it's as well to let her do what she likes the little while she is with us. But pray be careful of her, Alec, and not allow her to overwork," she whispered as she went out.

"That's exactly what I'm trying to do, ma'am, and rather a hard job I find it," he added, as he shut the door, for the dear aunts were dreadfully in his way sometimes.

Half an hour later came another interruption in the shape of Mac, who announced his arrival by the brief but elegant remark,

"Hullo! what new game is this?"

Rose explained, Mac gave a long whistle of surprise, and then took a promenade round the skeleton, observing gravely,

"Brother Bones looks very jolly, but I can't say much for his beauty."

"You mustn't make fun of him, for he's a good old fellow, and you'd be just as ugly if your flesh was off," said Rose, defending her new friend with warmth.

"I dare say, so I'll keep my flesh on, thank you. You are so busy you can't read to a fellow, I suppose?" asked Mac, whose eyes were better, but still too weak for books.

"Don't you want to come and join my class? Uncle explains it all to us, and you can take a look at the plates as they come along. We'll give up bones today and have eyes instead; that will be more interesting to you," added Rose, seeing no ardent thirst for physiological information in his face.

"Rose, we must not fly about from one thing to another in this way," began Dr. Alec, but she whispered quickly, with a nod towards Mac, whose goggles were turned wistfully in the direction of the forbidden books,

"He's blue to-day, and we must amuse him; give a little lecture on eyes, and it will do him good. No matter about me, uncle."

"Very well; the class will please be seated," and the Doctor gave a sounding rap on the table.

"Come, sit by me, dear, then we can both see the pictures; and if your head gets tired you can lie down," said Rose, generously opening her little college to a brother, and kindly providing for the weaknesses that all humanity is subject to.

Side by side they sat and listened to a very simple explanation of the mechanism of the eye, finding it as wonderful as a fairy tale, for fine plates illustrated it, and a very willing teacher did his best to make the lesson pleasant.

"Jove! if I'd known what mischief I was doing to that mighty delicate machine of mine, you wouldn't have caught me reading by firelight, or studying with a glare of sunshine on my book," said Mac, peering solemnly at a magnified eye-ball; then, pushing it away, he added indignantly, "Why isn't a fellow taught all about his works, and how to manage 'em, and not left to go blundering into all sorts of worries? Telling him after he's down isn't much use, for then he's found it out himself and won't thank you."

"Ah, Mac, that's just what I keep lecturing about, and people won't listen. You lads need that sort of knowledge so much, and fathers and mothers ought to be able to give it to you. Few of them are able, and so we all go blundering, as you say. Less Greek and Latin and more knowledge of the laws of health for my boys, if I had them. Mathematics are all very well, but morals are better, and I wish, how I wish that I could help teachers and parents to feel it as they ought."

"Some do; Aunt Jessie and her boys have capital talks, and I wish we could; but mother's so busy with her housekeeping, and father with his business, there never seems to be any time for that sort of thing; even if there was, it don't seem as if it would be easy to talk to them, because we've never got into the way of it, you know."

Poor Mac was right there, and expressed a want that many a boy and girl feels. Fathers and mothers are too absorbed in business and housekeeping to study their children, and cherish that sweet and natural confidence which is a child's surest safeguard, and a parent's subtlest power. So the young hearts hide trouble or temptation till the harm is done, and mutual regret comes too late. Happy the boys and girls who tell all things freely to father or mother, sure of pity, help, and pardon; and thrice happy the parents who, out of their own experience, and by their own virtues, can teach and uplift the souls for which they are responsible.

This longing stirred in the hearts of Rose and Mac, and by a natural impulse both turned to Dr. Alec, for in this queer world of ours, fatherly and motherly hearts often beat warm and wise in the breasts of bachelor uncles and maiden aunts; and it is my private opinion that these worthy creatures are a beautiful provision of nature for the cherishing of other people's children. They certainly get great comfort out of it, and receive much innocent affection that otherwise would be lost.

Dr. Alec was one of these, and his big heart had room for every one of the eight cousins, especially orphaned Rose and afflicted Mac; so, when the boy uttered that unconscious reproach to his parents, and Rose added with a sigh, "It must be beautiful to have a mother!" the good Doctor yearned over them, and, shutting his book with a decided slam, said in that cordial voice of his,

"Now, look here, children, you just come and tell me all your worries, and with God's help, I'll settle them for you. That is what I'm here for, I believe, and it will be a great happiness to me if you can trust me."

"We can, uncle, and we will!" both answered, with a heartiness that gratified him much.

"Good! now school is dismissed, and I advise you to go and refresh your 600,000,000 air cells by a brisk run in the garden. Come again whenever you like, Mac, and we'll teach you all we can about your 'works,' as you call them, so you can keep them running smoothly."

"We'll come, sir, much obliged," and the class in physiology went out to walk.

Mac did come again, glad to find something he could study in spite of his weak eyes, and learned much that was of more value than anything his school had ever taught him.

Of course, the other lads made great fun of the whole thing, and plagued Dr. Alec's students half out of their lives. But they kept on persistently, and one day something happened which made the other fellows behave themselves for ever after.

It was a holiday, and Rose up in her room thought she heard the voices of her cousins, so she ran down to welcome them, but found no one there.

"Never mind, they will be here soon, and then we'll have a frolic," she said to herself, and thinking she had been mistaken she went into the study to wait. She was lounging over the table looking at a map when an odd noise caught her ear. A gentle tapping somewhere, and following the sound it seemed to come from the inside of the long case in which the skeleton lived when not professionally engaged. This case stood upright in a niche between two book-cases at the back of the room, a darkish corner, where Brother Bones, as the boys would call him, was out of the way.

As Rose stood looking in that direction, and wondering if a rat had got shut in, the door of the case swung slowly open, and with a great start she saw a bony arm lifted, and a bony finger beckon to her. For a minute she was frightened, and ran to the study door with a fluttering heart, but just as she touched the handle a queer, stifled sort of giggle made her stop short and turn red with anger. She paused an instant to collect herself, and then went softly toward the bony beckoner. A nearer look revealed black threads tied to the arm and fingers, the ends of threads disappearing through holes bored in the back of the case. Peeping into the dark recess, she also caught sight of the tip of an elbow covered with a rough gray cloth which she knew very well.

Quick as a flash she understood the joke, her fear vanished, and with a wicked smile, she whipped out her scissors, cut the threads, and the bony arm dropped with a rattle. Before she could say, "Come out, Charlie, and let my skeleton alone," a sudden irruption of boys, all in a high state of tickle, proclaimed to the hidden rogue that his joke was a failure.

"I told him not to do it, because it might give you a start," explained Archie, emerging from the closet.

"I had a smelling bottle all ready if she fainted away," added Steve, popping up from behind the great chair.

"It's too bad of you not to squawk and run; we depended on it, it's such fun to howl after you," said Will and Geordie, rolling out from under the sofa in a promiscuous heap.

"You are getting altogether too strong-minded, Rose; most girls would have been in a jolly twitter to see this old fellow waggling his finger at them," complained Charlie, squeezing out from his tight quarters, dusty and disgusted.

"I'm used to your pranks now, so I'm always on the watch and prepared. But I won't have Brother Bones made fun of. I know uncle wouldn't like it, so please don't," began Rose just as Dr. Alec came in, and, seeing the state of the case at a glance, he said quietly,

"Hear how I got that skeleton, and then I'm sure you will treat it with respect."

The boys settled down at once on any article of furniture that was nearest and listened dutifully.

"Years ago, when I was in the hospital, a poor fellow was brought there with a rare and very painful disease. There was no hope for him, but we did our best, and he was so grateful that when he died he left us his body that we might discover the mysteries of his complaint, and so be able to help others afflicted in the same way. It did do good, and his brave patience made us remember him long after he was gone. He thought I had been kind to him, and said to a fellow-student of mine, 'Tell the Doctor I lave him me bones, for I've nothing else in the wide world, and I'll nos be wanting 'em at all, at all, when the great pain hat kilt me entirely.' So that is how they came to be mine, and why I've kept them carefully, for, though only a poor, ignorant fellow, Mike Nolan did what he could to help others, and prove his gratitude to those who tried to help him."

As Dr. Alec paused, Archie closed the door of the case as respectfully as if the mummy of an Egyptian king was inside; Will and Geordie looked solemnly at one another, evidently much impressed, and Charlie pensively remarked from the coal-hod where he sat,

"I've often heard of a skeleton in the house, but I think few people have one as useful and as interesting as ours."

Chapter 20—Under The Mistletoe

Rose made Phebe promise that she would bring her stocking into the "Bower," as she called her pretty room, on Christmas morning, because that first delicious rummage loses half its charm if two little night-caps at least do not meet over the treasures, and two happy voices Oh and Ah together.

So when Rose opened her eyes that day they fell upon faithful Phebe, rolled up in a shawl, sitting on the rug before a blazing fire, with her untouched stocking laid beside her.

"Merry Christmas!" cried the little mistress smiling gaily.

"Merry Christmas!" answered the little maid, so heartily that it did one good to hear her.

"Bring the stockings right away, Phebe, and let's see what we've got," said Rose, sitting up among the pillows, and looking as eager as a child.

A pair of long knobby hose were laid out upon the coverlet, and their contents examined with delight, though each knew every blessed thing that had been put into the other's stocking.

Never mind what they were; it is evident that they were quite satisfactory, for as Rose leaned back, she said, with a luxurious sigh of satisfaction, "Now, I believe I've got everything in the world that I want," and Phebe answered, smiling over a lapful of treasures, "This is the most splendid Christmas I ever had since I was born." Then she added with an important air,

"Do wish for something else, because I happen to know of two more presents outside the door this minute."

"Oh, me, what richness!" cried Rose, much excited. "I used to wish for a pair of glass slippers like Cinderella's, but as I can't have them, I really don't know what to ask for."

Phebe clapped her hands as she skipped off the bed and ran to the door, saying merrily, "One of them is for your feet, anyway. I don't know what you'll say to the other, but I think it's elegant."

So did Rose, when a shining pair of skates and a fine sled appeared.

"Uncle sent those; I know he did; and, now I see them, I remember that I did want to skate and coast. Isn't it a beauty? See! they fit nicely," and, sitting on the new sled, Rose tried a skate on her little bare foot, while Phebe stood by admiring the pretty tableau.

"Now we must hurry and get dressed, for there is a deal to do to-day, and I want to get through in time to try my sled before dinner."

"Gracious me, and I ought to be dusting my parlors this blessed minute!" and mistress and maid separated with such happy faces that anyone would have known what day it was without being told.

"Birnam Wood has come to Dunsinane, Rosy," said Dr. Alec, as he left the breakfast table to open the door for a procession of holly, hemlock, and cedar boughs that came marching up the steps.

Snowballs and "Merry Christmases!" flew about pretty briskly for several minutes; then all fell to work trimming the old house, for the family always dined together there on that day.

"I rode miles and mileses, as Ben says, to get this fine bit, and I'm going to hang it there as the last touch to the rig-a-madooning," said Charlie, as he fastened a dull green branch to the chandelier in the front parlor.

"It isn't very pretty," said Rose, who was trimming the chimney-piece with glossy holly sprays.

"Never mind that, it's mistletoe, and anyone who stands under it will get kissed whether they like it or not. Now's your time, ladies," answered the saucy Prince, keeping his place and looking sentimentally at the girls, who retired precipitately from the dangerous spot.

"You won't catch me," said Rose, with great dignity.

"See if I don't!"

"I've got my eye on Phebe," observed Will, in a patronising tone that made them all laugh.

"Bless the dear; I shan't mind it a bit," answered Phebe, with such a maternal air that Will's budding gallantry was chilled to death.

"Oh, the mistletoe bough," sang Rose.

"Oh, the mistletoe bough!" echoed all the boys, and the teasing ended in the plaintive ballad they all liked so well.

There was plenty of time to try the new skates before dinner, and then Rose took her first lesson on the little bay, which seemed to have frozen over for that express purpose. She found tumbling down and getting up again warm work for a time, but with six boys to teach her, she managed at last to stand alone; and, satisfied with that success, she refreshed herself with a dozen grand coasts on the Amazon, as her sled was called.

"Ah, that fatal colour! it breaks my heart to see it," croaked Aunt Myra, as Rose came down a little late, with cheeks almost as ruddy as the holly berries on the wall, and every curl as smooth as Phebe's careful hands could make it.

"I'm glad to see that Alec allows the poor child to make herself pretty in spite of his absurd notions," added Aunt Clara, taking infinite satisfaction in the fact that Rose's blue silk dress had three frills on it.

"She's a very intelligent child, and has a nice little manner of her own," observed Aunt Jane, with unusual affability; for Rose had just handed Mac a screen to guard his eyes from the brilliant fire.

"If I had a daughter like that to show my Jem when he gets home, I should be a very proud and happy woman," thought Aunt Jessie, and then reproached herself for not being perfectly satisfied with her four brave lads.

Aunt Plenty was too absorbed in the dinner to have an eye for anything else; if she had not been, she would have seen what an effect her new cap produced upon the boys. The good lady owned that she did "love a dressy cap," and on this occasion her head gear was magnificent; for the towering structure of lace was adorned with buff ribbons to such an extent that it looked as if a flock of yellow butterflies had settled on her dear old head. When she trotted about the rooms the ruches quivered, the little bows all stood erect, and the streamers waved in the breeze so comically that it was absolutely necessary for Archie to smother the Brats in the curtains till they had had their first laugh out.

Uncle Mac had brought Fun See to dinner, and it was a mercy he did, for the elder lads found a vent for their merriment in joking the young Chinaman on his improved appearance. He was in American costume now, with a cropped head, and spoke remarkably good English after six months at school; but, for all that, his yellow face and beady eyes made a curious contrast to the blonde Campbells all about him. Will called him the "Typhoon," meaning Tycoon, and the name stuck to him to his great disgust.

Aunt Peace was brought down and set in the chair of state at table, for she never failed to join the family on this day, and sat smiling at them all, "like an embodiment of Peace on earth," Uncle Alec said, as he took his place beside her, while Uncle Mac supported Aunt Plenty at the other end.

"I ate hardly any breakfast, and I've done everything I know to make myself extra hungry, but I really don't think I can eat straight through, unless I burst my buttons off," whispered Geordie to Will, as he surveyed the bounteous stores before him with a hopeless sigh.

"A fellow never knows what he can do till he tries," answered Will, attacking his heaped-up plate with an evident intention of doing his duty like a man.

Everybody knows what a Christmas dinner is, so we need waste no words in describing this one, but hasten at once to tell what happened at the end of it. The end, by the way, was so long in coming that the gas was lighted before dessert was over, for a snow flurry had come on and the wintry daylight faded fast. But that only made it all the jollier in the warm, bright rooms, full of happy souls. Everyone was very merry, but Archie seemed particularly uplifted so much so, that Charlie confided to Rose that he was afraid the Chief had been at the decanters.

Rose indignantly denied the insinuation, for when healths were drunk in the good old-fashioned way to suit the elders, she had observed that Aunt Jessie's boys filled their glasses with water, and had done the same herself in spite of the Prince's jokes about "the rosy."

But Archie certainly was unusually excited, and when someone remembered that it was the anniversary of Uncle Jem's wedding, and wished he was there to make a speech, his son electrified the family by trying to do it for him. It was rather incoherent and flowery, as maiden speeches are apt to be, but the end was considered superb; for, turning to his mother with a queer little choke in his voice, he said that she "deserved to be blessed with peace and plenty, to be crowned with roses and lads'-love, and to receive the cargo of happiness sailing home to her in spite of wind or tide to add another Jem to the family jewels."

That allusion to the Captain, now on his return trip, made Mrs. Jessie sob in her napkin, and set the boys cheering. Then, as if that was not sensation enough, Archie suddenly dashed out of the room, as if he had lost his wits.

"Too bashful to stay and be praised," began Charlie, excusing the peculiarities of his chief as in duty bound.

"Phebe beckoned to him; I saw her," cried Rose, staring hard at the door.

"Is it more presents coming?" asked Jamie, just as his brother re-appeared, looking more excited than ever.

"Yes; a present for mother, and here it is!" roared Archie, flinging wide the door to let in a tall man, who cried out,

"Where's my little woman? The first kiss for her, then the rest may come on as fast as they like."

Before the words were out of his mouth, Mrs. Jessie was half-hidden under his rough great-coat, and four boys were prancing about him clamouring for their turn.

Of course, there was a joyful tumult for a time, during which Rose slipped into the window recess and watched what went on, as if it were a chapter in a Christmas story. It was good to see bluff Uncle Jem look proudly at his tall son, and fondly hug the little ones. It was better still to see him shake his brothers' hands as if he would never leave off, and kiss all the sisters in a way that made even solemn Aunt Myra brighten up for a minute. But it was best of all to see him finally established in grandfather's chair, with his "little woman" beside him, his three youngest boys in his lap, and Archie hovering over him like a large-sized cherub. That really was, as Charlie said, "A landscape to do one's heart good."

"All hearty and all here, thank God!" said Captain Jem in the first pause that came, as he looked about him with a grateful face.

"All but Rose," answered loyal little Jamie, remembering the absent.

"Faith, I forgot the child! Where is George's little girl?" asked the Captain, who had not seen her since she was a baby.

"You'd better say Alec's great girl," said Uncle Mac, who professed to be madly jealous of his brother.

"Here I am, sir," and Rose appeared from behind the curtains, looking as if she had rather have stayed there.

"Saint George Germain, how the mite has grown!" cried Captain Jem, as he tumbled the boys out of his lap, and rose to greet the tall girl, like a gentleman as he was. But, somehow, when he shook her hand it looked so small in his big one, and her face reminded him so strongly of his dead brother, that he was not satisfied with so cold a welcome, and with a sudden softening of the keen eyes he took her up in his arms, whispering, with a rough cheek against her smooth one,

"God bless you, child! forgive me if I forgot you for a minute, and be sure that not one of your kinsfolk is happier to see you here than Uncle Jem."

That made it all right; and when he set her down, Rose's face was so bright it was evident that some spell had been used to banish the feeling of neglect that had kept her moping behind the curtain so long.

That everyone sat round and heard all about the voyage home how the Captain had set his heart on getting there in time to keep Christmas; how everything had conspired to thwart his plan; and how, at the very last minute, he had managed to do it, and had sent a telegram to Archie, bidding him keep the secret, and be ready for his father at any moment, for the ship got into another port, and he might be late.

Then Archie told how that telegram had burnt in his pocket all dinner-time; how he had to take Phebe into his confidence, and how clever she was to keep the Captain back till the speech was over and he could come in with effect.

The elders would have sat and talked all the evening, but the young folks were bent on having their usual Christmas frolic; so, after an hour of pleasant chat, they began to get restless, and having consulted together in dumb show, they devised a way to very effectually break up the family council.

Steve vanished, and, sooner than the boys imagined Dandy could get himself up, the skirl of the bag-pipe was heard in the hall, and the bonny piper came to lead Clan Campbell to the revel.

"Draw it mild, Stevie, my man; ye play unco weel, but ye mak a most infernal din," cried Uncle Jem, with his hands over his ears, for this accomplishment was new to him, and "took him all aback," as he expressed it.

So Steve droned out a Highland reel as softly as he could, and the boys danced it to a circle of admiring relations. Captain Jem was a true sailor, however, and could not stand idle while anything lively was going on; so, when the piper's breath gave out, he cut a splendid pigeon-wing into the middle of the hall, saying, "Who can dance a Fore and After?" and, waiting for no reply, began to whistle the air so invitingly that Mrs Jessie "set" to him laughing like a girl; Rose and Charlie took their places behind, and away went the four with a spirit and skill that inspired all the rest to "cut in" as fast as they could.

That was a grand beginning, and they had many another dance before anyone would own they were tired. Even Fun See distinguished himself with Aunt Plenty, whom he greatly admired as the stoutest lady in the company; plumpness being considered a beauty in his country. The merry old soul professed herself immensely flattered by his admiration, and the boys declared she "set her cap at him," else he would never have dared to catch her under the mistletoe, and, rising on the tips of his own toes, gallantly salute her fat cheek.

How they all laughed at her astonishment, and how Fun's little black eyes twinkled over this exploit! Charlie put him up to it, and Charlie was so bent on catching Rose, that he laid all sorts of pitfalls for her, and bribed the other lads to help him. But Rose was wide-awake, and escaped all his snares, professing great contempt for such foolish customs. Poor Phebe did not fare so well, and Archie was the only one who took a base advantage of her as she stood innocently offering tea to Aunt Myra, whom she happened to meet just under the fatal bough. If his father's arrival had not rather upset him, I doubt if the dignified Chief would have done it, for he apologized at once in the handsomest manner, and caught the tray that nearly dropped from Phebe's hands.

Jamie boldly invited all the ladies to come and salute him; and as for Uncle Jem, he behaved as if the entire room was a grove of mistletoe. Uncle Alec slyly laid a bit of it on Aunt Peace's cap, and then softly kissed her; which little joke seemed to please her very much, for she liked to have part in all the home pastimes, and Alec was her favourite nephew.

Charlie alone failed to catch his shy bird, and the oftener she escaped the more determined he was to ensnare her. When every other wile had been tried in vain, he got Archie to propose a game with forfeits.

"I understand that dodge," thought Rose, and was on her guard so carefully that not one among the pile soon collected belonged to her.

"Now let us redeem them and play something else," said Will, quite unconscious of the deeply-laid plots all about him.

"One more round and then we will," answered the Prince, who had now baited his trap anew.

Just as the question came to Rose, Jamie's voice was heard in the hall, crying distressfully, "Oh, come quick, quick!" Rose started up, missed the question, and was greeted with a general cry of "Forfeit! forfeit!" in which the little traitor came to join.

"Now I've got her," thought the young rascal, exulting in his fun-loving soul.

"Now I'm lost," thought Rose, as she gave up her pin-cushion with a sternly defiant look that would have daunted anyone but the reckless Prince. In fact, it made even him think twice, and resolve to "let Rose off easy," she had been so clever.

"Here's a very pretty pawn, and what shall be done to redeem it?" asked Steve, holding the pin-cushion over Charlie's head, for he had insisted on being judge, and kept that for the last.

"Fine or superfine?"

"Super."

"Hum, well, she shall take old Mac under the mistletoe, and kiss him prettily. Won't he be mad, though?" and this bad boy chuckled over the discomfort he had caused two harmless beings.

There was an impressive pause among the young folks in their corner, for they all knew that Mac would "be mad," since he hated nonsense of this sort, and had gone to talk with the elders when the game began. At this moment he was standing before the fire, listening to a discussion between his uncles and his father, looking as wise as a young owl, and blissfully unconscious of the plots against him.

Charlie expected that Rose would say, "I won't!" therefore he was rather astonished, not to say gratified, when, after a look at the victim, she laughed suddenly, and, going up to the group of gentlemen, drew her uncle Mac under the mistletoe and surprised him with a hearty kiss.

"Thank you, my dear," said the innocent gentleman, looking much pleased at the unexpected honour.

"Oh, come; that's not fair," began Charlie. But Rose cut him short by saying, as she made him a fine courtesy,

"You said 'Old Mac,' and though it was very disrespectful, I did it. That was your last chance, sir, and you've lost it."

He certainly had, for, as he spoke, Rose pulled down the mistletoe and threw it into the fire, while the boys jeered at the crestfallen Prince, and exalted quick-witted Rose to the skies.

"What's the joke?" asked young Mac, waked out of a brown study by the laughter, in which the elders joined.

But there was a regular shout when, the matter having been explained to him, Mac took a meditative stare at Rose through his goggles, and said in a philosophical tone, "Well, I don't think I should have minded much if she had done it."

That tickled the lads immensely, and nothing but the appearance of a slight refection would have induced them to stop chaffing the poor Worm, who could not see anything funny in the beautiful resignation he had shown on this trying occasion.

Soon after this, the discovery of Jamie curled up in the sofa corner, as sound asleep as a dormouse, suggested the propriety of going home, and a general move was made.

They were all standing about the hall lingering over the good-nights, when the sound of a voice softly singing "Sweet Home," made them pause and listen. It was Phebe, poor little Phebe, who never had a home, never knew the love of father or mother, brother or sister; who stood all alone in the wide world, yet was not sad nor afraid, but took her bits of happiness gratefully, and sung over her work without a thought of discontent.

I fancy the happy family standing there together remembered this and felt the beauty of it, for when the solitary voice came to the burden of its song, other voices took it up and finished it so sweetly, that the old house seemed to echo the word "Home" in the ears of both the orphan girls, who had just spent their first Christmas under its hospitable roof.

Chapter 21—A Scare
"Brother Alec, you surely don't mean to allow that child to go out such a bitter cold day as this," said Mrs. Myra, looking into the study, where the Doctor sat reading his paper, one February morning.

"Why not? If a delicate invalid like yourself can bear it, surely my hearty girl can, especially as she is dressed for cold weather," answered Dr. Alec with provoking confidence.

"But you have no idea how sharp the wind is. I am chilled to the very marrow of my bones," answered Aunt Myra, chafing the end of her purple nose with her sombre glove.

"I don't doubt it, ma'am, if you will wear crape and silk instead of fur and flannel. Rosy goes out in all weathers, and will be none the worse for an hour's brisk skating."

"Well, I warn you that you are trifling with the child's health, and depending too much on the seeming improvement she has made this year. She is a delicate creature for all that, and will drop away suddenly at the first serious attack, as her poor mother did," croaked Aunt Myra, with a despondent wag of the big bonnet.

"I'll risk it," answered Dr. Alec, knitting his brows, as he always did when any allusion was made to that other Rose.

"Mark my words, you will repent it," and with that awful prophecy, Aunt Myra departed like a black shadow.

Now it must be confessed that among the Doctor's failings and he had his share was a very masculine dislike of advice which was thrust upon him unasked. He always listened with respect to the great-aunts, and often consulted Mrs. Jessie; but the other three ladies tried his patience sorely, by constant warnings, complaints and counsels. Aunt Myra was an especial trial, and he always turned contrary the moment she began to talk. He could not help it, and often laughed about it with comic frankness. Here now was a sample of it, for he had just been thinking that Rose had better defer her run till the wind went down and the sun was warmer. But Aunt Myra spoke, and he could not resist the temptation to make light of her advice, and let Rose brave the cold. He had no fear of its harming her, for she went out every day, and it was a great satisfaction to him to see her run down the avenue a minute afterward, with her skates on her arm, looking like a rosy-faced Esquimaux in her seal-skin suit, as she smiled at Aunt Myra stalking along as solemnly as a crow.

"I hope the child won't stay out long, for this wind is enough to chill the marrow in younger bones than Myra's," thought Dr. Alec, half an hour later, as he drove toward the city to see the few patients he had consented to take for old acquaintance' sake.

The thought returned several times that morning, for it was truly a bitter day, and, in spite of his bear-skin coat, the Doctor shivered. But he had great faith in Rose's good sense, and it never occurred to him that she was making a little Casabianca of herself, with the difference of freezing instead of burning at her post.

You see, Mac had made an appointment to meet her at a certain spot, and have a grand skating bout as soon as the few lessons he was allowed were over. She had promised to wait for him, and did so with a faithfulness that cost her dear, because Mac forgot his appointment when the lessons were done, and became absorbed in a chemical experiment, till a general combustion of gases drove him out of his laboratory. Then he suddenly remembered Rose, and would gladly have hurried away to her, but his mother forbade his going out, for the sharp wind would hurt his eyes.

"She will wait and wait, mother, for she always keeps her word, and I told her to hold on till I came," explained Mac, with visions of a shivering little figure watching on the windy hill-top.

"Of course, your uncle won't let her go out such a day as this. If he does, she will have the sense to come here for you, or to go home again when you don't appear," said Aunt Jane, returning to her "Watts on the Mind."

"I wish Steve would just cut up and see if she's there, since I can't go," began Mac, anxiously.

"Steve won't stir a peg, thank you. He's got his own toes to thaw out, and wants his dinner," answered Dandy, just in from school, and wrestling impatiently with his boots.

So Mac resigned himself, and Rose waited dutifully till dinner-time assured her that her waiting was in vain. She had done her best to keep warm, had skated till she was tired and hot, then stood watching others till she was chilled; tried to get up a glow again by trotting up and down the road, but failed to do so, and finally cuddled disconsolately under a pine-tree to wait and watch. When she at length started for home, she was benumbed with cold, and could hardly make her way against the wind that buffeted the frost-bitten rose most unmercifully.

Dr. Alec was basking in the warmth of the study fire, after his drive, when the sound of a stifled sob made him hurry to the door and look anxiously into the hall. Rose lay in a shivering bunch near the register, with her things half off, wringing her hands, and trying not to cry with the pain returning warmth brought to her half-frozen fingers.

"My darling, what is it?" and Uncle Alec had her in his arms in a minute.

"Mac didn't come I can't get warm the fire makes me ache!" and with a long shiver Rose burst out crying, while her teeth chattered, and her poor little nose was so blue, it made one's heart ache to see it.

In less time than it takes to tell it, Dr. Alec had her on the sofa rolled up in the bear-skin coat, with Phebe rubbing her cold feet while he rubbed the aching hands, and Aunt Plenty made a comfortable hot drink, and Aunt Peace sent down her own foot-warmer and embroidered blanket "for the dear."

Full of remorseful tenderness, Uncle Alec worked over his new patient till she declared she was all right again. He would not let her get up to dinner, but fed her himself, and then forgot his own while he sat watching her fall into a drowse, for Aunt Plenty's cordial made her sleepy.

She lay so several hours for the drowse deepened into a heavy sleep, and Uncle Alec, still at his post, saw with growing anxiety that a feverish colour began to burn in her cheeks, that her breathing was quick and uneven, and now and then she gave a little moan, as if in pain. Suddenly she woke up with a start, and seeing Aunt Plenty bending over her, put out her arms like a sick child, saying wearily,

"Please, could I go to bed?"

"The best place for you, deary. Take her right up, Alec; I've got the hot water ready, and after a nice bath, she shall have a cup of my sage tea, and be rolled up in blankets to sleep off her cold," answered the old lady, cheerily, as she bustled away to give orders.

"Are you in pain, darling?" asked Uncle Alec, as he carried her up.

"My side aches when I breathe, and I feel stiff and queer; but it isn't bad, so don't be troubled, uncle," whispered Rose, with a little hot hand against his cheek.

But the poor doctor did look troubled, and had cause to do so, for just then Rose tried to laugh at Dolly charging into the room with a warming-pan, but could not, for the sharp pain took her breath away and made her cry out.

"Pleurisy," sighed Aunt Plenty, from the depths of the bath-tub.

"Pewmonia!" groaned Dolly, burrowing among the bedclothes with the long-handled pan, as if bent on fishing up that treacherous disease.

"Oh, is it bad?" asked Phebe, nearly dropping a pail of hot water in her dismay, for she knew nothing of sickness, and Dolly's suggestion had a peculiarly dreadful sound to her.

"Hush!" ordered the Doctor, in a tone that silenced all further predictions, and made everyone work with a will.

"Make her as comfortable as you can, and when she is in her little bed I'll come and say good-night," he added, when the bath was ready and the blankets browning nicely before the fire.

Then he went away to talk quite cheerfully to Aunt Peace about its being "only a chill"; after which he tramped up and down the hall, pulling his beard and knitting his brows, sure signs of great inward perturbation.

"I thought it would be too good luck to get through the year without a downfall. Confound my perversity! Why couldn't I take Myra's advice and keep Rose at home. It's not fair that the poor child should suffer for my sinful over-confidence. She shall not suffer for it! Pneumonia, indeed! I defy it," and he shook his fist in the ugly face of an Indian idol that happened to be before him, as if that particularly hideous god had some spite against his own little goddess.

In spite of his defiance his heart sunk when he saw Rose again, for the pain was worse, and the bath and blankets, the warming-pan and piping-hot sage tea, were all in vain. For several hours there was no rest for the poor child, and all manner of gloomy forebodings haunted the minds of those who hovered about her with faces full of the tenderest anxiety.

In the midst of the worst paroxysm Charlie came to leave a message from his mother, and was met by Phebe coming despondently downstairs with a mustard plaster that had brought no relief.

"What the dickens is the matter? You look as dismal as a tombstone," he said, as she held up her hand to stop his lively whistling.

"Miss Rose is dreadful sick."

"The deuce she is!"

"Don't swear, Mr. Charlie; she really is, and it's Mr. Mac's fault," and Phebe told the sad tale in a few sharp words, for she felt at war with the entire race of boys at that moment.

"I'll give it to him, make your mind easy about that," said Charlie, with an ominous doubling up of his fist. "But Rose isn't dangerously ill, is she?" he added anxiously, as Aunt Plenty was seen to trot across the upper hall, shaking a bottle violently as she went.

"Oh, but she is though. The Doctor don't say much, but he don't call it a 'chill' any more. It's 'pleurisy' now, and I'm so afraid it will be pewmonia to-morrow," answered Phebe, with a despairing glance at the plaster.

Charlie exploded into a stifled laugh at the new pronunciation of pneumonia, to Phebe's great indignation.

"How can you have the heart to do it, and she in such horrid pain? Hark to that, and then laugh if you darst," she said with a tragic gesture, and her black eyes full of fire.

Charlie listened and heard little moans that went to his heart and made his face as sober as Phebe's. "O uncle, please stop the pain, and let me rest a minute! Don't tell the boys I wasn't brave. I try to bear it, but it's so sharp I can't help crying."

Neither could Charlie, when he heard the broken voice say that; but, boy-like, he wouldn't own it, and said pettishly, as he rubbed his sleeve across his eyes,

"Don't hold that confounded thing right under my nose; the mustard makes my eyes smart."

"Don't see how it can, when it hasn't any more strength in it than meal. The Doctor said so, and I'm going to get some better," began Phebe, not a bit ashamed of the great tears that were bedewing the condemned plaster.

"I'll go!" and Charlie was off like a shot, glad of an excuse to get out of sight for a few minutes.

When he came back all inconvenient emotion had been disposed of, and, having delivered a box of the hottest mustard procurable for money, he departed to "blow up" Mac, that being his next duty in his opinion. He did it so energetically and thoroughly that the poor Worm was cast into the depths of remorseful despair, and went to bed that evening feeling that he was an outcast from among men, and bore the mark of Cain upon his brow.

Thanks to the skill of the Doctor, and the devotion of his helpers, Rose grew easier about midnight, and all hoped that the worst was over. Phebe was making tea by the study fire, for the Doctor had forgotten to eat and drink since Rose was ill, and Aunt Plenty insisted on his having a "good cordial dish of tea" after his exertions. A tap on the window startled Phebe, and, looking up, she saw a face peering in. She was not afraid, for a second look showed her that it was neither ghost nor burglar, but Mac, looking pale and wild in the wintry moonlight.

"Come and let a fellow in," he said in a low tone, and when he stood in the hall he clutched Phebe's arm, whispering gruffly, "How is Rose?"

"Thanks be to goodness, she's better," answered Phebe, with a smile that was like broad sunshine to the poor lad's anxious heart.

"And she will be all right again to-morrow?"

"Oh, dear no! Dolly says she's sure to have rheumatic fever, if she don't have noo-monia!" answered Phebe, careful to pronounce the word rightly this time.

Down went Mac's face, and remorse began to gnaw at him again as he gave a great sigh and said doubtfully,

"I suppose I couldn't see her?"

"Of course not at this time of night, when we want her to go to sleep!"

Mac opened his mouth to say something more, when a sneeze came upon him unawares, and a loud "Ah rash hoo!" awoke the echoes of the quiet house.

"Why didn't you stop it?" said Phebe reproachfully. "I dare say you've waked her up."

"Didn't know it was coming. Just my luck!" groaned Mac, turning to go before his unfortunate presence did more harm.

But a voice from the stair-head called softly, "Mac, come up; Rose wants to see you."

Up he went, and found his uncle waiting for him.

"What brings you here at this hour, my boy?" asked the Doctor in a whisper.

"Charlie said it was all my fault, and if she died I'd killed her. I couldn't sleep, so I came to see how she was, and no one knows it but Steve," he said with such a troubled face and voice that the Doctor had not the heart to blame him.

Before he could say anything more a feeble voice called "Mac!" and with a hasty "Stay a minute just to please her, and then slip away, for I want her to sleep," the Doctor led him into the room.

The face on the pillow looked very pale and childish, and the smile that welcomed Mac was very faint, for Rose was spent with pain, yet could not rest till she had said a word of comfort to her cousin.

"I knew your funny sneeze, and I guessed that you came to see how I did, though it is very late. Don't be worried, I'm better now, and it is my fault I was ill, not yours; for I needn't have been so silly as to wait in the cold just because I said I would."

Mac hastened to explain, to load himself with reproaches, and to beg her not to die on any account, for Charlie's lecture had made a deep impression on the poor boy's mind.

"I didn't know there was any danger of my dying," and Rose looked up at him with a solemn expression in her great eyes.

"Oh, I hope not; but people do sometimes go suddenly, you know, and I couldn't rest till I'd asked you to forgive me," faltered Mac, thinking that Rose looked very like an angel already, with the golden hair loose on the pillow, and the meekness of suffering on her little white face.

"I don't think I shall die; uncle won't let me; but if I do, remember I forgave you."

She looked at him with a tender light in her eyes, and, seeing how pathetic his dumb grief was, she added softly, drawing his head down, "I wouldn't kiss you under the mistletoe, but I will now, for I want you to be sure I do forgive and love you just the same."

That quite upset poor Mac; he could only murmur his thanks and get out of the room as fast as possible, to grope his way to the couch at the far end of the hall, and lie there till he fell asleep, worn out with trying not to "make a baby" of himself.

Chapter 22—Something to do

Whatever danger there might have been from the effects of that sudden chill, it was soon over, though, of course, Aunt Myra refused to believe it, and Dr. Alec cherished his girl with redoubled vigilance and tenderness for months afterward. Rose quite enjoyed being sick, because as soon as the pain ended the fun began, and for a week or two she led the life of a little princess secluded in the Bower, while every one served, amused, and watched over her in the most delightful manner. But the doctor was called away to see an old friend, who was dangerously ill, and then Rose felt like a young bird deprived of its mother's sheltering wing; especially on one afternoon when the aunts were taking their naps, and the house was very still within while snow fell softly without.

"I'll go and hunt up Phebe, she is always nice and busy, and likes to have me help her. If Dolly is out of the way we can make caramels and surprise the boys when they come," Rose said to herself, as she threw down her book and felt ready for society of some sort.

She took the precaution to peep through the slide before she entered the kitchen, for Dolly allowed no messing when she was round. But the coast was clear, and no one but Phebe appeared, sitting at the table with her head on her arms apparently asleep. Rose was just about to wake her with a "Boo!" when she lifted her head, dried her wet eyes with her blue apron, and fell to work with a resolute face on something she was evidently much interested in. Rose could not make out what it was, and her curiosity was greatly excited, for Phebe was writing with a sputtering pen on some bits of brown paper, apparently copying something from a little book.

"I must know what the dear thing is about, and why she cried, and then set her lips tight and went to work with all her might," thought Rose, forgetting all about the caramels, and, going round to the door, she entered the kitchen, saying pleasantly,

"Phebe, I want something to do. Can't you let me help you about anything, or shall I be in the way?"

"Oh, dear no, miss; I always love to have you round when things are tidy. What would you like to do?" answered Phebe, opening a drawer as if about to sweep her own affairs out of sight; but Rose stopped her, exclaiming, like a curious child,

"Let me see! What is it? I won't tell if you'd rather not have Dolly know."

"I'm only trying to study a bit; but I'm so stupid I don't get on much," answered the girl reluctantly, permitting her little mistress to examine the poor contrivances she was trying to work with.

A broken slate that had blown off the roof, an inch or two of pencil, an old almanac for a reader, several bits of brown or yellow paper ironed smoothly and sewn together for a copy-book, and the copies sundry receipts written in Aunt Plenty's neat hand. These, with a small bottle of ink and a rusty pen, made up Phebe's outfit, and it was little wonder that she did not "get on" in spite of the patient persistence that dried the desponding tears and drove along the sputtering pen with a will.

"You may laugh if you want to, Miss Rose, I know my things are queer, and that's why I hide 'em; but I don't mind since you've found me out, and I ain't a bit ashamed except of being so backward at my age," said Phebe humbly, though her cheeks grew redder as she washed out some crooked capitals with a tear or two not yet dried upon the slate.

"Laugh at you! I feel more like crying to think what a selfish girl I am, to have loads of books and things and never remember to give you some. Why didn't you come and ask me, and not go struggling along alone in this way? It was very wrong of you, Phebe, and I'll never forgive you if you do so again," answered Rose, with one hand on Phebe's shoulder, while the other gently turned the leaves of the poor little copy-book.

"I didn't like to ask for anything more when you are so good to me all the time, miss, dear," began Phebe, looking up with grateful eyes.

"O you proud thing! just as if it wasn't fun to give away, and I had the best of it. Now, see here, I've got a plan and you mustn't say no, or I shall scold. I want something to do, and I'm going to teach you all I know; it won't take long," and Rose laughed as she put her arm around Phebe's neck, and patted the smooth dark head with the kind little hand that so loved to give.

"It would be just heavenly!" and Phebe's face shone at the mere idea; but fell again as she added wistfully, "Only I'm afraid I ought not to let you do it, Miss Rose. It will take time, and maybe the Doctor wouldn't like it."

"He didn't want me to study much, but he never said a word about teaching, and I don't believe he will mind a bit. Anyway, we can try it till he comes, so pack up your things and go right to my room and we'll begin this very day; I'd truly like to do it, and we'll have nice times, see if we don't!" cried Rose eagerly.

It was a pretty sight to see Phebe bundle her humble outfit into her apron, and spring up as if the desire of her heart had suddenly been made a happy fact to her; it was a still prettier sight to see Rose run gaily on before, smiling like a good fairy as she beckoned to the other, singing as she went,

> "The way into my parlour is up a winding stair,
> And many are the curious things I'll show you when you're there.
> Will you, will you walk in, Phebe dear?"

"Oh, won't I!" answered Phebe fervently, adding, as they entered the Bower, "You are the dearest spider that ever was, and I'm the happiest fly."

"I'm going to be very strict, so sit down in that chair and don't say a word till school is ready to open," ordered Rose, delighted with the prospect of such a useful and pleasant "something to do."

So Phebe sat demurely in her place while her new teacher laid forth books and slates, a pretty inkstand and a little globe; hastily tore a bit off her big sponge, sharpened pencils with more energy than skill, and when all was ready gave a prance of satisfaction that set the pupil laughing.

"Now the school is open, and I shall hear you read, so that I may know in which class to put you, Miss Moore," began Rose with great dignity, as she laid a book before her scholar, and sat down in the easy chair with a long rule in her hand.

Phebe did pretty well, only tripping now and then over a hard word, and pronouncing identical "identickle," in a sober way that tickled Rose, though never a smile betrayed her. The spelling lesson which followed was rather discouraging; Phebe's ideas of geography were very vague, and grammar was nowhere, though the pupil protested that she tried so hard to "talk nice like educated folks" that Dolly called her "a stuck-up piece who didn't know her place."

"Dolly's an old goose, so don't you mind her, for she will say 'nater,' 'vittles,' and 'doos' as long as she lives, and insist that they are right. You do talk very nicely, Phebe, I've observed it, and grammar will help you, and show you some things are right and others ain't are not, I mean," added Rose, correcting herself, and feeling that she must mind her own parts of speech if she was to serve as an example for Phebe.

112

When the arithmetic came, the little teacher was surprised to find her scholar quicker in some things than herself, for Phebe had worked away at the columns in the butcher's and baker's books till she could add so quickly and correctly that Rose was amazed, and felt that in this branch the pupil would soon excel the teacher if she kept on at the same pace. Her praise cheered Phebe immensely, and they went bravely on, both getting so interested that time flew unheeded till Aunt Plenty appeared, exclaiming, as she stared at the two heads bent over one slate,

"Bless my heart, what is going on now?"

"School, aunty. I'm teaching Phebe, and it's great fun!" cried Rose, looking up with a bright face.

But Phebe's was brighter, though she added with a wistful look,

"Maybe I ought to have asked leave first; only when Miss Rose proposed this, I was so happy I forgot to. Shall I stop, ma'am?"

"Of course not, child; I'm glad to see you fond of your book, and to find Rose helping you along. My blessed mother used to sit at work with her maids about her, teaching them many a useful thing in the good old fashion that's gone by now. Only don't neglect your work, dear, or let the books interfere with the duties."

As Aunt Plenty spoke, with her kind old face beaming approvingly upon the girls, Phebe glanced at the clock, saw that it pointed to five, knew that Dolly would soon be down, expecting to find preparations for supper under way, and, hastily dropping her pencil, she jumped up, saying,

"Please, can I go? I'll clear up after I've done my chores."

"School is dismissed," answered Rose, and with a grateful "Thank you, heaps and heaps!" Phebe ran away singing the multiplication table as she set the tea ditto.

That was the way it began, and for a week the class of one went on with great pleasure and profit to all concerned; for the pupil proved a bright one, and came to her lessons as to a feast, while the young teacher did her best to be worthy the high opinion held of her, for Phebe firmly believed that Miss Rose knew everything in the way of learning.

Of course the lads found out what was going on, and chaffed the girls about the "Seminary," as they called the new enterprise; but they thought it a good thing on the whole, kindly offered to give lessons in Greek and Latin gratis, and decided among themselves that "Rose was a little trump to give the Phebe-bird such a capital boost."

Rose herself had some doubts as to how it would strike her uncle, and concocted a wheedlesome speech which should at once convince him that it was the most useful, wholesome, and delightful plan ever devised. But she got no chance to deliver her address, for Dr. Alec came upon her so unexpectedly that it went out of her head entirely. She was sitting on the floor in the library, poring over a big book laid open in her lap, and knew nothing of the long-desired arrival till two large, warm hands met under her chin and gently turned her head back, so that someone could kiss her heartily on either cheek, while a fatherly voice said, half reproachfully, "Why is my girl brooding over a dusty Encyclopedia when she ought to be running to meet the old gentleman who couldn't get on another minute without her?"

"O uncle! I'm so glad! and so sorry! Why didn't you let us know what time you'd be here, or call out the minute you came? Haven't I been home-sick for you? and now I'm so happy to have you back I could hug your dear old curly head off," cried Rose, as the Encyclopedia went down with a bang, and she up with a spring that carried her into Dr. Alec's arms, to be kept there in the sort of embrace a man gives to the dearest creature the world holds for him.

Presently he was in his easy chair with Rose upon his knee smiling up in his face and talking as fast as her tongue could go, while he watched her with an expression of supreme content, as he stroked the smooth round cheek, or held the little hand in his, rejoicing to see how rosy was the one, how plump and strong the other.

"Have you had a good time? Did you save the poor lady? Aren't you glad to be home again with your girl to torment you?"

"Yes, to all those questions. Now tell me what you've been at, little sinner? Aunty Plen says you want to consult me about some new and remarkable project which you have dared to start in my absence."

"She didn't tell you, I hope?"

"Not a word more expect that you were rather doubtful how I'd take it, and so wanted to 'fess' yourself and get round me as you always try to do, though you don't often succeed. Now, then, own up and take the consequences."

So Rose told about her school in her pretty, earnest way, dwelling on Phebe's hunger for knowledge, and the delight it was to help her, adding, with a wise nod,

"And it helps me too, uncle, for she is so quick and eager I have to do my best or she will get ahead of me in some things. To-day, now, she had the word 'cotton' in a lesson and asked all about it, and I was ashamed to find I really knew so little that I could only say that it was a plant that grew down South in a kind of a pod, and was made into cloth. That's what I was reading up when you came, and to-morrow I shall tell her all about it, and indigo too. So you see it teaches me also, and is as good as a general review of what I've learned, in a pleasanter way than going over it alone."

"You artful little baggage! that's the way you expect to get round me, is it? That's not studying, I suppose?"

"No, sir, it's teaching; and please, I like it much better than having a good time by myself. Besides, you know, I adopted Phebe and promised to be a sister to her, so I am bound to keep my word, am I not?" answered Rose, looking both anxious and resolute as she waited for her sentence.

Dr. Alec was evidently already won, for Rose had described the old slate and brown paper copy-book with pathetic effect, and the excellent man had not only decided to send Phebe to school long before the story was done, but reproached himself for forgetting his duty to one little girl in his love for another. So when Rose tried to look meek and failed utterly, he laughed and pinched her cheek, and answered in that genial way which adds such warmth and grace to any favour,

"I haven't the slightest objection in the world. In fact, I was beginning to think I might let you go at your books again, moderately, since you are so well; and this is an excellent way to try your powers. Phebe is a brave, bright lass, and shall have a fair chance in the world, if we can give it to her, so that if she ever finds her friends they need not be ashamed of her."

"I think she has found some already," began Rose eagerly.

"Hey? what? has anyone turned up since I've been gone?" asked Dr. Alec quickly, for it was a firm belief in the family that Phebe would prove to be "somebody" sooner or later.

114

"No, her best friend turned up when you came home, uncle," answered Rose with an approving pat, adding gratefully, "I can't half thank you for being so good to my girl, but she will, because I know she is going to make a woman to be proud of, she's so strong and true, and loving."

"Bless your dear heart, I haven't begun to do anything yet, more shame to me! But I'm going at it now, and as soon as she gets on a bit, she shall go to school as long as she likes. How will that do for a beginning?"

"It will be 'just heavenly,' as Phebe says, for it is the wish of her life to 'get lots of schooling,' and she will be too happy when I tell her. May I, please? it will be so lovely to see the dear thing open her big eyes and clap her hands at the splendid news."

"No one shall have a finger in this nice little pie; you shall do it all yourself, only don't go too fast, or make too many castles in the air, my dear; for time and patience must go into this pie of ours if it is to turn out well."

"Yes, uncle, only when it is opened won't 'the birds begin to sing?'" laughed Rose, taking a turn about the room as a vent for the joyful emotions that made her eyes shine. All of a sudden she stopped and asked soberly,

"If Phebe goes to school who will do her work? I'm willing, if I can."

"Come here and I'll tell you a secret. Dolly's 'bones' are getting so troublesome, and her dear old temper so bad, that the aunts have decided to pension her off and let her go and live with her daughter, who has married very well. I saw her this week, and she'd like to have her mother come, so in the spring we shall have a grand change, and get a new cook and chamber-girl if any can be found to suit our honoured relatives."

"Oh, me! how can I ever get on without Phebe? Couldn't she stay, just so I could see her? I'd pay her board rather than have her go, I'm so fond of her."

How Dr. Alec laughed at that proposal, and how satisfied Rose was when he explained that Phebe was still to be her maid, with no duties except such as she could easily perform between school-hours.

"She is a proud creature, for all her humble ways, and even from us would not take a favour if she did not earn it somewhere. So this arrangement makes it all square and comfortable, you see, and she will pay for the schooling by curling these goldilocks a dozen times a day if you let her."

"Your plans are always so wise and kind! That's why they work so well, I suppose, and why people let you do what you like with them. I really don't see how other girls get along without an Uncle Alec!" answered Rose, with a sigh of pity for those who had missed so great a blessing.

When Phebe was told the splendid news, she did not "stand on her head with rapture," as Charlie prophesied she would, but took it quietly, because it was such a happy thing she had no words "big and beautiful enough to thank them in," she said; but every hour of her day was brightened by this granted wish, and dedicated to the service of those who gave it.

Her heart was so full of content that if overflowed in music, and the sweet voice singing all about the house gave thanks so blithely that no other words were needed. Her willing feet were never tired of taking steps for those who had smoothed her way; her skilful hands were always busy in some labour of love for them, and on the face fast growing in comeliness there was an almost womanly expression of devotion, which proved how well Phebe had already learned one of life's great lessons gratitude.

Chapter 23—Peace-Making

"Steve, I want you to tell me something," said Rose to Dandy, who was making faces at himself in the glass, while he waited for an answer to the note he brought from his mother to Aunt Plenty.

"P'raps I will, and p'raps I won't. What is it?"

"Haven't Arch and Charlie quarrelled?"

"Dare say; we fellows are always having little rows, you know. I do believe a sty is coming on my star-board eye," and Steve affected to be absorbed in a survey of his yellow lashes.

"No, that won't do; I want to know all about it; for I'm sure something more serious than a 'little row' is the matter. Come, please tell me, Stenie, there's a dear."

"Botheration! you don't want me to turn telltale, do you?" growled Steve, pulling his top-knot, as he always did when perplexed.

"Yes, I do," was Rose's decided answer for she saw from his manner that she was right, and determined to have the secret out of him if coaxing would do it. "I don't wish you to tell things to everyone, of course, but to me you may, and you must, because I have a right to know. You boys need somebody to look after you, and I'm going to do it, for girls are nice peacemakers, and know how to manage people. Uncle said so, and he is never wrong."

Steve was about to indulge in a derisive hoot at the idea of her looking after them, but a sudden thought restrained him, and suggested a way in which he could satisfy Rose, and better himself at the same time.

"What will you give me if I'll tell you every bit about it?" he asked, with a sudden red in his cheeks and an uneasy look in his eyes, for he was half ashamed of the proposition.

"What do you want?" and Rose looked up rather surprised at his question.

"I'd like to borrow some money. I shouldn't think of asking you, only Mac never has a cent. since he's set up his old chemical shop, where he'll blow himself to bits some day, and you and uncle will have the fun of putting him together again," and Steve tried to look as if the idea amused him.

"I'll lend it to you with pleasure, so tell away," said Rose, bound to get at the secret.

Evidently much relieved by the promise, Steve set his top-knot cheerfully erect again, and briefly stated the case.

"As you say, it's all right to tell you, but don't let the boys know I blabbed, or Prince will take my head off. You see, Archie don't like some of the fellows Charlie goes with, and cuts 'em. That makes Prince mad, and he holds on just to plague Arch, so they don't speak to one another, if they can help it, and that's the row."

116

"Are those boys bad?" asked Rose, anxiously.

"Guess not, only rather wild. They are older than our fellows, but they like Prince, he's such a jolly boy; sings so well, dances jigs and breakdowns, you know, and plays any game that's going. He beat Morse at billiards, and that's something to brag of, for Morse thinks he knows everything. I saw the match, and it was great fun!"

Steve got quite excited over the prowess of Charlie, whom he admired immensely, and tried to imitate. Rose did not know half the danger of such gifts and tastes as Charlie's, but felt instinctively that something must be wrong if Archie disapproved.

"If Prince likes any billiard-playing boy better than Archie, I don't think much of his sense," she said severely.

"Of course he doesn't; but, you see, Charlie and Arch are both as proud as they can be, and won't give in. I suppose Arch is right, but I don't blame Charlie a bit for liking to be with the others sometimes, they are such a jolly set," and Steve shook his head morally, even while his eye twinkled over the memory of some of the exploits of the "jolly set."

"Oh, dear me!" sighed Rose, "I don't see what I can do about it, but I wish the boys would make up, for Prince can't come to any harm with Archie, he's so good and sensible."

"That's the trouble; Arch preaches, and Prince won't stand it. He told Arch he was a prig and a parson, and Arch told him he wasn't a gentleman. My boots! weren't they both mad, though! I thought for a minute they'd pitch into one another and have it out. Wish they had, and not gone stalking round stiff and glum ever since. Mac and I settle our rows with a bat or so over the head, and then we are all right."

Rose couldn't help laughing as Steve sparred away at a fat sofa-pillow, to illustrate his meaning; and, having given it several scientific whacks, he pulled down his cuffs and smiled upon her with benign pity for her feminine ignorance of this summary way of settling a quarrel.

"What droll things boys are!" she said, with a mixture of admiration and perplexity in her face, which Steve accepted as a compliment to his sex.

"We're a pretty clever invention, miss, and you can't get on without us," he answered, with his nose in the air. Then, taking a sudden plunge into business, he added, "How about that bit of money you were going to lend me? I've told, now you pay up."

"Of course I will! How much do you want?" and Rose pulled out her purse.

"Could you spare five dollars? I want to pay a little debt of honour that is rather pressing," and Steve put on a mannish air that was comical to see.

"Aren't all debts honourable?" asked innocent Rose.

"Yes, of course; but this is a bet I made, and it ought to be settled up at once," began Steve, finding it awkward to explain.

"Oh, don't bet, it's not right, and I know your father wouldn't like it. Promise you won't do so again; please promise!" and Rose held fast the hand into which she had just put the money.

"Well, I won't. It's worried me a good deal, but I was joked into it. Much obliged, cousin, I'm all right now," and Steve departed hastily.

117

Having decided to be a peace-maker, Rose waited for an opportunity, and very soon it came.

She was spending the day with Aunt Clara, who had been entertaining some young guests, and invited Rose to meet them, for she thought it high time her niece conquered her bashfulness and saw a little of society. Dinner was over, and everyone had gone. Aunt Clara was resting before going out to an evening party, and Rose was waiting for Charlie to come and take her home.

She sat alone in the elegant drawing-room, feeling particularly nice and pretty, for she had her best frock on, a pair of gold bands her aunt had just given her, and a tea-rose bud in her sash, like the beautiful Miss Van Tassel, whom everyone admired. She had spread out her little skirts to the best advantage, and, leaning back in a luxurious chair, sat admiring her own feet in new slippers with rosettes almost as big as dahlias. Presently Charlie came lounging in, looking rather sleepy and queer, Rose thought. On seeing her, however, he roused up and said with a smile that ended in a gape,

"I thought you were with mother, so I took forty winks after I got those girls off. Now, I'm at your service, Rosamunda, whenever you like."

"You look as if your head ached. If it does, don't mind me. I'm not afraid to run home alone, it's so early," answered Rose, observing the flushed cheeks and heavy eyes of her cousin.

"I think I see myself letting you do it. Champagne always makes my headache, but the air will set me up."

"Why do you drink it, then?" asked Rose, anxiously.

"Can't help it, when I'm host. Now, don't you begin to lecture; I've had enough of Archie's old-fashioned notions, and I don't want any more."

Charlie's tone was decidedly cross, and his whole manner so unlike his usual merry good-nature, that Rose felt crushed, and answered meekly,

"I wasn't going to lecture, only when people like other people, they can't bear to see them suffer pain."

That brought Charlie round at once, for Rose's lips trembled a little, though she tried to hide it by smelling the flower she pulled from her sash.

"I'm a regular bear, and I beg your pardon for being so cross, Rosy," he said in the old frank way that was so winning.

"I wish you'd beg Archie's too, and be good friends again. You never were cross when he was your chum," Rose said, looking up at him as he bent toward her from the low chimney-piece, where he had been leaning his elbows.

In an instant he stood as stiff and straight as a ramrod, and the heavy eyes kindled with an angry spark as he said, in his high and mighty manner,

"You'd better not meddle with what you don't understand, cousin."

"But I do understand, and it troubles me very much to see you so cold and stiff to one another. You always used to be together, and now you hardly speak. You are so ready to beg my pardon I don't see why you can't beg Archie's, if you are in the wrong."

"I'm not!" this was so short and sharp that Rose started, and Charlie added in a calmer but still very haughty tone: "A gentleman always begs pardon when he has been rude to a lady, but one man doesn't apologize to another man who has insulted him."

"Oh, my heart, what a pepperpot!" thought Rose, and, hoping to make him laugh, she added slyly: "I was not talking about men, but boys, and one of them a Prince, who ought to set a good example to his subjects."

But Charlie would not relent, and tried to turn the subject by saying gravely, as he unfastened the little gold ring from his watch-guard,

"I've broken my word, so I want to give this back and free you from the bargain. I'm sorry, but I think it a foolish promise, and don't intend to keep it. Choose a pair of ear-rings to suit yourself, as my forfeit. You have a right to wear them now."

"No, I can only wear one, and that is no use, for Archie will keep his word I'm sure!" Rose was so mortified and grieved at this downfall of her hopes that she spoke sharply, and would not take the ring the deserter offered her.

He shrugged his shoulders, and threw it into her lap, trying to look cool and careless, but failing entirely, for he was ashamed of himself, and out of sorts generally. Rose wanted to cry, but pride would not let her, and, being very angry, she relieved herself by talk instead of tears. Looking pale and excited, she rose out of her chair, cast away the ring, and said in a voice that she vainly tried to keep steady,

"You are not at all the boy I thought you were, and I don't respect you one bit. I've tried to help you be good, but you won't let me, and I shall not try any more. You talk a great deal about being a gentleman, but you are not, for you've broken your word, and I can never trust you again. I don't wish you to go home with me. I'd rather have Mary. Good-night."

And with that last dreadful blow, Rose walked out of the room, leaving Charlie as much astonished as if one of his pet pigeons had flown in his face and pecked at him. She was so seldom angry, that when her temper did get the better of her it made a deep impression on the lads, for it was generally a righteous sort of indignation at some injustice or wrong-doing, not childish passion.

Her little thunderstorm cleared off in a sob or two as she put on her things in the entry-closet, and when she emerged she looked the brighter for the shower. A hasty good-night to Aunt Clara now under the hands of the hairdresser and then she crept down to find Mary the maid. But Mary was out, so was the man, and Rose slipped away by the back-door, flattering herself that she had escaped the awkwardness of having Charlie for escort.

There she was mistaken, however, for the gate had hardly closed behind her when a well-known tramp was heard, and the Prince was beside her, saying in a tone of penitent politeness that banished Rose's wrath like magic,

"You needn't speak to me if you don't choose, but I must see you safely home, cousin."

She turned at once, put out her hand, and answered heartily,

"I was the cross one. Please forgive me, and let's be friends again."

Now that was better than a dozen sermons on the beauty of forgiveness, and did Charlie more good, for it showed him how sweet humility was, and proved that Rose practised as she preached.

He shook the hand warmly, then drew it through his arm and said, as if anxious to recover the good opinion with the loss of which he had been threatened,

"Look here, Rosy, I've put the ring back, and I'm going to try again. But you don't know how hard it is to stand being laughed at."

"Yes, I do! Ariadne plagues me every time I see her, because I don't wear ear-rings after all the trouble I had getting ready for them."

"Ah, but her twaddle isn't half as bad as the chaffing I get. It takes a deal of pluck to hold out when you are told you are tied to an apron string, and all that sort of thing," sighed Charlie.

"I thought you had a 'deal of pluck,' as you call it. The boys all say you are the bravest of the seven," said Rose.

"So I am about some things, but I cannot bear to be laughed at."

"It is hard, but if one is right won't that make it easier?"

"Not to me; it might to a pious parson like Arch."

"Please don't call him names! I guess he has what is called moral courage, and you physical courage. Uncle explained the difference to me, and moral is the best, though often it doesn't look so," said Rose thoughtfully.

Charlie didn't like that, and answered quickly, "I don't believe he'd stand it any better than I do, if he had those fellows at him."

"Perhaps that's why he keeps out of their way, and wants you to."

Rose had him there, and Charlie felt it, but would not give in just yet, though he was going fast, for somehow, in the dark he seemed to see things clearer than in the light, and found it very easy to be confidential when it was "only Rose."

"If he was my brother, now, he'd have some right to interfere," began Charlie, in an injured tone.

"I wish he was!" cried Rose.

"So do I," answered Charlie, and then they both laughed at his inconsistency.

The laugh did them good, and when Prince spoke again, it was in a different tone pensive, not proud nor perverse.

"You see, it's hard upon me that I have no brothers and sisters. The others are better off and needn't go abroad for chums if they don't like. I am all alone, and I'd be thankful even for a little sister."

Rose thought that very pathetic, and, overlooking the uncomplimentary word "even" in that last sentence, she said, with a timid sort of earnestness that conquered her cousin at once,

"Play I was a little sister. I know I'm silly, but perhaps I'm better than nothing, and I'd dearly love to do it."

"So should I! and we will, for you are not silly, my dear, but a very sensible girl, we all think, and I'm proud to have you for a sister. There, now!" and Charlie looked down at the curly head bobbing along beside him with real affection in his face.

Rose gave a skip of pleasure, and laid one seal-skin mitten over the other on his arm, as she said happily,

"That's so nice of you! Now, you needn't be lonely any more, and I'll try to fill Archie's place till he comes back, for I know he will, as soon as you let him."

"Well, I don't mind telling you that while he was my mate I never missed brothers and sisters, or wanted anyone else; but since he cast me off, I'll be hanged if I don't feel as forlorn as old Crusoe before Friday turned up."

This burst of confidence confirmed Rose in her purpose of winning Charlie's Mentor back to him, but she said no more, contented to have done so well. They parted excellent friends, and Prince went home, wondering why "a fellow didn't mind saying things to a girl or woman which they would die before they'd own to another fellow."

Rose also had some sage reflections upon the subject, and fell asleep thinking that there were a great many curious things in this world, and feeling that she was beginning to find out some of them.

Next day she trudged up the hill to see Archie, and having told him as much as she thought best about her talk with Charlie, begged him to forget and forgive.

"I've been thinking that perhaps I ought to, though I am in the right. I'm no end fond of Charlie, and he's the best-hearted lad alive; but he can't say No, and that will play the mischief with him, if he does not take care," said Archie in his grave, kind way.

"While father was home, I was very busy with him, so Prince got into a set I don't like. They try to be fast, and think it's manly, and they flatter him, and lead him on to do all sorts of things play for money, and bet, and loaf about. I hate to have him do so, and tried to stop it, but went to work the wrong way, so we got into a mess."

"He is all ready to make up if you don't say much, for he owned to me he was wrong; but I don't think he will own it to you, in words," began Rose.

"I don't care for that; if he'll just drop those row-dies and come back, I'll hold my tongue and not preach. I wonder if he owes those fellows money, and so doesn't like to break off till he can pay it. I hope not, but don't dare to ask; though, perhaps, Steve knows, he's always after Prince, more's the pity," and Archie looked anxious.

"I think Steve does know, for he talked about debts of honour the day I gave him—" There Rose stopped short and turned scarlet.

But Archie ordered her to "fess," and had the whole story in five minutes, for none dared disobey the Chief. He completed her affliction by putting a five-dollar bill into her pocket by main force, looking both indignant and resolute as he said,

"Never do so again; but send Steve to me, if he is afraid to go to his father. Charlie had nothing to do with that; he wouldn't borrow a penny of a girl, don't think it. But that's the harm he does Steve, who adores him, and tries to be like him in all things. Don't say a word; I'll make it all right, and no one shall blame you."

121

"Oh me! I always make trouble by trying to help, and then letting out the wrong thing," sighed Rose, much depressed by her slip of the tongue.

Archie comforted her with the novel remark that it was always best to tell the truth, and made her quite cheerful by promising to heal the breach with Charlie as soon as possible.

He kept his word so well that the very next afternoon, as Rose looked out of the window, she beheld the joyful spectacle of Archie and Prince coming up the avenue, arm-in-arm, as of old, talking away as if to make up for the unhappy silence of the past weeks.

Rose dropped her work, hurried to the door, and, opening it wide, stood there smiling down upon them so happily, that the faces of the lads brightened as they ran up the steps eager to show that all was well with them.

"Here's our little peace-maker!" said Archie, shaking hands with vigour.

But Charlie added, with a look that made Rose very proud and happy, "And my little sister."

Chapter 24—Which?

"Uncle, I have discovered what girls are made for," said Rose, the day after the reconciliation of Archie and the Prince.

"Well, my dear, what is it?" asked Dr. Alec, who was "planking the deck," as he called his daily promenade up and down the hall.

"To take care of boys," answered Rose, quite beaming with satisfaction as she spoke. "Phebe laughed when I told her, and said she thought girls had better learn to take care of themselves first. But that's because she hasn't got seven boy-cousins as I have."

"She is right, nevertheless, Rosy, and so are you, for the two things go together, and in helping seven lads you are unconsciously doing much to improve one lass," said Dr. Alec, stopping to nod and smile at the bright-faced figure resting on the old bamboo chair, after a lively game of battledore and shuttlecock, in place of a run which a storm prevented.

"Am I? I'm glad of that; but really, uncle, I do feel as if I must take care of the boys, for they come to me in all sorts of troubles, and ask advice, and I like it so much. Only I don't always know what to do, and I'm going to consult you privately and then surprise them with my wisdom."

"All right, my dear; what's the first worry? I see you have something on your little mind, so come and tell uncle."

Rose put her arm in his, and, pacing to and fro, told him all about Charlie, asking what she could do to keep him straight, and be a real sister to him.

"Could you make up your mind to go and stay with Aunt Clara a month?" asked the Doctor, when she ended.

"Yes, sir; but I shouldn't like it. Do you really want me to go?"

"The best cure for Charlie is a daily dose of Rose water, or Rose and water, or Rose and water; will you go and see that he takes it?" laughed Dr. Alec.

"You mean that if I'm there and try to make it pleasant, he will stay at home and keep out of mischief?"

"Exactly."

"But could I make it pleasant? He would want the boys."

"No danger but he'd have the boys, for they swarm after you like bees after their queen. Haven't you found that out?"

"Aunt Plen often says they never used to be here half so much before I came, but I never thought I made the difference, it seemed so natural to have them round."

"Little modesty doesn't know what a magnet she is; but she will find it out some day," and the Doctor softly stroked the cheek that had grown rosy with pleasure at the thought of being so much loved. "Now, you see, if I move the magnet to Aunt Clara's, the lads will go there as sure as iron to steel, and Charlie will be so happy at home he won't care for these mischievous mates of his I hope," added the Doctor, well knowing how hard it was to wean a seventeen-year-old boy from his first taste of what is called "seeing life," which, alas! often ends in seeing death.

"I'll go, uncle, right away! Aunt Clara is always asking me, and will be glad to get me. I shall have to dress and dine late, and see lots of company, and be very fashionable, but I'll try not to let it hurt me; and if I get in a puzzle or worried about anything I can run to you," answered Rose, good-will conquering timidity.

So it was decided, and without saying much about the real reason for this visit, Rose was transplanted to Aunt Clara's, feeling that she had a work to do, and very eager to do it well.

Dr. Alec was right about the bees, for the boys did follow their queen, and astonished Mrs. Clara by their sudden assiduity in making calls, dropping in to dinner, and getting up evening frolics. Charlie was a devoted host, and tried to show his gratitude by being very kind to his "little sister," for he guessed why she came, and his heart was touched by her artless endeavours to "help him be good."

Rose often longed to be back in the old house with the simpler pleasures and more useful duties of the life there; but, having made up her mind, in spite of Phebe, that "girls were made to take care of boys," here motherly little soul found much to enjoy in the new task she had undertaken.

It was a pretty sight to see the one earnest, sweet-faced girl among the flock of tall lads, trying to understand, to help and please them with a patient affection that worked many a small miracle unperceived. Slang, rough manners, and careless habits were banished or bettered by the presence of a little gentlewoman; and all the manly virtues cropping up were encouraged by the hearty admiration bestowed upon them by one whose good opinion all valued more than they confessed; while Rose tried to imitate the good qualities she praised in them, to put away her girlish vanities and fears, to be strong and just, and frank and brave, as well as modest, kind, and beautiful.

This trial worked so well that when the month was over, Mac and Steve demanded a visit in their turn, and Rose went, feeling that she would like to hear grim Aunt Jane say, as Aunt Clara did at parting, "I wish I could keep you all my life, dear."

After Mac and Steve had had their turn, Archie and Company bore her away for some weeks; and with them she was so happy, she felt as if she would like to stay for ever, if she could have Uncle Alec also.

Of course, Aunt Myra could not be neglected, and, with secret despair, Rose went to the "Mausoleum," as the boys called her gloomy abode. Fortunately, she was very near home, and Dr. Alec dropped in so often that her visit was far less dismal than she expected. Between them, they actually made Aunt Myra laugh heartily more than once; and Rose did her so much good by letting in the sunshine, singing about the silent house, cooking wholesome messes, and amusing the old lady with funny little lectures on physiology, that she forgot to take her pills and gave up "Mum's Elixir," because she slept so well, after the long walks and drives she was beguiled into taking, that she needed no narcotic.

So the winter flew rapidly away, and it was May before Rose was fairly settled again at home. They called her the "Monthly Rose," because she had spent a month with each of the aunts, and left such pleasant memories of bloom and fragrance behind her, that all wanted the family flower back again.

Dr. Alec rejoiced greatly over his recovered treasure; but as the time drew near when his year of experiment ended, he had many a secret fear that Rose might like to make her home for the next twelve month with Aunt Jessie, or even Aunt Clara, for Charlie's sake. He said nothing, but waited with much anxiety for the day when the matter should be decided; and while he waited he did his best to finish as far as possible the task he had begun so well.

Rose was very happy now, being out nearly all day enjoying the beautiful awakening of the world, for spring came bright and early, as if anxious to do its part. The old horse-chestnuts budded round her windows, green things sprung up like magic in the garden under her hands, hardy flowers bloomed as fast as they could, the birds sang blithely overhead, and every day a chorus of pleasant voices cried, "Good morning, cousin, isn't it jolly weather?"

No one remembered the date of the eventful conversation which resulted in the Doctor's experiment (no one but himself at least); so when the aunts were invited to tea one Saturday they came quite unsuspiciously, and were all sitting together having a social chat, when Brother Alec entered with two photographs in his hand.

"Do you remember that?" he said, showing one to Aunt Clara, who happened to be nearest.

"Yes, indeed; it is very like her when she came. Quite her sad, unchildlike expression, and thin little face, with the big dark eyes."

The picture was passed round, and all agreed that "it was very like Rose a year ago." This point being settled, the Doctor showed the second picture, which was received with great approbation, and pronounced a "charming likeness."

It certainly was, and a striking contrast to the first one, for it was a blooming, smiling face, full of girlish spirit and health, with no sign of melancholy, though the soft eyes were thoughtful, and the lines about the lips betrayed a sensitive nature.

Dr. Alec set both photographs on the chimneypiece, and, falling back a step or two, surveyed them with infinite satisfaction for several minutes, then wheeled round, saying briefly, as he pointed to the two faces,

"Time is up; how do you think my experiment has succeeded, ladies?"

124

"Bless me, so it is!" cried Aunt Plenty, dropping a stitch in her surprise.

"Beautifully, dear," answered Aunt Peace, smiling entire approval.

"She certainly has improved, but appearances are deceitful, and she had no constitution to build upon," croaked Aunt Myra.

"I am willing to allow that, as far as mere health goes, the experiment is a success," graciously observed Aunt Jane, unable to forget Rose's kindness to her Mac.

"So am I; and I'll go farther, for I really do believe Alec has done wonders for the child; she will be a beauty in two or three years," added Aunt Clara, feeling that she could say nothing better than that.

"I always knew he would succeed, and I'm so glad you all allow it, for he deserves more credit than you know, and more praise than he will ever get," cried Aunt Jessie, clapping her hands with an enthusiasm that caused Jamie's little red stocking to wave like a triumphal banner in the air.

Dr. Alec made them a splendid bow, looking much gratified, and then said soberly,

"Thank you; now the question is, shall I go on? for this is only the beginning. None of you know the hindrances I've had, the mistakes I've made, the study I've given the case, and the anxiety I've often felt. Sister Myra is right is one thing Rose is a delicate creature, quick to flourish in the sunshine, and as quick to droop without it. She has no special weakness, but inherits her mother's sensitive nature, and needs the wisest, tenderest care, to keep a very ardent little soul from wearing out a finely organised little body. I think I have found the right treatment, and; with you to help me, I believe we may build up a lovely and a noble woman, who will be a pride and comfort to us all."

There Dr. Alec stopped to get his breath, for he had spoken very earnestly, and his voice got a little husky over the last words. A gentle murmur from the aunts seemed to encourage him, and he went on with an engaging smile, for the good man was slyly trying to win all the ladies to vote for him when the time came.

"Now, I don't wish to be selfish or arbitrary, because I am her guardian, and I shall leave Rose free to choose for herself. We all want her, and if she likes to make her home with any of you rather than with me, she shall do so. In fact, I encouraged her visits last winter, that she might see what we can all offer her, and judge where she will be happiest. Is not that the fairest way? Will you agree to abide by her choice, as I do?"

"Yes, we will," said all the aunts, in quite a flutter of excitement at the prospect of having Rose for a whole year.

"Good! she will be here directly, and then we will settle the question for another year. A most important year, mind you, for she has got a good start, and will blossom rapidly now if all goes well with her. So I beg of you don't undo my work, but deal very wisely and gently with my little girl, for if any harm come to her, I think it would break my heart."

As he spoke, Dr. Alec turned his back abruptly and affected to be examining the pictures again; but the aunts understood how dear the child was to the solitary man who had loved her mother years ago, and who now found his happiness in cherishing the little Rose who was so like her. The good ladies nodded and sighed, and telegraphed to one another that none of them would complain if not chosen, or ever try to rob Brother Alec of his "Heart's Delight," as the boys called Rose.

Just then a pleasant sound of happy voices came up from the garden, and smiles broke out on all serious faces. Dr. Alec turned at once, saying, as he threw back his head, "There she is; now for it!"

The cousins had been a-Maying, and soon came flocking in laden with the spoils.

"Here is our bonny Scotch rose with all her thorns about her," said Dr. Alec, surveying her with unusual pride and tenderness, as she went to show Aunt Peace her basket full of early flowers, fresh leaves, and curious lichens.

"Leave your clutter in the hall, boys, and sit quietly down if you choose to stop here, for we are busy," said Aunt Plenty, shaking her finger at the turbulent Clan, who were bubbling over with the jollity born of spring sunshine and healthy exercise.

"Of course, we choose to stay! Wouldn't miss our Saturday high tea for anything," said the Chief, as he restored order among his men with a nod, a word, and an occasional shake.

"What is up? a court-martial?" asked Charlie, looking at the assembled ladies with affected awe and real curiosity, for these faces betrayed that some interesting business was afloat.

Dr. Alec explained in a few words, which he made as brief and calm as he could; but the effect was exciting, nevertheless, for each of the lads began at once to bribe, entice, and wheedle "our cousin" to choose his home.

"You really ought to come to us for mother's sake, as a relish, you know, for she must be perfectly satiated with boys," began Archie, using the strongest argument he could think of at the moment.

"Oh, do! we'll never slam, or bounce at you or call you 'fraid cat,' if you only will," besought Geordie and Will, distorting their countenances in the attempt to smile with overpowering sweetness.

"And I'll always wash my hands 'fore I touch you, and you shall be my dolly, 'cause Pokey's gone away, and I'll love you *hard*," cried Jamie, clinging to her with his chubby face full of affection.

"Brothers and sister ought to live together; especially when the brother needs some one to make home pleasant for him," added Charlie, with the wheedlesome tone and look that Rose always found so difficult to resist.

"You had her longest, and it's our turn now; Mac needs her more than you do, Prince, for she's 'the light of his eyes,' he says. Come, Rose, choose us, and I'll never use the musky pomade you hate again as long as I live," said Steve, with his most killing air, as he offered this noble sacrifice.

Mac peered wistfully over his goggles, saying in an unusually wide-awake and earnest way, --

"Do, cousin, then we can study chemistry together. My experiments don't blow up very often now, and the gases aren't at all bad when you get used to them."

Rose meantime had stood quite still, with the flowers dropping from her hands as her eyes went from one eager face to another, while smiles rippled over her own at the various enticements offered her. During the laugh that followed Mac's handsome proposition, she looked at her uncle, whose eyes were fixed on her with an expression of love and longing that went to her heart.

"Ah! yes," she thought, "he wants me most! I've often longed to give him something that he wished for very much, and now I can."

126

So, when, at a sudden gesture from Aunt Peace, silence fell, Rose said slowly, with a pretty colour in her cheeks, and a beseeching look about the room, as if asking pardon of the boys,

"It's very hard to choose when everybody is so fond of me; therefore I think I'd better go to the one who seems to need me most."

"No, dear, the one you love the best and will be happiest with," said Dr. Alec quickly, as a doleful sniff from Aunt Myra, and a murmur of "My sainted Caroline," made Rose pause and look that way.

"Take time, cousin; don't be in a hurry to make up your mind, and remember, 'Codlin's your friend,'" added Charlie, hopeful still.

"I don't want any time! I know who I love best, who I'm happiest with, and I choose uncle. Will he have me?" cried Rose, in a tone that produced a sympathetic thrill among the hearers, it was so full of tender confidence and love.

If she really had any doubt, the look in Dr. Alec's face banished it without a word, as he opened wide his arms, and she ran into them, feeling that home was there.

No one spoke for a minute, but there were signs of emotion among the aunts, which warned the boys to bestir themselves before the water-works began to play. So they took hands and began to prance about uncle and niece, singing, with sudden inspiration, the nursery rhyme,

"Ring around a Rosy!"

Of course that put an end to all sentiment, and Rose emerged laughing from Dr. Alec's bosom, with the mark of a waistcoat button nicely imprinted on her left cheek. He saw it, and said with a merry kiss that half effaced it, "This is my ewe lamb, and I have set my mark on her, so no one can steal her away."

That tickled the boys, and they set up a shout of,

"Uncle had a little lamb!"

But Rose hushed the noise by slipping into the circle, and making them dance prettily like lads and lasses round a May-pole; while Phebe, coming in with fresh water for the flowers, began to twitter, chirp, and coo, as if all the birds of the air had come to join in the spring revel of the eight cousins.

Preface

As authors may be supposed to know better than anyone else what they intended to do when writing a book, I beg leave to say that there is no moral to this story. Rose is not designed for a model girl, and the Sequel was simply written in fulfillment of a promise, hoping to afford some amusement, and perhaps here and there a helpful hint, to other roses getting ready to bloom.

L. M. Alcott

September 1876

## Chapter 1 COMING HOME

Three young men stood together on a wharf one bright October day awaiting the arrival of an ocean steamer with an impatience which found a vent in lively skirmishes with a small lad, who pervaded the premises like a will-o'-the-wisp and afforded much amusement to the other groups assembled there.

"They are the Campbells, waiting for their cousin, who has been abroad several years with her uncle, the doctor," whispered one lady to another as the handsomest of the young men touched his hat to her as he passed, lugging the boy, whom he had just rescued from a little expedition down among the piles.

"Which is that?" asked the stranger.

"Prince Charlie, as he's called a fine fellow, the most promising of the seven, but a little fast, people say," answered the first speaker with a shake of the head.

"Are the others his brothers?"

"No, cousins. The elder is Archie, a most exemplary young man. He has just gone into business with the merchant uncle and bids fair to be an honor to his family. The other, with the eyeglasses and no gloves, is Mac, the odd one, just out of college."

"And the boy?"

"Oh, he is Jamie, the youngest brother of Archibald, and the pet of the whole family. Mercy on us he'll be in if they don't hold on to him!"

The ladies' chat came to a sudden end just there, for by the time Jamie had been fished out of a hogshead, the steamer hove in sight and everything else was forgotten. As it swung slowly around to enter the dock, a boyish voice shouted, "There she is! I see her and Uncle and Phebe! Hooray for Cousin Rose!" And three small cheers were given with a will by Jamie as he stood on a post waving his arms like a windmill while his brother held onto the tail of his jacket.

Yes, there they were Uncle Alec swinging his hat like a boy, with Phebe smiling and nodding on one side and Rose kissing both hands delightedly on the other as she recognized familiar faces and heard familiar voices welcoming her home.

"Bless her dear heart, she's bonnier than ever! Looks like a Madonna doesn't she? with that blue cloak round her, and her bright hair flying in the wind!" said Charlie excitedly as they watched the group upon the deck with eager eyes.

"Madonnas don't wear hats like that. Rose hasn't changed much, but Phebe has. Why, she's a regular beauty!" answered Archie, staring with all his might at the dark-eyed young woman with the brilliant color and glossy black braids shining in the sun.

"Dear old Uncle! Doesn't it seem good to have him back?" was all Mac said, but he was not looking at "dear old uncle" as he made the fervent remark, for he saw only the slender blond girl nearby and stretched out his hands to meet hers, forgetful of the green water tumbling between them.

During the confusion that reigned for a moment as the steamer settled to her moorings, Rose looked down into the four faces upturned to hers and seemed to read in them something that both pleased and pained her. It was only a glance, and her own eyes were full, but through the mist of happy tears she received the impression that Archie was about the same, that Mac had decidedly improved, and that something was amiss with Charlie. There was no time for observation, however, for in a moment the shoreward rush began, and before she could grasp her traveling bag, Jamie was clinging to her like an ecstatic young bear. She was with difficulty released from his embrace to fall into the gentler ones of the elder cousins, who took advantage of the general excitement to welcome both blooming girls with affectionate impartiality. Then the wanderers were borne ashore in a triumphal procession, while Jamie danced rapturous jigs before them even on the gangway.

Archie remained to help his uncle get the luggage through the Custom House, and the others escorted the damsels home. No sooner were they shut up in a carriage, however, than a new and curious constraint seemed to fall upon the young people, for they realized, all at once, that their former playmates were men and women now. Fortunately, Jamie was quite free from this feeling of restraint and, sitting bodkinwise between the ladies, took all sorts of liberties with them and their belongings.

"Well, my mannikin, what do you think of us?" asked Rose, to break an awkward pause.

"You've both grown so pretty, I can't decide which I like best. Phebe is the biggest and brightest-looking, and I was always fond of Phebe, but somehow you are so kind of sweet and precious, I really think I must hug you again," and the small youth did it tempestuously.

"If you love me best, I shall not mind a bit about your thinking Phebe the handsomest, because she is. Isn't she, boys?" asked Rose, with a mischievous look at the gentlemen opposite, whose faces expressed a respectful admiration which much amused her.

"I'm so dazzled by the brilliancy and beauty that has suddenly burst upon me, I have no words to express my emotions," answered Charlie, gallantly dodging the dangerous question.

"I can't say yet, for I have not had time to look at anyone. I will now, if you don't mind." And, to the great amusement of the rest, Mac gravely adjusted his eyeglasses and took an observation.

"Well?" said Phebe, smiling and blushing under his honest stare, yet seeming not to resent it as she did the lordly sort of approval which made her answer the glance of Charlie's audacious blue eyes with a flash of her black ones.

"I think if you were my sister, I should be very proud of you, because your face shows what I admire more than its beauty truth and courage, Phebe," answered Mac with a little bow full of such genuine respect that surprise and pleasure brought a sudden dew to quench the fire of the girl's eyes and soothe the sensitive pride of the girl's heart.

Rose clapped her hands just as she used to do when anything delighted her, and beamed at Mac approvingly as she said: "Now that's a criticism worth having, and we are much obliged. I was sure you'd admire my Phebe when you knew her, but I didn't believe you would be wise enough to see it at once, and you have gone up many pegs in my estimation, I assure you."

"I was always fond of mineralogy you remember, and I've been tapping round a good deal lately, so I've learned to know precious metals when I see them," Mac said with his shrewd smile.

"That is the latest hobby, then? Your letters have amused us immensely, for each one had a new theory or experiment, and the latest was always the best. I thought Uncle would have died of laughter over the vegetarian mania it was so funny to imagine you living on bread and milk, baked apples, and potatoes roasted in your own fire," continued Rose, changing the subject again.

"This old chap was the laughingstock of his class. They called him Don Quixote, and the way he went at windmills of all sorts was a sight to see," put in Charlie, evidently feeling that Mac had been patted on the head quite as much as was good for him.

"But in spite of that the Don got through college with all the honors. Oh, wasn't I proud when Aunt Jane wrote to us about it and didn't she rejoice that her boy kept at the head of his class and won the medal!" cried Rose, shaking Mac by both hands in a way that caused Charlie to wish "the old chap" had been left behind with Dr. Alec.

"Oh, come, that's all Mother's nonsense. I began earlier than the other fellows and liked it better, so I don't deserve any praise. Prince is right, though. I did make a regular jack of myself, but on the whole I'm not sure that my wild oats weren't better than some I've seen sowed. Anyway, they didn't cost much, and I'm none the worse for them," said Mac placidly.

"I know what 'wild oats' means. I heard Uncle Mac say Charlie was sowing 'em too fast, and I asked Mama, so she told me. And I know that he was suspelled or expended, I don't remember which, but it was something bad, and Aunt Clara cried," added Jamie all in one breath, for he possessed a fatal gift of making malapropos remarks, which caused him to be a terror to his family.

"Do you want to go on the box again?" demanded Prince with a warning frown.

"No, I don't."

"Then hold your tongue."

"Well, Mac needn't kick me, for I was only..." began the culprit, innocently trying to make a bad matter worse.

"That will do," interrupted Charlie sternly, and James subsided, a crushed boy, consoling himself with Rose's new watch for the indignities he suffered at the hands of the "old fellows" as he vengefully called his elders.

Mac and Charlie immediately began to talk as hard as their tongues could wag, bringing up all sorts of pleasant subjects so successfully that peals of laughter made passersby look after the merry load with sympathetic smiles.

An avalanche of aunts fell upon Rose as soon as she reached home, and for the rest of the day the old house buzzed like a beehive. Evening found the whole tribe collected in the drawing rooms, with the exception of Aunt Peace, whose place was empty now.

Naturally enough, the elders settled into one group after a while, and the young fellows clustered about the girls like butterflies around two attractive flowers. Dr. Alec was the central figure in one room and Rose in the other, for the little girl, whom they had all loved and petted, had bloomed into a woman, and two years of absence had wrought a curious change in the relative positions of the cousins, especially the three elder ones, who eyed her with a mixture of boyish affection and manly admiration that was both new and pleasant.

Something sweet yet spirited about her charmed them and piqued their curiosity, for she was not quite like other girls, and rather startled them now and then by some independent little speech or act which made them look at one another with a sly smile, as if reminded that Rose was "Uncle's girl."

Let us listen, as in duty bound, to what the elders are saying first, for they are already building castles in air for the boys and girls to inhabit.

"Dear child how nice it is to see her safely back, so well and happy and like her sweet little self!" said Aunt Plenty, folding her hands as if giving thanks for a great happiness.

"I shouldn't wonder if you found that you'd brought a firebrand into the family, Alec. Two, in fact, for Phebe is a fine girl, and the lads have found it out already if I'm not mistaken," added Uncle Mac, with a nod toward the other room.

All eyes followed his, and a highly suggestive tableau presented itself to the paternal and maternal audience in the back parlor.

Rose and Phebe, sitting side by side on the sofa, had evidently assumed at once the places which they were destined to fill by right of youth, sex, and beauty, for Phebe had long since ceased to be the maid and become the friend, and Rose meant to have that fact established at once.

Jamie occupied the rug, on which Will and Geordie stood at ease, showing their uniforms to the best advantage, for they were now in a great school, where military drill was the delight of their souls. Steve posed gracefully in an armchair, with Mac lounging over the back of it, while Archie leaned on one corner of the low chimneypiece, looking down at Phebe as she listened to his chat with smiling lips and cheeks almost as rich in color as the carnations in her belt.

But Charlie was particularly effective, although he sat upon a music stool, that most trying position for any man not gifted with grace in the management of his legs. Fortunately Prince was, and had fallen into an easy attitude, with one arm over the back of the sofa, his handsome head bent a little, as he monopolized Rose, with a devoted air and a very becoming expression of contentment on his face.

Aunt Clara smiled as if well pleased; Aunt Jessie looked thoughtful; Aunt Jane's keen eyes went from dapper Steve to broad-shouldered Mac with an anxious glance; Mrs. Myra murmured something about her "blessed Caroline"; and Aunt Plenty said warmly, "Bless the dears! Anyone might be proud of such a bonny flock of bairns as that."

"I am all ready to play chaperon as soon as you please, Alec, for I suppose the dear girl will come out at once, as she did not before you went away. My services won't be wanted long, I fancy, for with her many advantages she will be carried off in her first season or I'm much mistaken," said Mrs. Clara, with significant nods and smiles.

"You must settle all those matters with Rose. I am no longer captain, only first mate now, you know," answered Dr. Alec, adding soberly, half to himself, half to his brother, "I wonder people are in such haste to 'bring out' their daughters, as it's called. To me there is something almost pathetic in the sight of a young girl standing on the threshold of the world, so innocent and hopeful, so ignorant of all that lies before her, and usually so ill prepared to meet the ups and downs of life. We do our duty better by the boys, but the poor little women are seldom provided with any armor worth having, and sooner or later they are sure to need it, for every one must fight her own battle, and only the brave and strong can win."

"You can't reproach yourself with neglect of that sort, Alec, for you have done your duty faithfully by George's girl, and I envy you the pride and happiness of having such a daughter, for she is that to you," answered old Mac, unexpectedly betraying the paternal sort of tenderness men seldom feel for their sons.

"I've tried, Mac, and I am both proud and happy, but with every year my anxiety seems to increase. I've done my best to fit Rose for what may come, as far as I can foresee it, but now she must stand alone, and all my care is powerless to keep her heart from aching, her life from being saddened by mistakes, or thwarted by the acts of others. I can only stand ready to share her joy and sorrow and watch her shape her life."

"Why, Alec, what is the child going to do that you need look so solemn?" exclaimed Mrs. Clara, who seemed to have assumed a sort of right to Rose already.

"Hark! And let her tell you herself," answered Dr. Alec, as Rose's voice was heard saying very earnestly, "Now, you have all told your plans for the future, why don't you ask us ours?"

"Because we know that there is only one thing for a pretty girl to do break a dozen or so hearts before she finds one to suit, then marry and settle," answered Charlie, as if no other reply was possible.

"That may be the case with many, but not with us, for Phebe and I believe that it is as much a right and a duty for women to do something with their lives as for men, and we are not going to be satisfied with such frivolous parts as you give us," cried Rose with kindling eyes. "I mean what I say, and you cannot laugh me down. Would you be contented to be told to enjoy yourself for a little while, then marry and do nothing more till you die?" she added, turning to Archie.

"Of course not that is only a part of a man's life," he answered decidedly.

"A very precious and lovely part, but not all," continued Rose. "Neither should it be for a woman, for we've got minds and souls as well as hearts; ambition and talents as well as beauty and accomplishments; and we want to live and learn as well as love and be loved. I'm sick of being told that is all a woman is fit for! I won't have anything to do with love till I prove that I am something besides a housekeeper and baby-tender!"

"Heaven preserve us! Here's woman's rights with a vengeance!" cried Charlie, starting up with mock horror, while the others regarded Rose with mingled surprise and amusement, evidently fancying it all a girlish outbreak.

"Ah, you needn't pretend to be shocked you will be in earnest presently, for this is only the beginning of my strong-mindedness," continued Rose, nothing daunted by the smiles of good-natured incredulity or derision on the faces of her cousins. "I have made up my mind not to be cheated out of the real things that make one good and happy and, just because I'm a rich girl, fold my hands and drift as so many do. I haven't lived with Phebe all these years in vain. I know what courage and self-reliance can do for one, and I sometimes wish I hadn't a penny in the world so that I could go and earn my bread with her, and be as brave and independent as she will be pretty soon."

It was evident that Rose was in earnest now, for as she spoke she turned to her friend with such respect as well as love in her face that the look told better than any words how heartily the rich girl appreciated the virtues hard experience had given the poor girl, and how eagerly she desired to earn what all her fortune could not buy for her.

Something in the glance exchanged between the friends impressed the young men in spite of their prejudices, and it was in a perfectly serious tone that Archie said, "I fancy you'll find your hands full, Cousin, if you want work, for I've heard people say that wealth has its troubles and trials as well as poverty."

"I know it, and I'm going to try and fill my place well. I've got some capital little plans all made, and have begun to study my profession already," answered Rose with an energetic nod.

"Could I ask what it is to be?" inquired Charlie in a tone of awe.

"Guess!" and Rose looked up at him with an expression half-earnest, half-merry.

"Well, I should say that you were fitted for a beauty and a belle, but as that is evidently not to your taste, I am afraid you are going to study medicine and be a doctor. Won't your patients have a heavenly time though? It will be easy dying with an angel to poison them."

"Now, Charlie, that's base of you, when you know how well women have succeeded in this profession and what a comfort Dr. Mary Kirk was to dear Aunt Peace. I did want to study medicine, but Uncle thought it wouldn't do to have so many M.D.'s in one family, since Mac thinks of trying it. Besides, I seem to have other work put into my hands that I am better fitted for."

"You are fitted for anything that is generous and good, and I'll stand by you, no matter what you've chosen," cried Mac heartily, for this was a new style of talk from a girl's lips, and he liked it immensely.

"Philanthropy is a generous, good, and beautiful profession, and I've chosen it for mine because I have much to give. I'm only the steward of the fortune Papa left me, and I think, if I use it wisely for the happiness of others, it will be more blest than if I keep it all for myself."

Very sweetly and simply was this said, but it was curious to see how differently the various hearers received it.

Charlie shot a quick look at his mother, who exclaimed, as if in spite of herself, "Now, Alec, are you going to let that girl squander a fine fortune on all sorts of charitable nonsense and wild schemes for the prevention of pauperism and crime?"

"'They who give to the poor lend to the Lord,' and practical Christianity is the kind He loves the best," was all Dr. Alec answered, but it silenced the aunts and caused even prudent Uncle Mac to think with sudden satisfaction of certain secret investments he had made which paid him no interest but the thanks of the poor.

Archie and Mac looked well pleased and promised their advice and assistance with the enthusiasm of generous young hearts. Steve shook his head, but said nothing, and the lads on the rug at once proposed founding a hospital for invalid dogs and horses, white mice, and wounded heroes.

"Don't you think that will be a better way for a woman to spend her life than in dancing, dressing, and husband-hunting, Charlie?" asked Rose, observing his silence and anxious for his approval.

"Very pretty for a little while, and very effective too, for I don't know anything more captivating than a sweet girl in a meek little bonnet going on charitable errands and glorifying poor people's houses with a delightful mixture of beauty and benevolence. Fortunately, the dear souls soon tire of it, but it's heavenly while it lasts."

Charlie spoke in a tone of mingled admiration and contempt, and smiled a superior sort of smile, as if he understood all the innocent delusions as well as the artful devices of the sex and expected nothing more from them. It both surprised and grieved Rose, for it did not sound like the Charlie she had left two years ago. But she only said, with a reproachful look and a proud little gesture of head and hand, as if she put the subject aside since it was not treated with respect: "I am sorry you have so low an opinion of women. There was a time when you believed in them sincerely."

"I do still, upon my word I do! They haven't a more devoted admirer and slave in the world than I am. Just try me and see," cried Charlie, gallantly kissing his hand to the sex in general.

But Rose was not appeased, and gave a disdainful shrug as she answered with a look in her eyes that his lordship did not like, "Thank you. I don't want admirers or slaves, but friends and helpers. I've lived so long with a wise, good man that I am rather hard to suit, perhaps, but I don't intend to lower my standard, and anyone who cares for my regard must at least try to live up to it."

"Whew! Here's a wrathful dove! Come and smooth her ruffled plumage, Mac. I'll dodge before I do further mischief," and Charlie strolled away into the other room, privately lamenting that Uncle Alec had spoiled a fine girl by making her strong-minded.

He wished himself back again in five minutes, for Mac said something that produced a gale of laughter, and when he took a look over his shoulder the "wrathful dove" was cooing so peacefully and pleasantly he was sorely tempted to return and share the fun. But Charlie had been spoiled by too much indulgence, and it was hard for him to own himself in the wrong even when he knew it. He always got what he wanted sooner or later, and having long ago made up his mind that Rose and her fortune were to be his, he was secretly displeased at the new plans and beliefs of the young lady, but flattered himself that they would soon be changed when she saw how unfashionable and inconvenient they were.

Musing over the delightful future he had laid out, he made himself comfortable in the sofa corner near his mother till the appearance of a slight refection caused both groups to melt into one. Aunt Plenty believed in eating and drinking, so the slightest excuse for festivity delighted her hospitable soul, and on this joyful occasion she surpassed herself.

It was during this informal banquet that Rose, roaming about from one admiring relative to another, came upon the three younger lads, who were having a quiet little scuffle in a secluded corner.

"Come out here and let me have a look at you," she said enticingly, for she predicted an explosion and public disgrace if peace was not speedily restored.

Hastily smoothing themselves down, the young gentlemen presented three flushed and merry countenances for inspection, feeling highly honored by the command.

"Dear me, how you two have grown! You big things how dare you get head of me in this way!" she said, standing on tiptoe to pat the curly pates before her, for Will and Geordie had shot up like weeds, and now grinned cheerfully down upon her as she surveyed them in comic amazement.

"The Campbells are all fine, tall fellows, and we mean to be the best of the lot. Shouldn't wonder if we were six-footers like Grandpa," observed Will proudly, looking so like a young Shanghai rooster, all legs and an insignificant head, that Rose kept her countenance with difficulty.

"We shall broaden out when we get our growth. We are taller than Steve now, a half a head, both of us," added Geordie, with his nose in the air.

Rose turned to look at Steve and, with a sudden smile, beckoned to him. He dropped his napkin and flew to obey the summons, for she was queen of the hour, and he had openly announced his deathless loyalty.

"Tell the other boys to come here. I've a fancy to stand you all in a row and look you over, as you did me that dreadful day when you nearly frightened me out of my wits," she said, laughing at the memory of it as she spoke.

They came in a body and, standing shoulder to shoulder, made such an imposing array that the young commander was rather daunted for a moment. But she had seen too much of the world lately to be abashed by a trifle, and the desire to see a girlish test gave her courage to face the line of smiling cousins with dignity and spirit.

"Now, I'm going to stare at you as you stared at me. It is my revenge on you seven bad boys for entrapping one poor little girl and enjoying her alarm. I'm not a bit afraid of you now, so tremble and beware!"

As she spoke, Rose looked up into Archie's face and nodded approvingly, for the steady gray eyes met hers fairly and softened as they did so a becoming change, for naturally they were rather keen than kind.

"A true Campbell, bless you!" she said, and shook his hand heartily as she passed on.

Charlie came next, and here she felt less satisfied, though scarcely conscious why, for, as she looked, there came a defiant sort of flash, changing suddenly to something warmer than anger, stronger than pride, making her shrink a little and say, hastily, "I don't find the Charlie I left, but the Prince is there still, I see."

Turning to Mac with a sense of relief, she gently took off his "winkers," as Jamie called them, and looked straight into the honest blue eyes that looked straight back at her, full of a frank and friendly affection that warmed her heart and made her own eyes brighten as she gave back the glasses, saying, with a look and tone of cordial satisfaction, "You are not changed, my dear old Mac, and I'm so glad of that!"

"Now say something extra sweet to me, because I'm the flower of the family," said Steve, twirling the blond moustache, which was evidently the pride of his life.

Rose saw at a glance that Dandy deserved his name more than ever, and promptly quenched his vanities by answering, with a provoking laugh, "Then the name of the flower of the family is Cockscomb."

"Ah, ha! who's got it now?" jeered Will.

"Let us off easy, please," whispered Geordie, mindful that their turn came next.

"You blessed beanstalks! I'm proud of you only don't grow quite out of sight, or even be ashamed to look a woman in the face," answered Rose, with a gentle pat on the cheek of either bashful young giant, for both were red as peonies, though their boyish eyes were as clear and calm as summer lakes.

"Now me!" and Jamie assumed his manliest air, feeling that he did not appear to advantage among his tall kinsmen. But he went to the head of the class in everyone's opinion when Rose put her arms around him, saying, with a kiss, "You must be my boy now, for all the others are too old, and I want a faithful little page to do my errands for me."

"I will, I will I'll marry you too, if you'll just hold on till I grow up!" cried Jamie, rather losing his head at this sudden promotion.

"Bless the baby, what is he talking about?" laughed Rose, looking down at her little knight as he clung about her with grateful ardor.

"Oh, I heard the aunts say that you'd better marry one of us, and keep the property in the family, so I speak first, because you are very fond of me, and I do love curls."

Alas for Jamie! This awful speech had hardly left his innocent lips when Will and Geordie swept him out of the room like a whirlwind, and the howls of that hapless boy were heard from the torture hall, where being shut into the skeleton case was one of the mildest punishments inflicted upon him.

Dismay fell upon the unfortunates who remained, but their confusion was soon ended, for Rose, with a look which they had never seen upon her face before, dismissed them with the brief command, "Break ranks the review is over," and walked away to Phebe.

"Confound that boy! You ought to shut him up or gag him!" fumed Charlie irritably.

"He shall be attended to," answered poor Archie, who was trying to bring up the little marplot with the success of most parents and guardians.

"The whole thing was deuced disagreeable," growled Steve, who felt that he had not distinguished himself in the late engagement.

"Truth generally is," observed Mac dryly as he strolled away with his odd smile.

As if he suspected discord somewhere, Dr. Alec proposed music at this crisis, and the young people felt that it was a happy thought.

"I want you to hear both my birds, for they have improved immensely, and I am very proud of them," said the doctor, twirling up the stool and pulling out the old music books.

"I had better come first, for after you have heard the nightingale you won't care for the canary," added Rose, wishing to put Phebe at her ease, for she sat among them looking like a picture, but rather shy and silent, remembering the days when her place was in the kitchen.

"I'll give you some of the dear old songs you used to like so much. This was a favorite, I think," and sitting down she sang the first familiar air that came, and sang it well in a pleasant, but by no means finished, manner.

It chanced to be "The Birks of Aberfeldie," and vividly recalled the time when Mac was ill and she took care of him. The memory was sweet to her, and involuntarily her eye wandered in search of him. He was not far away, sitting just as he used to sit when she soothed his most despondent moods astride of a chair with his head down on his arms, as if the song suggested the attitude. Her heart quite softened to him as she looked, and she decided to forgive him if no one else, for she was sure that he had no mercenary plans about her tiresome money.

Charlie had assumed a pensive air and fixed his fine eyes upon her with an expression of tender admiration, which made her laugh in spite of all her efforts to seem unconscious of it. She was both amused and annoyed at his very evident desire to remind her of certain sentimental passages in the last year of their girl- and boy-hood, and to change what she had considered a childish joke into romantic earnest. Rose had very serious ideas of love and had no intention of being beguiled into even a flirtation with her handsome cousin.

So Charlie attitudinized unnoticed and was getting rather out of temper when Phebe began to sing, and he forgot all about himself in admiration of her. It took everyone by surprise, for two years of foreign training added to several at home had worked wonders, and the beautiful voice that used to warble cheerily over pots and kettles now rang out melodiously or melted to a mellow music that woke a sympathetic thrill in those who listened. Rose glowed with pride as she accompanied her friend, for Phebe was in her own world now a lovely world where no depressing memory of poorhouse or kitchen, ignorance or loneliness, came to trouble her, a happy world where she could be herself and rule others by the magic of her sweet gift.

Yes, Phebe was herself now, and showed it in the change that came over her at the first note of music. No longer shy and silent, no longer the image of a handsome girl but a blooming woman, alive and full of the eloquence her art gave her, as she laid her hands softly together, fixed her eye on the light, and just poured out her song as simply and joyfully as the lark does soaring toward the sun.

"My faith, Alec that's the sort of voice that wins a man's heart out of his breast!" exclaimed Uncle Mac, wiping his eyes after one of the plaintive ballads that never grow old.

"So it would!" answered Dr. Alec delightedly.

"So it has," added Archie to himself; and he was right, for just at that moment he fell in love with Phebe. He actually did, and could fix the time almost to a second, for at a quarter past nine, he merely thought her a very charming young person; at twenty minutes past, he considered her the loveliest woman he ever beheld; at five and twenty minutes past, she was an angel singing his soul away; and at half after nine he was a lost man, floating over a delicious sea to that temporary heaven on earth where lovers usually land after the first rapturous plunge.

If anyone had mentioned this astonishing fact, nobody would have believed it; nevertheless, it was quite true, and sober, businesslike Archie suddenly discovered a fund of romance at the bottom of his hitherto well-conducted heart that amazed him. He was not quite clear what had happened to him at first, and sat about in a dazed sort of way, seeing, hearing, knowing nothing but Phebe, while the unconscious idol found something wanting in the cordial praise so modestly received because Mr. Archie never said a word.

This was one of the remarkable things which occurred that evening. Another was that Mac paid Rose a compliment, which was such an unprecedented fact, it produced a great sensation, though only one person heard it.

Everybody had gone but Mac and his father, who was busy with the doctor. Aunt Plenty was counting the teaspoons in the dining room, and Phebe was helping her as of old. Mac and Rose were alone he apparently in a brown study, leaning his elbows on the chimneypiece, and she lying back in a low chair looking thoughtfully at the fire. She was tired, and the quiet was grateful to her, so she kept silence and Mac respectfully held his tongue. Presently, however, she became conscious that he was looking at her as intently as eyes and glasses could do it, and without stirring from her comfortable attitude, she said, smiling up at him, "He looks as wise as an owl I wonder what he's thinking about?"

"You, Cousin."

"Something good, I hope?"

"I was thinking Leigh Hunt was about right when he said, 'A girl is the sweetest thing God ever made.'"

"Why, Mac!" and Rose sat bolt upright with an astonished face this was such an entirely unexpected sort of remark for the philosopher to make.

Evidently interested in the new discovery, Mac placidly continued, "Do you know, it seems as if I never really saw a girl before, or had any idea what agreeable creatures they could be. I fancy you are a remarkably good specimen, Rose."

"No, indeed! I'm only hearty and happy, and being safe at home again may make me look better than usual perhaps, but I'm no beauty except to Uncle."

"'Hearty and happy' that must be it," echoed Mac, soberly investigating the problem. "Most girls are sickly or silly, I think I have observed, and that is probably why I am so struck with you."

"Of all the queer boys you are the queerest! Do you really mean that you don't like or notice girls?" asked Rose, much amused at this new peculiarity of her studious cousin.

"Well, no, I am only conscious of two sorts noisy and quiet ones. I prefer the latter, but, as a general thing, I don't notice any of them much more than I do flies, unless they bother me, then I'd like to flap them away, but as that won't do, I hide."

Rose leaned back and laughed until her eyes were full. It was so comical to hear Mac sink his voice to a confidential whisper at the last words and see him smile with sinful satisfaction at the memory of the tormentors he had eluded.

"You needn't laugh it's a fact, I assure you. Charlie likes the creatures, and they spoil him. Steve follows suit, of course. Archie is a respectful slave when he can't help himself. As for me, I don't often give them a chance, and when I get caught I talk science and dead languages till they run for their lives. Now and then I find a sensible one, and then we get on excellently."

"A sad prospect for Phebe and me," sighed Rose, trying to keep sober.

"Phebe is evidently a quiet one. I know she is sensible, or you wouldn't care for her. I can see that she is pleasant to look at, so I fancy I shall like her. As for you, I helped bring you up, therefore I am a little anxious to see how you turn out. I was afraid your foreign polish might spoil you, but I think it has not. In fact, I find you quite satisfactory so far, if you don't mind my saying it. I don't quite know what the charm is, though. Must be the power of inward graces, since you insist that you have no outer ones."

Mac was peering at her with a shrewd smile on his lips, but such a kindly look behind the glasses that she found both words and glance very pleasant and answered merrily, "I am glad you approve of me, and much obliged for your care of my early youth. I hope to be a credit to you and depend on your keeping me straight, for I'm afraid I shall be spoilt among you all."

"I'll keep my eye on you upon one condition," replied the youthful mentor.

"Name it."

"If you are going to have a lot of lovers around, I wash my hands of you. If not, I'm your man."

"You must be sheep dog and help keep them away, for I don't want any yet awhile and, between ourselves, I don't believe I shall have any if it is known that I am strong-minded. That fact will scare most men away like a yellow flag," said Rose, for, thanks to Dr. Alec's guardianship, she had wasted neither heart nor time in the foolish flirtations so many girls fritter away their youth upon.

"Hum! I rather doubt that," muttered Mac as he surveyed the damsel before him.

She certainly did not look unpleasantly strong-minded, and she was beautiful in spite of her modest denials. Beautiful with the truest sort of beauty, for nobility of character lent its subtle charm to the bloom of youth, the freshness of health, the innocence of a nature whose sweet maidenliness Mac felt but could not describe. Gentle yet full of spirit, and all aglow with the earnestness that suggests lovely possibilities and makes one hope that such human flowers may have heaven's purest air and warmest sunshine to blossom in.

"Wait and see," answered Rose; then, as her uncle's voice was heard in the hall, she held out her hand, adding pleasantly, "The old times are to begin again, so come soon and tell me all your doings and help me with mine just as you used to do."

"You really mean it?" And Mac looked much pleased.

"I really do. You are so little altered, except to grow big, that I don't feel at all strange with you and want to begin where we left off."

"That will be capital. Good night, Cousin," and to her great amazement, he gave her a hearty kiss.

"Oh, but that is not the old way at all!" cried Rose, stepping back in merry confusion while the audacious youth assumed an air of mild surprise as he innocently asked: "Didn't we always say good night in that way? I had an impression that we did and were to begin just as we left off."

"Of course not. No power on earth would have bribed you to do it, as you know well enough. I don't mind the first night, but we are too old for that sort of thing now."

"I'll remember. It was the force of habit, I suppose, for I'm sure I must have done it in former times, it seemed so natural. Coming, Father!" and Mac retired, evidently convinced he was right.

"Dear old thing! He is as much a boy as ever, and that is such a comfort, for some of the others have grown up very fast," said Rose to herself, recalling Charlie's sentimental airs and Archie's beatified expression while Phebe sang.

Chapter 2 OLD FRIENDS WITH NEW FACES

"It is so good to be home again! I wonder how we ever made up our minds to go away!" exclaimed Rose as she went roaming about the old house next morning, full of the satisfaction one feels at revisiting familiar nooks and corners and finding them unchanged.

"That we might have the pleasure of coming back again," answered Phebe, walking down the hall beside her little mistress, as happy as she.

"Everything seems just as we left it, even to the rose leaves we used to tuck in here," continued the younger girl, peeping into one of the tall India jars that stood about the hall.

"Don't you remember how Jamie and Pokey used to play Forty Thieves with them, and how you tried to get into that blue one and got stuck, and the other boys found us before I could pull you out?" asked Phebe, laughing.

"Yes, indeed, and speaking of angels, one is apt to hear the rustling of their wings," added Rose, as a shrill whistle came up the avenue accompanied by the clatter of hoofs.

"It is the circus!" cried Phebe gaily as they both recalled the red cart and the charge of the clan.

There was only one boy now, alas, but he made noise enough for half a dozen, and before Rose could run to the door, Jamie came bouncing in with a "shining morning face," a bat over his shoulder, a red and white jockey cap on his head, one pocket bulging with a big ball, the other overflowing with cookies, and his mouth full of the apple he was just finishing off in hot haste.

"Morning! I just looked in to make sure you'd really come and see that you were all right," he observed, saluting with bat and doffing the gay cap with one effective twitch.

"Good morning, dear. Yes, we really are here, and getting to rights as fast as possible. But it seems to me you are rather gorgeous, Jamie. What do you belong to a fire company or a jockey club?" asked Rose, turning up the once chubby face, which now was getting brown and square about the chin.

"No, ma'am! Why, don't you know? I'm captain of the Base Ball Star Club. Look at that, will you?" And, as if the fact were one of national importance, Jamie flung open his jacket to display upon his proudly swelling chest an heart-shaped red flannel shield decorated with a white cotton star the size of a tea plate.

"Superb! I've been away so long I forgot there was such a game. And you the captain?" cried Rose, deeply impressed by the high honor to which her kinsman had arrived.

"I just am, and it's no joke you'd better believe, for we knock our teeth out, black our eyes, and split our fingers almost as well as the big fellows. You come down to the Common between one and two and see us play a match, then you'll understand what hard work it is. I'll teach you to bat now if you'll come out on the lawn," added Jamie, fired with a wish to exhibit his prowess.

"No, thank you, captain. The grass is wet, and you'll be late at school if you stay for us."

"I'm not afraid. Girls are not good for much generally, but you never used to mind a little wet and played cricket like a good one. Can't you ever do that sort of thing now?" asked the boy, with a pitying look at these hapless creatures debarred from the joys and perils of manly sports.

"I can run still and I'll get to the gate before you, see if I don't." And, yielding to the impulse of the moment, Rose darted down the steps before astonished Jamie could mount and follow.

He was off in a moment, but Rose had the start, and though old Sheltie did his best, she reached the goal just ahead, and stood there laughing and panting, all rosy with fresh October air, a pretty picture for several gentlemen who were driving by.

"Good for you, Rose!" said Archie, jumping out to shake hands while Will and Geordie saluted and Uncle Mac laughed at Jamie, who looked as if girls had risen slightly in his opinion.

"I'm glad it is you, because you won't be shocked. But I'm so happy to be back I forgot I was not little Rose still," said Atalanta, smoothing down her flying hair.

"You look very like her, with the curls on your shoulders in the old way. I missed them last night and wondered what it was. How are Uncle and Phebe?" asked Archie, whose eyes had been looking over Rose's head while he spoke toward the piazza, where a female figure was visible among the reddening woodbines.

"All well, thanks. Won't you come up and see for yourselves?"

"Can't, my dear, can't possibly. Business, you know, business. This fellow is my right-hand man, and I can't spare him a minute. Come, Arch, we must be off, or these boys will miss their train," answered Uncle Mac, pulling out his watch.

With a last look from the light-haired figure at the gate to the dark-haired one among the vines, Archie drove away and Jamie cantered after, consoling himself for his defeat with apple number two.

Rose lingered a moment, feeling much inclined to continue her run and pop in upon all the aunts in succession, but, remembering her uncovered head, was about to turn back when a cheerful "Ahoy! ahoy!" made her look up to see Mac approaching at a great pace, waving his hat as he came.

"The Campbells are coming, thick and fast this morning, and the more the merrier," she said, running to meet him. "You look like a good boy going to school, and virtuously conning your lesson by the way," she added, smiling to see him take his finger out of the book he had evidently been reading, and tuck it under his arm, just as he used to do years ago.

"I am a schoolboy, going to the school I like best," he answered, waving a plumy spray of asters as if pointing out the lovely autumn world about them, full of gay hues, fresh airs, and mellow sunshine.

"That reminds me that I didn't get a chance to hear much about your plans last night the other boys all talked at once, and you only got a word now and then. What have you decided to be, Mac?" asked Rose as they went up the avenue side by side.

"A man first, and a good one if possible. After that, what God pleases."

Something in the tone, as well as the words, made Rose look up quickly into Mac's face to see a new expression there. It was indescribable, but she felt as she had often done when watching the mists part suddenly, giving glimpses of some mountaintop, shining serene and high against the blue.

"I think you will be something splendid, for you really look quite glorified, walking under this arch of yellow leaves with the sunshine on your face," she exclaimed, conscious of a sudden admiration never felt before, for Mac was the plainest of all the cousins.

"I don't know about that, but I have my dreams and aspirations, and some of them are pretty high ones. Aim at the best, you know, and keep climbing if you want to get on," he said, looking at the asters with an inward sort of smile, as if he and they had some sweet secret between them.

"You are queerer than ever. But I like your ambition, and hope you will get on. Only mustn't you begin at something soon? I fancied you would study medicine with Uncle that used to be our plan, you know."

"I shall, for the present at least, because I quite agree with you that it is necessary to have an anchor somewhere and not go floating off into the world of imagination without ballast of the right sort. Uncle and I had some talk about it last night and I'm going to begin as soon as possible, for I've mooned long enough," and giving himself a shake, Mac threw down the pretty spray, adding half aloud:

"Chide me not, laborious band,
For the idle flowers I brought:

Every aster in my hand
Goes home laden with a thought."

Rose caught the words and smiled, thinking to herself, "Oh, that's it he is getting into the sentimental age and Aunt Jane has been lecturing him. Dear me, how we are growing up!"

"You look as if you didn't like the prospect very well," she said aloud, for Mac had rammed the volume of Shelley into his pocket and the glorified expression was so entirely gone, Rose fancied she had been mistaken about the mountaintop behind the mists.

"Yes, well enough I always thought the profession a grand one, and where could I find a better teacher than Uncle? I've got into lazy ways lately, and it is high time I went at something useful, so here I go," and Mac abruptly vanished into the study while Rose joined Phebe in Aunt Plenty's room.

The dear old lady had just decided, after long and earnest discussion, which of six favorite puddings should be served for dinner, and thus had a few moments to devote to sentiment, so when Rose came in she held out her arms, saying fondly: "I shall not feel as if I'd got my child back again until I have her in my lap a minute. No, you're not a bit too heavy, my rheumatism doesn't begin much before November, so sit here, darling, and put your two arms round my neck."

Rose obeyed, and neither spoke for a moment as the old woman held the young one close and appeased the two years' longing of a motherly heart by the caresses women give the creatures dearest to them. Right in the middle of a kiss, however, she stopped suddenly and, holding out one arm, caught Phebe, who was trying to steal away unobserved.

"Don't go there's room for both in my love, though there isn't in my lap. I'm so grateful to get my dear girls safely home again that I hardly know what I'm about," said Aunt Plenty, embracing Phebe so heartily that she could not feel left out in the cold and stood there with her black eyes shining through the happiest tears.

"There, now I've had a good hug, and feel as if I was all right again. I wish you'd set that cap in order, Rose I went to bed in such a hurry, I pulled the strings off it and left it all in a heap. Phebe, dear, you shall dust round a mite, just as you used to, for I haven't had anyone to do it as I like since you've been gone, and it will do me good to see all my knickknacks straightened out in your tidy way," said the elder lady, getting up with a refreshed expression on her rosy old face.

"Shall I dust in here too?" asked Phebe, glancing toward an inner room which used to be her care.

"No, dear, I'd rather do that myself. Go in if you like, nothing is changed. I must go and see to my pudding." And Aunt Plenty trotted abruptly away with a quiver of emotion in her voice which made even her last words pathetic.

Pausing on the threshold as if it was a sacred place, the girls looked in with eyes soon dimmed by tender tears, for it seemed as if the gentle occupant was still there. Sunshine shone on the old geraniums by the window; the cushioned chair stood in its accustomed place, with the white wrapper hung across it and the faded slippers lying ready. Books and basket, knitting and spectacles, were all just as she had left them, and the beautiful tranquility that always filled the room seemed so natural, both lookers turned involuntarily toward the bed, where Aunt Peace used to greet them with a smile. There was no sweet old face upon the pillow now, yet the tears that wet the blooming cheeks were not for her who had gone, but for her who was left, because they saw something which spoke eloquently of the love which outlives death and makes the humblest things beautiful and sacred.

143

A well-worn footstool stood beside the bed, and in the high-piled whiteness of the empty couch there was a little hollow where a gray head nightly rested while Aunt Plenty said the prayers her mother taught her seventy years ago.

Without a word, the girls softly shut the door. And while Phebe put the room in the most exquisite order, Rose retrimmed the plain white cap, where pink and yellow ribbons never rustled now, both feeling honored by their tasks and better for their knowledge of the faithful love and piety which sanctified a good old woman's life.

"You darling creature, I'm so glad to get you back! I know it's shamefully early, but I really couldn't keep away another minute. Let me help you I'm dying to see all your splendid things. I saw the trunks pass and I know you've quantities of treasures," cried Annabel Bliss all in one breath as she embraced Rose an hour later and glanced about the room bestrewn with a variety of agreeable objects.

"How well you are looking! Sit down and I'll show you my lovely photographs. Uncle chose all the best for me, and it's a treat to see them," answered Rose, putting a roll on the table and looking about for more.

"Oh, thanks! I haven't time now one needs hours to study such things. Show me your Paris dresses, there's a dear I'm perfectly aching to see the last styles," and Annabel cast a hungry eye toward certain large boxes delightfully suggestive of French finery.

"I haven't got any," said Rose, fondly surveying the fine photographs as she laid them away.

"Rose Campbell! You don't mean to say that you didn't get one Paris dress at least?" cried Annabel, scandalized at the bare idea of such neglect.

"Not one for myself. Aunt Clara ordered several, and will be charmed to show them when her box comes."

"Such a chance! Right there and plenty of money! How could you love your uncle after such cruelty?" sighed Annabel, with a face full of sympathy.

Rose looked puzzled for a minute, then seemed to understand, and assumed a superior air which became her very well as she said, good-naturedly opening a box of laces, "Uncle did not forbid my doing it, and I had money enough, but I chose not to spend it on things of that sort."

"Could and didn't! I can't believe it!" And Annabel sank into a chair, as if the thought was too much for her.

"I did rather want to at first, just for the fun of the thing. In fact, I went and looked at some amazing gowns. But they were very expensive, very much trimmed, and not my style at all, so I gave them up and kept what I valued more than all the gowns Worth every made."

"What in the world was it?" cried Annabel, hoping she would say diamonds.

"Uncle's good opinion," answered Rose, looking thoughtfully into the depths of a packing case, where lay the lovely picture that would always remind her of the little triumph over girlish vanity, which not only kept but increased "Uncle's good opinion."

"Oh, indeed!" said Annabel blankly, and fell to examining Aunt Plenty's lace while Rose went on with a happy smile in her eyes as she dived into another trunk.

144

"Uncle thinks one has no right to waste money on such things, but he is very generous and loves to give useful, beautiful, or curious gifts. See, all these pretty ornaments are for presents, and you shall choose first whatever you like."

"He's a perfect dear!" cried Annabel, reveling in the crystal, filigree, coral, and mosaic trinkets spread before her while Rose completed her rapture by adding sundry tasteful trifles fresh from Paris.

"Now tell me, when do you mean to have your coming-out party? I ask because I've nothing ready and want plenty of time, for I suppose it will be the event of the season," asked Annabel a few minutes later as she wavered between a pink coral and a blue lava set.

"I came out when I went to Europe, but I suppose Aunty Plen will want to have some sort of merry-making to celebrate our return. I shall begin as I mean to go on, and have a simple, sociable sort of party and invite everyone whom I like, no matter in what 'set' they happen to belong. No one shall ever say I am aristocratic and exclusive so prepare yourself to be shocked, for old friends and young, rich and poor, will be asked to all my parties."

"Oh, my heart! You are going to be odd, just as Mama predicted!" sighed Annabel, clasping her hands in despair and studying the effect of three bracelets on her chubby arm in the midst of her woe.

"In my own house I'm going to do as I think best, and if people call me odd, I can't help it. I shall endeavor not to do anything very dreadful, but I seem to inherit Uncle's love for experiments and mean to try some. I daresay they will fail and I shall get laughed at. I intend to do it nevertheless, so you had better drop me now before I begin," said Rose with an air of resolution that was rather alarming.

"What shall you wear at this new sort of party of yours?" asked Annabel, wisely turning a deaf ear to all delicate or dangerous topics and keeping to matters she understood.

"That white thing over there. It is fresh and pretty, and Phebe has one like it. I never want to dress more than she does, and gowns of that sort are always most becoming and appropriate to girls of our age."

"Phebe! You don't mean to say you are going to make a lady of her!" gasped Annabel, upsetting her treasures as she fell back with a gesture that made the little chair creak again, for Miss Bliss was as plump as a partridge.

"She is one already, and anybody who slights her slights me, for she is the best girl I know and the dearest," cried Rose warmly.

"Yes, of course I was only surprised you are quite right, for she may turn out to be somebody, and then how glad you'll feel that you were so good to her!" said Annabel, veering around at once, seeing which way the wind blew.

Before Rose could speak again, a cheery voice called from the hall, "Little mistress, where are you?"

"In my room, Phebe, dear," and up came the girl Rose was going to "make a lady of," looking so like one that Annabel opened her china-blue eyes and smiled involuntarily as Phebe dropped a little curtsey in playful imitation of her old manner and said quietly: "How do you do, Miss Bliss?"

"Glad to see you back, Miss Moore," answered Annabel, shaking hands in a way that settled the question of Phebe's place in her mind forever, for the stout damsel had a kind heart in spite of a weak head and was really fond of Rose. It was evidently "Love me, love my Phebe," so she made up her mind on the spot that Phebe was somebody, and that gave an air of romance even to the poorhouse.

She could not help staring a little as she watched the two friends work together and listened to their happy talk over each new treasure as it came to light, for every look and word plainly showed that years of close companionship had made them very dear to one another. It was pretty to see Rose try to do the hardest part of any little job herself still prettier to see Phebe circumvent her and untie the hard knots, fold the stiff papers, or lift the heavy trays with her own strong hands, and prettiest of all to hear her say in a motherly tone, as she put Rose into an easy chair: "Now, my deary, sit and rest, for you will have to see company all day, and I can't let you get tired out so early."

"That is no reason why I should let you either. Call Jane to help or I'll bob up again directly," answered Rose, with a very bad assumption of authority.

"Jane may take my place downstairs, but no one shall wait on you here except me, as long as I'm with you," said stately Phebe, stooping to put a hassock under the feet of her little mistress.

"It is very nice and pretty to see, but I don't know what people will say when she goes into society with the rest of us. I do hope Rose won't be very odd," said Annabel to herself as she went away to circulate the depressing news that there was to be no grand ball and, saddest disappointment of all, that Rose had not a single Paris costume with which to refresh the eyes and rouse the envy of her amiable friends.

"Now I've seen or heard from all the boys but Charlie, and I suppose he is too busy. I wonder what he is about," thought Rose, turning from the hall door, whither she had courteously accompanied her guest.

The wish was granted a moment after, for, going into the parlor to decide where some of her pictures should hang, she saw a pair of brown boots at one end of the sofa, a tawny-brown head at the other, and discovered that Charlie was busily occupied in doing nothing.

"The voice of the Bliss was heard in the land, so I dodged till she went upstairs, and then took a brief siesta while waiting to pay my respects to the distinguished traveler, Lady Hester Stanhope," he said, leaping up to make his best bow.

"The voice of the sluggard would be a more appropriate quotation, I think. Does Annabel still pine for you?" asked Rose, recalling certain youthful jokes upon the subject of unrequited affections.

"Not a bit of it. Fun has cut me out, and the fair Annabella will be Mrs. Tokio before the winter is over if I'm not much mistaken."

"What, little Fun See? How droll it seems to think of him grown up and married to Annabel of all people! She never said a word about him, but this accounts for her admiring my pretty Chinese things and being so interested in Canton."

"Little Fun is a great swell now, and much enamored of our fat friend, who will take to chopsticks whenever he says the word. I needn't ask how you do, Cousin, for you beat that Aurora all hollow in the way of color. I should have been up before, but I thought you'd like a good rest after your voyage."

"I was running a race with Jamie before nine o'clock. What were you doing, young man?"

"'Sleeping I dreamed, love, dreamed, love, of thee,'" began Charlie, but Rose cut him short by saying as reproachfully as she could, while the culprit stood regarding her with placid satisfaction: "You ought to have been up and at work like the rest of the boys. I felt like a drone in a hive of very busy bees when I saw them all hurrying off to their business."

"But, my dear girl, I've got no business. I'm making up my mind, you see, and do the ornamental while I'm deciding. There always ought to be one gentleman in a family, and that seems to be rather my line," answered Charlie, posing for the character with an assumption of languid elegance which would have been very effective if his twinkling eyes had not spoilt it.

"There are none but gentlemen in our family, I hope," answered Rose, with the proud air she always wore when anything was said derogatory to the name of Campbell.

"Of course, of course. I should have said gentleman of leisure. You see it is against my principles to slave as Archie does. What's the use? Don't need the money, got plenty, so why not enjoy it and keep jolly as long as possible? I'm sure cheerful people are public benefactors in this world of woe."

It was not easy to object to this proposition, especially when made by a comely young man who looked the picture of health and happiness as he sat on the arm of the sofa smiling at his cousin in the most engaging manner. Rose knew very well that the Epicurean philosophy was not the true one to begin life upon, but it was difficult to reason with Charlie because he always dodged sober subjects and was so full of cheery spirits, one hated to lessen the sort of sunshine which certainly is a public benefactor.

"You have such a clever way of putting things that I don't know how to contradict you, though I still think I'm right," she said gravely. "Mac likes to idle as well as you, but he is not going to do it because he knows it's bad for him to fritter away his time. He is going to study a profession like a wise boy, though he would much prefer to live among his beloved books or ride his hobbies in peace."

"That's all very well for him, because he doesn't care for society and may as well be studying medicine as philandering about the woods with his pockets full of musty philosophers and old-fashioned poets," answered Charlie with a shrug which plainly expressed his opinion of Mac.

"I wonder if musty philosophers, like Socrates and Aristotle, and old-fashioned poets, like Shakespeare and Milton, are not safer company for him to keep than some of the more modern friends you have?" said Rose, remembering Jamie's hints about wild oats, for she could be a little sharp sometimes and had not lectured "the boys" for so long it seemed unusually pleasant.

But Charlie changed the subject skillfully by exclaiming with an anxious expression: "I do believe you are going to be like Aunt Jane, for that's just the way she comes down on me whenever she gets the chance! Don't take her for a model, I beg she is a good woman but a mighty disagreeable one in my humble opinion."

The fear of being disagreeable is a great bugbear to a girl, as this artful young man well knew, and Rose fell into the trap at once, for Aunt Jane was far from being her model, though she could not help respecting her worth.

"Have you given up your painting?" she asked rather abruptly, turning to a gilded Fra Angelico angel which leaned in the sofa corner.

147

"Sweetest face I ever saw, and very like you about the eyes, isn't it?" said Charlie, who seemed to have a Yankee trick of replying to one question with another.

"I want an answer, not a compliment," and Rose tried to look severe as she put away the picture more quickly than she had taken it up.

"Have I given up painting? Oh, no! I daub a little in oils, slop a little in watercolors, sketch now and then, and poke about the studios when the artistic fit comes on."

"How is the music?"

"More flourishing. I don't practice much, but sing a good deal in company. Set up a guitar last summer and went troubadouring round in great style. The girls like it, and it's jolly among the fellows."

"Are you studying anything?"

"Well, I have some lawbooks on my table good, big, wise-looking chaps and I take a turn at them semioccasionally when pleasure palls or parents chide. But I doubt if I do more than learn what 'a allybi' is this year," and a sly laugh in Charlie's eye suggested that he sometimes availed himself of this bit of legal knowledge.

"What do you do then?"

"Fair catechist, I enjoy myself. Private theatricals have been the rage of late, and I have won such laurels that I seriously think of adopting the stage as my profession."

"Really!" cried Rose, alarmed.

"Why not? If I must go to work, isn't that as good as anything?"

"Not without more talent than I think you possess. With genius one can do anything without it one had better let the stage alone."

"There's a quencher for the 'star of the goodlie companie' to which I belong. Mac hasn't a ray of genius for anything, yet you admire him for trying to be an M.D.," cried Charlie, rather nettled at her words.

"It is respectable, at all events, and I'd rather be a second-rate doctor than a second-rate actor. But I know you don't mean it, and only say so to frighten me."

"Exactly. I always bring it up when anyone begins to lecture and it works wonders. Uncle Mac turns pale, the aunts hold up their hands in holy horror, and a general panic ensues. Then I magnanimously promise not to disgrace the family and in the first burst of gratitude the dear souls agree to everything I ask, so peace is restored and I go on my way rejoicing."

"Just the way you used to threaten to run off to sea if your mother objected to any of your whims. You are not changed in that respect, though you are in others. You had great plans and projects once, Charlie, and now you seem to be contented with being a 'jack of all trades and master of none'".

"Boyish nonsense! Time has brought wisdom, and I don't see the sense of tying myself down to one particular thing and grinding away at it year after year. People of one idea get so deucedly narrow and tame, I've no patience with them. Culture is the thing, and the sort one gets by ranging over a wide field is the easiest to acquire, the handiest to have, and the most successful in the end. At any rate, it is the kind I like and the only kind I intend to bother myself about."

With this declaration, Charlie smoothed his brow, clasped his hands over his head, and, leaning back, gently warbled the chorus of a college song as if it expressed his views of life better than he could:

> "While our rosy fillets shed
> Blushes o'er each fervid head,
> With many a cup and many a smile
> The festal moments we beguile."

"Some of my saints here were people of one idea, and though they were not very successful from a worldly point of view while alive, they were loved and canonized when dead," said Rose, who had been turning over a pile of photographs on the table and just then found her favorite, St. Francis, among them.

"This is more to my taste. Those worn-out, cadaverous fellows give me the blues, but here's a gentlemanly saint who takes things easy and does good as he goes along without howling over his own sins or making other people miserable by telling them of theirs." And Charlie laid a handsome St. Martin beside the brown-frocked monk.

Rose looked at both and understood why her cousin preferred the soldierly figure with the sword to the ascetic with his crucifix. One was riding bravely through the world in purple and fine linen, with horse and hound and squires at his back; and the other was in a lazar-house, praying over the dead and dying. The contrast was a strong one, and the girl's eyes lingered longest on the knight, though she said thoughtfully, "Yours is certainly the pleasantest and yet I never heard of any good deed he did, except divide his cloak with a beggar, while St. Francis gave himself to charity just when life was most tempting and spent years working for God without reward. He's old and poor, and in a dreadful place, but I won't give him up, and you may have your gay St. Martin if you want him."

"No, thank you, saints are not in my line but I'd like the golden-haired angel in the blue gown if you'll let me have her. She shall be my little Madonna, and I'll pray to her like a good Catholic," answered Charlie, turning to the delicate, deep-eyed figure with the lilies in its hand.

"With all my heart, and any others that you like. Choose some for your mother and give them to her with my love."

So Charlie sat down beside Rose to turn and talk over the pictures for a long and pleasant hour. But when they went away to lunch, if there had been anyone to observe so small but significant a trifle, good St. Francis lay face downward behind the sofa, while gallant St. Martin stood erect upon the chimneypiece.

Chapter 3 MISS CAMPBELL
While the travelers unpack their trunks, we will pick up, as briefly as possible, the dropped stitches in the little romance we are weaving.

Rose's life had been a very busy and quiet one for the four years following the May day when she made her choice. Study, exercise, housework, and many wholesome pleasures kept her a happy, hearty creature, yearly growing in womanly graces, yet always preserving the innocent freshness girls lose so soon when too early set upon the world's stage and given a part to play.

Not a remarkably gifted girl in any way, and far from perfect; full of all manner of youthful whims and fancies; a little spoiled by much love; rather apt to think all lives as safe and sweet as her own; and, when want or pain appealed to her, the tender heart overflowed with a remorseful charity which gave of its abundance recklessly. Yet, with all her human imperfections, the upright nature of the child kept her desires climbing toward the just and pure and true, as flowers struggle to the light; and the woman's soul was budding beautifully under the green leaves behind the little thorns.

At seventeen, Dr. Alec pronounced her ready for the voyage around the world, which he considered a better finishing off than any school could give her. But just then Aunt Peace began to fail and soon slipped quietly away to rejoin the lover she had waited for so long. Youth seemed to come back in a mysterious way to touch the dead face with lost loveliness, and all the romance of her past to gather around her memory. Unlike most aged women, her friends were among the young, and at her funeral the grayheads gave place to the band of loving girls who made the sweet old maiden ready for her rest, bore her pall, and covered her grave with the white flowers she had never worn.

When this was over poor Aunt Plenty seemed so lost without her lifelong charge that Dr. Alec would not leave her, and Rose gladly paid the debt she owed by the tender service which comforts without words. But Aunt Plenty, having lived for others all her days, soon rebelled against this willing sacrifice, soon found strength in her own sincere piety, solace in cheerful occupation, and amusement in nursing Aunt Myra, who was a capital patient, as she never died and never got well.

So at last the moment came when, with free minds, the travelers could set out, and on Rose's eighteenth birthday, with Uncle Alec and the faithful Phebe, she sailed away to see and study the big, beautiful world which lies ready for us all if we only know how to use and enjoy it.

Phebe was set to studying music in the best schools, and while she trained her lovely voice with happy industry, Rose and her uncle roamed about in the most delightful way till two years were gone like a dream and those at home clamored for their return.

Back they came, and now the heiress must make ready to take her place, for at twenty-one she came into possession of the fortune she had been trying to learn how to use well. Great plans fermented in her brain, for, though the heart was as generous as ever, time had taught her prudence and observation shown her that the wisest charity is that which helps the poor to help themselves.

Dr. Alec found it a little difficult to restrain the ardor of this young philanthropist who wanted to begin at once to endow hospitals, build homes, adopt children, and befriend all mankind.

"Take a little time to look about you and get your bearings, child. The world you have been living in is a much simpler, honester one than that you are now to enter. Test yourself a bit and see if the old ways seem best after all, for you are old enough to decide, and wise enough to discover, what is for your truest good, I hope," he said, trying to feel ready to let the bird escape from under his wing and make little flights alone.

"Now, Uncle, I'm very much afraid you are going to be disappointed in me," answered Rose with unusual hesitation yet a very strong desire visible in her eyes. "You like to have me quite honest, and I've learned to tell you all my foolish thoughts so I'll speak out, and if you find my wish very wrong and silly, please say so, for I don't want you to cast me off entirely, though I am grown up. You say, wait a little, test myself, and try if the old ways are best. I should like to do that, and can

I in a better way than leading the life other girls lead? Just for a little while," she added, as her uncle's face grew grave.

He was disappointed, yet acknowledged that the desire was natural and in a moment saw that a trial of this sort might have its advantages. Nevertheless, he dreaded it, for he had intended to choose her society carefully and try to keep her unspoiled by the world as long as possible, like many another fond parent and guardian. But the spirit of Eve is strong in all her daughters forbidden fruit will look rosier to them than any in their own orchards, and the temptation to take just one little bite proves irresistible to the wisest. So Rose, looking out from the safe seclusion of her girlhood into the woman's kingdom which she was about to take possession of, felt a sudden wish to try its pleasures before assuming its responsibilities, and was too sincere to hide the longing.

"Very well, my dear, try it if you like, only take care of your health be temperate in your gaiety and don't lose more than you gain, if that is possible," he added under his breath, endeavoring to speak cheerfully and not look anxious.

"I know it is foolish, but I do want to be a regular butterfly for a little while and see what it is like. You know I couldn't help seeing a good deal of fashionable life abroad, though we were not in it, and here at home the girls tell me about all sorts of pleasant things that are to happen this winter, so if you won't despise me very much, I should like to try it."

"For how long?"

"Would three months be too long? New Year is a good time to take a fresh start. Everyone is going to welcome me, so I must be gay in spite of myself, unless I'm willing to seem very ungrateful and morose," said Rose, glad to have so good a reason to offer for her new experiment.

"You may like it so well that the three months may become years. Pleasure is very sweet when we are young."

"Do you think it will intoxicate me?"

"We shall see, my dear."

"We shall!" And Rose marched away, looking as if she had taken a pledge of some sort, and meant to keep it.

It was a great relief to the public mind when it became known that Miss Campbell was really coming out at last, and invitations to Aunt Plenty's party were promptly accepted. Aunt Clara was much disappointed about the grand ball she had planned, but Rose stood firm, and the dear old lady had her way about everything.

The consequence was a delightfully informal gathering of friends to welcome the travelers home. Just a good, old-fashioned, hospitable housewarming, so simple, cordial, and genuine that those who came to criticize remained to enjoy, and many owned the charm they could neither describe nor imitate.

Much curiosity was felt about Phebe, and much gossip went on behind fans that evening, for those who had known her years ago found it hard to recognize the little housemaid in the handsome young woman who bore herself with such quiet dignity and charmed them all with her fine voice. "Cinderella has turned out a princess," was the general verdict, and Rose enjoyed the little sensation immensely, for she had had many battles to fight for her Phebe since she came among them, and now her faith was vindicated.

151

Miss Campbell herself was in great demand and did the honors so prettily that even Miss Bliss forgave her for her sad neglect of Worth, though she shook her head over the white gowns, just alike except that Phebe wore crimson and Rose, blue trimmings.

The girls swarmed eagerly around their recovered friend, for Rose had been a favorite before she went away and found her throne waiting for her now. The young men privately pronounced Phebe the handsomest "But then you know there's neither family nor money, so it's no use." Phebe, therefore, was admired as one of the ornamental properties belonging to the house and left respectfully alone.

But bonny Rose was "all right," as these amiable youths expressed it, and many a wistful eye followed the bright head as it flitted about the rooms as if it were a second Golden Fleece to be won with difficulty, for stalwart kinsmen hedged it round, and watchful aunts kept guard.

Little wonder that the girl found her new world an enchanting one and that her first sip of pleasure rather went to her head, for everybody welcomed and smiled on her, flattered and praised, whispered agreeable prophecies in her ear, and looked the compliments and congratulations they dared not utter till she felt as if she must have left her old self somewhere abroad and suddenly become a new and wonderfully gifted being.

"It is very nice, Uncle, and I'm not sure I mayn't want another three months of it when the first are gone," she whispered to Dr. Alec as he stood watching the dance she was leading with Charlie in the long hall after supper.

"Steady, my lass, steady, and remember that you are not really a butterfly but a mortal girl with a head that will ache tomorrow," he answered, watching the flushed and smiling face before him. "I almost wish there wasn't any tomorrow, but that tonight would last forever it is so pleasant, and everyone so kind," she said with a little sigh of happiness as she gathered up her fleecy skirts like a white bird pluming itself for flight.

"I'll ask your opinion about that at two A.M.," began her uncle with a warning nod.

"I'll give it honestly," was all Rose had time to say before Charlie swept her away into the particolored cloud before them.

"It's no use, Alec train a girl as wisely as you choose, she will break loose when the time comes and go in for pleasure as eagerly as the most frivolous, for 'tis their nature to,'" said Uncle Mac, keeping time to the music as if he would not mind "going in" for a bit of pleasure himself.

"My girl shall taste and try, but unless I'm much mistaken, a little bit of it will satisfy her. I want to see if she will stand the test, because if not, all my work is a failure and I'd like to know it," answered the doctor with a hopeful smile on his lips but an anxious look in his eyes.

"She will come out all right bless her heart! so let her sow her innocent wild oats and enjoy herself till she is ready to settle down. I wish all our young folks were likely to have as small a crop and get through as safely as she will," added Uncle Mac with a shake of the head as he glanced at some of the young men revolving before him.

"Nothing amiss with your lads, I hope?"

"No, thank heaven! So far I've had little trouble with either, though Mac is an odd stick and Steve a puppy. I don't complain, for both will outgrow that sort of thing and are good fellows at heart, thanks to their mother. But Clara's boy is in a bad way, and she will spoil him as a man as she has as a boy if his father doesn't interfere."

"I told brother Stephen all about him when I was in Calcutta last year, and he wrote to the boy, but Clara has got no end of plans in her head and so she insisted on keeping Charlie a year longer when his father ordered him off to India," replied the doctor as they walked away.

"It is too late to 'order' Charlie is a man now, and Stephen will find he has been too easy with him all these years. Poor fellow, it has been hard lines for him, and is likely to be harder, I fancy, unless he comes home and straightens things out."

"He won't do that if he can help it. He has lost all his energy living in that climate and hates worry more than ever, so you can imagine what an effort it would be to manage a foolish woman and a headstrong boy. We must lend a hand, Mac, and do our best for poor old Steve."

"The best we can do for the lad is to marry and settle him as soon as possible."

"My dear fellow, he is only three and twenty," began the doctor, as if the idea was preposterous. Then a sudden change came over him as he added with a melancholy smile, "I forget how much one can hope and suffer, even at twenty-three."

"And be all the better for, if bravely outlived," said Uncle Mac, with his hand on his brother's shoulder and the sincerest approval in his voice. Then, kindly returning to the younger people, he went on inquiringly, "You don't incline to Clara's view of a certain matter, I fancy?"

"Decidedly not. My girl must have the best, and Clara's training would spoil an angel," answered Dr. Alec quickly.

"But we shall find it hard to let our little Rose go out of the family. How would Archie do? He has been well brought up and is a thoroughly excellent lad."

The brothers had retired to the study by this time and were alone, yet Dr. Alec lowered his voice as he said with a tender sort of anxiety pleasant to see: "You know I do not approve of cousins marrying, so I'm in a quandary, Mac, for I love the child as if she were my own and feel as if I could not give her up to any man whom I did not know and trust entirely. It is of no use for us to plan, for she must choose for herself yet I do wish we could keep her among us and give one of our boys a wife worth having."

"We must, so never mind your theories but devote yourself to testing our elder lads and making one of them a happy fellow. All are heart-whole, I believe, and, though young still for this sort of thing, we can be gently shaping matters for them, since no one knows how soon the moment may come. My faith it is like living in a powder mill to be among a lot of young folks nowadays! All looks as calm as possible till a sudden spark produces an explosion, and heaven only knows where we find ourselves after it is over."

And Uncle Mac sat himself comfortably down to settle Rose's fate while the doctor paced the room, plucking at his beard and knitting his brows as if he found it hard to see his way.

"Yes, Archie is a good fellow," he said, answering the question he had ignored before. "An upright, steady, intelligent lad who will make an excellent husband if he ever finds out that he has a heart. I suppose I'm an old fool, but I do like a little more romance in a young man than he seems to have more warmth and enthusiasm, you know. Bless the boy! He might be forty instead of three or four and twenty, he's so sober, calm, and cool. I'm younger than he is, and could go a-wooing like a Romeo if I had any heart to offer a woman."

153

The doctor looked rather shamefaced as he spoke, and his brother burst out laughing. "See here, Alec, it's a pity so much romance and excellence as yours should be lost, so why don't you set these young fellows an example and go a-wooing yourself? Jessie has been wondering how you have managed to keep from falling in love with Phebe all this time, and Clara is quite sure that you waited only till she was safe under Aunt Plenty's wing to offer yourself in the good old-fashioned style."

"I!" And the doctor stood aghast at the mere idea, then he gave a resigned sort of sigh and added like a martyr, "If those dear women would let me alone, I'd thank them forever. Put the idea out of their minds for heaven's sake, Mac, or I shall be having that poor girl flung at my head and her comfort destroyed. She is a fine creature and I'm proud of her, but she deserves a better lot than to be tied to an old fellow like me whose only merit is his fidelity."

"As you please, I was only joking," and Uncle Mac dropped the subject with secret relief. The excellent man thought a good deal of family and had been rather worried at the hints of the ladies. After a moment's silence he returned to a former topic, which was rather a pet plan of his. "I don't think you do Archie justice, Alec. You don't know him as well as I do, but you'll find that he has heart enough under his cool, quiet manner. I've grown very fond of him, think highly of him, and don't see how you could do better for Rose than to give her to him."

"If she will go," said the doctor, smiling at his brother's businesslike way of disposing of the young people.

"She'll do anything to please you," began Uncle Mac in perfect good faith, for twenty-five years in the society of a very prosaic wife had taken nearly all the romance out of him.

"It is of no use for us to plan, and I shall never interfere except to advise, and if I were to choose one of the boys, I should incline to my godson," answered the doctor gravely.

"What, my Ugly Duckling!" exclaimed Uncle Mac in great surprise.

"The Ugly Duckling turned out a swan, you remember. I've always been fond of the boy because he's so genuine and original. Crude as a green apple now, but sound at the core, and only needs time to ripen. I'm sure he'll turn out a capital specimen of the Campbell variety."

"Much obliged, Alec, but it will never do at all. He's a good fellow, and may do something to be proud of by and by, but he's not the mate for our Rose. She needs someone who can manage her property when we are gone, and Archie is the man for that, depend upon it."

"Confound the property!" cried Dr. Alec impetuously. "I want her to be happy, and I don't care how soon she gets rid of her money if it is going to be a millstone round her neck. I declare to you, I dreaded the thought of this time so much that I've kept her away as long as I could and trembled whenever a young fellow joined us while we were abroad. Had one or two narrow escapes, and now I'm in for it, as you can see by tonight's 'success' as Clara calls it. Thank heaven I haven't many daughters to look after!"

"Come, come, don't be anxious take Archie and settle it right up safely and happily. That's my advice, and you'll find it sound," replied the elder conspirator, like one having experience.

"I'll think of it, but mind you, Mac, not a word of this to the sisters. We are a couple of old fools to be matchmaking so soon but I see what is before me and it's a comfort to free my mind to someone."

"So it is. Depend on me not a breath even to Jane," answered Uncle Mac, with a hearty shake and a sympathetic slap on the shoulder.

"Why, what dark and awful secrets are going on here? Is it a Freemason's Lodge and those the mystic signs?" asked a gay voice at the door; and there stood Rose, full of smiling wonder at the sight of her two uncles hand in hand, whispering and nodding to one another mysteriously.

They stared like schoolboys caught plotting mischief and looked so guilty that she took pity on them, innocently imagining the brothers were indulging in a little sentiment on this joyful occasion, so she added quickly, as she beckoned, without crossing the threshold, "Women not allowed, of course, but both of you dear Odd Fellows are wanted, for Aunt Plenty begs we will have an old-fashioned contra dance, and I'm to lead off with Uncle Mac. I chose you, sir, because you do it in style, pigeon wings and all. So, please come and Phebe is waiting for you, Uncle Alec. She is rather shy you know, but will enjoy it with you to take care of her."

"Thank you, thank you!" cried both gentlemen, following with great alacrity.

Unconscious, Rose enjoyed that Virginia reel immensely, for the pigeon wings were superb, and her partner conducted her through the convolutions of the dance without a fault, going down the middle in his most gallant style. Landing safely at the bottom, she stood aside to let him get his breath, for stout Uncle Mac was bound to do or die on that occasion and would have danced his pumps through without a murmur if she had desired it.

Leaning against the wall with his hair in his eyes, and a decidedly bored expression of countenance, was Mac, Jr., who had been surveying the gymnastics of his parent with respectful astonishment.

"Come and take a turn, my lad. Rose is fresh as a daisy, but we old fellows soon get enough of it, so you shall have my place," said his father, wiping his face, which glowed like a cheerful peony.

"No, thank you, sir I can't stand that sort of thing. I'll race you round the piazza with pleasure, Cousin, but his oven is too much for me," was Mac's uncivil reply as he backed toward the open window, as if glad of an excuse to escape.

"Fragile creature, don't stay on my account, I beg. I can't leave my guests for a moonlight run, even if I dared to take it on a frosty night in a thin dress," said Rose, fanning herself and not a bit ruffled by Mac's refusal, for she knew his ways and they amused her.

"Not half so bad as all this dust, gas, heat, and noise. What do you suppose lungs are made of?" demanded Mac, ready for a discussion then and there.

"I used to know, but I've forgotten now. Been so busy with other things that I've neglected the hobbies I used to ride five or six years ago," she said, laughing.

"Ah, those were times worth having! Are you going in for much of this sort of thing, Rose?" he asked with a disapproving glance at the dancers.

"About three months of it, I think."

"Then good-bye till New Year." And Mac vanished behind the curtains.

"Rose, my dear, you really must take that fellow in hand before he gets to be quite a bear. Since you have been gone he has lived in his books and got on so finely that we have let him alone, though his mother groans over his manners. Polish him up a bit, I beg of you, for it is high time he mended his odd ways and did justice to the fine gifts he hides behind them," said Uncle Mac, scandalized at the bluntness of his son.

"I know my chestnut burr too well to mind his prickles. But others do not, so I will take him in hand and make him a credit to his family," answered Rose readily.

"Take Archie for your model he's one of a thousand, and the girl who gets him gets a prize, I do assure you," added Uncle Mac, who found matchmaking to his taste and thought that closing remark a deep one.

"Oh, me, how tired I am!" cried Rose, dropping into a chair as the last carriage rolled away somewhere between one and two.

"What is your opinion now, Miss Campbell?" asked the doctor, addressing her for the first time by the name which had been uttered so often that night.

"My opinion is that Miss Campbell is likely to have a gay life if she goes on as she has begun, and that she finds it very delightful so far," answered the girl, with lips still smiling from their first taste of what the world calls pleasure.

Chapter 4 THORNS AMONG THE ROSES
For a time everything went smoothly, and Rose was a happy girl. The world seemed a beautiful and friendly place, and fulfillment of her brightest dreams appeared to be a possibility. Of course this could not last, and disappointment was inevitable, because young eyes look for a Paradise and weep when they find a workaday world which seems full of care and trouble till one learns to gladden and glorify it with high thoughts and holy living.

Those who loved her waited anxiously for the disillusion which must come in spite of all their cherishing, for till now Rose had been so busy with her studies, travels, and home duties that she knew very little of the triumphs, trials, and temptations of fashionable life. Birth and fortune placed her where she could not well escape some of them, and Dr. Alec, knowing that experience is the best teacher, wisely left her to learn this lesson as she must many another, devoutly hoping that it would not be a hard one.

October and November passed rapidly, and Christmas was at hand, with all its merry mysteries, home gatherings, and good wishes.

Rose sat in her own little sanctum, opening from the parlor, busily preparing gifts for the dear five hundred friends who seemed to grow fonder and fonder as the holidays drew near. The drawers of her commode stood open, giving glimpses of dainty trifles, which she was tying up with bright ribbons.

A young girl's face at such moments is apt to be a happy one, but Rose's was very grave as she worked, and now and then she threw a parcel into the drawer with a careless toss, as if no love made the gift precious. So unusual was this expression that it struck Dr. Alec as he came in and brought an anxious look to his eyes, for any cloud on that other countenance dropped its shadow over his.

"Can you spare a minute from your pretty work to take a stitch in my old glove?" he asked, coming up to the table strewn with ribbon, lace, and colored papers.

"Yes, Uncle, as many as you please."

The face brightened with sudden sunshine; both hands were put out to receive the shabby driving glove, and the voice was full of that affectionate alacrity which makes the smallest service sweet.

"My Lady Bountiful is hard at work, I see. Can I help in any way?" he asked, glancing at the display before him.

"No, thank you, unless you can make me as full of interest and pleasure in these things as I used to be. Don't you think preparing presents a great bore, except for those you love and who love you?" she added in a tone which had a slight tremor in it as she uttered the last words.

"I don't give to people whom I care nothing for. Can't do it, especially at Christmas, when goodwill should go into everything one does. If all these 'pretties' are for dear friends, you must have a great many."

"I thought they were friends, but I find many of them are not, and that's the trouble, sir."

"Tell me all about it, dear, and let the old glove go," he said, sitting down beside her with his most sympathetic air.

But she held the glove fast, saying eagerly, "No, no, I love to do this! I don't feel as if I could look at you while I tell what a bad, suspicious girl I am," she added, keeping her eyes on her work.

"Very well, I'm ready for confessions of any iniquity and glad to get them, for sometimes lately I've seen a cloud in my girl's eyes and caught a worried tone in her voice. Is there a bitter drop in the cup that promised to be so sweet, Rose?"

"Yes, Uncle. I've tried to think there was not, but it is there, and I don't like it. I'm ashamed to tell, and yet I want to, because you will show me how to make it sweet or assure me that I shall be the better for it, as you used to do when I took medicine."

She paused a minute, sewing swiftly; then out came the trouble all in one burst of girlish grief and chagrin.

"Uncle, half the people who are so kind to me don't care a bit for me, but for what I can give them, and that makes me unhappy, because I was so glad and proud to be liked. I do wish I hadn't a penny in the world, then I should know who my true friends were."

"Poor little lass! She has found out that all that glitters is not gold, and the disillusion has begun," said the doctor to himself, adding aloud, smiling yet pitiful, "And so all the pleasure is gone out of the pretty gifts and Christmas is a failure?"

"Oh, no not for those whom nothing can make me doubt! It is sweeter than ever to make these things, because my heart is in every stitch and I know that, poor as they are, they will be dear to you, Aunty Plen, Aunt Jessie, Phebe, and the boys."

She opened a drawer where lay a pile of pretty gifts, wrought with loving care by her own hands, touching them tenderly as she spoke and patting the sailor's knot of blue ribbon on one fat parcel with a smile that told how unshakable her faith in someone was. "But these," she said, pulling open another drawer and tossing over its gay contents with an air half sad, half scornful, "these I

157

bought and give because they are expected. These people care only for a rich gift, not one bit for the giver, whom they will secretly abuse if she is not as generous as they expect. How can I enjoy that sort of thing, Uncle?"

"You cannot, but perhaps you do some of them injustice, my dear. Don't let the envy or selfishness of a few poison your faith in all. Are you sure that none of these girls care for you?" he asked, reading a name here and there on the parcels scattered about.

"I'm afraid I am. You see I heard several talking together the other evening at Annabel's, only a few words, but it hurt me very much, for nearly everyone was speculating on what I would give them and hoping it would be something fine. 'She's so rich she ought to be generous,' said one. 'I've been perfectly devoted to her for weeks and hope she won't forget it,' said another. 'If she doesn't give me some of her gloves, I shall think she's very mean, for she has heaps, and I tried on a pair in fun so she could see they fitted and take a hint,' added a third. I did take the hint, you see." And Rose opened a handsome box in which lay several pairs of her best gloves, with buttons enough to satisfy the heart of the most covetous.

"Plenty of silver paper and perfume, but not much love went into that bundle, I fancy?" And Dr. Alec could not help smiling at the disdainful little gesture with which Rose pushed away the box.

"Not a particle, nor in most of these. I have given them what they wanted and taken back the confidence and respect they didn't care for. It is wrong, I know, but I can't bear to think all the seeming goodwill and friendliness I've been enjoying was insincere and for a purpose. That's not the way I treat people."

"I am sure of it. Take things for what they are worth, dear, and try to find the wheat among the tares, for there is plenty if one knows how to look. Is that all the trouble?"

"No, sir, that is the lightest part of it. I shall soon get over my disappointment in those girls and take them for what they are worth as you advise, but being deceived in them makes me suspicious of others, and that is hateful. If I cannot trust people I'd rather keep by myself and be happy. I do detest maneuvering and underhanded plots and plans!"

Rose spoke petulantly and twitched her silk till it broke, while regret seemed to give place to anger as she spoke.

"There is evidently another thorn pricking. Let us have it out, and then I'll kiss the place to make it well as I used to do when I took the splinters from the fingers you are pricking so unmercifully," said the doctor, anxious to relieve his pet patient as soon as possible.

Rose laughed, but the color deepened in her cheeks as she answered with a pretty mixture of maidenly shyness and natural candor.

"Aunt Clara worries me by warning me against half the young men I meet and insisting that they want only my money. Now that is dreadful, and I won't listen, but I can't help thinking of it sometimes, for they are very kind to me and I'm not vain enough to think it is my beauty. I suppose I am foolish, but I do like to feel that I am something besides an heiress."

The little quiver was in Rose's voice again as she ended, and Dr. Alec gave a quick sigh as he looked at the downcast face so full of the perplexity ingenuous spirits feel when doubt first mars their faith and dims the innocent beliefs still left from childhood. He had been expecting this and knew that what the girl just began to perceive and try modestly to tell had long ago been plain to worldlier eyes. The heiress was the attraction to most of the young men whom she met. Good fellows enough, but educated, as nearly all are nowadays, to believe that girls with beauty or money are brought to market to sell or buy as the case may be.

Rose could purchase anything she liked, as she combined both advantages, and was soon surrounded by many admirers, each striving to secure the prize. Not being trained to believe that the only end and aim of a woman's life was a good match, she was a little disturbed, when the first pleasing excitement was over, to discover that her fortune was her chief attraction.

It was impossible for her to help seeing, hearing, guessing this from a significant glance, a stray word, a slight hint here and there, and the quick instinct of a woman felt even before it understood the self-interest which chilled for her so many opening friendships. In her eyes love was a very sacred thing, hardly to be thought of till it came, reverently received and cherished faithfully to the end. Therefore, it is not strange that she shrank from hearing it flippantly discussed and marriage treated as a bargain to be haggled over, with little thought of its high duties, great responsibilities, and tender joys. Many things perplexed her, and sometimes a doubt of all that till now she had believed and trusted made her feel as if at sea without a compass, for the new world was so unlike the one she had been living in that it bewildered while it charmed the novice.

Dr. Alec understood the mood in which he found her and did his best to warn without saddening by too much worldly wisdom.

"You are something besides an heiress to those who know and love you, so take heart, my girl, and hold fast to the faith that is in you. There is a touchstone for all these things, and whatever does not ring true, doubt and avoid. Test and try men and women as they come along, and I am sure conscience, instinct, and experience will keep you from any dire mistake," he said, with a protecting arm about her and a trustful look that was very comforting.

After a moment's pause she answered, while a sudden smile dimpled around her mouth and the big glove went up to hide her telltale cheeks: "Uncle, if I must have lovers, I do wish they'd be more interesting. How can I like or respect men who go on as some of them do and then imagine women can feel honored by the offer of their hands? Hearts are out of fashion, so they don't say much about them."

"Ah, ha! That is the trouble, is it? And we begin to have delicate distresses, do we?" said Dr. Alec, glad to see her brightening and full of interest in the new topic, for he was a romantic old fellow, as he had confessed to his brother.

Rose put down the glove and looked up with a droll mixture of amusement and disgust in her face. "Uncle, it is perfectly disgraceful! I've wanted to tell you, but I was ashamed, because I never could boast of such things as some girls do, and they were so absurd I couldn't feel as if they were worth repeating even to you. Perhaps I ought, though, for you may think it proper to command me to make a good match, and of course I should have to obey," she added, trying to look meek.

"Tell, by all means. Don't I always keep your secrets and give you the best advice, like a model guardian? You must have a confidant, and where find a better one than here?" he asked, tapping his waistcoat with an inviting gesture.

"Nowhere so I'll tell all but the names. I'd best be prudent, for I'm afraid you may get a little fierce you do sometimes when people vex me," began Rose, rather liking the prospect of a confidential chat with Uncle, for he had kept himself a good deal in the background lately.

"You know our ideas are old-fashioned, so I was not prepared to have men propose at all times and places with no warning but a few smiles and soft speeches. I expected things of that sort would be very interesting and proper, not to say thrilling, on my part but they are not, and I find

159

myself laughing instead of crying, feeling angry instead of glad, and forgetting all about it very soon. Why, Uncle, one absurd boy proposed when we'd met only half a dozen times. But he was dreadfully in debt, so that accounted for it perhaps." And Rose dusted her fingers, as if she had soiled them.

"I know him, and I thought he'd do it," observed the doctor with a shrug.

"You see and know everything, so there's no need of going on, is there?"

"Do, do! Who else? I won't even guess."

"Well, another went down upon his knees in Mrs. Van's greenhouse and poured forth his passion manfully, with a great cactus pricking his poor legs all the while. Kitty found him there, and it was impossible to keep sober, so he has hated me ever since."

The doctor's "Ha! Ha!" was good to hear, and Rose joined him, for it was impossible to regard these episodes seriously, since no true sentiment redeemed them from absurdity.

"Another sent me reams of poetry and went on so Byronically that I began to wish I had red hair and my name was Betsy Ann. I burnt all the verses, so don't expect to see them, and he, poor fellow, is consoling himself with Emma. But the worst of all was the one who would make love in public and insisted on proposing in the middle of a dance. I seldom dance round dances except with our boys, but that night I did because the girls laughed at me for being so 'prudish,' as they called it. I don't mind them now, for I found I was right, and felt that I deserved my fate."

"Is that all?" asked her uncle, looking "fierce," as she predicted, at the idea of his beloved girl obliged to listen to a declaration, twirling on the arm of a lover.

"One more but him I shall not tell about, for I know he was in earnest and really suffered, though I was as kind as I knew how to be. I'm young in these things yet, so I grieved for him, and treat his love with the tenderest respect."

Rose's voice sank almost to a whisper as she ended, and Dr. Alec bent his head, as if involuntarily saluting a comrade in misfortune. Then he got up, saying with a keen look into the face he lifted by a finger under the chin: "Do you want another three months of this?"

"I'll tell you on New Year's Day, Uncle."

"Very well. Try to keep a straight course, my little captain, and if you see dirty weather ahead, call on your first mate."

"Aye, aye, sir. I'll remember."

Chapter 5 PRINCE CHARMING
The old glove lay upon the floor forgotten while Rose sat musing, till a quick step sounded in the hall and a voice drew near, tunefully humming.

"As he was walkin' doun the street
The city for to view,

Oh, there he spied a bonny lass,
The window lookin' through."

"Sae licht he jumpèd up the stair,
And tirled at the pin;
Oh, wha sae ready as hersel'
To let the laddie in?"

sang Rose as the voice paused and a tap came at the door.

"Good morning, Rosamunda, here are your letters, and your most devoted ready to execute any commissions you may have for him," was Charlie's greeting as he came in looking comely, gay, and debonair as usual.

"Thanks. I've no errands unless you mail my replies, if these need answering, so by your leave, Prince," and Rose began to open the handful of notes he threw into her lap.

"Ha! What sight is this to blast mine eyes?" ejaculated Charlie, as he pointed to the glove with a melodramatic start, for, like most accomplished amateur actors, he was fond of introducing private theatricals into his daily talk and conversation.

"Uncle left it."

"'Tis well. Methought perchance a rival had been here," and, picking it up, Charlie amused himself with putting it on the head of a little Psyche which ornamented the mantelpiece, softly singing as he did so, another verse of the old song:

"He set his Jenny on his knee,
All in his Highland dress;
For brawly well he kenned the way
To please a bonny lass."

Rose went on reading her letters, but all the while was thinking of her conversation with her uncle as well as something else suggested by the newcomer and his ditty.

During the three months since her return she had seen more of this cousin than any of the others, for he seemed to be the only one who had leisure to "play with Rose," as they used to say years ago. The other boys were all at work, even little Jamie, many of whose play hours were devoted to manful struggles with Latin grammar, the evil genius of his boyish life. Dr. Alec had many affairs to arrange after his long absence; Phebe was busy with her music; and Aunt Plenty still actively superintended her housekeeping. Thus it fell out, quite naturally, that Charlie should form the habit of lounging in at all hours with letters, messages, bits of news, and agreeable plans for Rose. He helped her with her sketching, rode with her, sang with her, and took her to parties as a matter of course, for Aunt Clara, being the gaiest of the sisters, played chaperon on all occasions.

For a time it was very pleasant, but, by and by, Rose began to wish Charlie would find something to do like the rest and not make dawdling after her the business of his life. The family was used to his self-indulgent ways, and there was an amiable delusion in the minds of the boys that he had a right to the best of everything, for to them he was still the Prince, the flower of the flock, and in time to be an honor to the name. No one exactly knew how, for, though full of talent, he seemed to have no especial gift or bias, and the elders began to shake their heads because, in spite of many grand promises and projects, the moment for decisive action never came.

Rose saw all this and longed to inspire her brilliant cousin with some manful purpose which should win for him respect as well as admiration. But she found it very hard, for though he listened with imperturbable good humor, and owned his shortcomings with delightful frankness, he always had some argument, reason, or excuse to offer and out-talked her in five minutes, leaving her silenced but unconvinced.

Of late she had observed that he seemed to feel as if her time and thoughts belonged exclusively to him and rather resented the approach of any other claimant. This annoyed her and suggested the idea that her affectionate interest and efforts were misunderstood by him, misrepresented and taken advantage of by Aunt Clara, who had been most urgent that she should "use her influence with the dear boy," though the fond mother resented all other interference. This troubled Rose and made her feel as if caught in a snare, for, while she owned to herself that Charlie was the most attractive of her cousins, she was not ready to be taken possession of in this masterful way, especially since other and sometimes better men sought her favor more humbly.

These thoughts were floating vaguely in her mind as she read her letters and unconsciously influenced her in the chat that followed.

"Only invitations, and I can't stop to answer them now or I shall never get through this job," she said, returning to her work.

"Let me help. You do up, and I'll direct. Have a secretary, do now, and see what a comfort it will be," proposed Charlie, who could turn his hand to anything and had made himself quite at home in the sanctum.

"I'd rather finish this myself, but you may answer the notes if you will. Just regrets to all but two or three. Read the names as you go along and I'll tell you which."

"To hear is to obey. Who says I'm a 'frivolous idler' now?" And Charlie sat down at the writing table with alacrity, for these hours in the little room were his best and happiest.

"Order is heaven's first law, and the view a lovely one, but I don't see any notepaper," he added, opening the desk and surveying its contents with interest.

"Right-hand drawer violet monogram for the notes, plain paper for the business letter. I'll see to that, though," answered Rose, trying to decide whether Annabel or Emma should have the laced handkerchief.

"Confiding creature! Suppose I open the wrong drawer and come upon the tender secrets of your soul?" continued the new secretary, rummaging out the delicate notepaper with masculine disregard of order.

"I haven't got any," answered Rose demurely.

"What, not one despairing scrawl, one cherished miniature, one faded floweret, etc., etc.? I can't believe it, Cousin," and he shook his head incredulously.

"If I had, I certainly should not show them to you, impertinent person! There are a few little souvenirs in that desk, but nothing very sentimental or interesting."

"How I'd like to see 'em! But I should never dare to ask," observed Charlie, peering over the top of the half-open lid with a most persuasive pair of eyes.

"You may if you want to, but you'll be disappointed, Paul Pry. Lower left-hand drawer with the key in it."

"'Angel of goodness, how shall I requite thee? Interesting moment, with what palpitating emotions art thou fraught!'" And, quoting from the "Mysteries of Udolpho," he unlocked and opened the drawer with a tragic gesture.

"Seven locks of hair in a box, all light, for 'here's your straw color, your orange tawny, your French crown color, and your perfect yellow' Shakespeare. They look very familiar, and I fancy I know the heads they thatched."

"Yes, you all gave me one when I went away, you know, and I carried them round the world with me in that very box."

"I wish the heads had gone too. Here's a jolly little amber god with a gold ring in his back and a most balmy breath," continued Charlie, taking a long sniff at the scent bottle.

"Uncle brought me that long ago, and I'm very fond of it."

"This now looks suspicious man's ring with a lotus cut on the stone and a note attached. I tremble as I ask, who, when, and where?"

"A gentleman, on my birthday, in Calcutta."

"I breathe again it was my sire?"

"Don't be absurd. Of course it was, and he did everything to make my visit pleasant. I wish you'd go and see him like a dutiful son, instead of idling here."

"That's what Uncle Mac is eternally telling me, but I don't intend to be lectured into the treadmill till I've had my fling first," muttered Charlie rebelliously.

"If you fling yourself in the wrong direction, you may find it hard to get back again," began Rose gravely.

"No fear, if you look after me as you seem to have promised to do, judging by the thanks you get in this note. Poor old governor! I should like to see him, for it's almost four years since he came home last and he must be getting on."

Charlie was the only one of the boys who ever called his father "governor," perhaps because the others knew and loved their fathers, while he had seen so little of his that the less respectful name came more readily to his lips, since the elder man in truth seemed a governor issuing requests or commands, which the younger too often neglected or resented.

Long ago Rose had discovered that Uncle Stephen found home made so distasteful by his wife's devotion to society that he preferred to exile himself, taking business as an excuse for his protracted absences.

The girl was thinking of this as she watched her cousin turn the ring about with a sudden sobriety which became him well; and, believing that the moment was propitious, she said earnestly: "He is getting on. Dear Charlie, do think of duty more than pleasure in this case and I'm sure you never will regret it."

"Do you want me to go?" he asked quickly.

163

"I think you ought."

"And I think you'd be much more charming if you wouldn't always be worrying about right and wrong! Uncle Alec taught you that along with the rest of his queer notions."

"I'm glad he did!" cried Rose warmly, then checked herself and said with a patient sort of sigh, "You know women always want the men they care for to be good and can't help trying to make them so."

"So they do, and we ought to be a set of angels, but I've a strong conviction that, if we were, the dear souls wouldn't like us half as well. Would they now?" asked Charlie with an insinuating smile.

"Perhaps not, but that is dodging the point. Will you go?" persisted Rose unwisely.

"No, I will not."

That was sufficiently decided and an uncomfortable pause followed, during which Rose tied a knot unnecessarily tight and Charlie went on exploring the drawer with more energy than interest.

"Why, here's an old thing I gave you ages ago!" he suddenly exclaimed in a pleased tone, holding up a little agate heart on a faded blue ribbon. "Will you let me take away the heart of stone and give you a heart of flesh?" he asked, half in earnest, half in jest, touched by the little trinket and the recollections it awakened.

"No, I will not," answered Rose bluntly, much displeased by the irreverent and audacious question.

Charlie looked rather abashed for a moment, but his natural lightheartedness made it easy for him to get the better of his own brief fits of waywardness and put others in good humor with him and themselves.

"Now we are even let's drop the subject and start afresh," he said with irresistible affability as he coolly put the little heart in his pocket and prepared to shut the drawer. But something caught his eye, and exclaiming, "What's this? What's this?" he snatched up a photograph which lay half under a pile of letters with foreign postmarks.

"Oh! I forgot that was there," said Rose hastily.

"Who is the man?" demanded Charlie, eyeing the good-looking countenance before him with a frown.

"That is the Honorable Gilbert Murray, who went up the Nile with us and shot crocodiles and other small game, being a mighty hunter, as I told you in my letters," answered Rose gaily, though ill pleased at the little discovery just then, for this had been one of the narrow escapes her uncle spoke of.

"And they haven't eaten him yet, I infer from the pile of letters?" said Charlie jealously.

"I hope not. His sister did not mention it when she wrote last."

"Ah! Then she is your correspondent? Sisters are dangerous things sometimes." And Charlie eyed the packet suspiciously.

"In this case, a very convenient thing, for she tells me all about her brother's wedding, as no one else would take the trouble to do."

"Oh! Well, if he's married, I don't care a straw about him. I fancied I'd found out why you are such a hard-hearted charmer. But if there is no secret idol, I'm all at sea again." And Charlie tossed the photograph into the drawer as if it no longer interested him.

"I'm hard-hearted because I'm particular and, as yet, do not find anyone at all to my taste."

"No one?" with a tender glance.

"No one" with a rebellious blush, and the truthful addition "I see much to admire and like in many persons, but none quite strong and good enough to suit me. My heroes are old-fashioned, you know."

"Prigs, like Guy Carleton, Count Altenberg, and John Halifax I know the pattern you goody girls like," sneered Charlie, who preferred the Guy Livingston, Beauclerc, and Rochester style.

"Then I'm not a 'goody girl,' for I don't like prigs. I want a gentleman in the best sense of the word, and I can wait, for I've seen one, and know there are more in the world."

"The deuce you have! Do I know him?" asked Charlie, much alarmed.

"You think you do," answered Rose with a mischievous sparkle in her eye.

"If it isn't Pem, I give it up. He's the best-bred fellow I know."

"Oh, dear, no! Far superior to Mr. Pemberton and many years older," said Rose, with so much respect that Charlie looked perplexed as well as anxious.

"Some apostolic minister, I fancy. You pious creatures always like to adore a parson. But all we know are married."

"He isn't."

"Give a name, for pity's sake I'm suffering tortures of suspense," begged Charlie.

"Alexander Campbell."

"Uncle? Well, upon my word, that's a relief, but mighty absurd all the same. So, when you find a young saint of that sort, you intend to marry him, do you?" demanded Charlie much amused and rather disappointed.

"When I find any man half as honest, good, and noble as Uncle, I shall be proud to marry him if he asks me," answered Rose decidedly.

"What odd tastes women have!" And Charlie leaned his chin on his hand to muse pensively for a moment over the blindness of one woman who could admire an excellent old uncle more than a dashing young cousin.

Rose, meanwhile, tied up her parcels industriously, hoping she had not been too severe, for it was very hard to lecture Charlie, though he seemed to like it sometimes and came to confession voluntarily, knowing that women love to forgive when the sinners are of his sort.

"It will be mail time before you are done," she said presently, for silence was less pleasant than his rattle.

Charlie took the hint and dashed off several notes in his best manner. Coming to the business letter, he glanced at it and asked, with a puzzled expression: "What is all this? Cost of repairs, etc., from a man named Buffum?"

"Never mind that I'll see to it by and by."

"But I do mind, for I'm interested in all your affairs, and though you think I've no head for business, you'll find I have if you'll try me."

"This is only about my two old houses in the city, which are being repaired and altered so that the rooms can be let singly."

"Going to make tenement houses of them? Well, that's not a bad idea such places pay well, I've heard."

"That is just what I'm not going to do. I wouldn't have a tenement house on my conscience for a million dollars not as they are now," said Rose decidedly.

"Why, what do you know about it, except that people live in them and the owners turn a pretty penny on the rents?"

"I know a good deal about them, for I've seen many such, both here and abroad. It was not all pleasure with us, I assure you. Uncle was interested in hospitals and prisons, and I sometimes went with him, but they made me sad so he suggested other charities that I could be of help about when we came home. I visited infant schools, working women's homes, orphan asylums, and places of that sort. You don't know how much good it did me and how glad I am that I have the means of lightening a little some of the misery in the world."

"But, my dear girl, you needn't make ducks and drakes of your fortune trying to feed and cure and clothe all the poor wretches you see. Give, of course everyone should do something in that line and no one likes it better than I. But don't, for mercy's sake, go at it as some women do and get so desperately earnest, practical, and charity-mad that there is no living in peace with you," protested Charlie, looking alarmed at the prospect.

"You can do as you please. I intend to do all the good I can by asking the advice and following the example of the most 'earnest,' 'practical,' and 'charitable' people I know so, if you don't approve, you can drop my acquaintance," answered Rose, emphasizing the obnoxious words and assuming the resolute air she always wore when defending her hobbies.

"You'll be laughed at."

"I'm used to that."

"And criticized and shunned."

"Not by people whose opinion I value."

"Women shouldn't go poking into such places."

"I've been taught that they should."

166

"Well, you'll get some dreadful disease and lose your beauty, and then where are you?" added Charlie, thinking that might daunt the young philanthropist.

But it did not, for Rose answered, with a sudden kindling of the eyes as she remembered her talk with Uncle Alec: "I shouldn't like it. But there would be one satisfaction in it, for when I'd lost my beauty and given away my money, I should know who really cared for me."

Charlie nibbled his pen in silence for a moment, then asked, meekly, "Could I respectfully inquire what great reform is to be carried on in the old houses which their amiable owner is repairing?"

"I am merely going to make them comfortable homes for poor but respectable women to live in. There is a class who cannot afford to pay much, yet suffer a great deal from being obliged to stay in noisy, dirty, crowded places like tenement houses and cheap lodgings. I can help a few of them and I'm going to try."

"May I humbly ask if these decayed gentlewomen are to inhabit their palatial retreat rent-free?"

"That was my first plan, but Uncle showed me that it was wiser not make genteel paupers of them, but let them pay a small rent and feel independent. I don't want the money, of course, and shall use it in keeping the houses tidy or helping other women in like case," said Rose, entirely ignoring her cousin's covert ridicule.

"Don't expect any gratitude, for you won't get it; nor much comfort with a lot of forlornities on your hands, and be sure that when it is too late you will tire of it all and wish you had done as other people do."

"Thanks for your cheerful prophecies, but I think I'll venture."

She looked so undaunted that Charlie was a little nettled and fired his last shot rather recklessly: "Well, one thing I do know you'll never get a husband if you go on in this absurd way, and by Jove! you need one to take care of you and keep the property together!"

Rose had a temper, but seldom let it get the better of her; now, however, it flashed up for a moment. Those last words were peculiarly unfortunate, because Aunt Clara had used them more than once when warning her against impecunious suitors and generous projects. She was disappointed in her cousin, annoyed at having her little plans laughed at, and indignant with him for his final suggestion.

"I'll never have one, if I must give up the liberty of doing what I know is right, and I'd rather go into the poorhouse tomorrow than 'keep the property together' in the selfish way you mean!"

That was all but Charlie saw that he had gone too far and hastened to make his peace with the skill of a lover, for, turning to the little cabinet piano behind him, he sang in his best style the sweet old song:

"Oh were thou in the cauld blast,"

dwelling with great effect, not only upon the tender assurance that "My plaid should shelter thee," 

but also that, even if a king,

"The brightest jewel in my crown
Wad be my queen, wad be my queen."

It was very evident that Prince Charming had not gone troubadouring in vain, for Orpheus himself could not have restored harmony more successfully. The tuneful apology was accepted with a forgiving smile and a frank "I'm sorry I was cross, but you haven't forgotten how to tease, and I'm rather out of sorts today. Late hours don't agree with me."

"Then you won't feel like going to Mrs. Hope's tomorrow, I'm afraid," and Charlie took up the last note with an expression of regret which was very flattering.

"I must go, because it is made for me, but I can come away early and make up lost sleep. I do hate to be so fractious," and Rose rubbed the forehead that ached with too much racketing.

"But the German does not begin till late I'm to lead and depend upon you. Just stay this once to oblige me," pleaded Charlie, for he had set his heart on distinguishing himself.

"No I promised Uncle to be temperate in my pleasures and I must keep my word. I'm so well now, it would be very foolish to get ill and make him anxious not to mention losing my beauty, as you are good enough to call it, for that depends on health, you know."

"But the fun doesn't begin till after supper. Everything will be delightful, I assure you, and we'll have a gay old time as we did last week at Emma's."

"Then I certainly will not, for I'm ashamed of myself when I remember what a romp that was and how sober Uncle looked as he let me in at three in the morning, all fagged out my dress in rags, my head aching, my feet so tired that I could hardly stand, and nothing to show for five hours' hard work but a pocketful of bonbons, artificial flowers, and tissue-paper fool's caps. Uncle said I'd better put one on and go to bed, for I looked as though I'd been to a French bal masque. I never want to hear him say so again, and I'll never let dawn catch me out in such a plight anymore."

"You were all right enough, for mother didn't object and I got you both home before daylight. Uncle is notional about such things, so I shouldn't mind, for we had a jolly time and we were none the worse for it."

"Indeed we were, every one of us! Aunt Clara hasn't gotten over her cold yet. I slept all the next day, and you looked like a ghost, for you'd been out every night for weeks, I think."

"Oh, nonsense! Everyone does it during the season, and you'll get used to the pace very soon," began Charlie, bent on making her go, for he was in his element in a ballroom and never happier than when he had his pretty cousin on his arm.

"Ah! But I don't want to get used to it, for it costs too much in the end. I don't wish to get used to being whisked about a hot room by men who have taken too much wine, to turn day into night, wasting time that might be better spent, and grow into a fashionable fast girl who can't get along without excitement. I don't deny that much of it is pleasant, but don't try to make me too fond of gaiety. Help me to resist what I know is hurtful, and please don't laugh me out of the good habits Uncle has tried so hard to give me."

Rose was quite sincere in her appeal, and Charlie knew she was right, but he always found it hard to give up anything he had set his heart on, no matter how trivial, for the maternal indulgence which had harmed the boy had fostered the habit of self-indulgence, which was ruining the man. So when Rose looked up at him, with a very honest desire to save him as well as herself from being swept into the giddy vortex which keeps so many young people revolving aimlessly, till they go down or are cast upon the shore, wrecks of what they might have been, he gave a shrug and answered briefly: "As you please. I'll bring you home as early as you like, and Effie Waring shall take your place in the German. What flowers shall I send you?"

168

Now, that was an artful speech of Charlie's, for Miss Waring was a fast and fashionable damsel who openly admired Prince Charming and had given him the name. Rose disliked her and was sure her influence was bad, for youth made frivolity forgivable, wit hid want of refinement, and beauty always covers a multitude of sins in a man's eyes. At the sound of Effie's name, Rose wavered, and would have yielded but for the memory of the "first mate's" last words. She did desire to "keep a straight course"; so, though the current of impulse set strongly in a southerly direction, principle, the only compass worth having, pointed due north, and she tried to obey it like a wise young navigator, saying steadily, while she directed to Annabel the parcel containing a capacious pair of slippers intended for Uncle Mac: "Don't trouble yourself about me. I can go with Uncle and slip away without disturbing anybody."

"I don't believe you'll have the heart to do it," said Charlie incredulously as he sealed the last note.

"Wait and see."

"I will, but I shall hope to the last." And kissing his hand to her, he departed to post her letters, quite sure that Miss Waring would not lead the German.

It certainly looked for a moment as if Miss Campbell would, because she ran to the door with the words "I'll go" upon her lips. But she did not open it till she had stood a minute staring hard at the old glove on Psyche's head; then like one who had suddenly gotten a bright idea, she gave a decided nod and walked slowly out of the room.

Chapter 6 POLISHING MAC

"Please could I say one word?" was the question three times repeated before a rough head bobbed out from the grotto of books in which Mac usually sat when he studied.

"Did anyone speak?" he asked, blinking in the flood of sunshine that entered with Rose.

"Only three times, thank you. Don't disturb yourself, I beg, for I merely want to say a word," answered Rose as she prevented him from offering the easy chair in which he sat.

"I was rather deep in a compound fracture and didn't hear. What can I do for you, Cousin?" And Mac shoved a stack of pamphlets off the chair near him with a hospitable wave of the hand that sent his papers flying in all directions.

Rose sat down, but did not seem to find her "word" an easy one to utter, for she twisted her handkerchief about her fingers in embarrassed silence till Mac put on his glasses and, after a keen look, asked soberly: "Is it a splinter, a cut, or a whitlow, ma'am?"

"It is neither. Do forget your tiresome surgery for a minute and be the kindest cousin that ever was," answered Rose, beginning rather sharply and ending with her most engaging smile.

"Can't promise in the dark," said the wary youth.

"It is a favor, a great favor, and one I don't choose to ask any of the other boys," answered the artful damsel.

Mac looked pleased and leaned forward, saying more affably, "Name it, and be sure I'll grant it if I can."

"Go with me to Mrs. Hope's party tomorrow night."

"What!" And Mac recoiled as if she had put a pistol to his head.

"I've left you in peace a long time, but it is your turn now, so do your duty like a man and a cousin."

"But I never go to parties!" cried the unhappy victim in great dismay.

"High time you began, sir."

"But I don't dance fit to be seen."

"I'll teach you."

"My dress coat isn't decent, I know."

"Archie will lend you one he isn't going."

"I'm afraid there's a lecture that I ought not to cut."

"No, there isn't I asked Uncle."

"I'm always so tired and dull in the evening."

"This sort of thing is just what you want to rest and freshen up your spirits."

Mac gave a groan and fell back vanquished, for it was evident that escape was impossible.

"What put such a perfectly wild idea into your head?" he demanded, rather roughly, for hitherto he had been left in peace and this sudden attack decidedly amazed him.

"Sheer necessity, but don't do it if it is so very dreadful to you. I must go to several more parties, because they are made for me, but after that I'll refuse, and then no one need be troubled with me."

Something in Rose's voice made Mac answer penitently, even while he knit his brows in perplexity. "I don't mean to be rude, and of course I'll go anywhere if I'm really needed. But I don't understand where the sudden necessity is, with three other fellows at command, all better dancers and beaus than I am."

"I don't want them, and I do want you, for I haven't the heart to drag Uncle out anymore, and you know I never go with any gentleman but those of my own family."

"Now look here, Rose if Steve has been doing anything to tease you, just mention it and I'll attend to him," cried Mac, plainly seeing that something was amiss and fancying that Dandy was at the bottom of it, as he had done escort duty several times lately.

"No, Steve has been very good, but I know he had rather be with Kitty Van, so of course I feel like a marplot, though he is too polite to hint it."

"What a noodle that boy is! But there's Archie he's steady as a church and has no sweetheart to interfere," continued Mac, bound to get at the truth and half suspecting what it was.

"He is on his feet all day, and Aunt Jessie wants him in the evening. He does not care for dancing as he used, and I suppose he really does prefer to rest and read." Rose might have added, "And hear Phebe sing," for Phebe did not go out as much as Rose did, and Aunt Jessie often came to sit with the old lady when the young folks were away and, of course, dutiful Archie came with her, so willingly of late!

"What's amiss with Charlie? I thought he was the prince of cavaliers. Annabel says he dances 'like an angel,' and I know a dozen mothers couldn't keep him at home of an evening. Have you had a tiff with Adonis and so fall back on poor me?" asked Mac, coming last to the person of whom he thought first but did not mention, feeling shy about alluding to a subject often discussed behind her back.

"Yes, I have, and I don't intend to go with him any more for some time. His ways do not suit me, and mine do not suit him, so I want to be quite independent, and you can help me if you will," said Rose, rather nervously spinning the big globe close by.

Mac gave a low whistle, looking wide awake all in a minute as he said with a gesture, as if he brushed a cobweb off his face: "Now, see here, Cousin, I'm not good at mysteries and shall only blunder if you put me blindfold into any nice maneuver. Just tell me straight out what you want and I'll do it if I can. Play I'm Uncle and free your mind come now."

He spoke so kindly, and the honest eyes were so full of merry goodwill, that Rose thought she might confide in him and answered as frankly as he could desire: "You are right, Mac, and I don't mind talking to you almost as freely as to Uncle, because you are such a reliable fellow and won't think me silly for trying to do what I believe to be right. Charlie does, and so makes it hard for me to hold to my resolutions. I want to keep early hours, dress simply, and behave properly no matter what fashionable people do. You will agree to that, I'm sure, and stand by me through thick and thin for principle's sake."

"I will, and begin by showing you that I understand the case. I don't wonder you are not pleased, for Charlie is too presuming, and you do need someone to help you head him off a bit. Hey, Cousin?"

"What a way to put it!" And Rose laughed in spite of herself, adding with an air of relief, "That is it, and I do want someone to help me make him understand that I don't choose to be taken possession of in that lordly way, as if I belonged to him more than to the rest of the family. I don't like it, for people begin to talk, and Charlie won't see how disagreeable it is to me."

"Tell him so," was Mac's blunt advice.

"I have, but he only laughs and promises to behave, and then he does it again when I am so placed that I can't say anything. You will never understand, and I cannot explain, for it is only a look, or a word, or some little thing but I won't have it, and the best way to cure him is to put it out of his power to annoy me so."

"He is a great flirt and wants to teach you how, I suppose. I'll speak to him if you like and tell him you don't want to learn. Shall I?" asked Mac, finding the case rather an interesting one.

"No, thank you that would only make trouble. If you will kindly play escort a few times, it will show Charlie that I am in earnest without more words and put a stop to the gossip," said Rose, coloring like a poppy at the recollection of what she heard one young man whisper to another as

171

Charlie led her through a crowded supper room with his most devoted air, "Lucky dog! He is sure to get the heiress, and we are nowhere."

"There's no danger of people gossiping about us, is there?" And Mac looked up with the oddest of all his odd expressions.

"Of course not you're only a boy."

"I'm twenty-one, thank you, and Prince is but a couple of years older," said Mac, promptly resenting the slight put upon his manhood.

"Yes, but he is like other young men, while you are a dear old bookworm. No one would ever mind what you did, so you may go to parties with me every night and not a word would be said or, if there was, I shouldn't mind since it is 'only Mac,'" answered Rose, smiling as she quoted a household phrase often used to excuse his vagaries.

"Then I am nobody?" he said, lifting his brows as if the discovery surprised and rather nettled him.

"Nobody in society as yet, but my very best cousin in private, and I've just proved my regard by making you my confidant and choosing you for my knight," said Rose, hastening to soothe the feelings her careless words seemed to have ruffled slightly.

"Much good that is likely to do me," grumbled Mac.

"You ungrateful boy, not to appreciate the honor I've conferred upon you! I know a dozen who would be proud of the place, but you only care for compound fractures, so I won't detain you any longer, except to ask if I may consider myself provided with an escort for tomorrow night?" said Rose, a trifle hurt at his indifference, for she was not used to refusals.

"If I may hope for the honor." And, rising, he made her a bow which was such a capital imitation of Charlie's grand manner that she forgave him at once, exclaiming with amused surprise: "Why, Mac! I didn't know you could be so elegant!"

"A fellow can be almost anything he likes if he tries hard enough," he answered, standing very straight and looking so tall and dignified that Rose was quite impressed, and with a stately courtesy she retired, saying graciously: "I accept with thanks. Good morning, Dr. Alexander Mackenzie Campbell."

When Friday evening came and word was sent up that her escort had arrived, Rose ran down, devoutly hoping that he had not come in a velveteen jacket, top-boots, black gloves, or made any trifling mistake of that sort. A young gentleman was standing before the long mirror, apparently intent upon the arrangement of his hair, and Rose paused suddenly as her eye went from the glossy broadcloth to the white-gloved hands, busy with an unruly lock that would not stay in place.

"Why, Charlie, I thought—" she began with an accent of surprise in her voice, but got no further, for the gentleman turned and she beheld Mac in immaculate evening costume, with his hair parted sweetly on his brow, a superior posy at his buttonhole, and the expression of a martyr on his face.

"Ah, don't you wish it was? No one but yourself to thank that it isn't he. Am I right? Dandy got me up, and he ought to know what is what," demanded Mac, folding his hands and standing as stiff as a ramrod.

"You are so regularly splendid that I don't know you."

172

"Neither do I."

"I really had no idea you could look so like a gentleman," added Rose, surveying him with great approval.

"Nor that I could feel so like a fool."

"Poor boy! He does look rather miserable. What can I do to cheer him up in return for the sacrifice he is making?"

"Stop calling me a boy. It will soothe my agony immensely and give me courage to appear in a low-necked coat and curl on my forehead, for I'm not used to such elegancies and I find them no end of a trial."

Mac spoke in such a pathetic tone, and gave such a gloomy glare at the aforesaid curl, that Rose laughed in his face and added to his woe by handing him her cloak. He surveyed it gravely for a minute, then carefully put it on wrong side out and gave the swan's-down hood a good pull over the head, to the utter destruction of all smoothness to the curls inside.

Rose uttered a cry and cast off the cloak, bidding him learn to do it properly, which he meekly did and then led her down the hall without walking on her skirts more than three times on the way. But at the door she discovered that she had forgotten her furred overshoes and bade Mac get them.

"Never mind it's not wet," he said, pulling his cap over his eyes and plunging into his coat, regardless of the "elegancies" that afflicted him.

"But I can't walk on cold stones with thin slippers, can I?" began Rose, showing him a little white foot.

"You needn't, for there you are, my lady." And, unceremoniously picking her up, Mac landed her in the carriage before she could say a word.

"What an escort!" she exclaimed in comic dismay, as she rescued her delicate dress from a rug in which he was about to tuck her up like a mummy.

"It's 'only Mac,' so don't mind," and he cast himself into an opposite corner with the air of a man who had nerved himself to the accomplishment of many painful duties and was bound to do them or die.

"But gentlemen don't catch up ladies like bags of meal and poke them into carriages in this way. It is evident that you need looking after, and it is high time I undertook your society manners. Now, do mind what you are about and don't get yourself or me into a scrape if you can help it," besought Rose, feeling that on many accounts she had gone further and fared worse.

"I'll behave like a Turveydrop see if I don't."

Mac's idea of the immortal Turveydrop's behavior seemed to be a peculiar one; for, after dancing once with his cousin, he left her to her own devices and soon forgot all about her in a long conversation with Professor Stumph, the learned geologist. Rose did not care, for one dance proved to her that that branch of Mac's education had been sadly neglected, and she was glad to glide smoothly about with Steve, though he was only an inch or two taller than herself. She had plenty of partners, however, and plenty of chaperons, for all the young men were her most devoted, and all the matrons beamed upon her with maternal benignity.

Charlie was not there, for when he found that Rose stood firm, and had moreover engaged Mac as a permanency, he would not go at all and retired in high dudgeon to console himself with more dangerous pastimes. Rose feared it would be so, and even in the midst of the gaiety about her an anxious mood came over her now and then and made her thoughtful for a moment. She felt her power and wanted to use it wisely, but did not know how to be kind to Charlie without being untrue to herself and giving him false hopes.

"I wish we were all children again, with no hearts to perplex us and no great temptations to try us," she said to herself as she rested a minute in a quiet nook while her partner went to get a glass of water. Right in the midst of this half-sad, half-sentimental reverie, she heard a familiar voice behind her say earnestly: "And allophite is the new hydrous silicate of alumina and magnesia, much resembling pseudophite, which Websky found in Silesia."

"What is Mac talking about!" she thought, and, peeping behind a great azalea in full bloom, she saw her cousin in deep conversation with the professor, evidently having a capital time, for his face had lost its melancholy expression and was all alive with interest, while the elder man was listening as if his remarks were both intelligent and agreeable.

"What is it?" asked Steve, coming up with the water and seeing a smile on Rose's face.

She pointed out the scientific tete-a-tete going on behind the azalea, and Steve grinned as he peeped, then grew sober and said in a tone of despair: "If you had seen the pains I took with that fellow, the patience with which I brushed his wig, the time I spent trying to convince him that he must wear thin boots, and the fight I had to get him into that coat, you'd understand my feelings when I see him now."

"Why, what's the matter with him?" asked Rose.

"Will you take a look and see what a spectacle he has made of himself. He'd better be sent home at once or he will disgrace the family by looking as if he'd been in a row."

Steve spoke in such a tragic tone that Rose took another peep and did sympathize with Dandy, for Mac's elegance was quite gone. His tie was under one ear, his posy hung upside down, his gloves were rolled into a ball, which he absently squeezed and pounded as he talked, and his hair looked as if a whirlwind had passed over it, for his ten fingers set it on end now and then, as they had a habit of doing when he studied or talked earnestly. But he looked so happy and wide awake, in spite of his dishevelment, that Rose gave an approving nod and said behind her fan: "It is a trying spectacle, Steve yet, on the whole, I think his own odd ways suit him best and I fancy we shall be proud of him, for he knows more than all the rest of us put together. Hear that now." And Rose paused that they might listen to the following burst of eloquence from Mac's lips: "You know Frenzal has shown that the globular forms of silicate of bismuth at Schneeburg and Johanngeorgenstadt are not isometric, but monoclinic in crystalline form, and consequently he separates them from the old eulytite and gives them the new name Agricolite."

"Isn't it awful? Let us get out of this before there's another avalanche or we shall be globular silicates and isometric crystals in spite of ourselves," whispered Steve with a panic-stricken air, and they fled from the hailstorm of hard words that rattled about their ears, leaving Mac to enjoy himself in his own way.

But when Rose was ready to go home and looked about for her escort, he was nowhere to be seen, for the professor had departed, and Mac with him, so absorbed in some new topic that he entirely

174

forgot his cousin and went placidly home, still pondering on the charms of geology. When this pleasing fact dawned upon Rose her feelings may be imagined. She was both angry and amused it was so like Mac to go mooning off and leave her to her fate. Not a hard one, however; for, though Steve was gone with Kitty before her plight was discovered, Mrs. Bliss was only too glad to take the deserted damsel under her wing and bear her safely home.

Rose was warming her feet and sipping the chocolate which Phebe always had ready for her, as she never ate supper, when a hurried tap came at the long window whence the light streamed and Mac's voice was heard softly asking to be let in "just for one minute."

Curious to know what had befallen him, Rose bade Phebe obey his call and the delinquent cavalier appeared, breathless, anxious, and more dilapidated than ever, for he had forgotten his overcoat; his tie was at the back of his neck now; and his hair as rampantly erect as if all the winds of heaven had been blowing freely through it, as they had, for he had been tearing to and fro the last half hour, trying to undo the dreadful deed he had so innocently committed.

"Don't take any notice of me, for I don't deserve it. I only came to see that you were safe, Cousin, and then go hang myself, as Steve advised," he began in a remorseful tone that would have been very effective if he had not been obliged to catch his breath with a comical gasp now and then.

"I never thought you would be the one to desert me," said Rose with a reproachful look, thinking it best not to relent too soon, though she was quite ready to do it when she saw how sincerely distressed he was.

"It was that confounded man! He was a regular walking encyclopedia, and, finding I could get a good deal out of him, I went in for general information, as the time was short. You know I always forget everything else when I get hold of such a fellow."

"That is evident. I wonder how you came to remember me at all," answered Rose, on the brink of a laugh it was so absurd.

"I didn't till Steve said something that reminded me then it burst upon me, in one awful shock, that I'd gone and left you, and you might have knocked me down with a feather," said honest Mac, hiding none of his iniquity.

"What did you do then?"

"Do! I went off like a shot and never stopped till I reached the Hopes'"

"You didn't walk all the way?" cried Rose.

"Bless you, no I ran. But you were gone with Mrs. Bliss, so I pelted back again to see with my own eyes that you were safe at home," answered Mac with a sigh of relief, wiping his hot forehead.

"But it is three miles at least each way, and twelve o'clock, and dark and cold. Oh, Mac! How could you!" exclaimed Rose, suddenly realizing what he had done as she heard his labored breathing, saw the state of the thin boots, and detected the absence of an overcoat.

"Couldn't do less, could I?" asked Mac, leaning up against the door and trying not to pant.

"There was no need of half killing yourself for such a trifle. You might have known I could take care of myself for once, at least, with so many friends about. Sit down this minute. Bring another cup, please, Phebe this boy isn't going home till he is rested and refreshed after such a run as that," commanded Rose.

"Don't be good to me I'd rather take a scolding than a chair, and drink hemlock instead of chocolate if you happen to have any ready," answered Mac with a pathetic puff as he subsided onto the sofa and meekly took the draft Phebe brought him.

"If you had anything the matter with your heart, sir, a race of this sort might be the death of you so never do it again," said Rose, offering her fan to cool his heated countenance.

"Haven't got any heart."

"Yes, you have, for I hear it beating like a trip-hammer, and it is my fault I ought to have stopped as we went by and told you I was all right."

"It's the mortification, not the miles, that upsets me. I often take that run for exercise and think nothing of it but tonight I was so mad I made extra-good time, I fancy. Now don't you worry, but compose your mind and 'sip your dish of tea,' as Evelina says," answered Mac, artfully turning the conversation from himself.

"What do you know about Evelina?" asked Rose in great surprise.

"All about her. Do you suppose I never read a novel?"

"I thought you read nothing but Greek and Latin, with an occasional glance at Websky's pseudophites and the monoclinics of Johanngeorgenstadt."

Mac opened his eyes wide at this reply, then seemed to see the joke and joined in the laugh with such heartiness that Aunt Plenty's voice was heard demanding from above with sleepy anxiety: "Is the house afire?"

"No, ma'am, everything is safe, and I'm only saying good night," answered Mac, diving for his cap.

"Then go at once and let that child have her sleep," added the old lady, retiring to her bed.

Rose ran into the hall, and catching up her uncle's fur coat, met Mac as he came out of the study, absently looking about for his own.

"You haven't any, you benighted boy! So take this, and have your wits about you next time or I won't let you off so easily," she said, holding up the heavy garment and peeping over it, with no sign of displeasure in her laughing eyes.

"Next time! Then you do forgive me? You will try me again, and give me a chance to prove that I'm not a fool?" cried Mac, embracing the big coat with emotion.

"Of course I will, and, so far from thinking you a fool, I was much impressed with your learning tonight and told Steve that we ought to be proud of our philosopher."

"Learning be hanged! I'll show you that I'm not a bookworm but as much a man as any of them, and then you may be proud or not, as you like!" cried Mac with a defiant nod that caused the glasses to leap wildly off his nose as he caught up his hat and departed as he came.

A day or two later Rose went to call upon Aunt Jane, as she dutifully did once or twice a week. On her way upstairs she heard a singular sound in the drawing room and involuntarily stopped to listen.

"One, two, three, slide! One, two, three, turn! Now, then, come on!" said one voice impatiently.

"It's very easy to say 'come on,' but what the dickens do I do with my left leg while I'm turning and sliding with my right?" demanded another voice in a breathless and mournful tone.

Then the whistling and thumping went on more vigorously than before, and Rose, recognizing the voices, peeped through the half-open door to behold a sight which made her shake with suppressed laughter. Steve, with a red tablecloth tied around his waist, languished upon Mac's shoulder, dancing in perfect time to the air he whistled, for Dandy was proficient in the graceful art and plumed himself upon his skill. Mac, with a flushed face and dizzy eye, clutched his brother by the small of his back, vainly endeavoring to steer him down the long room without entangling his own legs in the tablecloth, treading on his partner's toes, or colliding with the furniture. It was very droll, and Rose enjoyed the spectacle till Mac, in a frantic attempt to swing around, dashed himself against the wall and landed Steve upon the floor. Then it was impossible to restrain her laughter any longer and she walked in upon them, saying merrily: "It was splendid! Do it again, and I'll play for you."

Steve sprang up and tore off the tablecloth in great confusion, while Mac, still rubbing his head, dropped into a chair, trying to look quite calm and cheerful as he gasped out: "How are you, Cousin? When did you come? John should have told us."

"I'm glad he didn't, for then I should have missed this touching tableau of cousinly devotion and brotherly love. Getting ready for our next party, I see."

"Trying to, but there are so many things to remember all at once keep time, steer straight, dodge the petticoats, and manage my confounded legs that it isn't easy to get on at first," answered Mac with a sigh of exhaustion, wiping his hot forehead.

"Hardest job I ever undertook and, as I'm not a battering ram, I decline to be knocked round any longer," growled Steve, dusting his knees and ruefully surveying the feet that had been trampled on till they tingled, for his boots and broadcloth were dear to the heart of the dapper youth.

"Very good of you, and I'm much obliged. I've got the pace, I think, and can practice with a chair to keep my hand in," said Mac with such a comic mixture of gratitude and resignation that Rose went off again so irresistibly that her cousins joined her with a hearty roar.

"As you are making a martyr of yourself in my service, the least I can do is lend a hand. Play for us, Steve, and I'll give Mac a lesson, unless he prefers the chair." And, throwing off her hat and cloak, Rose beckoned so invitingly that the gravest philosopher would have yielded.

"A thousand thanks, but I'm afraid I shall hurt you," began Mac, much gratified, but mindful of past mishaps.

"I'm not. Steve didn't manage his train well, for good dancers always loop theirs up. I have none at all, so that trouble is gone and the music will make it much easier to keep step. Just do as I tell you, and you'll go beautifully after a few turns."

"I will, I will! Pipe up, Steve! Now, Rose!" And, brushing his hair out of his eyes with an air of stern determination, Mac grasped Rose and returned to the charge bent on distinguishing himself if he died in the attempt.

The second lesson prospered, for Steve marked the time by a series of emphatic bangs; Mac obeyed orders as promptly as if his life depended on it; and, after several narrow escapes at exciting

177

moments, Rose had the satisfaction of being steered safely down the room and landed with a grand pirouette at the bottom. Steve applauded, and Mac, much elated, exclaimed with artless candor: "There really is a sort of inspiration about you, Rose. I always detested dancing before, but now, do you know, I rather like it."

"I knew you would, only you mustn't stand with your arm round your partner in this way when you are done. You must seat and fan her, if she likes it," said Rose, anxious to perfect a pupil who seemed so lamentably in need of a teacher.

"Yes, of course, I know how they do it." And, releasing his cousin, Mac raised a small whirlwind around her with a folded newspaper, so full of zeal that she had not the heart to chide him again.

"Well done, old fellow. I begin to have hopes of you and will order you a new dress coat at once, since you are really going in for the proprieties of life," said Steve from the music stool, with the approving nod of one who was a judge of said proprieties. "Now, Rose, if you will just coach him a little in his small talk, he won't make a laughingstock of himself as he did the other night," added Steve. "I don't mean his geological gabble that was bad enough, but his chat with Emma Curtis was much worse. Tell her, Mac, and see if she doesn't think poor Emma had a right to think you a first-class bore."

"I don't see why, when I merely tried to have a little sensible conversation," began Mac with reluctance, for he had been unmercifully chaffed by his cousins, to whom his brother had betrayed him.

"What did you say? I won't laugh if I can help it," said Rose, curious to hear, for Steve's eyes were twinkling with fun.

"Well, I knew she was fond of theaters, so I tried that first and got on pretty well till I began to tell her how they managed those things in Greece. Most interesting subject, you know?"

"Very. Did you give her one of the choruses or a bit of Agamemnon, as you did when you described it to me?" asked Rose, keeping sober with difficulty as she recalled that serio-comic scene.

"Of course not, but I was advising her to read Prometheus when she gaped behind her fan and began to talk about Phebe. What a 'nice creature' she was, 'kept her place,' dressed according to her station, and that sort of twaddle. I suppose it was rather rude, but being pulled up so short confused me a bit, and I said the first thing that came into my head, which was that I thought Phebe the best-dressed woman in the room because she wasn't all fuss and feathers like most of the girls."

"Oh, Mac! That to Emma, who makes it the labor of her life to be always in the height of fashion and was particularly splendid that night. What did she say?" cried Rose, full of sympathy for both parties.

"She bridled and looked daggers at me."

"And what did you do?"

"I bit my tongue and tumbled out of one scrape into another. Following her example, I changed the subject by talking about the charity concert for the orphans, and when she gushed about the 'little darlings,' I advised her to adopt one and wondered why young ladies didn't do that sort of thing, instead of cuddling cats and lapdogs."

"Unhappy boy! Her pug is the idol of her life, and she hates babies," said Rose.

"More fool she! Well, she got my opinion on the subject, anyway, and she's very welcome, for I went on to say that I thought it would not only be a lovely charity, but excellent training for the time when they had little darlings of their own. No end of poor things die through the ignorance of mothers, you know," added Mac, so seriously that Rose dared not smile at what went before.

"Imagine Emma trotting round with a pauper baby under her arm instead of her cherished Toto," said Steve with an ecstatic twirl on the stool.

"Did she seem to like your advice, Monsieur Malapropos?" asked Rose, wishing she had been there.

"No, she gave a little shriek and said, 'Good gracious, Mr. Campbell, how droll you are! Take me to Mama, please,' which I did with a thankful heart. Catch me setting her pug's leg again," ended Mac with a grim shake of the head.

"Never mind. You were unfortunate in your listener that time. Don't think all girls are so foolish. I can show you a dozen sensible ones who would discuss dress reform and charity with you and enjoy Greek tragedy if you did the chorus for them as you did for me," said Rose consolingly, for Steve would only jeer.

"Give me a list of them, please, and I'll cultivate their acquaintance. A fellow must have some reward for making a teetotum of himself."

"I will with pleasure; and if you dance well they will make it very pleasant for you, and you'll enjoy parties in spite of yourself."

"I cannot be a 'glass of fashion and a mold of form' like Dandy here, but I'll do my best: only, if I had my choice, I'd much rather go round the streets with an organ and a monkey," answered Mac despondently.

"Thank you kindly for the compliment," and Rose made him a low courtesy, while Steve cried, "Now you have done it!" in a tone of reproach which reminded the culprit, all too late, that he was Rose's chosen escort.

"By the gods, so I have!" And casting away the newspaper with a gesture of comic despair, Mac strode from the room, chanting tragically the words of Cassandra, "'Woe! woe! O Earth! O Apollo! I will dare to die; I will accost the gates of Hades, and make my prayer that I may receive a mortal blow!'"

Chapter 7 PHEBE

While Rose was making discoveries and having experiences, Phebe was doing the same in a quieter way, but though they usually compared notes during the bedtime tete-a-tete which always ended their day, certain topics were never mentioned, so each had a little world of her own into which even the eye of friendship did not peep.

Rose's life just now was the gaiest but Phebe's the happiest. Both went out a good deal, for the beautiful voice was welcomed everywhere, and many were ready to patronize the singer who would have been slow to recognize the woman. Phebe knew this and made no attempt to assert herself, content to know that those whose regard she valued felt her worth and hopeful of a time when she could gracefully take the place she was meant to fill.

Proud as a princess was Phebe about some things, though in most as humble as a child; therefore, when each year lessened the service she loved to give and increased the obligations she would have refused from any other source, dependence became a burden which even the most fervent gratitude could not lighten. Hitherto the children had gone on together, finding no obstacles to their companionship in the secluded world in which they lived. Now that they were women their paths inevitably diverged, and both reluctantly felt that they must part before long.

It had been settled, when they were abroad, that on their return Phebe should take her one gift in her hand and try her fortunes. On no other terms would she accept the teaching which was to fit her for the independence she desired. Faithfully had she used the facilities so generously afforded both at home and abroad and now was ready to prove that they had not been in vain. Much encouraged by the small successes she won in drawing rooms, and the praise bestowed by interested friends, she began to feel that she might venture on a larger field and begin her career as a concert singer, for she aimed no higher.

Just at this time much interest was felt in a new asylum for orphan girls, which could not be completed for want of funds. The Campbells well had borne their part and still labored to accomplish the much-needed charity. Several fairs had been given for this purpose, followed by a series of concerts. Rose had thrown herself into the work with all her heart and now proposed that Phebe should make her debut at the last concert, which was to be a peculiarly interesting one, as all the orphans were to be present and were expected to plead their own cause by the sight of their innocent helplessness as well as touch hearts by the simple airs they were to sing.

Some of the family thought Phebe would object to so humble a beginning, but Rose knew her better and was not disappointed, for when she made her proposal Phebe answered readily: "Where could I find a fitter time and place to come before the public than here among my little sisters in misfortune? I'll sing for them with all my heart only I must be one of them and have no flourish made about me."

"You shall arrange it as you like, and as there is to be little vocal music but yours and the children's, I'll see that you have everything as you please," promised Rose.

It was well she did, for the family got much excited over the prospect of "our Phebe's debut" and would have made a flourish if the girls had not resisted. Aunt Clara was in despair about the dress because Phebe decided to wear a plain claret-colored merino with frills at neck and wrists so that she might look, as much as possible, like the other orphans in their stuff gowns and white aprons. Aunt Plenty wanted to have a little supper afterward in honor of the occasion, but Phebe begged her to change it to a Christmas dinner for the poor children. The boys planned to throw bushels of flowers, and Charlie claimed the honor of leading the singer in. But Phebe, with tears in her eyes, declined their kindly offers, saying earnestly: "I had better begin as I am to go on and depend upon myself entirely. Indeed, Mr. Charlie, I'd rather walk in alone, for you'd be out of place among us and spoil the pathetic effect we wish to produce." And a smile sparkled through the tears as Phebe looked at the piece of elegance before her and thought of the brown gowns and pinafores.

So, after much discussion, it was decided that she should have her way in all things and the family content themselves with applauding from the front.

"We'll blister our hands every man of us, and carry you home in a chariot and four see if we don't, you perverse prima donna!" threatened Steve, not at all satisfied with the simplicity of the affair.

"A chariot and two will be very acceptable as soon as I'm done. I shall be quite steady till my part is all over, and then I may feel a little upset, so I'd like to get away before the confusion begins. Indeed, I don't mean to be perverse, but you are all so kind to me, my heart is full whenever I think of it, and that wouldn't do if I'm to sing," said Phebe, dropping one of the tears on the little frill she was making.

"No diamond could have adorned it better," Archie thought as he watched it shine there for a moment, and felt like shaking Steve for daring to pat the dark head with an encouraging "All right. I'll be on hand and whisk you away while the rest are splitting their gloves. No fear of your breaking down. If you feel the least bit like it, though, just look at me and I'll glare at you and shake my fist, since kindness upsets you."

"I wish you would, because one of my ballads is rather touching and I always want to cry when I sing it. The sight of you trying to glare will make me want to laugh and that will steady me nicely, so sit in front, please, ready to slip out when I come off the last time."

"Depend upon me!" And the little man departed, taking great credit to himself for his influence over tall, handsome Phebe.

If he had known what was going on in the mind of the silent young gentleman behind the newspaper, Steve would have been much astonished, for Archie, though apparently engrossed by business, was fathoms deep in love by this time. No one suspected this but Rose, for he did his wooing with his eyes, and only Phebe knew how eloquent they could be. He had discovered what the matter was long ago had made many attempts to reason himself out of it, but, finding it a hopeless task, had given up trying and let himself drift deliciously. The knowledge that the family would not approve only seemed to add ardor to his love and strength to his purpose, for the same energy and persistence which he brought to business went into everything he did, and having once made up his mind to marry Phebe, nothing could change this plan except a word from her.

He watched and waited for three months, so that he might not be accused of precipitation, though it did not take him one to decide that this was the woman to make him happy. Her steadfast nature, quiet, busy ways, and the reserved power and passion betrayed sometimes by a flash of the black eyes, a quiver of the firm lips, suited Archie, who possessed many of the same attributes himself. The obscurity of her birth and isolation of her lot, which would have deterred some lovers, not only appealed to his kindly heart, but touched the hidden romance which ran like a vein of gold through his strong common sense and made practical, steady-going Archie a poet when he fell in love. If Uncle Mac had guessed what dreams and fancies went on in the head bent over his ledgers, and what emotions were fermenting in the bosom of his staid "right-hand man," he would have tapped his forehead and suggested a lunatic asylum. The boys thought Archie had sobered down too soon. His mother began to fear that the air of the counting room did not suit him, and Dr. Alec was deluded into the belief that the fellow really began to "think of Rose," he came so often in the evening, seeming quite content to sit beside her worktable and snip tape or draw patterns while they chatted.

No one observed that, though he talked to Rose on these occasions, he looked at Phebe, in her low chair close by, busy but silent, for she always tried to efface herself when Rose was near and often mourned that she was too big to keep out of sight. No matter what he talked about, Archie always saw the glossy black braids on the other side of the table, the damask cheek curving down into the firm white throat, and the dark lashes, lifted now and then, showing eyes so deep and soft he dared not look into them long. Even the swift needle charmed him, the little brooch which rose and fell with her quiet breath, the plain work she did, and the tidy way she gathered her bits of thread into a tiny bag. He seldom spoke to her; never touched her basket, though he ravaged Rose's if he wanted string or scissors; very rarely ventured to bring her some curious or pretty thing when ships came in from China only sat and thought of her, imagined that this was his parlor, this her worktable, and they two sitting there alone a happy man and wife.

At this stage of the little evening drama he would be conscious of such a strong desire to do something rash that he took refuge in a new form of intoxication and proposed music, sometimes so abruptly that Rose would pause in the middle of a sentence and look at him, surprised to meet a curiously excited look in the usually cool gray eyes.

Then Phebe, folding up her work, would go to the piano, as if glad to find a vent for the inner life which she seemed to have no power of expressing except in song. Rose would follow to accompany her, and Archie, moving to a certain shady corner whence he could see Phebe's face as she sang, would give himself up to unmitigated rapture for half an hour. Phebe never sang so well as at such times, for the kindly atmosphere was like sunshine to a bird, criticisms were few and gentle, praises hearty and abundant, and she poured out her soul as freely as a spring gushes up when its hidden source is full.

In moments such as these Phebe was beautiful with the beauty that makes a man's eye brighten with honest admiration and fills his heart with a sense of womanly nobility and sweetness. Little wonder, then, that the chief spectator of this agreeable tableau grew nightly more enamored, and while the elders were deep in whist, the young people were playing that still more absorbing game in which hearts are always trumps.

Rose, having Dummy for a partner, soon discovered the fact and lately had begun to feel as she fancied Wall must have done when Pyramus wooed Thisbe through its chinks. She was a little startled at first, then amused, then anxious, then heartily interested, as every woman is in such affairs, and willingly continued to be a medium, though sometimes she quite tingled with the electricity which seemed to pervade the air. She said nothing, waiting for Phebe to speak, but Phebe was silent, seeming to doubt the truth till doubt became impossible, then to shrink as if suddenly conscious of wrongdoing and seize every possible pretext for absenting herself from the "girls' corner," as the pretty recess was called.

The concert plan afforded excellent opportunities for doing this, and evening after evening she slipped away to practice her songs upstairs while Archie sat staring disconsolately at the neglected work basket and mute piano. Rose pitied him and longed to say a word of comfort, but felt shy he was such a reserved fellow so left him to conduct his quiet wooing in his own way, feeling that the crisis would soon arrive.

She was sure of this as she sat beside him on the evening of the concert, for while the rest of the family nodded and smiled, chatted and laughed in great spirits, Archie was as mute as a fish and sat with his arms tightly folded, as if to keep in any unruly emotions which might attempt to escape. He never looked at the program, but Rose knew when Phebe's turn came by the quick breath he drew and the intent look, so absent before, that came into his eyes.

But her own excitement prevented much notice of his, for Rose was in a flutter of hope and fear, sympathy and delight, about Phebe and her success. The house was crowded; the audience sufficiently mixed to make the general opinion impartial; and the stage full of little orphans with shining faces, a most effective reminder of the object in view.

"Little dears, how nice they look!" "Poor things, so young to be fatherless and motherless." "It will be a disgrace to the city if those girls are not taken proper care of." "Subscriptions are always in order, you know, and pretty Miss Campbell will give you her sweetest smile if you hand her a handsome check." "I've heard this Phebe Moore, and she really has a delicious voice such a pity she won't fit herself for opera!" "Only sings three times tonight; that's modest, I'm sure, when

182

she's the chief attraction, so we must give her an encore after the Italian piece." "The orphans lead off, I see. Stop your ears if you like, but don't fail to applaud or the ladies will never forgive you."

Chat of this sort went on briskly while fans waved, programs rustled, and ushers flew about distractedly, till an important gentleman appeared, made his bow, skipped upon the leader's stand, and with a wave of his baton caused a general uprising of white pinafores as the orphans led off with that much-enduring melody "America" in shrill small voices, but with creditable attention to time and tune. Pity and patriotism produced a generous round of applause, and the little girls sat down, beaming with innocent satisfaction.

An instrumental piece followed, and then a youthful gentleman, with his hair in picturesque confusion, and what his friends called a "musical brow," bounded up the steps and, clutching a roll of music with a pair of tightly gloved hands, proceed to inform the audience, in a husky tenor voice, that "It was a lovely violet."

What else the song contained in the way of sense or sentiment it was impossible to discover as the three pages of music appeared to consist of variations upon that one line, ending with a prolonged quaver which flushed the musical brow and left the youth quite breathless when he made his bow.

"Now she's coming! Oh, Uncle, my heart beats as if it were myself!" whispered Rose, clutching Dr. Alec's arm with a little gasp as the piano was rolled forward, the leader's stand pushed back, and all eyes turned toward the anteroom door.

She forgot to glance at Archie, and it was as well perhaps, for his heart was thumping almost audibly as he waited for his Phebe. Not from the anteroom, but out among the children, where she had sat unseen in the shadow of the organ, came stately Phebe in her wine-colored dress, with no ornament but her fine hair and a white flower at her throat. Very pale, but quite composed, apparently, for she stepped slowly through the narrow lane of upturned faces, holding back her skirts lest they should rudely brush against some little head. Straight to the front she went, bowed hastily, and, with a gesture to the accompanist, stood waiting to begin, her eyes fixed on the great gilt clock at the opposite end of the hall.

They never wandered from that point while she sang, but as she ended they dropped for an instant on an eager, girlish countenance bending from a front seat; then, with her hasty little bow, she went quickly back among the children, who clapped and nodded as she passed, well pleased with the ballad she had sung.

Everyone courteously followed their example, but there was no enthusiasm, and it was evident that Phebe had not produced a particularly favorable impression.

"Never sang so badly in her life," muttered Charlie irefully.

"She was frightened, poor thing. Give her time, give her time," said Uncle Mac kindly.

"I know she was, and I glared like a gorgon, but she never looked at me," added Steve, smoothing his gloves and his brows at the same time.

"That first song was the hardest, and she got through much better than I expected," put in Dr. Alec, bound not to show the disappointment he felt.

"Don't be troubled. Phebe has courage enough for anything, and she'll astonish you before the evening's over," prophesied Mac with unabated confidence, for he knew something the rest did not.

Rose said nothing, but under cover of her burnous gave Archie's hand a sympathetic squeeze, for his arms were unfolded now, as if the strain was over, and one lay on his knee while with the other he wiped his hot forehead with an air of relief.

Friends about them murmured complimentary fibs and affected great delight and surprise at Miss Moore's "charming style," "exquisite simplicity," and "undoubted talent." But strangers freely criticized, and Rose was so indignant at some of their remarks, she could not listen to anything on the stage, though a fine overture was played, a man with a remarkable bass voice growled and roared melodiously, and the orphans sang a lively air with a chorus of "Tra, la, la," which was a great relief to little tongues unused to long silence.

"I've often heard that women's tongues were hung in the middle and went at both ends now I'm sure of it," whispered Charlie, trying to cheer her up by pointing out the comical effect of some seventy-five open mouths in each of which the unruly member was wagging briskly.

Rose laughed and let him fan her, leaning from his seat behind with the devoted air he always assumed in public, but her wounded feelings were not soothed and she continued to frown at the stout man on the left who had dared to say with a shrug and a glance at Phebe's next piece, "That young woman can no more sing this Italian thing than she can fly, and they ought not to let her attempt it."

Phebe did, however, and suddenly changed the stout man's opinion by singing it grandly, for the consciousness of her first failure pricked her pride and spurred her to do her best with the calm sort of determination which conquers fear, fires ambition, and changes defeat to success. She looked steadily at Rose now, or the flushed, intent face beside her, and throwing all her soul into the task, let her voice ring out like a silver clarion, filling the great hall and setting the hearers' blood a-tingle with the exulting strain.

That settled Phebe's fate as a cantatrice. The applause was genuine and spontaneous this time and broke out again and again with the generous desire to atone for former coldness. But she would not return, and the shadow of the great organ seemed to have swallowed her up, for no eye could find her, no pleasant clamor win her back.

"Now I can die content," said Rose, beaming with heartfelt satisfaction while Archie looked steadfastly at his program, trying to keep his face in order, and the rest of the family assumed a triumphant air, as if they had never doubted from the first.

"Very well, indeed," said the stout man with an approving nod. "Quite promising for a beginner. Shouldn't wonder if in time they made a second Cary or Kellogg of her."

"Now you'll forgive him, won't you?" murmured Charlie in his cousin's ear.

"Yes, and I'd like to pat him on the head. But take warning and never judge by first appearances again," whispered Rose, at peace now with all mankind.

Phebe's last song was another ballad; she meant to devote her talent to that much neglected but always attractive branch of her art. It was a great surprise, therefore, to all but one person in the hall when, instead of singing "Auld Robin Grey," she placed herself at the piano, and, with a smiling glance over her shoulder at the children, broke out in the old bird song which first won Rose. But the chirping, twittering, and cooing were now the burden to three verses of a charming little song, full of springtime and the awakening life that makes it lovely. A rippling accompaniment flowed through it all, and a burst of delighted laughter from the children filled up the first pause with a fitting answer to the voices that seemed calling to them from the vernal woods.

It was very beautiful, and novelty lent its charm to the surprise, for art and nature worked a pretty miracle and the clever imitation, first heard from a kitchen hearth, now became the favorite in a crowded concert room. Phebe was quite herself again; color in the cheeks now; eyes that wandered smiling to and fro; and lips that sang as gaily and far more sweetly than when she kept time to her blithe music with a scrubbing brush.

This song was evidently intended for the children, and they appreciated the kindly thought, for as Phebe went back among them, they clapped ecstatically, flapped their pinafores, and some caught her by the skirts with audible requests to "Do it again, please; do it again."

But Phebe shook her head and vanished, for it was getting late for such small people, several of whom "lay sweetly slumbering there" till roused by the clamor round them. The elders, however, were not to be denied and applauded persistently, especially Aunt Plenty, who seized Uncle Mac's cane and pounded with it as vigorously as "Mrs. Nubbles" at the play.

"Never mind your gloves, Steve; keep it up till she comes," cried Charlie, enjoying the fun like a boy while Jamie lost his head with excitement and, standing up, called "Phebe! Phebe!" in spite of his mother's attempts to silence him.

Even the stout man clapped, and Rose could only laugh delightedly as she turned to look at Archie, who seemed to have let himself loose at last and was stamping with a dogged energy funny to see.

So Phebe had to come, and stood there meekly bowing, with a moved look on her face that showed how glad and grateful she was, till a sudden hush came; then, as if inspired by the memory of the cause that brought her there, she looked down into the sea of friendly faces before her, with no trace of fear in her own, and sang the song that never will grow old.

That went straight to the hearts of those who heard her, for there was something inexpressibly touching in the sight of this sweet-voiced woman singing of home for the little creatures who were homeless, and Phebe made her tuneful plea irresistible by an almost involuntary gesture of the hands which had hung loosely clasped before her till, with the last echo of the beloved word, they fell apart and were half outstretched, as if pleading to be filled.

It was the touch of nature that works wonders, for it made full purses suddenly weigh heavily in pockets slow to open, brought tears to eyes unused to weep, and caused that group of red-gowned girls to grow very pathetic in the sight of fathers and mothers who had left little daughters safe asleep at home. This was evident from the stillness that remained unbroken for an instant after Phebe ended; and before people could get rid of their handkerchiefs she would have been gone if the sudden appearance of a mite in a pinafore, climbing up the stairs from the anteroom with a great bouquet grasped in both hands, had not arrested her.

Up came the little creature, intent on performing the mission for which rich bribes of sugarplums had been promised, and trotting bravely across the stage, she held up the lovely nosegay, saying in her baby voice, "Dis for you, ma'am." Then, startled by the sudden outburst of applause, she hid her face in Phebe's gown and began to sob with fright.

An awkward minute for poor Phebe, but she showed unexpected presence of mind and left behind her a pretty picture of the oldest and youngest orphan as she went quickly down the step, smiling over the great bouquet with the baby on her arm.

Nobody minded the closing piece, for people began to go, sleepy children to be carried off, and whispers grew into a buzz of conversation. In the general confusion Rose looked to see if Steve had remembered his promise to help Phebe slip away before the rush began. No, there he was putting on Kitty's cloak, quite oblivious to any other duty. Turning to ask Archie to hurry out, Rose found that he had already vanished, leaving his gloves behind him.

"Have you lost anything?" asked Dr. Alec, catching a glimpse of her face.

"No, sir, I've found something," she whispered back, giving him the gloves to pocket along with her fan and glass, adding hastily as the concert ended, "Please, Uncle, tell them all not to come with us. Phebe has had enough excitement and ought to rest."

Rose's word was law to the family in all things concerning Phebe. So word was passed that there were to be no congratulations until tomorrow, and Dr. Alec got his party off as soon as possible. But all the way home, while he and Aunt Plenty were prophesying a brilliant future for the singer, Rose sat rejoicing over the happy present of the woman. She was sure that Archie had spoken and imagined the whole scene with feminine delight how tenderly he had asked the momentous question, how gratefully Phebe had given the desired reply, and now how both were enjoying that delicious hour which Rose had been given to understand never came but once. Such a pity to shorten it, she thought, and begged her uncle to go home the longest way the night was so mild, the moonlight so clear, and herself so in need of fresh air after the excitement of the evening.

"I thought you would want to rush into Phebe's arms the instant she got done," said Aunt Plenty, innocently wondering at the whims girls took into their heads.

"So I should if I consulted my own wishes, but as Phebe asked to be let alone I want to gratify her," answered Rose, making the best excuse she could.

"A little piqued," thought the doctor, fancying he understood the case.

As the old lady's rheumatism forbade their driving about till midnight, home was reached much too soon, Rose thought, and tripped away to warn the lovers the instant she entered the house. But study, parlor, and boudoir were empty; and, when Jane appeared with cake and wine, she reported that "Miss Phebe went right upstairs and wished to be excused, please, being very tired."

"That isn't at all like Phebe I hope she isn't ill," began Aunt Plenty, sitting down to toast her feet.

"She may be a little hysterical, for she is a proud thing and represses her emotions as long as she can. I'll step up and see if she doesn't need a soothing draft of some sort." And Dr. Alec threw off his coat as he spoke.

"No, no, she's only tired. I'll run up to her she won't mind me and I'll report if anything is amiss."

Away went Rose, quite trembling with suspense, but Phebe's door was shut, no light shone underneath, and no sound came from the room within. She tapped and receiving no answer, went on to her own chamber, thinking to herself: "Love always makes people queer, I've heard, so I suppose they settled it all in the carriage and the dear thing ran away to think about her happiness alone. I'll not disturb her. Why, Phebe!" said Rose, surprised, for, entering her room, there was the cantatrice, busy about the nightly services she always rendered her little mistress.

"I'm waiting for you, dear. Where have you been so long?" asked Phebe, poking the fire as if anxious to get some color into cheeks that were unnaturally pale.

The instant she spoke Rose knew that something was wrong, and a glance at her face confirmed the fear. It was like a dash of cold water and quenched her happy fancies in a moment; but being a delicate-minded girl, she respected Phebe's mood and asked no questions, made no comments, and left her friend to speak or be silent as she chose.

186

"I was so excited I would take a turn in the moonlight to calm my nerves. Oh, dearest Phebe, I am so glad, so proud, so full of wonder at your courage and skill and sweet ways altogether that I cannot half tell you how I love and honor you!" she cried, kissing the white cheeks with such tender warmth they could not help glowing faintly as Phebe held her little mistress close, sure that nothing could disturb this innocent affection.

"It is all your work, dear, because but for you I might still be scrubbing floors and hardly dare to dream of anything like this," she said in her old grateful way, but in her voice there was a thrill of something deeper than gratitude, and at the last two words her head went up with a gesture of soft pride as if it had been newly crowned.

Rose heard and saw and guessed at the meaning of both tone and gesture, feeling that her Phebe deserved both the singer's laurel and the bride's myrtle wreath. But she only looked up, saying very wistfully: "Then it has been a happy night for you as well as for us."

"The happiest of my life, and the hardest," answered Phebe briefly as she looked away from the questioning eyes.

"You should have let us come nearer and help you through. I'm afraid you are very proud, my Jenny Lind."

"I have to be, for sometimes I feel as if I had nothing else to keep me up." She stopped short there, fearing that her voice would prove traitorous if she went on. In a moment she asked in a tone that was almost hard: "You think I did well tonight?"

"They all think so, and were so delighted they wanted to come in a body and tell you so, but I sent them home because I knew you'd be tired out. Perhaps I ought not to have done it and you'd rather have had a crowd about you than just me?"

"It was the kindest thing you ever did, and what could I like better than 'just you,' my darling?"

Phebe seldom called her that, and when she did her heart was in the little word, making it so tender that Rose thought it the sweetest in the world, next to Uncle Alec's "my little girl." Now it was almost passionate, and Phebe's face grew rather tragical as she looked down at Rose. It was impossible to seem unconscious any longer, and Rose said, caressing Phebe's cheek, which burned with a feverish color now: "Then don't shut me out if you have a trouble, but let me share it as I let you share all mine."

"I will! Little mistress, I've got to go away, sooner even than we planned."

"Why, Phebe?"

"Because Archie loves me."

"That's the very reason you should stay and make him happy."

"Not if it caused dissension in the family, and you know it would."

Rose opened her lips to deny this impetuously, but checked herself and answered honestly: "Uncle and I would be heartily glad, and I'm sure Aunt Jessie never could object if you loved Archie as he does you."

"She has other hopes, I think, and kind as she is, it would be a disappointment if he brought me home. She is right, they all are, and I alone am to blame. I should have gone long ago I knew I should, but it was so pleasant, I couldn't bear to go away alone."

"I kept you, and I am to blame if anyone, but indeed, dear Phebe, I cannot see why you should care even if Aunt Myra croaks and Aunt Clara exclaims or Aunt Jane makes disagreeable remarks. Be happy, and never mind them," cried Rose, so much excited by all this that she felt the spirit of revolt rise up within her and was ready to defy even that awe-inspiring institution "the family" for her friend's sake.

But Phebe shook her head with a sad smile and answered, still with the hard tone in her voice as if forcing back all emotion that she might see her duty clearly: "You could do that, but I never can. Answer me this, Rose, and answer truly as you love me. If you had been taken into a house, a friendless, penniless, forlorn girl, and for years been heaped with benefits, trusted, taught, loved, and made, oh, so happy! could you think it right to steal away something that these good people valued very much? To have them feel that you had been ungrateful, had deceived them, and meant to thrust yourself into a high place not fit for you when they had been generously helping you in other ways, far more than you deserved. Could you then say as you do now, 'Be happy, and never mind them'?"

Phebe held Rose by the shoulders now and searched her face so keenly that the other shrank a little, for the black eyes were full of fire and there was something almost grand about this girl who seemed suddenly to have become a woman. There was no need for words to answer the question so swiftly asked, for Rose put herself in Phebe's place in the drawing of a breath, and her own pride made her truthfully reply: "No I could not!"

"I knew you'd say that, and help me do my duty." And all the coldness melted out of Phebe's manner as she hugged her little mistress close, feeling the comfort of sympathy even through the blunt sincerity of Rose's words.

"I will if I know how. Now, come and tell me all about it." And, seating herself in the great chair which had often held them both, Rose stretched out her hands as if glad and ready to give help of any sort.

But Phebe would not take her accustomed place, for, as if coming to confession, she knelt down upon the rug and, leaning on the arm of the chair, told her love story in the simplest words.

"I never thought he cared for me until a little while ago. I fancied it was you, and even when I knew he liked to hear me sing I supposed it was because you helped, and so I did my best and was glad you were to be a happy girl. But his eyes told the truth. Then I saw what I had been doing and was frightened. He did not speak, so I believed, what is quite true, that he felt I was not a fit wife for him and would never ask me. It was right I was glad of it, yet I was proud and, though I did not ask or hope for anything, I did want him to see that I respected myself, remembered my duty, and could do right as well as he. I kept away. I planned to go as soon as possible and resolved that at this concert I would do so well, he should not be ashamed of poor Phebe and her one gift."

"It was this that made you so strange, then, preferring to go alone and refusing every little favor at our hands?" asked Rose, feeling very sure now about the state of Phebe's heart.

"Yes, I wanted to do everything myself and not owe one jot of my success, if I had any, to even the dearest friend I've got. It was bad and foolish of me, and I was punished by the first dreadful failure. I was so frightened, Rose! My breath was all gone, my eyes so dizzy I could hardly see, and that great crowd of faces seemed so near, I dared not look. If it had not been for the clock I never should have gotten through, and when I did, not knowing in the least how I'd sung, one look at your distressed face told me I'd failed."

"But I smiled, Phebe indeed I did as sweetly as I could, for I was sure it was only fright," protested Rose eagerly.

"So you did, but the smile was full of pity, not of pride, as I wanted it to be, and I rushed into a dark place behind the organ, feeling ready to kill myself. How angry and miserable I was! I set my teeth, clenched my hands, and vowed that I would do well next time or never sing another note. I was quite desperate when my turn came, and felt as if I could do almost anything, for I remembered that he was there. I'm not sure how it was, but it seemed as if I was all voice, for I let myself go, trying to forget everything except that two people must not be disappointed, though I died when the song was done."

"Oh, Phebe, it was splendid! I nearly cried, I was so proud and glad to see you do yourself justice at last."

"And he?" whispered Phebe, with her face half hidden on the arm of the chair.

"Said not a word, but I saw his lips tremble and his eyes shine and I knew he was the happiest creature there, because I was sure he did think you fit to be his wife and did mean to speak very soon."

Phebe made no answer for a moment, seeming to forget the small success in the greater one which followed and to comfort her sore heart with the knowledge that Rose was right.

"He sent the flowers, he came for me, and, on the way home, showed me how wrong I had been to doubt him for an hour. Don't ask me to tell that part, but be sure I was the happiest creature in the world then."

And Phebe hid her face again, all wet with tender tears that fell soft and sudden as a summer shower.

Rose let them flow undisturbed while she silently caressed the bent head, wondering, with a wistful look in her own wet eyes, what this mysterious passion was which could so move, ennoble, and beautify the beings whom it blessed.

An impertinent little clock upon the chimneypiece striking eleven broke the silence and reminded Phebe that she could not indulge in love dreams there. She started up, brushed off her tears, and said resolutely: "That is enough for tonight. Go happily to bed, and leave the troubles for tomorrow."

"But, Phebe, I must know what you said," cried Rose, like a child defrauded of half its bedtime story.

"I said, 'No.'"

"Ah! But it will change to 'yes' by and by, I'm sure of that so I'll let you go to dream of him. The Campbells are rather proud of being descendants of Robert the Bruce, but they have common sense and love you dearly, as you'll see tomorrow."

"Perhaps." And with a good night kiss, poor Phebe went away, to lie awake till dawn.

Chapter 8 BREAKERS AHEAD

Anxious to smooth the way for Phebe, Rose was up betimes and slipped into Aunt Plenty's room before the old lady had gotten her cap on.

"Aunty, I've something pleasant to tell you, and while you listen, I'll brush your hair, as you like to have me," she began, well aware that the proposed process was a very soothing one.

"Yes, dear only don't be too particular, because I'm late and must hurry down or Jane won't get things straight, and it does fidget me to have the saltcellars uneven, the tea strainer forgotten, and your uncle's paper not aired," returned Miss Plenty, briskly unrolling the two gray curls she wore at her temples.

Then Rose, brushing away at the scanty back hair, led skillfully up to the crisis of her tale by describing Phebe's panic and brave efforts to conquer it; all about the flowers Archie sent her; and how Steve forgot, and dear, thoughtful Archie took his place. So far it went well and Aunt Plenty was full of interest, sympathy, and approbation, but when Rose added, as if it was quite a matter of course, "So, on the way home, he told her he loved her," a great start twitched the gray locks out of her hands as the old lady turned around, with the little curls standing erect, exclaiming, in undisguised dismay: "Not seriously, Rose?"

"Yes, Aunty, very seriously. He never jokes about such things."

"Mercy on us! What shall we do about it?"

"Nothing, ma'am, but be as glad as we ought and congratulate him as soon as she says 'yes.'?

"Do you mean to say she didn't accept at once?"

"She never will if we don't welcome her as kindly as if she belonged to one of our best families, and I don't blame her."

"I'm glad the girl has so much sense. Of course we can't do anything of the sort, and I'm surprised at Archie's forgetting what he owes to the family in this rash manner. Give me my cap, child I must speak to Alec at once." And Aunt Plenty twisted her hair into a button at the back of her head with one energetic twirl.

"Do speak kindly, Aunty, and remember that it was not Phebe's fault. She never thought of this till very lately and began at once to prepare for going away," said Rose pleadingly.

"She ought to have gone long ago. I told Myra we should have trouble somewhere as soon as I saw what a good-looking creature she was, and here it is as bad as can be. Dear, dear! Why can't young people have a little prudence?"

"I don't see that anyone need object if Uncle Jem and Aunt Jessie approve, and I do think it will be very, very unkind to scold poor Phebe for being well-bred, pretty, and good, after doing all we could to make her so."

"Child, you don't understand these things yet, but you ought to feel your duty toward your family and do all you can to keep the name as honorable as it always has been. What do you suppose our blessed ancestress Lady Marget would say to our oldest boy taking a wife from the poorhouse?"

As she spoke, Miss Plenty looked up, almost apprehensively, at one of the wooden-faced old portraits with which her room was hung, as if asking pardon of the severe-nosed matron who stared back at her from under the sort of blue dish cover which formed her headgear.

"As Lady Marget died about two hundred years ago, I don't care a pin what she would say, especially as she looks like a very narrow-minded, haughty woman. But I do care very much what Miss Plenty Campbell says, for she is a very sensible, generous, discreet, and dear old lady who wouldn't hurt a fly, much less a good and faithful girl who has been a sister to me. Would she?" entreated Rose, knowing well that the elder aunt led all the rest more or less.

But Miss Plenty had her cap on now and consequently felt herself twice the woman she was without it, so she not only gave it a somewhat belligerent air by setting it well up, but she shook her head decidedly, smoothed down her stiff white apron, and stood up as if ready for battle.

"I shall do my duty, Rose, and expect the same of others. Don't say any more now I must turn the matter over in my mind, for it has come upon me suddenly and needs serious consideration."

With which unusually solemn address she took up her keys and trotted away, leaving her niece to follow with an anxious countenance, uncertain whether her championship had done good or ill to the cause she had at heart.

She was much cheered by the sound of Phebe's voice in the study, for Rose was sure that if Uncle Alec was on their side all would be well. But the clouds lowered again when they came in to breakfast, for Phebe's heavy eyes and pale cheeks did not look encouraging, while Dr. Alec was as sober as a judge and sent an inquiring glance toward Rose now and then as if curious to discover how she bore the news.

An uncomfortable meal, though all tried to seem as usual and talked over last night's events with all the interest they could. But the old peace was disturbed by a word, as a pebble thrown into a quiet pool sends telltale circles rippling its surface far and wide. Aunt Plenty, while "turning the subject over in her mind," also seemed intent on upsetting everything she touched and made sad havoc in her tea tray; Dr. Alec unsociably read his paper; Rose, having salted instead of sugared her oatmeal, absently ate it, feeling that the sweetness had gone out of everything; and Phebe, after choking down a cup of tea and crumbling a roll, excused herself and went away, sternly resolving not to be a bone of contention to this beloved family.

As soon as the door was shut Rose pushed away her plate and, going to Dr. Alec, she peeped over the paper with such an anxious face that he put it down at once.

"Uncle, this is a serious matter, and we must take our stand at once, for you are Phebe's guardian and I am her sister," began Rose with pretty solemnity. "You have often been disappointed in me," she continued, "but I know I never shall be in you because you are too wise and good to let any worldly pride or prudence spoil your sympathy with Archie and our Phebe. You won't desert them, will you?"

"Never!" answered Dr. Alec with gratifying energy.

"Thank you! Thank you!" cried Rose. "Now, if I have you and Aunty on my side, I'm not afraid of anybody."

"Gently, gently, child. I don't intend to desert the lovers, but I certainly shall advise them to consider well what they are about. I'll own I am rather disappointed, because Archie is young to decide his life in this way and Phebe's career seemed settled in another fashion. Old people don't like to have their plans upset, you know," he added more lightly, for Rose's face fell as he went on.

"Old people shouldn't plan too much for the young ones, then. We are very grateful, I'm sure, but we cannot always be disposed of in the most prudent and sensible way, so don't set your hearts on little arrangements of that sort, I beg," And Rose looked wondrous wise, for she could not help suspecting even her best uncle of "plans" in her behalf.

"You are quite right-we shouldn't, yet it is very hard to help it," confessed Dr. Alec with a conscious air, and, returning hastily to the lovers, he added kindly: "I was much pleased with the straightforward way in which Phebe came to me this morning and told me all about it, as if I really was her guardian. She did not own it in words, but it was perfectly evident that she loves Archie with all her heart, yet, knowing the objections which will be made, very sensibly and bravely proposes to go away at once and end the matter as if that were possible, poor child." And the tenderhearted man gave a sigh of sympathy that did Rose good to hear and mollified her rising indignation at the bare idea of ending Phebe's love affairs in such a summary way.

"You don't think she ought to go, I hope?"

"I think she will go."

"We must not let her."

"We have no right to keep her."

"Oh, Uncle, surely we have! Our Phebe, whom we all love so much."

"You forget that she is a woman now, and we have no claim on her. Because we've befriended her for years is the very reason we should not make our benefits a burden, but leave her free, and if she chooses to do this in spite of Archie, we must let her with a Godspeed."

Before Rose could answer, Aunt Plenty spoke out like one having authority, for old-fashioned ways were dear to her soul and she thought even love affairs should be conducted with a proper regard to the powers that be.

"The family must talk the matter over and decide what is best for the children, who of course will listen to reason and do nothing ill advised. For my part, I am quite upset by the news, but shall not commit myself till I've seen Jessie and the boy. Jane, clear away, and bring me the hot water."

That ended the morning conference. And, leaving the old lady to soothe her mind by polishing spoons and washing cups, Rose went away to find Phebe while the doctor retired to laugh over the downfall of brother Mac's matchmaking schemes.

The Campbells did not gossip about their concerns in public, but being a very united family, it had long been the custom to "talk over" any interesting event which occurred to any member thereof, and everyone gave his or her opinion, advice, or censure with the utmost candor. Therefore the first engagement, if such it could be called, created a great sensation, among the aunts especially, and they were in as much of a flutter as a flock of maternal birds when their young begin to hop out of the nest. So at all hours the excellent ladies were seen excitedly nodding their caps together as they discussed the affair in all its bearings, without ever arriving at any unanimous decision.

The boys took it much more calmly. Mac was the only one who came out strongly in Archie's favor. Charlie thought the Chief ought to do better and called Phebe "a siren who had bewitched the sage youth." Steve was scandalized and delivered long orations upon one's duty to society, keeping the old name up, and the danger of mésalliances, while all the time he secretly sympathized with Archie, being much smitten with Kitty Van himself. Will and Geordie, unfortunately home for the holidays, considered it "a jolly lark," and little Jamie nearly drove his elder brother distracted by curious inquiries as to "how folks felt when they were in love."

Uncle Mac's dismay was so comical that it kept Dr. Alec in good spirits, for he alone knew how deep was the deluded man's chagrin at the failure of the little plot which he fancied was prospering finely.

"I'll never set my heart on anything of the sort again, and the young rascals may marry whom they like. I'm prepared for anything now—so if Steve brings home the washerwoman's daughter, and Mac runs away with our pretty chambermaid, I shall say, 'Bless you my children,' with mournful resignation, for, upon my soul, that is all that's left for a modern parent to do."

With which tragic burst, poor Uncle Mac washed his hands of the whole affair and buried himself in the countinghouse while the storm raged.

About this time Archie might have echoed Rose's childish wish, that she had not quite so many aunts, for the tongues of those interested relatives made sad havoc with his little romance and caused him to long fervently for a desert island where he could woo and win his love in delicious peace. That nothing of the sort was possible soon became evident, since every word uttered only confirmed Phebe's resolution to go away and proved to Rose how mistaken she had been in believing that she could bring everyone to her way of thinking.

Prejudices are unmanageable things, and the good aunts, like most women, possessed a plentiful supply, so Rose found it like beating her head against a wall to try and convince them that Archie was wise in loving poor Phebe. His mother, who had hoped to have Rose for her daughter not because of her fortune, but the tender affection she felt for her put away her disappointment without a word and welcomed Phebe as kindly as she could for her boy's sake. But the girl felt the truth with the quickness of a nature made sensitive by love and clung to her resolve all the more tenaciously, though grateful for the motherly words that would have been so sweet if genuine happiness had prompted them.

Aunt Jane called it romantic nonsense and advised strong measures "kind, but firm, Jessie." Aunt Clara was sadly distressed about "what people would say" if one of "our boys" married a nobody's daughter. And Aunt Myra not only seconded her views by painting portraits of Phebe's unknown relations in the darkest colors but uttered direful prophecies regarding the disreputable beings who would start up in swarms the moment the girl made a good match.

These suggestions so wrought upon Aunt Plenty that she turned a deaf ear to the benevolent emotions native to her breast and, taking refuge behind "our blessed ancestress, Lady Marget," refused to sanction any engagement which could bring discredit upon the stainless name which was her pride.

So it all ended where it began, for Archie steadily refused to listen to anyone but Phebe, and she as steadily reiterated her bitter "No!" fortifying herself half unconsciously with the hope that, by and by, when she had won a name, fate might be kinder.

While the rest talked, she had been working, for every hour showed her that her instinct had been a true one and pride would not let her stay, though love pleaded eloquently. So, after a Christmas anything but merry, Phebe packed her trunks, rich in gifts from those who generously gave her all but the one thing she desired, and, with a pocketful of letters to people who could further her plans, she went away to seek her fortune, with a brave face and a very heavy heart.

"Write often, and let me know all you do, my Phebe, and remember I shall never be contented till you come back again," whispered Rose, clinging to her till the last.

"She will come back, for in a year I'm going to bring her home, please God," said Archie, pale with the pain of parting but as resolute as she.

"I'll earn my welcome then perhaps it will be easier for them to give and me to receive it," answered Phebe, with a backward glance at the group of caps in the hall as she went down the steps on Dr. Alec's arm.

"You earned it long ago, and it is always waiting for you while I am here. Remember that, and God bless you, my good girl," he said, with a paternal kiss that warmed her heart.

"I never shall forget it!" And Phebe never did.

Chapter 9 NEW YEAR'S CALLS
"Now I'm going to turn over a new leaf, as I promised. I wonder what I shall find on the next page?" said Rose, coming down on New Year's morning with a serious face and a thick letter in her hand.

"Tired of frivolity, my dear?" asked her uncle, pausing in his walk up and down the hall to glance at her with a quick, bright look she liked to bring into his eyes.

"No, sir, and that's the sad part of it, but I've made up my mind to stop while I can because I'm sure it is not good for me. I've had some very sober thoughts lately, for since my Phebe went away I've had no heart for gaiety, so it is a good place to stop and make a fresh start," answered Rose, taking his arm and walking on with him.

"An excellent time! Now, how are you going to fill the aching void?" he asked, well pleased.

"By trying to be as unselfish, brave, and good as she is." And Rose held the letter against her bosom with a tender touch, for Phebe's strength had inspired her with a desire to be as self-reliant. "I'm going to set about living in earnest, as she has; though I think it will be harder for me than for her, because she stands alone and has a career marked out for her. I'm nothing but a commonplace sort of girl, with no end of relations to be consulted every time I wink and a dreadful fortune hanging like a millstone round my neck to weigh me down if I try to fly. It is a hard case, Uncle, and I get low in my mind when I think about it," sighed Rose, oppressed with her blessings.

"Afflicted child! How can I relieve you?" And there was amusement as well as sympathy in Dr. Alec's face as he patted the hand upon his arm.

"Please don't laugh, for I really am trying to be good. In the first place, help me to wean myself from foolish pleasures and show me how to occupy my thoughts and time so that I may not idle about and dream instead of doing great things."

"Good! We'll begin at once. Come to town with me this morning and see your houses. They are all ready, and Mrs. Gardner has half a dozen poor souls waiting to go in as soon as you give the word," answered the doctor promptly, glad to get his girl back again, though not surprised that she still looked with regretful eyes at the Vanity Fair, always so enticing when we are young.

"I'll give it today, and make the new year a happy one to those poor souls at least. I'm so sorry that it's impossible for me to go with you, but you know I must help Aunty Plen receive. We haven't been here for so long that she had set her heart on having a grand time today, and I particularly want to please her because I have not been as amiable as I ought lately. I really couldn't forgive her for siding against Phebe."

"She did what she thought was right, so we must not blame her. I am going to make my New Year's calls today and, as my friends live down that way, I'll get the list of names from Mrs. G. and tell the poor ladies, with Miss Campbell's compliments, that their new home is ready. Shall I?"

"Yes, Uncle, but take all the credit to yourself, for I never should have thought of it if you had not proposed the plan."

"Bless your heart! I'm only your agent, and suggest now and then. I've nothing to offer but advice, so I lavish that on all occasions."

"You have nothing because you've given your substance all away as generously as you do your advice. Never mind you shall never come to want while I live. I'll save enough for us two, though I do make 'ducks and drakes of my fortune.'"

Dr. Alec laughed at the toss of the head with which she quoted Charlie's offensive words, then offered to take the letter, saying, as he looked at his watch: "I'll post that for you in time for the early mail. I like a run before breakfast."

But Rose held her letter fast, dimpling with sudden smiles, half merry and half shy.

"No thank you, sir. Archie likes to do that, and never fails to call for all I write. He gets a peep at Phebe's in return and I cheer him up a bit, for, though he says nothing, he has a hard time of it, poor fellow."

"How many letters in five days?"

"Four, sir, to me. She doesn't write to him, Uncle."

"As yet. Well, you show hers, so it's all right and you are a set of sentimental youngsters." And the doctor walked away, looking as if he enjoyed the sentiment as much as any of them.

Old Miss Campbell was nearly as great a favorite as young Miss Campbell, so a succession of black coats and white gloves flowed in and out of the hospitable mansion pretty steadily all day. The clan was out in great force, and came by in installments to pay their duty to Aunt Plenty and wish the compliments of the season to "our cousin." Archie appeared first, looking sad but steadfast, and went away with Phebe's letter in his left breast pocket feeling that life was still endurable, though his love was torn from him, for Rose had many comfortable things to say and read him delicious bits from the voluminous correspondence lately begun.

Hardly was he gone when Will and Geordie came marching in, looking as fine as gray uniforms with much scarlet piping could make them and feeling peculiarly important, as this was their first essay in New Year's call-making. Brief was their stay, for they planned to visit every friend they had, and Rose could not help laughing at the droll mixture of manly dignity and boyish delight with which they drove off in their own carriage, both as erect as ramrods, arms folded, and caps stuck at exactly the same angle on each blond head.

"Here comes the other couple Steve, in full feather, with a big bouquet for Kitty, and poor Mac, looking like a gentleman and feeling like a martyr, I'm sure," said Rose, watching one carriage turn in as the other turned out of the great gate, with its arch of holly, ivy, and evergreen.

"Here he is. I've got him in tow for the day and want you to cheer him up with a word of praise, for he came without a struggle though planning to bolt somewhere with Uncle," cried Steve, falling back to display his brother, who came in looking remarkably well in his state and festival array, for polishing had begun to tell.

"A happy New Year, Aunty, same to you, Cousin, and best wishes for as many more as you deserve," said Mac, heeding Steve no more than if he had been a fly as he gave the old lady a hearty kiss and offered Rose a quaint little nosegay of pansies.

"Heart's-ease do you think I need it?" she asked, looking up with sudden sobriety.

"We all do. Could I give you anything better on a day like this?"

"No thank you very much." And a sudden dew came to Rose's eyes, for, though often blunt in speech, when Mac did do a tender thing, it always touched her because he seemed to understand her moods so well.

"Has Archie been here? He said he shouldn't go anywhere else, but I hope you talked that nonsense out of his head," said Steve, settling his tie before the mirror.

"Yes, dear, he came but looked so out of spirits I really felt reproached. Rose cheered him up a little, but I don't believe he will feel equal to making calls and I hope he won't, for his face tells the whole story much too plainly," answered Aunty Plenty, rustling about her bountiful table in her richest black silk with all her old lace on.

"Oh, he'll get over it in a month or two, and Phebe will soon find another lover, so don't be worried about him, Aunty," said Steve, with the air of a man who knew all about that sort of thing.

"If Archie does forget, I shall despise him, and I know Phebe won't try to find another lover, though she'll probably have them she is so sweet and good!" cried Rose indignantly, for, having taken the pair under her protection, she defended them valiantly.

"Then you'd have Arch hope against hope and never give up, would you?" asked Mac, putting on his glasses to survey the thin boots which were his especial abomination.

"Yes, I would, for a lover is not worth having if he's not in earnest!"

"Exactly. So you'd like them to wait and work and keep on loving till they made you relent or plainly proved that it was no use."

"If they were good as well as constant, I think I should relent in time."

"I'll mention that to Pemberton, for he seemed to be hit the hardest, and a ray of hope will do him good, whether he is equal to the ten years' wait or not," put in Steve, who liked to rally Rose about her lovers.

"I'll never forgive you if you say a word to anyone. It is only Mac's odd way of asking questions, and I ought not to answer them. You will talk about such things and I can't stop you, but I don't like it," said Rose, much annoyed.

"Poor little Penelope! She shall not be teased about her suitors but left in peace till her Ulysses comes home," said Mac, sitting down to read the mottoes sticking out of certain fanciful bonbons on the table.

"It is this fuss about Archie which has demoralized us all. Even the owl waked up and hasn't got over the excitement yet, you see. He's had no experience, poor fellow, so he doesn't know how to behave," observed Steve, regarding his bouquet with tender interest.

"That's true, and I asked for information because I may be in love myself someday and all this will be useful, don't you see?"

"You in love!" And Steve could not restrain a laugh at the idea of the bookworm a slave to the tender passion.

Quite unruffled, Mac leaned his chin in both hands, regarding them with a meditative eye as he answered in his whimsical way: "Why not? I intend to study love as well as medicine, for it is one of the most mysterious and remarkable diseases that afflict mankind, and the best way to understand it is to have it. I may catch it someday, and then I should like to know how to treat and cure it."

"If you take it as badly as you did measles and whooping cough, it will go hard with you, old fellow," said Steve, much amused with the fancy.

"I want it to. No great experience comes or goes easily, and this is the greatest we can know, I believe, except death."

Something in Mac's quiet tone and thoughtful eyes made Rose look at him in surprise, for she had never heard him speak in that way before. Steve also stared for an instant, equally amazed, then said below his breath, with an air of mock anxiety: "He's been catching something at the hospital, typhoid probably, and is beginning to wander. I'll take him quietly away before he gets any wilder. Come, old lunatic, we must be off."

"Don't be alarmed. I'm all right and much obliged for your advice, for I fancy I shall be a desperate lover when my time comes, if it ever does. You don't think it impossible, do you?" And Mac put the question so soberly that there was a general smile.

"Certainly not you'll be a regular Douglas, tender and true," answered Rose, wondering what queer question would come next.

"Thank you. The fact is, I've been with Archie so much in his trouble lately that I've gotten interested in this matter and very naturally want to investigate the subject as every rational man must, sooner or later, that's all. Now, Steve, I'm ready." And Mac got up as if the lesson was over.

"My dear, that boy is either a fool or a genius, and I'm sure I should be glad to know which," said Aunt Plenty, putting her bonbons to rights with a puzzled shake of her best cap.

"Time will show, but I incline to think that he is not a fool by any means," answered the girl, pulling a cluster of white roses out of her bosom to make room for the pansies, though they did not suit the blue gown half so well.

Just then Aunt Jessie came in to help them receive, with Jamie to make himself generally useful, which he proceeded to do by hovering around the table like a fly about a honey pot when not flattening his nose against the windowpanes to announce excitedly, "Here's another man coming up the drive!"

197

Charlie arrived next in his most sunshiny humor, for anything social and festive was his delight, and when in this mood the Prince was quite irresistible. He brought a pretty bracelet for Rose and was graciously allowed to put it on while she chid him gently for his extravagance.

"I am only following your example, for you know 'nothing is too good for those we love, and giving away is the best thing one can do,'" he retorted, quoting words of her own.

"I wish you would follow my example in some other things as well as you do in this," said Rose soberly as Aunt Plenty called him to come and see if the punch was right.

"Must conform to the customs of society. Aunty's heart would be broken if we did not drink her health in the good old fashion. But don't be alarmed I've a strong head of my own, and that's lucky, for I shall need it before I get through," laughed Charlie, showing a long list as he turned away to gratify the old lady with all sorts of merry and affectionate compliments as the glasses touched.

Rose did feel rather alarmed, for if he drank the health of all the owners of those names, she felt sure that Charlie would need a very strong head indeed. It was hard to say anything then and there without seeming disrespect to Aunt Plenty, yet she longed to remind her cousin of the example she tried to set him in this respect, for Rose never touched wine, and the boys knew it. She was thoughtfully turning the bracelet, with its pretty device of turquoise forget-me-nots, when the giver came back to her, still bubbling over with good spirits.

"Dear little saint, you look as if you'd like to smash all the punch bowls in the city, and save us jolly young fellows from tomorrow's headache."

"I should, for such headaches sometimes end in heartaches, I'm afraid. Dear Charlie, don't be angry, but you know better than I that this is a dangerous day for such as you so do be careful for my sake," she added, with an unwonted touch of tenderness in her voice, for, looking at the gallant figure before her, it was impossible to repress the womanly longing to keep it always as brave and blithe as now.

Charlie saw that new softness in the eyes that never looked unkindly on him, fancied that it meant more than it did, and, with a sudden fervor in his own voice, answered quickly: "My darling, I will!"

The glow which had risen to his face was reflected in hers, for at that moment it seemed as if it would be possible to love this cousin who was so willing to be led by her and so much needed some helpful influence to make a noble man of him. The thought came and went like a flash, but gave her a quick heartthrob, as if the old affection was trembling on the verge of some warmer sentiment, and left her with a sense of responsibility never felt before. Obeying the impulse, she said, with a pretty blending of earnestness and playfulness, "If I wear the bracelet to remember you by, you must wear this to remind you of your promise."

"And you," whispered Charlie, bending his head to kiss the hands that put a little white rose in his buttonhole.

Just at that most interesting moment they became aware of an arrival in the front drawing room, whither Aunt Plenty had discreetly retired. Rose felt grateful for the interruption, because, not being at all sure of the state of her heart as yet, she was afraid of letting a sudden impulse lead her too far. But Charlie, conscious that a very propitious instant had been spoiled, regarded the newcomer with anything but a benignant expression of countenance and, whispering, "Good-bye, my Rose, I shall look in this evening to see how you are after the fatigues of the day," he went away, with such a cool nod to poor Fun See that the amiable Asiatic thought he must have mortally offended him.

Rose had little leisure to analyze the new emotions of which she was conscious, for Mr. Tokio came up at once to make his compliments with a comical mingling of Chinese courtesy and American awkwardness, and before he had got his hat on Jamie shouted with admiring energy: "Here's another! Oh, such a swell!"

They now came thick and fast for many hours, and the ladies stood bravely at their posts till late into the evening. Then Aunt Jessie went home, escorted by a very sleepy little son, and Aunt Plenty retired to bed, used up. Dr. Alec had returned in good season, for his friends were not fashionable ones, but Aunt Myra had sent up for him in hot haste and he had good-naturedly obeyed the summons. In fact, he was quite used to them now, for Mrs. Myra, having tried a variety of dangerous diseases, had finally decided upon heart complaint as the one most likely to keep her friends in a chronic state of anxiety and was continually sending word that she was dying. One gets used to palpitations as well as everything else, so the doctor felt no alarm but always went and prescribed some harmless remedy with the most amiable sobriety and patience.

Rose was tired but not sleepy and wanted to think over several things, so instead of going to bed she sat down before the open fire in the study to wait for her uncle and perhaps Charlie, though she did not expect him so late.

Aunt Myra's palpitations must have been unusually severe, for the clock struck twelve before Dr. Alec came, and Rose was preparing to end her reverie when the sound of someone fumbling at the hall door made her jump up, saying to herself: "Poor man! His hands are so cold he can't get his latchkey in. Is that you, Uncle?" she added, running to admit him, for Jane was slow and the night as bitter as it was brilliant.

A voice answered, "Yes." And as the door swung open, in walked, not Dr. Alec, but Charlie, who immediately took one of the hall chairs and sat there with his hat on, rubbing his gloveless hands and blinking as if the light dazzled him, as he said in a rapid, abrupt sort of tone, "I told you I'd come left the fellows keeping it up gloriously going to see the old year out, you know. But I promised never break my word and here I am. Angel in blue, did you slay your thousands?"

"Hush! The waiters are still about. Come to the study fire and warm yourself, you must be frozen," said Rose, going before to roll up the easy chair.

"Not at all never warmer looks very comfortable, though. Where's Uncle?" asked Charlie, following with his hat still on, his hands in his pockets, and his eye fixed steadily on the bright head in front of him.

"Aunt Myra sent for him, and I was waiting up to see how she was," answered Rose, busily mending the fire.

Charlie laughed and sat down upon a corner of the library table. "Poor old soul! What a pity she doesn't die before he is quite worn out. A little too much ether some of these times would send her off quite comfortably, you know."

"Don't speak in that way. Uncle says imaginary troubles are often as hard to bear as real ones," said Rose, turning around displeased.

Till now she had not fairly looked at him, for recollections of the morning made her a little shy. His attitude and appearance surprised her as much as his words, and the quick change in her face seemed to remind him of his manners. Getting up, he hastily took off his hat and stood looking at her with a curiously fixed yet absent look as he said in the same rapid, abrupt way, as if, when once started, he found it hard to stop, "I beg pardon only joking very bad taste I know, and won't do it again. The heat of the room makes me a little dizzy, and I think I got a chill coming out. It is cold I am frozen, I daresay though I drove like the devil."

"Not that bad horse of yours, I hope? I know it is dangerous, so late and alone," said Rose, shrinking behind the big chair as Charlie approached the fire, carefully avoiding a footstool in his way.

"Danger is exciting that's why I like it. No man ever called me a coward let him try it once. I never give in and that horse shall not conquer me. I'll break his neck, if he breaks my spirit doing it. No I don't mean that never mind it's all right," and Charlie laughed in a way that troubled her, because there was no mirth in it.

"Have you had a pleasant day?" asked Rose, looking at him intently as he stood pondering over the cigar and match which he held, as if doubtful which to strike and which to smoke.

"Day? Oh, yes, capital. About two thousand calls, and a nice little supper at the Club. Randal can't sing any more than a crow, but I left him with a glass of champagne upside down, trying to give them my old favorite:

"'Tis better to laugh than be sighing,"

and Charlie burst forth in that bacchanalian melody at the top of his voice, waving an allumette holder over his head to represent Randal's inverted wineglass.

"Hush! You'll wake Aunty," cried Rose in a tone so commanding that he broke off in the middle of a roulade to stare at her with a blank look as he said apologetically, "I was merely showing how it should be done. Don't be angry, dearest look at me as you did this morning, and I'll swear never to sing another note if you say so. I'm only a little gay we drank your health handsomely, and they all congratulated me. Told 'em it wasn't out yet. Stop, though I didn't mean to mention that. No matter I'm always in a scrape, but you always forgive me in the sweetest way. Do it now, and don't be angry, little darling." And, dropping the vase, he went toward her with a sudden excitement that made her shrink behind the chair.

She was not angry, but shocked and frightened, for she knew now what the matter was and grew so pale, he saw it and asked pardon before she could utter a rebuke.

"We'll talk of that tomorrow. It is very late. Go home now, please, before Uncle comes," she said, trying to speak naturally yet betraying her distress by the tremor of her voice and the sad anxiety in her eyes.

"Yes, yes, I will go you are tired I'll make it all right tomorrow." And as if the sound of his uncle's name steadied him for an instant, Charlie made for the door with an unevenness of gait which would have told the shameful truth if his words had not already done so. Before he reached it, however, the sound of wheels arrested him and, leaning against the wall, he listened with a look of dismay mingled with amusement creeping over his face. "Brutus has bolted now I am in a fix. Can't walk home with this horrid dizziness in my head. It's the cold, Rose, nothing else, I do assure you, and a chill yes, a chill. See here! Let one of those fellows there lend me an arm no use to go after that brute. Won't Mother be frightened though when he gets home?" And with that empty laugh again, he fumbled for the door handle.

"No, no don't let them see you! Don't let anyone know! Stay here till Uncle comes, and he'll take care of you. Oh, Charlie! How could you do it! How could you when you promised?" And, forgetting fear in the sudden sense of shame and anguish that came over her, Rose ran to him, caught his hand from the lock, and turned the key; then, as if she could not bear to see him standing there with that vacant smile on his lips, she dropped into a chair and covered up her face.

The cry, the act, and, more than all, the sight of the bowed head would have sobered poor Charlie if it had not been too late. He looked about the room with a vague, despairing look, as if to find reason fast slipping from his control, but heat and cold, excitement and reckless pledging of many healths had done their work too well to make instant sobriety possible, and owning his defeat with a groan, he turned away and threw himself face-downward on the sofa, one of the saddest sights the new year looked upon as it came in.

As she sat there with hidden eyes, Rose felt that something dear to her was dead forever. The ideal, which all women cherish, look for, and too often think they have found when love glorifies a mortal man, is hard to give up, especially when it comes in the likeness of the first lover who touches a young girl's heart. Rose had just begun to feel that perhaps this cousin, despite his faults, might yet become the hero that he sometimes looked, and the thought that she might be his inspiration was growing sweet to her, although she had not entertained it until very lately. Alas, how short the tender dream had been, how rude the awakening! How impossible it would be ever again to surround that fallen figure with all the romance of an innocent fancy or gift it with the high attributes beloved by a noble nature!

Breathing heavily in the sudden sleep that kindly brought a brief oblivion of himself, he lay with flushed cheeks, disordered hair, and at his feet the little rose that never would be fresh and fair again a pitiful contrast now to the brave, blithe young man who went so gaily out that morning to be so ignominiously overthrown at night.

Many girls would have made light of a trespass so readily forgiven by the world, but Rose had not yet learned to offer temptation with a smile and shut her eyes to the weakness that makes a man a brute. It always grieved or disgusted her to see it in others, and now it was very terrible to have it brought so near not in its worst form, by any means, but bad enough to wring her heart with shame and sorrow and fill her mind with dark forebodings for the future. So she could only sit mourning for the Charlie that might have been while watching the Charlie that was with an ache in her heart which found no relief till, putting her hands there as if to ease the pain, they touched the pansies, faded but still showing gold among the somber purple, and then two great tears dropped on them as she sighed: "Ah, me! I do need heart's-ease sooner than I thought!"

Her uncle's step made her spring up and unlock the door, showing him such an altered face that he stopped short, ejaculating in dismay, "Good heavens, child! What's the matter?" adding, as she pointed to the sofa in pathetic silence, "Is he hurt? ill? dead?"

"No, Uncle, he is—" She could not utter the ugly word but whispered with a sob in her throat, "Be kind to him," and fled away to her own room, feeling as if a great disgrace had fallen on the house.

Chapter 10 THE SAD AND SOBER PART

"How will he look? What will he say? Can anything make us forget and be happy again?" were the first questions Rose asked herself as soon as she woke from the brief sleep which followed a long, sad vigil. It seemed as if the whole world must be changed because a trouble darkened it for her. She was too young yet to know how possible it is to forgive much greater sins than this, forget far heavier disappointments, outlive higher hopes, and bury loves compared to which hers was but a girlish fancy. She wished it had not been so bright a day, wondered how her birds could sing with such shrill gaiety, put no ribbon in her hair, and said, as she looked at the reflection of her own tired face in the glass, "Poor thing! You thought the new leaf would have something pleasant on it. The story has been very sweet and easy to read so far, but the sad and sober part is coming now."

A tap at the door reminded her that, in spite of her afflictions, breakfast must be eaten, and the sudden thought that Charlie might still be in the house made her hurry to the door, to find Dr. Alec waiting for her with his morning smile. She drew him in and whispered anxiously, as if someone lay dangerously ill nearby, "Is he better, Uncle? Tell me all about it I can bear it now."

Some men would have smiled at her innocent distress and told her this was only what was to be expected and endured, but Dr. Alec believed in the pure instincts that make youth beautiful, desired to keep them true, and hoped his girl would never learn to look unmoved by pain and pity upon any human being vanquished by a vice, no matter how trivial it seemed, how venial it was held. So his face grew grave, though his voice was cheerful as he answered: "All right, I daresay, by this time, for sleep is the best medicine in such cases. I took him home last night, and no one knows he came but you and I."

"No one ever shall. How did you do it, Uncle?"

"Just slipped out of the long study window and got him cannily off, for the air and motion, after a dash of cold water, brought him around, and he was glad to be safely landed at home. His rooms are below, you know, so no one was disturbed, and I left him sleeping nicely."

"Thank you so much," sighed Rose. "And Brutus? Weren't they frightened when he got back alone?"

"Not at all. The sagacious beast went quietly to the stable, and the sleepy groom asked no questions, for Charlie often sends the horse round by himself when it is late or stormy. Rest easy, dear no eye but ours saw the poor lad come and go, and we'll forgive it for love's sake."

"Yes, but not forget it. I never can, and he will never be again to me the Charlie I've been so proud and fond of all these years. Oh, Uncle, such a pity! Such a pity!"

"Don't break your tender heart about it, child, for it is not incurable, thank God! I don't make light of it, but I am sure that under better influences Charlie will redeem himself because his impulses are good and this his only vice. I can hardly blame him for what he is, because his mother did the harm. I declare to you, Rose, I sometimes feel as if I must break out against that woman and thunder in her ears that she is ruining the immortal soul for which she is responsible to heaven!"

Dr. Alec seldom spoke in this way, and when he did it was rather awful, for his indignation was of the righteous sort and such thunder often rouses up a drowsy soul when sunshine has no effect. Rose liked it, and sincerely wished Aunt Clara had been there to get the benefit of the outbreak, for she needed just such an awakening from the self-indulgent dream in which she lived.

"Do it, and save Charlie before it is too late!" she cried, kindling herself as she watched him, for he looked like a roused lion as he walked about the room with his hand clenched and a spark in his eye, evidently in desperate earnest and ready to do almost anything.

"Will you help?" he asked, stopping suddenly with a look that made her stand up straight and strong as she answered with an eager voice: "I will."

"Then don't love him yet."

That startled her, but she asked steadily, though her heart began to beat and her color to come: "Why not?"

"Firstly, because no woman should give her happiness into the keeping of a man without fixed principles; secondly, because the hope of being worthy of you will help him more than any prayers or preaching of mine. Thirdly, because it will need all our wit and patience to undo the work of nearly four and twenty years. You understand what I mean?"

"Yes, sir."

"Can you say 'no' when he asks you to say 'yes' and wait a little for your happiness?"

"I can."

"And will you?"

"I will."

"Then I'm satisfied, and a great weight taken off my heart. I can't help seeing what goes on, or trembling when I think of you setting sail with no better pilot than poor Charlie. Now you answer as I hoped you would, and I am proud of my girl!"

They had been standing with the width of the room between them, Dr. Alec looking very much like a commander issuing orders, Rose like a well-drilled private obediently receiving them, and both wore the air of soldiers getting ready for a battle, with the bracing of nerves and quickening of the blood brave souls feel as they put on their armor. At the last words he went to her, brushed back the hair, and kissed her on the forehead with a tender sort of gravity and a look that made her feel as if he had endowed her with the Victoria Cross for courage on the field.

No more was said then, for Aunt Plenty called them down and the day's duties began. But that brief talk showed Rose what to do and fitted her to do it, for it set her to thinking of the duty one owes one's self in loving as in all the other great passions or experiences which make or mar a life.

She had plenty of time for quiet meditation that day because everyone was resting after yesterday's festivity, and she sat in her little room planning out a new year so full of good works, grand successes, and beautiful romances that if it could have been realized, the Millennium would have begun. It was a great comfort to her, however, and lightened the long hours haunted by a secret desire to know when Charlie would come and a secret fear of the first meeting. She was sure he would be bowed down with humiliation and repentance, and a struggle took place in her mind between the pity she could not help feeling and the disapprobation she ought to show. She decided to be gentle, but very frank; to reprove, but also to console; and to try to improve the softened moment by inspiring the culprit with a wish for all the virtues which make a perfect man.

The fond delusion grew quite absorbing, and her mind was full of it as she sat watching the sun set from her western window and admiring with dreamy eyes the fine effect of the distant hills clear and dark against a daffodil sky when the bang of a door made her sit suddenly erect in her low chair and say with a catch in her breath: "He's coming! I must remember what I promised Uncle and be very firm."

Usually Charlie announced his approach with music of some sort. Now he neither whistled, hummed, nor sang, but came so quietly Rose was sure that he dreaded this meeting as much as she did and, compassionating his natural confusion, did not look around as the steps drew near. She thought perhaps he would go down upon his knees, as he used to after a boyish offense, but hoped not, for too much humility distressed her, so she waited for the first demonstration anxiously.

It was rather a shock when it came, however, for a great nosegay dropped into her lap and a voice, bold and gay as usual, said lightly: "Here she is, as pretty and pensive as you please. Is the world hollow, our doll stuffed with sawdust, and do we want to go into a nunnery today, Cousin?"

Rose was so taken aback by this unexpected coolness that the flowers lay unnoticed as she looked up with a face so full of surprise, reproach, and something like shame that it was impossible to mistake its meaning. Charlie did not, and had the grace to redden deeply, and his eyes fell as he said quickly, though in the same light tone: "I humbly apologize for coming so late last night. Don't be hard upon me, Cousin. You know America expects every man to do his duty on New Year's Day."

"I am tired of forgiving! You make and break promises as easily as you did years ago, and I shall never ask you for another," answered Rose, putting the bouquet away, for the apology did not satisfy her and she would not be bribed to silence.

"But, my dear girl, you are so very exacting, so peculiar in your notions, and so angry about trifles that a poor fellow can't please you, try as he will," began Charlie, ill at ease, but too proud to show half the penitence he felt, not so much for the fault as for her discovery of it.

"I am not angry I am grieved and disappointed, for I expect every man to do his duty in another way and keep his word to the uttermost, as I try to do. If that is exacting, I'm sorry, and won't trouble you with my old-fashioned notions anymore."

"Bless my soul! What a rout about nothing! I own that I forgot I know I acted like a fool and I beg pardon. What more can I do?"

"Act like a man, and never let me be so terribly ashamed of you again as I was last night." And Rose gave a little shiver as she thought of it.

That involuntary act hurt Charlie more than her words, and it was his turn now to feel "terribly ashamed," for the events of the previous evening were very hazy in his mind and fear magnified them greatly. Turning sharply away, he went and stood by the fire, quite at a loss how to make his peace this time, because Rose was so unlike herself. Usually a word of excuse sufficed, and she seemed glad to pardon and forget; now, though very quiet, there was something almost stern about her that surprised and daunted him, for how could he know that all the while her pitiful heart was pleading for him and the very effort to control it made her a little hard and cold?

As he stood there, restlessly fingering the ornaments upon the chimneypiece, his eye brightened suddenly and, taking up the pretty bracelet lying there, he went slowly back to her, saying in a tone that was humble and serious enough now: "I will act like a man, and you shall never be ashamed again. Only be kind to me. Let me put this on, and promise afresh this time I swear I'll keep it. Won't you trust me, Rose?"

It was very hard to resist the pleading voice and eyes, for this humility was dangerous; and, but for Uncle Alec, Rose would have answered "yes." The blue forget-me-nots reminded her of her own promise, and she kept it with difficulty now, to be glad always afterward. Putting back the offered trinket with a gentle touch, she said firmly, though she dared not look up into the anxious face bending toward her: "No, Charlie I can't wear it. My hands must be free if I'm to help you as I ought. I will be kind, I will trust you, but don't swear anything, only try to resist temptation, and we'll all stand by you."

Charlie did not like that and lost the ground he had gained by saying impetuously: "I don't want anyone but you to stand by me, and I must be sure you won't desert me, else, while I'm mortifying soul and body to please you, some stranger will come and steal your heart away from me. I couldn't bear that, so I give you fair warning, in such a case I'll break the bargain, and go straight to the devil."

The last sentence spoiled it all, for it was both masterful and defiant. Rose had the Campbell spirit in her, though it seldom showed; as yet she valued her liberty more than any love offered her, and she resented the authority he assumed too soon resented it all the more warmly because of the effort she was making to reinstate her hero, who would insist on being a very faulty and ungrateful man. She rose straight out of her chair, saying with a look and tone which rather startled her hearer and convinced him that she was no longer a tenderhearted child but a woman with a will of her own and a spirit as proud and fiery as any of her race: "My heart is my own, to dispose of as I please. Don't shut yourself out of it by presuming too much, for you have no claim on me but that of cousinship, and you never will have unless you earn it. Remember that, and neither threaten nor defy me anymore."

For a minute it was doubtful whether Charlie would answer this flash with another, and a general explosion ensue, or wisely quench the flame with the mild answer which turneth away wrath. He chose the latter course and made it very effective by throwing himself down before his offended goddess, as he had often done in jest. This time it was not acting, but serious, earnest, and there was real passion in his voice as he caught Rose's dress in both hands, saying eagerly: "No, no! Don't shut your heart against me or I shall turn desperate. I'm not half good enough for such a saint as you, but you can do what you will with me. I only need a motive to make a man of me, and where can I find a stronger one than in trying to keep your love?"

"It is not yours yet," began Rose, much moved, though all the while she felt as if she were on a stage and had a part to play, for Charlie had made life so like a melodrama that it was hard for him to be quite simple even when most sincere.

"Let me earn it, then. Show me how, and I'll do anything, for you are my good angel, Rose, and if you cast me off, I feel as if I shouldn't care how soon there was an end of me," cried Charlie, getting tragic in his earnestness and putting both arms around her, as if his only safety lay in clinging to this beloved fellow creature.

Behind footlights it would have been irresistible, but somehow it did not touch the one spectator, though she had neither time nor skill to discover why. For all their ardor the words did not ring quite true. Despite the grace of the attitude, she would have liked him better manfully erect upon his feet, and though the gesture was full of tenderness, a subtle instinct made her shrink away as she said with a composure that surprised herself even more than it did him: "Please don't. No, I will promise nothing yet, for I must respect the man I love."

That brought Charlie to his feet, pale with something deeper than anger, for the recoil told him more plainly than the words how much he had fallen in her regard since yesterday. The memory of the happy moment when she gave the rose with that new softness in her eyes, the shy color, the sweet "for my sake" came back with sudden vividness, contrasting sharply with the now averted face, the hand outstretched to put him back, the shrinking figure, and in that instant's silence, poor Charlie realized what he had lost, for a girl's first thought of love is as delicate a thing as the rosy morning glory, which a breath of air can shatter. Only a hint of evil, only an hour's debasement for him, a moment's glimpse for her of the coarser pleasures men know, and the innocent heart, just opening to bless and to be blessed, closed again like a sensitive plant and shut him out perhaps forever.

The consciousness of this turned him pale with fear, for his love was deeper than she knew, and he proved this when he said in a tone so full of mingled pain and patience that it touched her to the heart: "You shall respect me if I can make you, and when I've earned it, may I hope for something more?"

She looked up then, saw in his face the noble shame, the humble sort of courage that shows repentance to be genuine and gives promise of success, and, with a hopeful smile that was a cordial to him, answered heartily: "You may."

"Bless you for that! I'll make no promises, I'll ask for none only trust me, Rose, and while you treat me like a cousin, remember that no matter how many lovers you may have you'll never be to any of them as dear as you are to me."

A traitorous break in his voice warned Charlie to stop there, and with no other good-bye, he very wisely went away, leaving Rose to put the neglected flowers into water with remorseful care and lay away the bracelet, saying to herself: "I'll never wear it till I feel as I did before. Then he shall put it on and I'll say 'yes.'"

Chapter 11 SMALL TEMPTATIONS
"Oh, Rose, I've got something so exciting to tell you!" cried Kitty Van Tassel, skipping into the carriage next morning when her friend called for her to go shopping.

Kitty always did have some "perfectly thrilling" communication to make and Rose had learned to take them quietly, but the next demonstration was a new one, for, regardless alike of curious observers outside and disordered hats within, Kitty caught Rose around the neck, exclaiming in a rapturous whisper: "My dearest creature, I'm engaged!"

"I'm so glad! Of course it is Steve?"

"Dear fellow, he did it last night in the nicest way, and Mama is so delighted. Now what shall I be married in?" And Kitty composed herself with a face full of the deepest anxiety.

"How can you talk of that so soon? Why, Kit, you unromantic girl, you ought to be thinking of your lover and not your clothes," said Rose, amused yet rather scandalized at such want of sentiment.

"I am thinking of my lover, for he says he will not have a long engagement, so I must begin to think about the most important things at once, mustn't I?"

"Ah, he wants to be sure of you, for you are such a slippery creature he is afraid you'll treat him as you did poor Jackson and the rest," interrupted Rose, shaking her finger at her prospective cousin, who had tried this pastime twice before and was rather proud than otherwise of her brief engagements.

"You needn't scold, for I know I'm right, and when you've been in society as long as I have you'll find that the only way to really know a man is to be engaged to him. While they want you they are all devotion, but when they think they've got you, then you find out what wretches they are," answered Kitty with an air of worldly wisdom which contrasted oddly with her youthful face and giddy manners.

"A sad prospect for poor Steve, unless I give him a hint to look well to his ways."

"Oh, my dear child, I'm sure of him, for my experience has made me very sharp and I'm convinced I can manage him without a bit of trouble. We've known each other for ages" Steve was twenty and Kitty eighteen "and always been the best of friends. Besides, he is quite my ideal man. I never could bear big hands and feet, and his are simply adorable. Then he's the best dancer I know and dresses in perfect taste. I really do believe I fell in love with his pocket handkerchiefs first, they were so enchanting I couldn't resist," laughed Kitty, pulling a large one out of her pocket and burying her little nose in the folds, which shed a delicious fragrance upon the air.

"Now, that looks promising, and I begin to think you have got a little sentiment after all," said Rose, well pleased, for the merry brown eyes had softened suddenly and a quick color came up in Kitty's cheek as she answered, still half hiding her face in the beloved handkerchief: "Of course I have, lots of it, only I'm ashamed to show it to most people, because it's the style to take everything in the most nonchalant way. My gracious, Rose, you'd have thought me a romantic goose last night while Steve proposed in the back parlor, for I actually cried, he was so dreadfully in earnest when I pretended that I didn't care for him, and so very dear and nice when I told the truth. I didn't know he had it in him, but he came out delightfully and never cared a particle, though I dropped tears all over his lovely shirtfront. Wasn't that good of him? For you know he hates his things to be mussed."

"He's a true Campbell, and has got a good warm heart of his own under those fine fronts of his. Aunt Jane doesn't believe in sentiment, so he has been trained never to show any, but it is there, and you must encourage him to let it out, not foolishly, but in a way to make him more manly and serious."

"I will if I can, for though I wouldn't own this to everybody, I like it in him very much and feel as if Steve and I should get on beautifully. Here we are now, be sure not to breathe a word if we meet anyone. I want it to be a profound secret for a week at least," added Kitty, whisking her handkerchief out of sight as the carriage stopped before the fashionable store they were about to visit.

Rose promised with a smile, for Kitty's face betrayed her without words, so full was it of the happiness which few eyes fail to understand whenever they see it.

"Just a glance at the silks. You ask my opinion about white ones, and I'll look at the colors. Mama says satin, but that is out now, and I've set my heart on the heaviest corded thing I can find," whispered Kitty as they went rustling by the long counters strewn with all that could delight the feminine eye and tempt the feminine pocket.

"Isn't that opal the loveliest thing you ever saw? I'm afraid I'm too dark to wear it, but it would just suit you. You'll need a variety, you know," added Kitty in a significant aside as Rose stood among the white silks while her companion affected great interest in the delicate hues laid before her.

"But I have a variety now, and don't need a new dress of any sort."

"No matter, get it, else it will be gone. You've worn all yours several times already and must have a new one whether you need it or not. Dear me! If I had as much pocket money as you have, I'd

207

come out in a fresh toilet at every party I went to," answered Kitty, casting an envious eye upon the rainbow piles before her.

The quick-witted shopman saw that a wedding was afoot, for when two pretty girls whisper, smile, and blush over their shopping, clerks scent bridal finery and a transient gleam of interest brightens their imperturbable countenances and lends a brief energy to languid voices weary with crying, "Cash!" Gathering both silks with a practiced turn of the hand, he held them up for inspection, detecting at a glance which was the bride-elect and which the friend, for Kitty fell back to study the effect of silvery white folds with an absorbing interest impossible to mistake while Rose sat looking at the opal as if she scarcely heard a bland voice saying, with the rustle of silk so dear to girlish ears: "A superb thing, just opened; all the rage in Paris; very rare shade; trying to most, as the lady says, but quite perfect for a blonde."

Rose was not listening to those words but to others which Aunt Clara had lately uttered, laughed at then, but thought over more than once since.

"I'm tired of hearing people wonder why Miss Campbell does not dress more. Simplicity is all very well for schoolgirls and women who can't afford anything better, but you can, and you really ought. Your things are pretty enough in their way, and I rather like you to have a style of your own, but it looks odd and people will think you are mean if you don't make more show. Besides, you don't do justice to your beauty, which would be both peculiar and striking if you'd devote your mind to getting up ravishing costumes."

Much more to the same effect did her aunt say, discussing the subject quite artistically and unconsciously appealing to several of Rose's ruling passions. One was a love for the delicate fabrics, colors, and ornaments which refined tastes enjoy and whose costliness keeps them from ever growing common; another, her strong desire to please the eyes of those she cared for and gratify their wishes in the smallest matter if she could. And last, but not least, the natural desire of a young and pretty woman to enhance the beauty which she so soon discovers to be her most potent charm for the other sex, her passport to a high place among her maiden peers.

She had thought seriously of surprising and delighting everyone by appearing in a costume which should do justice to the loveliness which was so modest that it was apt to forget itself in admiring others what girls call a "ravishing" dress, such as she could imagine and easily procure by the magic of the Fortunatus' purse in her pocket. She had planned it all, the shimmer of pale silk through lace like woven frostwork, ornaments of some classic pattern, and all the dainty accessories as perfect as time, taste, and money could make them.

She knew that Uncle Alec's healthful training had given her a figure that could venture on any fashion and Nature blessed her with a complexion that defied all hues. So it was little wonder that she felt a strong desire to use these gifts, not for the pleasure of display, but to seem fair in the eyes that seldom looked at her without a tender sort of admiration, all the more winning when no words marred the involuntary homage women love.

These thoughts were busy in Rose's mind as she sat looking at the lovely silk and wondering what Charlie would say if she should some night burst upon him in a pale rosy cloud, like the Aurora to whom he often likened her. She knew it would please him very much and she longed to do all she honestly could to gratify the poor fellow, for her tender heart already felt some remorseful pangs, remembering how severe she had been the night before. She could not revoke her words, because she meant them every one, but she might be kind and show that she did not wholly shut him out from her regard by asking him to go with her to Kitty's ball and gratify his artistic taste by a lovely costume. A very girlish but kindly plan, for that ball was to be the last of her frivolities, so she wanted it to be a pleasant one and felt that "being friends" with Charlie would add much to her enjoyment.

This idea made her fingers tighten on the gleaming fabric so temptingly upheld, and she was about to take it when, "If ye please, sir, would ye kindly tell me where I'd be finding the flannel place?" said a voice behind her, and, glancing up, she saw a meek little Irishwoman looking quite lost and out of place among the luxuries around her.

"Downstairs, turn to the left," was the clerk's hasty reply, with a vague wave of the hand which left the inquirer more in the dark than ever.

Rose saw the woman's perplexity and said kindly, "I'll show you this way."

"I'm ashamed to be throublin' ye, miss, but it's strange I am in it, and wouldn't be comin' here at all, at all, barrin' they tould me I'd get the bit I'm wantin' chaper in this big shop than the little ones more becomin' the like o' me," explained the little woman humbly.

Rose looked again as she led the way through a well-dressed crowd of busy shoppers, and something in the anxious, tired face under the old woolen hood the bare, purple hands holding fast a meager wallet and a faded scrap of the dotted flannel little children's frocks are so often made of touched the generous heart that never could see want without an impulse to relieve it. She had meant only to point the way, but, following a new impulse, she went on, listening to the poor soul's motherly prattle about "me baby" and the "throuble" it was to "find clothes for the growin' childer when me man is out av work and the bit and sup inconvaynient these hard times" as they descended to that darksome lower world where necessities take refuge when luxuries crowd them out from the gayer place above.

The presence of a lady made Mrs. Sullivan's shopping very easy now, and her one poor "bit" of flannel grew miraculously into yards of several colors, since the shabby purse was no lighter when she went away, wiping her eyes on the corner of a big, brown bundle. A very little thing, and no one saw it but a wooden-faced clerk, who never told, yet it did Rose good and sent her up into the light again with a sober face, thinking self-reproachfully, "What right have I to more gay gowns when some poor babies have none, or to spend time making myself fine while there is so much bitter want in the world?"

Nevertheless the pretty things were just as tempting as ever, and she yearned for the opal silk with a renewed yearning when she got back. It is not certain that it would not have been bought in spite of her better self if a good angel in the likeness of a stout lady with silvery curls about the benevolent face, enshrined in a plain bonnet, had not accosted her as she joined Kitty, still brooding over the wedding gowns.

"I waited a moment for you, my dear, because I'm in haste, and very glad to save myself a journey or a note," began the newcomer in a low tone as Rose shook hands with the most affectionate respect. "You know the great box factory was burned a day or two ago and over a hundred girls thrown out of work. Some were hurt and are in the hospital, many have no homes to go to, and nearly all need temporary help of some sort. We've had so many calls this winter I hardly know which way to turn, for want is pressing, and I've had my finger in so many purses I'm almost ashamed to ask again. Any little contribution ah, thank you, I was sure you wouldn't fail me, my good child," and Mrs. Gardener warmly pressed the hand that went so quickly into the little porte-monnaie and came out so generously filled.

"Let me know how else I can help, and thank you very much for allowing me to have a share in your good works," said Rose, forgetting all about gay gowns as she watched the black bonnet go briskly away with an approving smile on the fine old face inside it.

"You extravagant thing! How could you give so much?" whispered Kitty, whose curious eye had seen three figures on the single bill which had so rapidly changed hands.

"I believe if Mrs. Gardener asked me for my head I should give it to her," answered Rose lightly, then, turning to the silks, she asked, "Which have you decided upon, the yellow white or the blue, the corded or the striped?"

"I've decided nothing; except that you are to have the pink and wear it at my ahem! ball," said Kitty, who had made up her mind, but could not give her orders till Mama had been consulted.

"No, I can't afford it just yet. I never overstep my allowance, and I shall have to if I get any more finery. Come, we ought not to waste time here if you have all the patterns you want." And Rose walked quickly away, glad that it was out of her power to break through two resolutions which hitherto had been faithfully kept one to dress simply for example's sake, the other not to be extravagant for charity's sake.

As Rosamond had her day of misfortunes, so this seemed to be one of small temptations to Rose. After she had set Kitty down at home and been to see her new houses, she drove about doing various errands for the aunts and, while waiting in the carriage for the execution of an order, young Pemberton came by.

As Steve said, this gentleman had been "hard hit" and still hovered mothlike about the forbidden light. Being the most eligible parti of the season, his regard was considered a distinction to be proud of, and Rose had been well scolded by Aunt Clara for refusing so honorable a mate. The girl liked him, and he was the suitor of whom she had spoken so respectfully to Dr. Alec because he had no need of the heiress and had sincerely loved Rose. He had been away, and she hoped had gotten over his disappointment as happily as the rest, but now when he saw her, and came hurrying up so hungry for a word, she felt that he had not forgotten and was too kind to chill him with the bow which plainly says "Don't stop."

A personable youth was Pemberton, and had brought with him from the wilds of Canada a sable-lined overcoat which was the envy of every masculine and the admiration of every feminine friend he had, and as he stood at her carriage window Rose knew that this luxurious garment and its stalwart wearer were objects of interest to the passersby. It chanced that the tide of shoppers flowed in that direction and, as she chatted, familiar faces often passed with glances, smiles, and nods of varying curiosity, significance, and wonder.

She could not help feeling a certain satisfaction in giving him a moment's pleasure, since she could do no more, but it was not that amiable desire alone which made her ignore the neat white parcels which the druggist's boy deposited on the front seat and kept her lingering a little longer to enjoy one of the small triumphs which girls often risk more than a cold in the head to display. The sight of several snowflakes on the broad shoulders which partially obstructed her view, as well as the rapidly increasing animation of Pemberton's chat, reminded her that it was high time to go.

"I mustn't keep you it is beginning to storm," she said, taking up her muff, much to old Jacob's satisfaction, for small talk is not exciting to a hungry man whose nose feels like an icicle.

"Is it? I thought the sun was shining." And the absorbed gentleman turned to the outer world with visible reluctance, for it looked very warm and cozy in the red-lined carriage.

"Wise people say we must carry our sunshine with us," answered Rose, taking refuge in commonplaces, for the face at the window grew pensive suddenly as he answered, with a longing look, "I wish I could." Then, smiling gratefully, he added, "Thank you for giving me a little of yours."

"You are very welcome." And Rose offered him her hand while her eyes mutely asked pardon for withholding her leave to keep it.

He pressed it silently and, shouldering the umbrella which he forgot to open, turned away with an "up again and take another" expression, which caused the soft eyes to follow him admiringly.

"I ought not to have kept him a minute longer than I could help, for it wasn't all pity; it was my foolish wish to show off and do as I liked for a minute, to pay for being good about the gown. Oh, me! How weak and silly I am in spite of all my trying!" And Miss Campbell fell into a remorseful reverie, which lasted till she got home.

"Now, young man, what brought you out in this driving storm?" asked Rose as Jamie came stamping in that same afternoon.

"Mama sent you a new book thought you'd like it. I don't mind your old storms!" replied the boy, wrestling his way out of his coat and presenting a face as round and red and shiny as a well-polished Baldwin apple.

"Much obliged it is just the day to enjoy it and I was longing for something nice to read," said Rose as Jamie sat down upon the lower stair for a protracted struggle with his rubber boots.

"Here you are, then no yes I do believe I've forgotten it, after all!" cried Jamie, slapping his pockets one after the other with a dismayed expression of countenance.

"Never mind, I'll hunt up something else. Let me help you with those your hands are so cold." And Rose good-naturedly gave a tug at the boots while Jamie clutched the banisters, murmuring somewhat incoherently as his legs flew up and down: "I'll go back if you want me to. I'm so sorry! It's very good of you, I'm sure. Getting these horrid things on made me forget. Mother would make me wear 'em, though I told her they'd stick like like gumdrops," he added, inspired by recollections of certain dire disappointments when the above-mentioned sweetmeat melted in his pockets and refused to come out.

"Now what shall we do?" asked Rose when he was finally extricated. "Since I've nothing to read, I may as well play."

"I'll teach you to pitch and toss. You catch very well for a girl, but you can't throw worth a cent," replied Jamie, gamboling down the hall in his slippers and producing a ball from some of the mysterious receptacles in which boys have the art of storing rubbish enough to fill a peck measure.

Of course Rose agreed and cheerfully risked getting her eyes blackened and her fingers bruised till her young receptor gratefully observed that "it was no fun playing where you had to look out for windows and jars and things, so I'd like that jolly book about Captain Nemo and the Nautilus, please."

Being gratified, he spread himself upon the couch, crossed his legs in the air, and without another word dived Twenty Thousand Leagues Under the Sea, where he remained for two mortal hours, to the general satisfaction of his relatives.

Bereft both of her unexpected playfellow and the much desired book, Rose went into the parlor, there to discover a French novel which Kitty had taken from a library and left in the carriage among the bundles. Settling herself in her favorite lounging chair, she read as diligently as Jamie while the wind howled and snow fell fast without.

For an hour nothing disturbed the cozy quiet of the house for Aunt Plenty was napping upstairs and Dr. Alec writing in his own sanctum; at least Rose thought so, till his step made her hastily drop the book and look up with very much the expression she used to wear when caught in mischief years ago.

"Did I startle you? Have a screen you are burning your face before this hot fire." And Dr. Alec pulled one forward.

"Thank you, Uncle. I didn't feel it." And the color seemed to deepen in spite of the screen while the uneasy eyes fell upon the book in her lap.

"Have you got the Quarterly there? I want to glance at an article in it if you can spare it for a moment," he said, leaning toward her with an inquiring glance.

"No, sir, I am reading." And, without mentioning the name, Rose put the book into his hand.

The instant his eye fell on the title he understood the look she wore and knew what "mischief" she had been in. He knit his brows, then smiled, because it was impossible to help it Rose looked so conscience-stricken in spite of her twenty years.

"How do you find it? Interesting?"

"Oh, very! I felt as if I was in another world and forgot all about this."

"Not a very good world, I fancy, if you were afraid or ashamed to be found in it. Where did this come from?" asked Dr. Alec, surveying the book with great disfavor. Rose told him, and added slowly, "I particularly wanted to read it, and fancied I might, because you did when it was so much talked about the winter we were in Rome."

"I did read it to see if it was fit for you."

"And decided that it was not, I suppose, since you never gave it to me!"

"Yes."

"Then I won't finish it. But, Uncle, I don't see why I should not," added Rose wistfully, for she had reached the heart of the romance and found it wonderfully fascinating.

"You may not see, but don't you feel why not?" asked Dr. Alec gravely.

Rose leaned her flushed cheek on her hand and thought a minute, then looked up and answered honestly, "Yes, I do, but can't explain it, except that I know something must be wrong, because I blushed and started when you came in."

"Exactly." And the doctor gave an emphatic nod, as if the symptoms pleased him.

"But I really don't see any harm in the book so far. It is by a famous author, wonderfully well written, as you know, and the characters so lifelike that I feel as if I should really meet them somewhere."

"I hope not!" ejaculated the doctor, shutting the book quickly, as if to keep the objectionable beings from escaping.

Rose laughed, but persisted in her defense, for she did want to finish the absorbing story, yet would not without leave.

"I have read French novels before, and you gave them to me. Not many, to be sure, but the best, so I think I know what is good and shouldn't like this if it was harmful."

Her uncle's answer was to reopen the volume and turn the leaves an instant as if to find a particular place. Then he put it into her hand, saying quietly: "Read a page or two aloud, translating as you go. You used to like that try it again."

Rose obeyed and went glibly down a page, doing her best to give the sense in her purest English. Presently she went more slowly, then skipped a sentence here and there, and finally stopped short, looking as if she needed a screen again.

"What's the matter?" asked her uncle, who had been watching her with a serious eye.

"Some phrases are untranslatable, and it only spoils them to try. They are not amiss in French, but sound coarse and bad in our blunt English," she said a little pettishly, for she felt annoyed by her failure to prove the contested point.

"Ah, my dear, if the fine phrases won't bear putting into honest English, the thoughts they express won't bear putting into your innocent mind! That chapter is the key to the whole book, and if you had been led up, or rather down, to it artfully and artistically, you might have read it to yourself without seeing how bad it is. All the worse for the undeniable talent which hides the evil so subtly and makes the danger so delightful."

He paused a moment, then added with an anxious glance at the book, over which she was still bending, "Finish it if you choose only remember, my girl, that one may read at forty what is unsafe at twenty, and that we never can be too careful what food we give that precious yet perilous thing called imagination."

And taking his Review, he went away to look over a learned article which interested him much less than the workings of a young mind nearby.

Another long silence, broken only by an occasional excited bounce from Jamie when the sociable cuttlefish looked in at the windows or the Nautilus scuttled a ship or two in its terrific course. A bell rang, and the doctor popped his head out to see if he was wanted. It was only a message for Aunt Plenty, and he was about to pop in again when his eye was caught by a square parcel on the slab.

"What's this?" he asked, taking it up.

"Rose wants me to leave it at Kitty Van's when I go. I forgot to bring her book from Mama, so I shall go and get it as soon as ever I've done this," replied Jamie from his nest.

As the volume in his hands was a corpulent one, and Jamie only a third of the way through, Dr. Alec thought Rose's prospect rather doubtful and, slipping the parcel into his pocket, he walked away, saying with a satisfied air: "Virtue doesn't always get rewarded, but it shall be this time if I can do it."

More than half an hour afterward, Rose woke from a little nap and found the various old favorites with which she had tried to solace herself replaced by the simple, wholesome story promised by Aunt Jessie.

"Good boy! I'll go and thank him," she said half aloud, jumping up, wide awake and much pleased.

But she did not go, for just then she spied her uncle standing on the rug warming his hands with a generally fresh and breezy look about him which suggested a recent struggle with the elements.

"How did this come?" she asked suspiciously.

"A man brought it."

"This man? Oh, Uncle! Why did you take so much trouble just to gratify a wish of mine?" she cried, taking both the cold hands in hers with a tenderly reproachful glance from the storm without to the ruddy face above her.

"Because, having taken away your French bonbons with the poisonous color on them, I wanted to get you something better. Here it is, all pure sugar, the sort that sweetens the heart as well as the tongue and leaves no bad taste behind."

"How good you are to me! I don't deserve it, for I didn't resist temptation, though I tried. Uncle, after I'd put the book away, I thought I must just see how it ended, and I'm afraid I should have read it all if it had not been gone," said Rose, laying her face down on the hands she held as humbly as a repentant child.

But Uncle Alec lifted up the bent head and, looking into the eyes that met his frankly, though either held a tear, he said, with the energy that always made his words remembered: "My little girl, I would face a dozen storms far worse than this to keep your soul as stainless as snow, for it is the small temptations which undermine integrity unless we watch and pray and never think them too trivial to be resisted."

Some people would consider Dr. Alec an overcareful man, but Rose felt that he was right, and when she said her prayers that night, added a meek petition to be kept from yielding to three of the small temptations which beset a rich, pretty, and romantic girl extravagance, coquetry, and novel reading.

Chapter 12 AT KITTY'S BALL

Rose had no new gown to wear on this festive occasion, and gave one little sigh of regret as she put on the pale blue silk refreshed with clouds of gaze de Chambéry. But a smile followed, very bright and sweet, as she added the clusters of forget-me-not which Charlie had conjured up through the agency of an old German florist, for one part of her plan had been carried out, and Prince was invited to be her escort, much to his delight, though he wisely made no protestations of any sort and showed his gratitude by being a model gentleman. This pleased Rose, for the late humiliation and a very sincere desire to atone for it gave him an air of pensive dignity which was very effective.

Aunt Clara could not go, for a certain new cosmetic, privately used to improve the once fine complexion, which had been her pride till late hours impaired it, had brought out an unsightly eruption, reducing her to the depths of woe and leaving her no solace for her disappointment but the sight of the elegant velvet dress spread forth upon her bed in melancholy state.

214

So Aunt Jessie was chaperon, to Rose's great satisfaction, and looked as "pretty as a pink," Archie thought, in her matronly pearl-colored gown with a dainty trifle of rich lace on her still abundant hair. He was very proud of his little mama, and as devoted as a lover, "to keep his hand in against Phebe's return," she said laughingly when he brought her a nosegay of blush roses to light up her quiet costume.

A happier mother did not live than Mrs. Jessie as she sat contentedly beside Sister Jane (who graced the frivolous scene in a serious black gown with a diadem of purple asters nodding above her severe brow), both watching their boys with the maternal conviction that no other parent could show such remarkable specimens as these. Each had done her best according to her light, and years of faithful care were now beginning to bear fruit in the promise of goodly men, so dear to the hearts of true mothers.

Mrs. Jessie watched her three tall sons with something like wonder, for Archie was a fine fellow, grave and rather stately, but full of the cordial courtesy and respect we see so little of nowadays and which is the sure sign of good home training. "The cadets," as Will and Geordie called themselves, were there as gorgeous as you please, and the agonies they suffered that night with tight boots and stiff collars no pen can fitly tell. But only to one another did they confide these sufferings and the rare moments of repose when they could stand on one aching foot with heads comfortably sunken inside the excruciating collars, which rasped their ears and made the lobes thereof a pleasing scarlet. Brief were these moments, however, and the Spartan boys danced on with smiling faces, undaunted by the hidden anguish which preyed upon them "fore and aft," as Will expressed it.

Mrs. Jane's pair were an odd contrast, and even the stern disciplinarian herself could not help smiling as she watched them. Steve was superb, and might have been married on the spot, so superfine was his broad-cloth, glossy his linen, and perfect the fit of his gloves. While pride and happiness so fermented in his youthful bosom, there would have been danger of spontaneous combustion if dancing had not proved a safety valve, for his strong sense of the proprieties would not permit him to vent his emotions in any other way.

Kitty felt no such restraint, and looked like a blissful little gypsy, with her brunet prettiness set off by a dashing costume of cardinal and cream color and every hair on her head curled in a Merry Pecksniffian crop, for youth was her strong point, and she much enjoyed the fact that she had been engaged three times before she was nineteen.

To see her and Steve spin around the room was a sight to bring a smile to the lips of the crustiest bachelor or saddest spinster, for happy lovers are always a pleasing spectacle, and two such merry little grigs as these are seldom seen.

Mac, meantime, with glasses astride his nose, surveyed his brother's performances "on the light fantastic" very much as a benevolent Newfoundland would the gambols of a toy terrier, receiving with thanks the hasty hints for his guidance which Steve breathed into his ear as he passed and forgetting all about them the next minute. When not thus engaged Mac stood about with his thumbs in his vest pockets, regarding the lively crowd like a meditative philosopher of a cheerful aspect, often smiling to himself at some whimsical fancy of his own, knitting his brows as some bit of ill-natured gossip met his ear, or staring with undisguised admiration as a beautiful face or figure caught his eye.

"I hope that girl knows what a treasure she has got. But I doubt if she ever fully appreciates it," said Mrs. Jane, bringing her spectacles to bear upon Kitty as she whisked by, causing quite a gale with her flying skirts.

"I think she will, for Steve has been so well brought up, she cannot but see and feel the worth of what she has never had, and being so young she will profit by it," answered Mrs. Jessie softly, thinking of the days when she and her Jem danced together, just betrothed.

"I've done my duty by both the boys, and done it thoroughly, or their father would have spoilt them, for he's no more idea of discipline than a child." And Aunt Jane gave her own palm a smart rap with her closed fan, emphasizing the word "thoroughly" in a most suggestive manner.

"I've often wished I had your firmness, Jane but after all, I'm not sure that I don't like my own way best, at least with my boys, for plenty of love, and plenty of patience, seem to have succeeded pretty well." And Aunt Jessie lifted the nosegay from her lap, feeling as if that unfailing love and patience were already blooming into her life as beautifully as the sweet-breathed roses given by her boy refreshed and brightened these long hours of patient waiting in a corner.

"I don't deny that you've done well, Jessie, but you've been let alone and had no one to hold your hand or interfere. If my Mac had gone to sea as your Jem did, I never should have been as severe as I am. Men are so perverse and shortsighted, they don't trouble about the future as long as things are quiet and comfortable in the present," continued Mrs. Jane, quite forgetting that the shortsighted partner of the firm, physically speaking at least, was herself.

"Ah, yes! We mothers love to foresee and foretell our children's lives even before they are born, and are very apt to be disappointed if they do not turn out as we planned. I know I am yet I really have no cause to complain and am learning to see that all we can do is to give the dear boys good principles and the best training we may, then leave them to finish what we have begun." And Mrs. Jessie's eye wandered away to Archie, dancing with Rose, quite unconscious what a pretty little castle in the air tumbled down when he fell in love with Phebe.

"Right, quite right on that point we agree exactly. I have spared nothing to give my boys good principles and good habits, and I am willing to trust them anywhere. Nine times did I whip my Steve to cure him of fibbing, and over and over again did Mac go without his dinner rather than wash his hands. But I whipped and starved them both into obedience, and now I have my reward," concluded the "stern parent" with a proud wave of the fan, which looked very like a ferule, being as big, hard, and uncompromising as such an article could be.

Mrs. Jessie gave a mild murmur of assent, but could not help thinking, with a smile, that in spite of their early tribulations the sins for which the boys suffered had gotten a little mixed in their result, for fibbing Steve was now the tidy one, and careless Mac the truth teller. But such small contradictions will happen in the best-regulated families, and all perplexed parents can do is to keep up a steadfast preaching and practicing in the hope that it will bear fruit sometime, for according to an old proverb, Children pick up words as pigeons pease, To utter them again as God shall please.

"I hope they won't dance the child to death among them, for each one seems bound to have his turn, even your sober Mac," said Mrs. Jessie a few minutes later as she saw Archie hand Rose over to his cousin, who carried her off with an air of triumph from several other claimants.

"She's very good to him, and her influence is excellent, for he is of an age now when a young woman's opinion has more weight than an old one's. Though he is always good to his mother, and I feel as if I should take great comfort in him. He's one of the sort who will not marry till late, if ever, being fond of books and a quiet life," responded Mrs. Jane, remembering how often her son had expressed his belief that philosophers should not marry and brought up Plato as an example of the serene wisdom to be attained only by a single man while her husband sided with Socrates, for whom he felt a profound sympathy, though he didn't dare to own it.

"Well, I don't know about that. Since my Archie surprised me by losing his heart as he did, I'm prepared for anything, and advise you to do likewise. I really shouldn't wonder if Mac did something remarkable in that line, though he shows no sign of it yet, I confess," answered Mrs. Jessie, laughing.

"It won't be in that direction, you may be sure, for her fate is sealed. Dear me, how sad it is to see a superior girl like that about to throw herself away on a handsome scapegrace. I won't mention names, but you understand me." And Mrs. Jane shook her head, as if she could mention the name of one superior girl who had thrown herself away and now saw the folly of it.

"I'm very anxious, of course, and so is Alec, but it may be the saving of one party and the happiness of the other, for some women love to give more than they receive," said Mrs. Jessie, privately wondering, for the thousandth time, why brother Mac ever married the learned Miss Humphries.

"You'll see that it won't prosper, and I shall always maintain that a wife cannot entirely undo a mother's work. Rose will have her hands full if she tries to set all Clara's mistakes right," answered Aunt Jane grimly, then began to fan violently as their hostess approached to have a dish of chat about "our dear young people."

Rose was in a merry mood that night, and found Mac quite ready for fun, which was fortunate, since her first remark set them off on a droll subject.

"Oh, Mac! Annabel has just confided to me that she is engaged to Fun See! Think of her going to housekeeping in Canton someday and having to order rats, puppies, and bird's-nest soup for dinner," whispered Rose, too much amused to keep the news to herself.

"By Confucius! Isn't that a sweet prospect?" And Mac burst out laughing, to the great surprise of his neighbors, who wondered what there was amusing about the Chinese sage. "It is rather alarming, though, to have these infants going on at this rate. Seems to be catching, a new sort of scarlet fever, to judge by Annabel's cheeks and Kitty's gown," he added, regarding the aforesaid ladies with eyes still twinkling with merriment.

"Don't be ungallant, but go and do likewise, for it is all the fashion. I heard Mrs. Van tell old Mrs. Joy that it was going to be a marrying year, so you'll be sure to catch it," answered Rose, reefing her skirts, for, with all his training, Mac still found it difficult to keep his long legs out of the man-traps.

"It doesn't look like a painful disease, but I must be careful, for I've no time to be ill now. What are the symptoms?" asked Mac, trying to combine business with pleasure and improve his mind while doing his duty.

"If you ever come back I'll tell you," laughed Rose as he danced away into the wrong corner, bumped smartly against another gentleman, and returned as soberly as if that was the proper figure.

"Well, tell me 'how not to do it,'" he said, subsiding for a moment's talk when Rose had floated to and fro in her turn.

"Oh! You see some young girl who strikes you as particularly charming whether she really is or not doesn't matter a bit and you begin to think about her a great deal, to want to see her, and to get generally sentimental and absurd," began Rose, finding it difficult to give a diagnosis of the most mysterious disease under the sun.

"Don't think it sounds enticing. Can't I find an antidote somewhere, for if it is in the air this year I'm sure to get it, and it may be fatal," said Mac, who felt pretty lively and liked to make Rose merry, for he suspected that she had a little trouble from a hint Dr. Alec had given him.

"I hope you will catch it, because you'll be so funny."

"Will you take care of me as you did before, or have you got your hands full?"

"I'll help, but really with Archie and Steve and Charlie, I shall have enough to do. You'd better take it lightly the first time, and so won't need much care."

"Very well, how shall I begin? Enlighten my ignorance and start me right, I beg."

"Go about and see people, make yourself agreeable, and not sit in corners observing other people as if they were puppets dancing for your amusement. I heard Mrs. Van once say that propinquity works wonders, and she ought to know, having married off two daughters, and just engaged a third to 'a most charming young man.'?

"Good lack! The cure sounds worse than the disease. Propinquity, hey? Why, I may be in danger this identical moment and can't flee for my life," said Mac, gently catching her round the waist for a general waltz.

"Don't be alarmed, but mind your steps, for Charlie is looking at us, and I want you to do your best. That's perfect take me quite round, for I love to waltz and seldom get a good turn except with you boys," said Rose, smiling up at him approvingly as his strong arm guided her among the revolving couples and his feet kept time without a fault.

"This certainly is a great improvement on the chair business, to which I have devoted myself with such energy that I've broken the backs of two partners and dislocated the arm of the old rocker. I took an occasional turn with that heavy party, thinking it good practice in case I ever happen to dance with stout ladies." And Mac nodded toward Annabel, pounding gaily with Mr. Tokio, whose yellow countenance beamed as his beady eyes rested on his plump fiancée.

Pausing in the midst of her merriment at the image of Mac and the old rocking chair, Rose said reprovingly, "Though a heathen Chinee, Fun puts you to shame, for he did not ask foolish questions but went a-wooing like a sensible little man, and I've no doubt Annabel will be very happy."

"Choose me a suitable divinity and I will try to adore. Can I do more than that to retrieve my character?" answered Mac, safely landing his partner and plying the fan according to instructions.

"How would Emma do?" inquired Rose, whose sense of the ludicrous was strong and who could not resist the temptation of horrifying Mac by the suggestion.

"Never! It sets my teeth on edge to look at her tonight. I suppose that dress is 'a sweet thing just out,' but upon my word she reminds me of nothing but a Harlequin ice," and Mac turned his back on her with a shudder, for he was sensitive to discords of all kinds.

"She certainly does, and that mixture of chocolate, pea green, and pink is simply detestable, though many people would consider it decidedly 'chic,' to use her favorite word. I suppose you will dress your wife like a Spartan matron of the time of Lycurgus," added Rose, much tickled by his new conceit.

"I'll wait till I get her before I decide. But one thing I'm sure of she shall not dress like a Greek dancer of the time of Pericles," answered Mac, regarding with great disfavor a young lady who, having a statuesque figure, affected drapery of the scanty and clinging description.

"Then it is of no use to suggest that classic creature, so as you reject my first attempts, I won't go on but look about me quietly, and you had better do the same. Seriously, Mac, more gaiety and less study would do you good, for you will grow old before your time if you shut yourself up and pore over books so much."

"I don't believe there is a younger or a jollier-feeling fellow in the room than I am, though I may not conduct myself like a dancing dervish. But I own you may be right about the books, for there are many sorts of intemperance, and a library is as irresistible to me as a barroom to a toper. I shall have to sign a pledge and cork up the only bottle that tempts me my ink-stand."

"I'll tell you how to make it easier to abstain. Stop studying and write a novel into which you can put all your wise things, and so clear your brains for a new start by and by. Do I should so like to read it," cried Rose, delighted with the project, for she was sure Mac could do anything he liked in that line.

"First live, then write. How can I go to romancing till I know what romance means?" he asked soberly, feeling that so far he had had very little in his life.

"Then you must find out, and nothing will help you more than to love someone very much. Do as I've advised and be a modern Diogenes going about with spectacles instead of a lantern in search, not of an honest man, but a perfect woman. I do hope you will be successful." And Rose made her curtsey as the dance ended.

"I don't expect perfection, but I should like one as good as they ever make them nowadays. If you are looking for the honest man, I wish you success in return," said Mac, relinquishing her fan with a glance of such sympathetic significance that a quick flush of feeling rose to the girl's face as she answered very low, "If honesty was all I wanted, I certainly have found it in you."

Then she went away with Charlie, who was waiting for his turn, and Mac roamed about, wondering if anywhere in all that crowd his future wife was hidden, saying to himself, as he glanced from face to face, quite unresponsive to the various allurements displayed,

> "What care I how fair she be,
> If she be not fair for me?"

Just before supper several young ladies met in the dressing room to repair damages and, being friends, they fell into discourse as they smoothed their locks and had their tattered furbelows sewed or pinned up by the neat-handed Phillis-in-waiting.

When each had asked the other, "How do I look tonight, dear?" and been answered with reciprocal enthusiasm, "Perfectly lovely, darling!" Kitty said to Rose, who was helping her to restore order out of the chaos to which much exercise had reduced her curls: "By the way, young Randal is dying to be presented to you. May I after supper?"

"No, thank you," answered Rose very decidedly.

"Well, I'm sure I don't see why not," began Kitty, looking displeased but not surprised.

"I think you do, else why didn't you present him when he asked? You seldom stop to think of etiquette why did you now?"

"I didn't like to do it till I had you are so particular I thought you'd say 'no,' but I couldn't tell him so," stammered Kitty, feeling that she had better have settled the matter herself, for Rose was very particular and had especial reason to dislike this person because he was not only a dissipated young reprobate himself but seemed possessed of Satan to lead others astray likewise.

"I don't wish to be rude, dear, but I really must decline, for I cannot know such people, even though I meet them here," said Rose, remembering Charlie's revelations on New Year's night and hardening her heart against the man who had been his undoing on that as well as on other occasions, she had reason to believe.

"I couldn't help it! Old Mr. Randal and Papa are friends, and though I spoke of it, brother Alf wouldn't hear of passing that bad boy over," explained Kitty eagerly.

"Yet Alf forbade you driving or skating with him, for he knows better than we how unfit he is to come among us."

"I'd drop him tomorrow if I could, but I must be civil in my own house. His mother brought him, and he won't dare to behave here as he does at their bachelor parties."

"She ought not to have brought him till he had shown some desire to mend his ways. It is none of my business, I know, but I do wish people wouldn't be so inconsistent, letting boys go to destruction and then expecting us girls to receive them like decent people." Rose spoke in an energetic whisper, but Annabel heard her and exclaimed, as she turned round with a powder puff in her hand: "My goodness, Rose! What is all that about going to destruction?"

"She is being strong-minded, and I don't very much blame her in this case. But it leaves me in a dreadful scrape," said Kitty, supporting her spirits with a sniff of aromatic vinegar.

"I appeal to you, since you heard me, and there's no one here but ourselves do you consider young Randal a nice person to know?" And Rose turned to Annabel and Emma with an anxious eye, for she did not find it easy to abide by her principles when so doing annoyed friends.

"No, indeed, he's perfectly horrid! Papa says he and Gorham are the wildest young men he knows, and enough to spoil the whole set. I'm so glad I've got no brothers," responded Annabel, placidly powdering her pink arms, quite undeterred by the memory of sundry white streaks left on sundry coat sleeves.

"I think that sort of scrupulousness is very ill-bred, if you'll excuse my saying so, Rose. We are not supposed to know anything about fastness, and wildness, and so on, but to treat every man alike and not be fussy and prudish," said Emma, settling her many-colored streamers with the superior air of a woman of the world, aged twenty.

"Ah! But we do know, and if our silence and civility have no effect, we ought to try something else and not encourage wickedness of any kind. We needn't scold and preach, but we can refuse to know such people and that will do some good, for they don't like to be shunned and shut out from respectable society. Uncle Alec told me not to know that man, and I won't." Rose spoke with unusual warmth, forgetting that she could not tell the real reason for her strong prejudice against "that man."

"Well, I know him. I think him very jolly, and I'm engaged to dance the German with him after supper. He leads quite as well as your cousin Charlie and is quite as fascinating, some people think," returned Emma, tossing her head disdainfully, for Prince Charming did not worship at her shrine and it piqued her vanity.

In spite of her quandary, Rose could not help smiling as she recalled Mac's comparison, for Emma turned so red with spiteful chagrin, she seemed to have added strawberry ice to the other varieties composing the Harlequin.

"Each must judge for herself. I shall follow Aunt Jessie's advice and try to keep my atmosphere as pure as I can, for she says every woman has her own little circle and in it can use her influence for good, if she will. I do will heartily, and I'll prove that I'm neither proud nor fussy by receiving, here or at home, any respectable man you like to present to me, no matter how poor or plain or insignificant he may be."

With which declaration Rose ended her protest, and the four damsels streamed downstairs together like a wandering rainbow. But Kitty laid to heart what she had said; Annabel took credit herself for siding with her; and Emma owned that she was not trying to keep her atmosphere pure when she came to dance with the objectionable Randal. So Rose's "little circle" was the better for the influence she tried to exert, although she never knew it.

At suppertime Charlie kept near her, and she was quite content with him, for he drank only coffee, and she saw him shake his head with a frown when young Van beckoned him toward an anteroom, from whence the sound of popping corks had issued with increasing frequency as the evening wore on.

"Dear fellow, he does try," thought Rose, longing to show how she admired his self-denial, but she could only say, as they left the supper room with the aunts, who were going early: "If I had not promised Uncle to get home as soon after midnight as possible, I'd stay and dance the German with you, for you deserve a reward tonight."

"A thousand thanks, but I am going when you do," answered Charlie, understanding both her look and words and very grateful for them.

"Really?" cried Rose, delighted.

"Really. I'll be in the hall when you come down." And Charlie thought the Fra Angelico angel was not half so bright and beautiful as the one who looked back at him out of a pale blue cloud as Rose went upstairs as if on wings.

When she came down again Charlie was not in the hall, however, and, after waiting a few minutes, Mac offered to go and find him, for Aunt Jane was still hunting a lost rubber above.

"Please say I'm ready, but he needn't come if he doesn't want to," said Rose, not wishing to demand too much of her promising penitent.

"If he has gone into that barroom, I'll have him out, no matter who is there!" growled Mac to himself as he made his way to the small apartment whither the gentlemen retired for a little private refreshment when the spirit moved, as it often did.

The door was ajar, and Charlie seemed to have just entered, for Mac heard a familiar voice call out in a jovial tone: "Come, Prince! You're just in time to help us drink Steve's health with all the honors."

"Can't stop, only ran in to say good night, Van. Had a capital time, but I'm on duty and must go."

"That's a new dodge. Take a stirrup cup anyway, and come back in time for a merry-go-rounder when you've disposed of the ladies," answered the young host, diving into the wine cooler for another bottle.

"Charlie's going in for sanctity, and it doesn't seem to agree with him," laughed one of the two other young men who occupied several chairs apiece, resting their soles in every sense of the word.

"Apron strings are coming into fashion the bluer the better hey, Prince?" added the other, trying to be witty, with the usual success.

"You'd better go home early yourself, Barrow, or that tongue of yours will get you into trouble," retorted Charlie, conscious that he ought to take his own advice, yet lingering, nervously putting on his gloves while the glasses were being filled.

"Now, brother-in-law, fire away! Here you are, Prince." And Steve handed a glass across the table to his cousin, feeling too much elated with various pleasurable emotions to think what he was doing, for the boys all knew Charlie's weakness and usually tried to defend him from it.

Before the glass could be taken, however, Mac entered in a great hurry, delivering his message in an abbreviated and rather peremptory form: "Rose is waiting for you. Hurry up!"

"All right. Good night, old fellows!" And Charlie was off, as if the name had power to stop him in the very act of breaking the promise made to himself.

"Come, Solon, take a social drop, and give us an epithalamium in your best Greek. Here's to you!" And Steve was lifting the wine to his own lips when Mac knocked the glass out of his hand with a flash of the eye that caused his brother to stare at him with his mouth open in an imbecile sort of way, which seemed to excite Mac still more, for, turning to his young host, he said, in a low voice, and with a look that made the gentlemen on the chairs sit up suddenly: "I beg pardon, Van, for making a mess, but I can't stand by and see my own brother tempt another man beyond his strength or make a brute of himself. That's plain English, but I can't help speaking out, for I know not one of you would willingly hurt Charlie, and you will if you don't let him alone."

"What do you pitch into me for? I've done nothing. A fellow must be civil in his own house, mustn't he?" asked Van good-humoredly as he faced about, corkscrew in hand.

"Yes, but it is not civil to urge or joke a guest into doing what you know and he knows is bad for him. That's only a glass of wine to you, but it is perdition to Charlie, and if Steve knew what he was about, he'd cut his right hand off before he'd offer it."

"Do you mean to say I'm tipsy?" demanded Steve, ruffling up like a little gamecock, for though he saw now what he had done and was ashamed of it, he hated to have Mac air his peculiar notions before other people.

"With excitement, not champagne, I hope, for I wouldn't own you if you were," answered Mac, in whom indignation was effervescing like the wine in the forgotten bottle, for the men were all young, friends of Steve's and admirers of Charlie's. "Look here, boys," he went on more quietly, "I know I ought not to explode in this violent sort of way, but upon my life I couldn't help it when I heard what you were saying and saw what Steve was doing. Since I have begun, I may as well finish and tell you straight out that Prince can't stand this sort of thing. He is trying to flee temptation, and whoever leads him into it does a cowardly and sinful act, for the loss of one's own self-respect is bad enough, without losing the more precious things that make life worth having. Don't tell him I've said this, but lend a hand if you can, and never have to reproach yourselves with the knowledge that you helped to ruin a fellow creature, soul and body."

It was well for the success of Mac's first crusade that his hearers were gentlemen and sober, so his outburst was not received with jeers or laughter but listened to in silence, while the expression of the faces changed from one of surprise to regret and respect, for earnestness is always effective and championship of this sort seldom fails to touch hearts as yet unspoiled. As he paused with an eloquent little quiver in his eager voice, Van corked the bottle at a blow, threw down the corkscrew, and offered Mac his hand, saying heartily, in spite of his slang: "You are a first-class old brick! I'll lend a hand for one, and do my best to back up Charlie, for he's the finest fellow I know, and shan't go to the devil like poor Randal if I can help it."

Murmurs of applause from the others seemed to express a general assent to this vigorous statement, and, giving the hand a grateful shake, Mac retreated to the door, anxious to be off now that he had freed his mind with such unusual impetuosity.

"Count on me for anything I can do in return for this, Van. I'm sorry to be such a marplot, but you can take it out in quizzing me after I'm gone. I'm fair game, and Steve can set you going."

With that, Mac departed as abruptly as he had come, feeling that he had "made a mess" of it, but comforting himself with the thought that perhaps he had secured help for Charlie at his own expense and thinking with a droll smile as he went back to his mother: "My romance begins by looking after other girls' lovers instead of finding a sweetheart for myself, but I can't tell Rose, so she won't laugh at me."

## Chapter 13 BOTH SIDES

Steve's engagement made a great stir in the family a pleasant one this time, for nobody objected, everything seemed felicitous, and the course of true love ran very smoothly for the young couple, who promised to remove the only obstacle to their union by growing old and wise as soon as possible. If he had not been so genuinely happy, the little lover's airs would have been unbearable, for he patronized all mankind in general, his brother and elder cousins in particular.

"Now, that is the way to manage matters," he declared, standing before the fire in Aunt Clara's billiard room a day or two after the ball, with his hands behind his back. "No nonsense, no delay, no domestic rows or tragic separations. Just choose with taste and judgment, make yourself agreeable through thick and thin, and when it is perfectly evident that the dear creature adores the ground you walk on, say the word like a man, and there you are."

"All very easy to do that with a girl like Kitty, who has no confounded notions to spoil her and trip you up every time you don't exactly toe the mark," muttered Charlie, knocking the balls about as if it were a relief to hit something, for he was in a gloriously bad humor that evening, because time hung heavy on his hands since he had forsworn the company he could not keep without danger to himself.

"You should humor those little notions, for all women have them, and it needs tact to steer clear of them. Kitty's got dozens, but I treat them with respect, have my own way when I can, give in without growling when I can't, and we get on like a couple of—"

"Spoons," put in Charlie, who felt that he had not steered clear and so suffered shipwreck in sight of land.

Steve meant to have said "doves," but his cousin's levity caused him to add with calm dignity, "reasonable beings," and then revenged himself by making a good shot which won him the game.

"You always were a lucky little dog, Steve. I don't begrudge you a particle of your happiness, but it does seem as if things weren't quite fair sometimes," said Archie, suppressing an envious sigh, for, though he seldom complained, it was impossible to contrast his own and his cousin's prospects with perfect equanimity.

"His worth shines forth the brightest who in hope
Always confides: the Abject soul despairs,"

observed Mac, quoting Euripides in a conversational tone as he lay upon a divan reposing after a hard day's work.

"Thank you," said Archie, brightening a little, for a hopeful word from any source was very comfortable.

"That's your favorite Rip, isn't it? He was a wise old boy, but you could find advice as good as that nearer home," put in Steve, who just then felt equal to slapping Plato on the shoulder, so elated was he at being engaged "first of all the lot," as he gracefully expressed it.

"Don't halloo till you are out of the wood, Dandy Mrs. Kit has jilted two men, and may a third, so you'd better not brag of your wisdom too soon, for she may make a fool of you yet," said Charlie, cynically, his views of life being very gloomy about this time.

"No, she won't, Steve, if you do your part honestly. There's the making of a good little woman in Kitty, and she has proved it by taking you instead of those other fellows. You are not a Solomon, but you're not spoilt yet, and she had the sense to see it," said Mac encouragingly from his corner, for he and his brother were better friends than even since the little scene at the Van Tassels'.

"Hear! Hear!" cried Steve, looking more than ever like a cheerful young cockerel trying to crow as he stood upon the hearth rug with his hands under his coat tails, rising and falling alternately upon the toes and heels of his neat little boots.

"Come, you've given them each a pat on the head haven't you got one for me? I need it enough, for if ever there was a poor devil born under an evil star, it is C. C. Campbell," exclaimed Charlie, leaning his chin on his cue with a discontented expression of countenance, for trying to be good is often very hard work till one gets used to it.

"Oh, yes! I can accommodate you." And, as if his words suggested the selection, Mac, still lying flat upon his back, repeated one of his favorite bits from Beaumont and Fletcher, for he had a wonderful memory and could reel off poetry by the hour together.

"Man is his own star; and the soul that can
Render an honest and a perfect man
Commands all light, all influence, all fate.
Nothing to him falls early or too late.

Our acts our angels are; or good or ill,
Our fatal shadows that walk by us still."

"Confoundedly bad angels they are too," muttered Charlie ruefully, remembering the one that undid him.

His cousins never knew exactly what occurred on New Year's night, but suspected that something was amiss, for Charlie had the blues, and Rose, though as kind as ever, expressed no surprise at his long absences. They had all observed and wondered at this state of things, yet discreetly made no remark till Steve, who was as inquisitive as a magpie, seized this opportunity to say in a friendly tone, which showed that he bore no malice for the dark prophecy regarding his Kitty's faithfulness: "What's the trouble, Prince? You are so seldom in a bad humor that we don't know what to make of it and all feel out of spirits when you have the blues. Had a tiff with Rose?"

"Never you mind, little boy, but this I will say the better women are, the more unreasonable they are. They don't require us to be saints like themselves, which is lucky, but they do expect us to render an 'honest and a perfect man' sometimes, and that is asking rather too much in a fallen world like this," said Charlie, glad to get a little sympathy, though he had no intention of confessing his transgressions.

"No, it isn't," said Mac, decidedly.

"Much you know about it," began Charlie, ill pleased to be so flatly contradicted.

"Well, I know this much," added Mac, suddenly sitting up with his hair in a highly disheveled condition. "It is very unreasonable in us to ask women to be saints and then expect them to feel honored when we offer them our damaged hearts or, at best, one not half as good as theirs. If they weren't blinded by love, they'd see what a mean advantage we take of them and not make such bad bargains."

"Upon my word, the philosopher is coming out strong upon the subject! We shall have him preaching 'Women's Rights' directly," said Steve, much amazed at this outburst.

"I've begun, you see, and much good may it do you," answered Mac, laying himself placidly down again.

"Well, but look here, man you are arguing on the wrong side," put in Archie, quite agreeing with him, but feeling that he must stand by his order at all costs.

"Never mind sides, uphold the right wherever you find it. You needn't stare, Steve I told you I was going to look into this matter, and I am. You think I'm wrapped up in books, but I see a great deal more of what is going on around me than you imagine, and I'm getting on in this new branch, let me tell you, quite as fast as is good for me, I daresay."

"Going in for perfection, are you?" asked Charlie, both amused and interested, for he respected Mac more than he owned even to himself, and though he had never alluded to the timely warning, neither forgot.

"Yes, I think of it."

"How will you begin?"

"Do my best all-round keep good company, read good books, love good things, and cultivate soul and body as faithfully and wisely as I can."

"And you expect to succeed, do you?"

"Please God, I will."

The quiet energy of Mac's last words produced a momentary silence. Charlie thoughtfully studied the carpet; Archie, who had been absently poking the fire, looked over at Mac as if he thanked him again, and Steve, forgetting his self-conceit, began to wonder if it was not possible to improve himself a little for Kitty's sake. Only a minute, for young men do not give much time to thoughts of this kind, even when love stirs up the noblest impulses within them. To act rather than to talk is more natural to most of them, as Charlie's next question showed, for, having the matter much at heart, he ventured to ask in an offhand way as he laughed and twirled his cue: "Do you intend to reach the highest point of perfection before you address one of the fair saints, or shall you ask her to lend a hand somewhere short of that?"

"As it takes a long lifetime to do what I plan, I think I shall ask some good woman 'to lend a hand' when I've got anything worth offering her. Not a saint, for I never shall be one myself, but a gentle creature who will help me, as I shall try to help her, so that we can go on together and finish our work hereafter, if we haven't time to do it here."

If Mac had been a lover, he would not have discussed the subject in this simple and sincere fashion, though he might have felt it far more deeply, but being quite heart-free, he frankly showed his interest and, curiously enough, out of his wise young head unconsciously gave the three lovers before him counsel which they valued, because he practiced what he preached.

"Well, I hope you'll find her!" said Charlie heartily as he went back to his game.

"I think I shall." And while the others played, Mac lay staring at the window curtain as contentedly as if, through it, he beheld "a dream of fair women" from which to choose his future mate.

A few days after this talk in the billiard room, Kitty went to call upon Rose, for as she was about to enter the family she felt it her duty to become acquainted with all its branches. This branch, however, she cultivated more assiduously than any other and was continually running in to confer with "Cousin Rose," whom she considered the wisest, dearest, kindest girl ever created. And Rose, finding that, in spite of her flighty head, Kitty had a good heart of her own, did her best to encourage all the new hopes and aspirations springing up in it under the warmth of the first genuine affection she had ever known.

"My dear, I want to have some serious conversation with you upon a subject in which I take an interest for the first time in my life," began Miss Kitty, seating herself and pulling off her gloves as if the subject was one which needed a firm grasp.

"Tell away, and don't mind if I go on working, as I want to finish this job today," answered Rose, with a long-handled paintbrush in her hand and a great pair of shears at her side.

"You are always so busy! What is it now? Let me help I can talk faster when I'm doing something," which seemed hardly possible, for Kitty's tongue went like a mill clapper at all hours.

"Making picture books for my sick babies at the hospital. Pretty work, isn't it? You cut out, and I'll paste them on these squares of gay cambric then we just tie up a few pages with a ribbon and there is a nice, light, durable book for the poor dears to look at as they lie in their little beds."

"A capital idea. Do you go there often? How ever do you find the time for such things?" asked Kitty, busily cutting from a big sheet the touching picture of a parent bird with a red head and a blue tail offering what looked like a small boa constrictor to one of its nestlings, a fat young squab with a green head, yellow body, and no tail at all.

"I have plenty of time now I don't go out so much, for a party uses up two days generally one to prepare for it and one to get over it, you know."

"People think it is so odd of you to give up society all of a sudden. They say you have 'turned pious' and it is owing to your peculiar bringing-up. I always take your part and say it is a pity other girls haven't as sensible an education, for I don't know one who is as satisfactory on the whole as you are."

"Much obliged. You may also tell people I gave up gaiety because I value health more. But I haven't forsworn everything of the kind, Kit. I go to concerts and lectures, and all sorts of early things, and have nice times at home, as you know. I like fun as well as ever, but I'm getting on, you see, and must be preparing a little for the serious part of life. One never knows when it may come," said Rose, thoughtfully as she pasted a squirrel upside down on the pink cotton page before her.

"That reminds me of what I wanted to say. If you'll believe me, my dear, Steve has got that very idea into his head! Did you or Mac put it there?" asked Kitty, industriously clashing her shears.

"No, I've given up lecturing the boys lately they are so big now they don't like it, and I fancy I'd got into a way that was rather tiresome."

"Well, then, he is 'turning pious' too. And what is very singular, I like it. Now don't smile I really do and I want to be getting ready for the 'serious part of life,' as you call it. That is, I want to grow better as fast as I can, for Steve says he isn't half good enough for me. Just think of that!"

Kitty looked so surprised and pleased and proud that Rose felt no desire to laugh at her sudden fancy for sobriety but said in her most sympathetic tone: "I'm very glad to hear it, for it shows that he loves you in the right way."

"Is there more than one way?"

"Yes, I fancy so, because some people improve so much after they fall in love, and others do not at all. Have you never observed that?"

"I never learned how to observe. Of course I know that some matches turn out well and some don't, but I never thought much about it."

"Well, I have, for I was rather interested in the subject lately and had a talk with Aunt Jessie and Uncle about it."

"Gracious! You don't talk to them about such things, do you?"

"Yes, indeed. I ask any questions I like, and always get a good answer. It is such a nice way to learn, Kitty, for you don't have to pore over books, but as things come along you talk about them and remember, and when they are spoken of afterward you understand and are interested, though you don't say a word," explained Rose.

"It must be nice, but I haven't anyone to do so for me. Papa is too busy, and Mama always says when I ask question, 'Don't trouble your head with such things, child,' so I don't. What did you learn about matches turning out well? I'm interested in that, because I want mine to be quite perfect in all respects."

"After thinking it over, I came to the conclusion that Uncle was right, and it is not always safe to marry a person just because you love him," began Rose, trying to enlighten Kitty without betraying herself.

"Of course not if they haven't money or are bad. But otherwise I don't see what more is needed," said Kitty wonderingly.

"One should stop and see if it is a wise love, likely to help both parties and wear well, for you know it ought to last all one's lifetime, and it is very sad if it doesn't."

"I declare it quite scares me to think of it, for I don't usually go beyond my wedding day in making plans. I remember, though, that when I was engaged the first time you don't know the man; it was just after you went away, and I was only sixteen someone very ill-naturedly said I should 'marry in haste and repent at leisure,' and that made me try to imagine how it would seem to go on year after year with Gustavus who had a dreadful temper, by the way and it worried me so to think of it that I broke the engagement, and was so glad ever afterward."

"You were a wise girl and I hope you'll do it again if you find, after a time, that you and Steve do not truly trust and respect as well as love one another. If you don't, you'll be miserable when it is too late, as so many people are who do marry in haste and have a lifetime to repent it. Aunt Jessie says so, and she knows."

"Don't be solemn, Rose. It fidgets me to think about life-times, and respecting, and all those responsible things. I'm not used to it, and I don't know how to do it."

"But you must think, and you must learn how before you take the responsibility upon yourself. That is what your life is for, and you mustn't spoil it by doing a very solemn thing without seeing if you are ready for it."

"Do you think about all this?" asked Kitty, shrugging up her shoulders as if responsibility of any sort did not sit comfortably on them.

"One has to sometimes, you know. But is that all you wanted to tell me?" added Rose, anxious to turn the conversation from herself.

"Oh, dear, no! The most serious thing of all is this. Steve is putting himself in order generally, and so I want to do my part, and I must begin right away before my thoughts get distracted with clothes and all sorts of dear, delightful, frivolous things that I can't help liking. Now I wish you'd tell me where to begin. Shouldn't I improve my mind by reading something solid?" And Kitty looked over at the well-filled bookcase as if to see if it contained anything large and dry enough to be considered "solid."

"It would be an excellent plan, and we'll look up something. What do you feel as if you needed most?"

"A little of everything I should say, for when I look into my mind there really doesn't seem to be much there but odds and ends, and yet I'm sure I've read a great deal more than some girls do. I suppose novels don't count, though, and are of no use, for, goodness knows, the people and things they describe aren't a bit like the real ones."

"Some novels are very useful and do as much good as sermons, I've heard Uncle say, because they not only describe truly, but teach so pleasantly that people like to learn in that way," said Rose, who knew the sort of books Kitty had read and did not wonder that she felt rather astray when she tried to guide herself by their teaching.

"You pick me out some of the right kind, and I'll apply my mind to them. Then I ought to have some 'serious views' and 'methods' and 'principles.' Steve said 'principles,' good firm ones, you know." And Kitty gave a little pull at the bit of cambric she was cutting as housewives pull cotton or calico when they want "a good firm article."

Rose could not help laughing now, though much pleased, for Kitty was so prettily in earnest, and yet so perfectly ignorant how to begin on the self-improvement she very much needed, that it was pathetic as well as comical to see and hear her.

"You certainly want some of those, and must begin at once to get them, but Aunt Jessie can help you there better than I can, or Aunt Jane, for she has very 'firm' ones, I assure you," said Rose, sobering down as quickly as possible.

"Mercy on us! I should never dare to say a word about it to Mrs. Mac, for I'm dreadfully afraid of her, she is so stern, and how I'm ever to get on when she is my mother-in-law I don't know!" cried Kitty, clasping her hands in dismay at the idea.

"She isn't half as stern as she looks, and if you go to her without fear, you've no idea how sensible and helpful she is. I used to be frightened out of my wits with her, but now I'm not a bit, and we get on nicely. Indeed, I'm fond of her, she is so reliable and upright in all things."

"She certainly is the straightest woman I ever saw, and the most precise. I never shall forget how scared I was when Steve took me up to see her that first time. I put on all my plainest things, did my hair in a meek knob, and tried to act like a sober, sedate young woman. Steve would laugh at me and say I looked like a pretty nun, so I couldn't be as proper as I wished. Mrs. Mac was very kind, of course, but her eye was so sharp I felt as if she saw right through me, and knew that I'd pinned on my bonnet strings, lost a button off my boot, and didn't brush my hair for ten minutes every night," said Kitty in an awe-stricken tone.

"She likes you, though, and so does Uncle, and he's set his heart on having you live with them by and by, so don't mind her eyes but look straight up at her, and you'll see how kind they can grow."

"Mac likes me, too, and that did please me, for he doesn't like girls generally. Steve told me he said I had the 'making of a capital little woman in me.' Wasn't it nice of him? Steve was so proud, though he does laugh at Mac sometimes."

"Don't disappoint them, dear. Encourage Steve in all the good things he likes or wants, make friends with Mac, love Aunt Jane, and be a daughter to Uncle, and you'll find yourself a very happy girl."

"I truly will, and thank you very much for not making fun of me. I know I'm a little goose, but lately I've felt as if I might come to something if I had the right sort of help. I'll go up and see Aunt Jessie tomorrow. I'm not a bit afraid of her, and then if you'll just quietly find out from Uncle Doctor what I must read, I'll work as hard as I can. Don't tell anyone, please, they'll think it odd and affected, and I can't bear to be laughed at, though I daresay it is good discipline."

Rose promised, and both worked in silence for a moment, then Kitty asked rather timidly: "Are you and Charlie trying this plan too? Since you've left off going out so much, he keeps away also, and we don't know what to make of it."

"He has had what he calls an 'artistic fit' lately, set up a studio, and is doing some crayon sketches of us all. If he'd only finish his things, they would be excellent, but he likes to try a great variety at once. I'll take you in sometime, and perhaps he will do a portrait of you for Steve. He likes girls' faces and gets the likenesses wonderfully well."

"People say you are engaged but I contradict it, because, of course, I should know if you were."

"We are not."

"I'm glad of it, for really, Rose, I'm afraid Charlie hasn't got 'firm principles,' though he is a fascinating fellow and one can't scold him. You don't mind my saying so, do you, dear?" added Kitty, for Rose did not answer at once.

"Not in the least, for you are one of us now, and I can speak frankly and I will, for I think in one way you can help Steve very much. You are right about Charlie, both as to the principles and the fascination. Steve admires him exceedingly, and always from a boy liked to imitate his pleasant ways. Some of them are very harmless and do Steve good, but some are not. I needn't talk about it, only you must show your boy that you depend on him to keep out of harm and help him do it."

"I will, I will! And then perhaps, when he is a perfect model, Charlie will imitate him. I really begin to feel as if I had a great deal to do." And Kitty looked as if she was beginning to like it also.

"We all have and the sooner we go to work the better for us and those we love. You wouldn't think now that Phebe was doing anything for Archie, but she is, and writes such splendid letters, they stir him up wonderfully and make us all love and admire her more than ever."

"How is she getting on?" asked Kitty, who, though she called herself a "little goose," had tact enough to see that Rose did not care to talk about Charlie.

"Nicely, for you know she used to sing in our choir, so that was a good recommendation for another. She got a fine place in the new church at L——, and that gives her a comfortable salary, though she has something put away. She was always a saving creature and kept her wages carefully. Uncle invested them, and she begins to feel quite independent already. No fear but my Phebe will get on she has such energy and manages so well. I sometimes wish I could run away and work with her."

"Ah, my dear! We rich girls have our trials as well as poor ones, though we don't get as much pity as they do," sighed Kitty. "Nobody knows what I suffer sometimes from worries that I can't talk about, and I shouldn't get much sympathy if I did, just because I live in a big house, wear good gowns, and have lots of lovers. Annabel used to say she envied me above all created beings, but she doesn't now, and is perfectly absorbed in her dear little Chinaman. Do you see how she ever could like him?"

So they began to gossip, and the sober talk was over for that time, but when Kitty departed, after criticizing all her dear friends and their respective sweethearts, she had a helpful little book in her muff, a resolute expression on her bright face, and so many excellent plans for self-improvement in her busy brain that she and Steve bid fair to turn out the model couple of the century.

Chapter 14 AUNT CLARA'S PLAN

Being seriously alarmed by the fear of losing the desire of his heart, Charlie had gone resolutely to work and, like many another young reformer, he rather overdid the matter, for in trying to keep out of the way of temptation, he denied himself much innocent enjoyment. The "artistic fit" was a good excuse for the seclusion which he fancied would be a proper penance, and he sat listlessly plying crayon or paintbrush, with daily wild rides on black Brutus, which seemed to do him good, for danger of that sort was his delight.

People were used to his whims and made light of what they considered a new one, but when it lasted week after week and all attempts to draw him out were vain, his jolly comrades gave him up and the family began to say approvingly, "Now he really is going to settle down and do something." Fortunately, his mother let him alone, for though Dr. Alec had not "thundered in her ear" as he threatened, he had talked with her in a way which first made her very angry, then anxious, and, lastly, quite submissive, for her heart was set on the boy's winning Rose and she would have had him put on sackcloth and ashes if that would have secured the prize. She made light of the cause of Rose's displeasure, considering her extremely foolish and straitlaced, "for all young men of any spirit had their little vices, and came out well enough when the wild oats were sowed." So she indulged Charlie in his new vagary, as she had in all his others, and treated him like an ill-used being, which was neither an inspiring nor helpful course on her part. Poor soul! She saw her mistake by and by, and when too late repented of it bitterly.

Rose wanted to be kind, and tried in various ways to help her cousin, feeling very sure she should succeed as many another hopeful woman has done, quite unconscious how much stronger an undisciplined will is than the truest love, and what a difficult task the wisest find it to undo the mistakes of a bad education. But it was a hard thing to do, for at the least hint of commendation or encouragement, he looked so hopeful that she was afraid of seeming to promise too much, and, of all things, she desired to escape the accusation of having trifled with him.

So life was not very comfortable to either just then; and while Charlie was "mortifying soul and body" to please her, she was studying how to serve him best. Aunt Jessie helped her very much, and no one guessed, when they saw pretty Miss Campbell going up and down the hill with such a serious face, that she was intent upon anything except taking, with praiseworthy regularity, the constitutionals which gave her such a charming color.

Matters were in this state when one day a note came to Rose from Mrs. Clara.

MY SWEET CHILD, Do take pity on my poor boy and cheer him up with a sight of you, for he is so triste it breaks my heart to see him. He has a new plan in his head, which strikes me as an excellent one, if you will only favor it. Let him come and take you for a drive this fine afternoon and talk things over. It will do him a world of good and deeply oblige

Your ever loving

AUNT CLARA.

Rose read the note twice and stood a moment pondering, with her eyes absently fixed on the little bay before her window. The sight of several black figures moving briskly to and fro across its frozen surface seemed to suggest a mode of escape from the drive she dreaded in more ways than one. "That will be safer and pleasanter," she said, and going to her desk wrote her answer.

DEAR AUNTY, I'm afraid of Brutus, but if Charlie will go skating with me, I should enjoy it very much and it would do us both good. I can listen to the new plan with an undivided mind there, so give him my love, please, and say I shall expect him at three.

Affectionately, ROSE.

Punctually at three Charlie appeared with his skates over his arm and with a very contented face, which brightened wonderfully as Rose came downstairs in a sealskin suit and scarlet skirt, so like the one she wore years ago that he involuntarily exclaimed as he took her skates: "You look so like little Rose I hardly know you, and it seems so like old times I feel sixteen again."

"That is just the way one ought to feel on such a day as this. Now let us be off and have a good spin before anyone comes. There are only a few children there now, but it is Saturday, you know, and everybody will be out before long," answered Rose, carefully putting on her mittens as she talked, for her heart was not as light as the one little Rose carried under the brown jacket, and the boy of sixteen never looked at her with the love and longing she read in the eyes of the young man before her.

Away they went, and were soon almost as merry and warm as the children around them, for the ice was in good condition, the February sunshine brilliant, and the keen wind set their blood a-tingle with a healthful glow.

"Now tell me the plan your mother spoke of," began Rose as they went gliding across the wide expanse before them, for Charlie seemed to have forgotten everything but the bliss of having her all to himself for a little while.

"Plan? Oh, yes! It is simply this. I'm going out to Father next month."

"Really?" and Rose looked both surprised and incredulous, for this plan was not a new one.

"Really. You don't believe it, but I am, and mother means to go with me. We've had another letter from the governor, and he says if she can't part from her big baby to come along too, and all be happy together. What do you think of that?" he asked, eyeing her intently, for they were face to face as she went backward and he held both of her hands to steer and steady her.

"I like it immensely, and do believe it now only it rather takes my breath away to think of Aunty's going, when she never would hear of it before."

"She doesn't like the plan very well now and consents to go only on one condition."

"What is that?" asked Rose, trying to free her hands, for a look at Charlie made her suspect what was coming.

"That you go with us." And, holding the hands fast, he added rapidly, "Let me finish before you speak. I don't mean that anything is to be changed till you are ready, but if you go, I am willing to give up everything else and live anywhere as long as you like. Why shouldn't you come to us for a year or two? We've never had our share. Father would be delighted, mother contented, and I the happiest man alive."

"Who made this plan?" asked Rose as soon as she got the breath which certainly had been rather taken away by this entirely new and by no means agreeable scheme.

"Mother suggested it I shouldn't have dared even to dream of such richness. I'd made up my mind to go alone, and when I told her, she was in despair till this superb idea came into her head. After that, of course, it was easy enough for me to stick to the resolution I'd made."

"Why did you decide to go, Charlie?" And Rose looked up into the eyes that were fixed beseechingly on hers.

They wavered and glanced aside, then met hers honestly yet full of humility, which made her own fall as he answered very low: "Because I don't dare to stay."

"Is it so hard?" she said pitifully.

"Very hard. I haven't the moral courage to own up and face ridicule, and it seems so mean to hide for fear of breaking my word. I will keep it this time, Rose, if I go to the ends of the earth to do it."

"It is not cowardly to flee temptation, and nobody whose opinion is worth having will ridicule any brave attempt to conquer one's self. Don't mind it, Charlie, but stand fast, and I am sure you will succeed."

"You don't know what it is, and I can't tell you, for till I tried to give it up I never guessed what a grip it had on me. I thought it was only a habit, easy to drop when I liked, but it is stronger than I, and sometimes I feel as if possessed of a devil that will get the better of me, try as I may."

He dropped her hands abruptly as he said that, with the energy of despair; and, as if afraid of saying too much, he left her for a minute, striking away at full speed, as if in truth he would "go to the ends of the earth" to escape the enemy within himself.

Rose stood still, appalled by this sudden knowledge of how much greater the evil was than she had dreamed. What ought she to do? Go with her cousin, and by so doing tacitly pledge herself as his companion on that longer journey for which he was as yet so poorly equipped? Both heart and conscience protested against this so strongly that she put the thought away. But compassion pleaded for him tenderly, and the spirit of self-sacrifice, which makes women love to give more than they receive, caused her to feel as if in a measure this man's fate lay in her hands, to be decided for good or ill through her. How should she be true both to him and to herself?

Before this question could be answered, he was back again, looking as if he had left his care behind him, for his moods varied like the wind. Her attitude, as she stood motionless and alone with downcast face, was so unlike the cheerful creature who came to meet him an hour ago, it filled him with self-reproach, and, coming up, he drew one hand through his arm, saying, as she involuntarily followed him, "You must not stand still. Forget my heroics and answer my question. Will you go with us, Rose?"

"Not now that is asking too much, Charlie, and I will promise nothing, because I cannot do it honestly," she answered, so firmly that he knew appeal was useless.

"Am I to go alone, then, leaving all I care for behind me?"

"No, take your mother with you, and do your best to reunite your parents. You could not give yourself to a better task."

"She won't go without you."

"I think she will if you hold fast to your resolution. You won't give that up, I hope?"

"No I must go somewhere, for I can't stay here, and it may as well be India, since that pleases Father," answered Charlie doggedly.

"It will more than you can imagine. Tell him all the truth, and see how glad he will be to help you, and how sincerely he will respect you for what you've done."

"If you respect me, I don't care much about the opinion of anyone else," answered Charlie, clinging with a lover's pertinacity to the hope that was dearest.

"I shall, if you go manfully away and do the duty you owe your father and yourself."

"And when I've done it, may I come back to be rewarded, Rose?" he asked, taking possession of the hand on his arm as if it was already his.

"I wish I could say what you want me to. But how can I promise when I am not sure of anything? I don't love you as I ought, and perhaps I never shall so why persist in making me bind myself in this way? Be generous, Charlie, and don't ask it," implored Rose, much afflicted by his persistence.

"I thought you did love me it looked very like it a month ago, unless you have turned coquette, and I can't quite believe that," he answered bitterly.

"I was beginning to love you, but you made me afraid to go on," murmured Rose, trying to tell the truth kindly.

"That cursed custom! What can a man do when his hostess asks him to drink wine with her?" And Charlie looked as if he could have cursed himself even more heartily.

"He can say 'no.'"

"I can't."

"Ah, that's the trouble! You never learned to say it even to yourself, and now it is so hard, you want me to help you."

"And you won't."

"Yes, I will, by showing you that I can say it to myself, for your sake." And Rose looked up with a face so full of tender sorrow he could not doubt the words which both reproached and comforted him.

"My little saint! I don't deserve one half your goodness to me, but I will, and go away without one complaint to do my best, for your sake," he cried, touched by her grief and stirred to emulation by the example of courage and integrity she tried to set him.

Here Kitty and Steve bore down upon them; and, obeying the impulse to put care behind them, which makes it possible for young hearts to ache one minute and dance the next, Rose and Charlie banished their troubles, joined in the sport that soon turned the lonely little bay into a ballroom, and enjoyed the splendors of a winter sunset forgetful of separation and Calcutta.

Chapter 15 ALAS FOR CHARLIE!
In spite of much internal rebellion, Charlie held fast to his resolution, and Aunt Clara, finding all persuasions vain, gave in and in a state of chronic indignation against the world in general and Rose in particular, prepared to accompany him. The poor girl had a hard time of it and, but for her uncle, would have fared still worse. He was a sort of shield upon which Mrs. Clara's lamentations, reproaches, and irate glances fell unavailingly instead of wounding the heart against which they were aimed.

The days passed very quickly now, for everyone seemed anxious to have the parting over and preparations went on rapidly. The big house was made ready to shut up for a year at least, comforts for the long voyage laid in, and farewell visits paid. The general activity and excitement rendered it impossible for Charlie to lead the life of an artistic hermit any longer and he fell into a restless condition which caused Rose to long for the departure of the Rajah when she felt that he would be safe, for these farewell festivities were dangerous to one who was just learning to say "no."

"Half the month safely gone. If we can only get well over these last weeks, a great weight will be off my mind," thought Rose as she went down one wild, wet morning toward the end of February.

Opening the study door to greet her uncle, she exclaimed, "Why, Archie!" then paused upon the threshold, transfixed by fear, for in her cousin's white face she read the tidings of some great affliction.

"Hush! Don't be frightened. Come in and I'll tell you," he whispered, putting down the bottle he had just taken from the doctor's medicine closet.

Rose understood and obeyed, for Aunt Plenty was poorly with her rheumatism and depended on her morning doze.

"What is it?" she said, looking about the room with a shiver, as if expecting to see again what she saw there New Year's night. Archie was alone, however, and, drawing her toward the closet, answered with an evident effort to be quite calm and steady "Charlie is hurt! Uncle wants more ether and the wide bandages in some drawer or other. He told me, but I forget. You keep this place in order find them for me. Quick!"

Before he had done, Rose was at the drawer, turning over the bandages with hands that trembled as they searched.

"All narrow! I must make some. Can you wait?" And, catching up a piece of old linen, she tore it into wide strips, adding, in the same quick tone, as she began to roll them, "Now, tell me."

"I can wait those are not needed just yet. I didn't mean anyone should know, you least of all," began Archie, smoothing out the strips as they lay across the table and evidently surprised at the girl's nerve and skill.

"I can bear it make haste! Is he much hurt?"

"I'm afraid he is. Uncle looks sober, and the poor boy suffers so, I couldn't stay," answered Archie, turning still whiter about the lips that never had so hard a tale to tell before.

"You see, he went to town last evening to meet the man who is going to buy Brutus."

"And Brutus did it? I knew he would!" cried Rose, dropping her work to wring her hands, as if she guessed the ending of the story now.

"Yes, and if he wasn't shot already I'd do it myself with pleasure, for he's done his best to kill Charlie," muttered Charlie's mate with a grim look, then gave a great sigh and added with averted face, "I shouldn't blame the brute, it wasn't his fault. He needed a firm hand and—" He stopped there, but Rose said quickly: "Go on. I must know."

"Charlie met some of his old cronies, quite by accident; there was a dinner party, and they made him go, just for a good-bye, they said. He couldn't refuse, and it was too much for him. He would come home alone in the storm, though they tried to keep him, as he wasn't fit. Down by the new bridge that high embankment, you know the wind had put the lantern out he forgot or something scared Brutus, and all went down together."

Archie had spoken fast and brokenly but Rose understood and at the last word hid her face with a little moan, as if she saw it all.

"Drink this and never mind the rest," he said, dashing into the next room and coming back with a glass of water, longing to be done and away, for this sort of pain seemed almost as bad as that he had left.

Rose drank, but held his arm tightly, as he would have turned away, saying in a tone of command he could not disobey: "Don't keep anything back tell me the worst at once."

"We knew nothing of it," he went on obediently. "Aunt Clara thought he was with me, and no one found him till early this morning. A workman recognized him and he was brought home, dead they thought. I came for Uncle an hour ago. Charlie is conscious now, but awfully hurt, and I'm afraid from the way Mac and Uncle looked at one another that Oh! Think of it, Rose! Crushed and helpless, alone in the rain all night, and I never knew, I never knew!"

With that, poor Archie broke down entirely and, flinging himself into a chair, laid his face on the table, sobbing like a girl. Rose had never seen a man cry before, and it was so unlike a woman's gentler grief that it moved her very much. Putting by her own anguish, she tried to comfort his and, going to him, lifted up his head and made him lean on her, for in such hours as this women are the stronger. It was a very little to do, but it did comfort Archie, for the poor fellow felt as if fate was very hard upon him just then, and in this faithful bosom he could pour his brief but pathetic plaint.

"Phebe's gone, and now if Charlie's taken, I don't see how I can bear it!"

"Phebe will come back, dear, and let us hope poor Charlie isn't going to be taken yet. Such things always seem worst at first, I've heard people say, so cheer up and hope for the best," answered Rose, seeking for some comfortable words to say and finding very few.

They took effect, however, for Archie did cheer up like a man. Wiping away the tears which he so seldom shed that they did not know where to go, he got up, gave himself a little shake, and said with a long breath, as if he had been underwater: "Now I'm all right, thank you. I couldn't help it the shock of being waked suddenly to find the dear old fellow in such a pitiful state upset me. I ought to go are these ready?"

"In a minute. Tell Uncle to send for me if I can be of any use. Oh, poor Aunt Clara! How does she bear it?"

"Almost distracted. I took Mother to her, and she will do all that anybody can. Heaven only knows what Aunt will do if—"

"And only heaven can help her," added Rose as Archie stopped at the words he could not utter. "Now take them, and let me know often."

"You brave little soul, I will." And Archie went away through the rain with his sad burden, wondering how Rose could be so calm when the beloved Prince might be dying.

A long dark day followed, with nothing to break its melancholy monotony except the bulletins that came from hour to hour reporting little change either for better or for worse. Rose broke the news gently to Aunt Plenty and set herself to the task of keeping up the old lady's spirits, for, being helpless, the good soul felt as if everything would go wrong without her. At dusk she fell asleep, and Rose went down to order lights and fire in the parlor, with tea ready to serve at any moment, for she felt sure some of the men would come and that a cheerful greeting and creature comforts would suit them better than tears, darkness, and desolation.

Presently Mac arrived, saying the instant he entered the room: "More comfortable, Cousin."

"Thank heaven!" cried Rose, unclasping her hands. Then seeing how worn out, wet, and weary Mac looked as he came into the light, she added in a tone that was a cordial in itself, "Poor boy, how tired you are! Come here, and let me make you comfortable."

"I was going home to freshen up a bit, for I must be back in an hour. Mother took my place, so I could be spared, and came off, as Uncle refused to stir."

"Don't go home, for if Aunty isn't there it will be very dismal. Step into Uncle's room and refresh, then come back and I'll give you your tea. Let me, let me! I can't help in any other way, and I must do something, this waiting is so dreadful."

Her last words betrayed how much suspense was trying her, and Mac yielded at once, glad to comfort and be comforted. When he came back, looking much revived, a tempting little tea table stood before the fire and Rose went to meet him, saying with a faint smile, as she liberally bedewed him with the contents of a cologne flask: "I can't bear the smell of ether it suggests such dreadful things."

"What curious creatures women are! Archie told us you bore the news like a hero, and now you turn pale at a whiff of bad air. I can't explain it," mused Mac as he meekly endured the fragrant shower bath.

"Neither can I, but I've been imagining horrors all day and made myself nervous. Don't let us talk about it, but come and have some tea."

"That's another queer thing. Tea is your panacea for all human ills yet there isn't any nourishment in it. I'd rather have a glass of milk, thank you," said Mac, taking an easy chair and stretching his feet to the fire.

She brought it to him and made him eat something; then, as he shut his eyes wearily, she went away to the piano and, having no heart to sing, played softly till he seemed asleep. But at the stroke of six he was up and ready to be off again.

"He gave me that. Take it with you and put some on his hair. He likes it, and I do so want to help a little," she said, slipping the pretty flagon into his pocket with such a wistful look Mac never thought of smiling at this very feminine request.

"I'll tell him. Is there anything else I can do for you, Cousin?" he asked, holding the cold hand that had been serving him so helpfully.

"Only this if there is any sudden change, promise to send for me, no matter at what hour it is. I must say 'good-bye'".

"I will come for you. But, Rose, I am sure you may sleep in peace tonight, and I hope to have good news for you in the morning."

"Bless you for that! Come early, and let me see him soon. I will be very good, and I know it will not do him any harm."

237

"No fear of that. The first thing he said when he could speak was 'Tell Rose carefully,' and as I came away he guessed where I was going and tried to kiss his hand in the old way, you know."

Mac thought it would cheer her to hear that Charlie remembered her, but the sudden thought that she might never see the familiar little gesture anymore was the last drop that made her full heart overflow, and Mac saw the "hero" of the morning sink down at his feet in a passion of tears that frightened him. He took her to the sofa and tried to comfort her, but as soon as the bitter sobbing quieted she looked up and said quite steadily, great drops rolling down her cheeks the while: "Let me cry it is what I need, and I shall be all the better for it by and by. Go to Charlie now and tell him I said with all my heart, 'Good night!'?

"I will!" And Mac trudged away, marveling in his turn at the curiously blended strength and weakness of womankind.

That was the longest night Rose ever spent, but joy came in the morning with the early message: "He is better. You are to come by and by." Then Aunt Plenty forgot her lumbago and arose; Aunt Myra, who had come to have a social croak, took off her black bonnet as if it would not be needed at present, and the girl made ready to go and say "Welcome back," not the hard "Good-bye."

It seemed very long to wait, for no summons came till afternoon, then her uncle arrived, and at the first sight of his face Rose began to tremble.

"I came for my little girl myself, because we must go back at once," he said as she hurried toward him hat in hand.

"I'm ready, sir." But her hands shook as she tried to tie the ribbons, and her eyes never left the face that was full of tender pity for her.

He took her quickly into the carriage and, as they rolled away, said with the quiet directness which soothes such agitation better than any sympathetic demonstration: "Charlie is worse. I feared it when the pain went so suddenly this morning, but the chief injuries are internal and one can never tell what the chances are. He insists that he is better, but he will soon begin to fail, I fear, become unconscious, and slip away without more suffering. This is the time for you to see him, for he has set his heart on it, and nothing can hurt him now. My child, it is very hard, but we must help each other bear it."

Rose tried to say, "Yes, Uncle" bravely, but the words would not come, and she could only slip her hand into his with a look of mute submission. He laid her head on his shoulder and went on talking so quietly that anyone who did not see how worn and haggard his face had grown with two days and a night of sharp anxiety might have thought him cold.

"Jessie has gone home to rest, and Jane is with poor Clara, who has dropped asleep at last. I've sent for Steve and the other boys. There will be time for them later, but he so begged to see you now, I thought it best to come while this temporary strength keeps him up. I have told him how it is, but he will not believe me. If he asks you, answer honestly and try to fit him a little for this sudden ending of so many hopes."

"How soon, Uncle?"

"A few hours, probably. This tranquil moment is yours make the most of it and, when we can do no more for him, we'll comfort one another."

Mac met them in the hall, but Rose hardly saw him. She was conscious only of the task before her and, when her uncle led her to the door, she said quietly, "Let me go in alone, please."

Archie, who had been hanging over the bed, slipped away into the inner room as she appeared, and Rose found Charlie waiting for her with such a happy face, she could not believe what she had heard and found it easy to say almost cheerfully as she took his eager hand in both of hers: "Dear Charlie, I'm so glad you sent for me. I longed to come, but waited till you were better. You surely are?" she added, as a second glance showed to her the indescribable change which had come upon the face which at first seemed to have both light and color in it.

"Uncle says not, but I think he is mistaken, because the agony is all gone, and except for this odd sinking now and then, I don't feel so much amiss," he answered feebly but with something of the old lightness in his voice.

"You will hardly be able to sail in the Rajah, I fear, but you won't mind waiting a little while we nurse you," said poor Rose, trying to talk on quietly, with her heart growing heavier every minute.

"I shall go if I'm carried! I'll keep that promise, though it costs me my life. Oh, Rose! You know? They've told you?" And, with a sudden memory of what brought him there, he hid his face in the pillow.

"You broke no promise, for I would not let you make one, you remember. Forget all that, and let us talk about the better time that may be coming for you."

"Always so generous, so kind!" he murmured, with her hand against his feverish cheek; then, looking up, he went on in a tone so humbly contrite it made her eyes fill with slow, hot tears.

"I tried to flee temptation I tried to say 'no,' but I am so pitiably weak, I couldn't. You must despise me. But don't give me up entirely, for if I live, I'll do better. I'll go away to Father and begin again."

Rose tried to keep back the bitter drops, but they would fall, to hear him still speak hopefully when there was no hope. Something in the mute anguish of her face seemed to tell him what she could not speak, and a quick change came over him as he grasped her hand tighter, saying in a sharp whisper: "Have I really got to die, Rose?"

Her only answer was to kneel down and put her arms about him, as if she tried to keep death away a little longer. He believed it then, and lay so still, she looked up in a moment, fearing she knew not what.

But Charlie bore it manfully, for he had the courage which can face a great danger bravely, though not the strength to fight a bosom sin and conquer it. His eyes were fixed, as if trying to look into the unseen world whither he was going, and his lips firmly set that no word of complaint should spoil the proof he meant to give that, though he had not known how to live, he did know how to die. It seemed to Rose as if for one brief instant she saw the man that might have been if early training had taught him how to rule himself; and the first words he uttered with a long sigh, as his eye came back to her, showed that he felt the failure and owned it with pathetic candor.

"Better so, perhaps; better go before I bring any more sorrow to you and shame to myself. I'd like to stay a little longer and try to redeem the past; it seems so wasted now, but if I can't, don't grieve, Rose. I'm no loss to anyone, and perhaps it is too late to mend."

"Oh, don't say that! No one will find your place among us we never can forget how much we loved you, and you must believe how freely we forgive as we would be forgiven," cried Rose, steadied by the pale despair that had fallen on Charlie's face with those bitter words.

"'Forgive us our trespasses!' Yes, I should say that. Rose, I'm not ready, it is so sudden. What can I do?" he whispered, clinging to her as if he had no anchor except the creature whom he loved so much.

"Uncle will tell you I am not good enough I can only pray for you." And she moved as if to call in the help so sorely needed.

"No, no, not yet! Stay by me, darling read something there, in Grandfather's old book, some prayer for such as I. It will do me more good from you than any minister alive."

She got the venerable book given to Charlie because he bore the good man's name and, turning to the "Prayer for the Dying," read it brokenly while the voice beside her echoed now and then some word that reproved or comforted.

"The testimony of a good conscience." "By the sadness of his countenance may his heart be made better." "Christian patience and fortitude." "Leave the world in peace." "Amen."

There was silence for a little; then Rose, seeing how wan he looked, said softly, "Shall I call Uncle now?"

"If you will. But first don't smile at my foolishness, dear I want my little heart. They took it off please give it back and let me keep it always," he answered with the old fondness strong as ever, even when he could show it only by holding fast the childish trinket which she found and had given him the old agate heart with the faded ribbon. "Put it on, and never let them take it off," he said, and when she asked if there was anything else she could do for him, he tried to stretch out his arms to her with a look which asked for more.

She kissed him very tenderly on lips and forehead, tried to say "good-bye," but could not speak, and groped her way to the door. Turning for a last look, Charlie's hopeful spirit rose for a moment, as if anxious to send her away more cheerful, and he said with a shadow of the old blithe smile, a feeble attempt at the familiar farewell gesture: "Till tomorrow, Rose."

Alas for Charlie! His tomorrow never came, and when she saw him next, he lay there looking so serene and noble, it seemed as if it must be well with him, for all the pain was past; temptation ended; doubt and fear, hope and love, could no more stir his quiet heart, and in solemn truth he had gone to meet his Father, and begin again.

Chapter 16 GOOD WORKS

The Rajah was delayed awhile, and when it sailed poor Mrs. Clara was on board, for everything was ready. All thought she had better go to comfort her husband, and since her boy died she seemed to care very little what became of her. So, with friends to cheer the long voyage, she sailed away, a heavyhearted woman, yet not quite disconsolate, for she knew her mourning was excessively becoming and felt sure that Stephen would not find her altered by her trials as much as might have been expected.

Then nothing was left of that gay household but the empty rooms, silence never broken by a blithe voice anymore, and pictures full of promise, but all unfinished, like poor Charlie's life.

There was much mourning for the bonny Prince, but no need to tell of it except as it affected Rose, for it is with her we have most to do, the other characters being of secondary importance.

When time had soothed the first shock of sudden loss, she was surprised to find the memory of his faults and failings, short life and piteous death, grew dim, as if a kindly hand had wiped out the record and given him back to her in the likeness of the brave, bright boy she had loved, not as the wayward, passionate young man who had loved her.

This comforted her very much, and folding down the last blotted leaf where his name was written, she gladly turned back to reopen and reread the happier chapters which painted the youthful knight before he went out to fall in his first battle. None of the bitterness of love bereaved marred this memory for Rose, because she found that the warmer sentiment, just budding in her heart, had died with Charlie and lay cold and quiet in his grave. She wondered, yet was glad, though sometimes a remorseful pang smote her when she discovered how possible it was to go on without him, feeling almost as if a burden had been lifted off, since his happiness was taken out of her hands. The time had not yet come when the knowledge that a man's heart was in her keeping would make the pride and joy of her life, and while she waited for that moment she enjoyed the liberty she seemed to have recovered.

Such being her inward state, it much annoyed her to be regarded as a brokenhearted girl and pitied for the loss of her young lover. She could not explain to all the world, so let it pass, and occupied her mind with the good works which always lie ready to be taken up and carried on. Having chosen philanthropy as her profession, she felt that it was high time to begin the task too long neglected.

Her projects were excellent, but did not prosper as rapidly as she hoped, for, having to deal with people, not things, unexpected obstacles were constantly arising. The "Home for Decayed Gentlewomen," as the boys insisted on calling her two newly repaired houses, started finely and it was a pleasant sight to see the comfortable rooms filled with respectable women busy at their various tasks, surrounded by the decencies and many of the comforts which make life endurable. But, presently, Rose was disturbed to find that the good people expected her to take care of them in a way she had not bargained for. Buffum, her agent, was constantly reporting complaints, new wants, and general discontent if they were not attended to. Things were very neglected, water pipes froze and burst, drains got out of order, yards were in a mess, and rents behind-hand. Worst of all, outsiders, instead of sympathizing, only laughed and said, "We told you so," which is a most discouraging remark to older and wiser workers than Rose.

Uncle Alec, however, stood by her staunchly and helped her out of many of her woes by good advice and an occasional visit of inspection, which did much to impress upon the dwellers there the fact that, if they did not do their part, their leases would be short ones.

"I didn't expect to make anything out of it, but I did think they would be grateful," said Rose on one occasion when several complaints had come in at once and Buffum had reported great difficulty in collecting the low rents.

"If you do this thing for the sake of the gratitude, then it is a failure but if it is done for the love of helping those who need help, it is a success, for in spite of their worry every one of these women feel what privileges they enjoy and value them highly," said Dr. Alec as they went home after one of these unsatisfactory calls.

"Then the least they can do is to say 'thank you.' I'm afraid I have thought more of the gratitude than the work, but if there isn't any, I must make up my mind to go without," answered Rose, feeling defrauded of her due.

"Favors often separate instead of attracting people nearer to one another, and I've seen many a friendship spoilt by the obligation being all on one side. Can't explain it, but it is so, and I've come to the conclusion that it is as hard to give in the right spirit as it is to receive. Puzzle it out, my dear, while you are learning to do good for its own sake."

"I know one sort of people who are grateful and I'm going to devote my mind to them. They thank me in many ways, and helping them is all pleasure and no worry. Come into the hospital and see the dear babies, or the Asylum, and carry oranges to Phebe's orphans they don't complain and fidget one's life out, bless their hearts!" cried Rose, cheering up suddenly.

After that she left Buffum to manage the "Retreat," and devoted her energies to the little folks, always so ready to receive the smallest gift and repay the giver with their artless thanks. Here she found plenty to do, and did it with such sweet goodwill that she won her way like sunshine, making many a little heart dance over splendid dolls, gay picture books, and pots of flowers, as well as food, fire, and clothes for the small bodies pinched with want and pain.

As spring came new plans sprang up as naturally as dandelions. The poor children longed for the country; and, as the green fields could not come to them, Rose carried them to the green fields. Down on the Point stood an old farmhouse, often used by the Campbell tribe for summer holidays. That spring it was set to rights unusually early, several women installed as housekeeper, cook, and nurses, and when the May days grew bright and warm, squads of pale children came to toddle in the grass, run over the rocks, and play upon the smooth sands of the beach. A pretty sight, and one that well repaid those who brought it to pass.

Everyone took an interest in the "Rose Garden," as Mac named it, and the womenfolk were continually driving over to the Point for something for the "poor dears." Aunt Plenty sowed gingerbread broadcast; Aunt Jessie made pinafores by the dozen while Aunt Jane "kept her eye" on the nurses, and Aunt Myra supplied medicines so liberally that the mortality would have been awful if Dr. Alec had not taken them in charge. To him this was the most delightful spot in the world and well it might be, for he suggested the idea and gave Rose all the credit of it. He was often there, and his appearance was always greeted with shrieks of rapture, as the children gathered from all quarters creeping, running, hopping on crutches, or carried in arms which they gladly left to sit on "Uncle Doctor's" knee, for that was the title by which he went among them.

He seemed as young as any of his comrades, though the curly head was getting gray, and the frolics that went on when he arrived were better than any medicine to children who had never learned to play. It was a standing joke among the friends that the bachelor brother had the largest family and was the most domestic man of the remaining four, though Uncle Mac did his part manfully and kept Aunt Jane in a constant fidget by his rash propositions to adopt the heartiest boys and prettiest girls to amuse him and employ her.

On one occasion Aunt Jane had a very narrow escape, and the culprit being her son, not her husband, she felt free to repay herself for many scares of this sort by a good scolding, which, unlike many, produced excellent results.

One bright June day, as Rose came cantering home from the Point on her pretty bay pony, she saw a man sitting on a fallen tree beside the road and something in his despondent attitude arrested her attention. As she drew nearer he turned his head, and she stopped short, exclaiming in great surprise: "Why, Mac! What are you doing here?"

242

"Trying to solve a problem," he answered, looking up with a whimsical expression of perplexity and amusement in his face which made Rose smile till his next words turned her sober in a twinkling: "I've eloped with a young lady, and don't know what to do with her. I took her home, of course, but mother turned her out of the house, and I'm in a quandary."

"Is that her baggage?" asked Rose, pointing with her whip to the large bundle which he held while the wild idea flashed through her head that perhaps he really had done some rash deed of this sort.

"No, this is the young lady herself." And, opening a corner of the brown shawl, he displayed a child of three so pale, so thin and tiny that she looked like a small scared bird just fallen from the nest as she shrank away from the light with great frightened eyes and a hand like a little claw tightly clutched a button of Mac's coat.

"Poor baby! Where did it come from?" cried Rose, leaning down to look.

"I'll tell you the story, and then you shall advise me what to do. At our hospital we've had a poor woman who got hurt and died two days ago. I had nothing to do with her, only took her a bit of fruit once or twice, for she had big, wistful sort of eyes that haunted me. The day she died I stopped a minute, and the nurse said she'd been wanting to speak to me but didn't dare. So I asked if I could do anything for her and, though she could hardly breathe for pain being almost gone she implored me to take care of baby. I found out where the child was, and promised I'd see after her for the poor soul couldn't seem to die till I'd given her that comfort. I never can forget the look in her eyes as I held her hand and said, 'Baby shall be taken care of.' She tried to thank me, and died soon after quite peacefully. Well, I went today and hunted up the poor little wretch. Found her in a miserable place, left in the care of an old hag who had shut her up alone to keep her out of the way, and there this mite was, huddled in a corner, crying 'Marmar, marmar!' fit to touch a heart of stone. I blew up at the woman and took the baby straightaway, for she had been abused. It was high time. Look there, will you?"

Mac turned the little skinny arm and showed a blue mark which made Rose drop her reins and stretch out both hands, crying with a tender sort of indignation: "How dared they do it? Give her to me, poor little motherless thing!"

Mac laid the bundle in her arms, and Rose began to cuddle it in the fond, foolish way women have a most comfortable and effective way, nevertheless and baby evidently felt that things were changing for the better when warm lips touched her cheeks, a soft hand smoothed her tumbled hair, and a womanly face bent over her with the inarticulate cooings and purrings mothers make. The frightened eyes went up to this gentle countenance and rested there as if reassured; the little claw crept to the girl's neck, and poor baby nestled to her with a long sigh and a plaintive murmur of "Marmar, marmar" that certainly would have touched a stony heart.

"Now, go on. No, Rosa, not you," said the new nurse as the intelligent animal looked around to see if things were all right before she proceeded.

"I took the child home to mother, not knowing what else to do, but she wouldn't have it at any price, even for a night. She doesn't like children, you know, and Father has joked so much about 'the Pointers' that she is quite rampant at the mere idea of a child in the house. She told me to take it to the Rose Garden. I said it was running over now, and no room even for a mite like this. 'Go to the Hospital,' says she. 'Baby isn't ill, ma'am,' says I. 'Orphan Asylum,' says she. 'Not an orphan got a father who can't take care of her,' says I. 'Take her to the Foundling place, or Mrs. Gardener, or someone whose business it is. I will not have the creature here, sick and dirty and noisy. Carry it back, and ask Rose to tell you what to do with it.' So my cruel parent cast me forth but relented as I shouldered baby, gave me a shawl to put her in, a jumble to feed her with, and

243

money to pay her board in some good place. Mother's bark is always worse than her bite, you know."

"And you were trying to think of the 'good place' as you sat here?" asked Rose, looking down at him with great approval as he stood patting Rosa's glossy neck.

"Exactly. I didn't want to trouble you, for you have your house full already, and I really couldn't lay my hand on any good soul who would be bothered with this little forlornity. She has nothing to recommend her, you see not pretty; feeble; shy as a mouse; no end of care, I daresay yet she needs every bit she can get to keep soul and body together, if I'm any judge."

Rose opened her lips impulsively, but closed them without speaking and sat a minute looking straight between Rosa's ears, as if forcing herself to think twice before she spoke. Mac watched her out of the corner of his eyes as he said, in a musing tone, tucking the shawl around a pair of shabby little feet the while, "This seems to be one of the charities that no one wants to undertake, yet I can't help feeling that my promise to the mother binds me to something more than merely handing baby over to some busy matron or careless nurse in any of our overcrowded institutions. She is such a frail creature she won't trouble anyone long, perhaps, and I should like to give her just a taste of comfort, if not love, before she finds her 'Marmar' again."

"Lead Rosa I'm going to take this child home, and if Uncle is willing, I'll adopt her, and she shall be happy!" cried Rose, with the sudden glow of feeling that always made her lovely. And gathering poor baby close, she went on her way like a modern Britomart, ready to redress the wrongs of any who had need of her.

As he led the slowly stepping horse along the quiet road, Mac could not help thinking that they looked a little like the Flight into Egypt, but he did not say so, being a reverent youth only glanced back now and then at the figure above him, for Rose had taken off her hat to keep the light from baby's eyes and sat with the sunshine turning her uncovered hair to gold as she looked down at the little creature resting on the saddle before her with the sweet thoughtfulness one sees in some of Correggio's young Madonnas.

No one else saw the picture, but Mac long remembered it, and ever after there was a touch of reverence added to the warm affection he had always borne his cousin Rose.

"What is the child's name?" was the sudden question which disturbed a brief silence, broken only by the sound of pacing hoofs, the rustle of green boughs overhead, and the blithe caroling of birds.

"I'm sure I don't know," answered Mac, suddenly aware that he had fallen out of one quandary into another.

"Didn't you ask?"

"No, the mother called her 'Baby,' and the old woman, 'Brat.' And that is all I know of the first name the last is Kennedy. You may christen her what you like."

"Then I shall name her Dulcinea, as you are her knight, and call her Dulce for short. That is a sweet diminutive, I'm sure," laughed Rose, much amused at the idea.

Don Quixote looked pleased and vowed to defend his little lady stoutly, beginning his services on the spot by filling the small hands with buttercups, thereby winning for himself the first smile baby's face had known for weeks.

When they got home Aunt Plenty received her new guest with her accustomed hospitality and, on learning the story, was as warmly interested as even enthusiastic Rose could desire, bustling about to make the child comfortable with an energy pleasant to see, for the grandmotherly instincts were strong in the old lady and of late had been beautifully developed.

In less than half an hour from the time baby went upstairs, she came down again on Rose's arm, freshly washed and brushed, in a pink gown much too large and a white apron decidedly too small; an immaculate pair of socks, but no shoes; a neat bandage on the bruised arm, and a string of spools for a plaything hanging on the other. A resigned expression sat upon her little face, but the frightened eyes were only shy now, and the forlorn heart evidently much comforted.

"There! How do you like your Dulce now?" said Rose, proudly displaying the work of her hands as she came in with her habit pinned up and carrying a silver porringer of bread and milk.

Mac knelt down, took the small, reluctant hand, and kissed it as devoutly as ever good Alonzo Quixada did that of the Duchess while he said, merrily quoting from the immortal story: "'High and Sovereign Lady, thine till death, the Knight of the Rueful Countenance.'"

But baby had no heart for play and, withdrawing her hand, pointed to the porringer with the suggestive remark: "Din-din, now."

So Rose sat down and fed the Duchess while the Don stood by and watched the feast with much satisfaction.

"How nice she looks! Do you consider shoes unhealthy?" he asked, surveying the socks with respectful interest.

"No, her shoes are drying. You must have let her go in the mud."

"I only put her down for a minute when she howled, and she made for a puddle, like a duck. I'll buy her some new ones clothes too. Where do I go, what do I ask for, and how much do I get?" he said, diving for his pocketbook, amiably anxious but pitiably ignorant.

"I'll see to that. We always have things on hand for the Pointers as they come along and can soon fit Dulce out. You may make some inquiries about the father if you will, for I don't want to have her taken away just as I get fond of her. Do you know anything about him?"

"Only that he is in State Prison for twenty-one years, and not likely to trouble you."

"How dreadful! I really think Phebe was better off to have none at all. I'll go to work at once, then, and try to bring up the convict's little daughter to be a good woman so that she will have an honest name of her own, since he has nothing but disgrace to give her."

"Uncle can show you how to do that if you need any help. He has been so successful in his first attempt, I fancy you won't require much," said Mac, picking up the spools for the sixth time.

"Yes, I shall, for it is a great responsibility, and I do not undertake it lightly," answered Rose soberly, though the double-barreled compliment pleased her very much.

"I'm sure Phebe has turned out splendidly, and you began very early with her."

"So I did! That's encouraging. Dear thing, how bewildered she looked when I proposed adopting her. I remember all about it, for Uncle had just come and I was quite crazy over a box of presents and rushed at Phebe as she was cleaning brasses. How little I thought my childish offer would end so well!" And Rose fell a-musing with a happy smile on her face while baby picked the last morsels out of the porringer with her own busy fingers.

It certainly had ended well, for Phebe at the end of six months not only had a good place as choir singer but several young pupils and excellent prospects for the next winter.

"Accept the blessing of a poor young man, Whose lucky steps have led him to your door, and let me help as much as I can. Good-bye, my Dulcinea."

And, with a farewell stroke of the smooth head, Mac went away to report his success to his mother, who, in spite of her seeming harshness, was already planning how she could best befriend this inconvenient baby.


Chapter 17 AMONG THE HAYCOCKS
Uncle Alec did not object and, finding that no one had any claim upon the child, permitted Rose to keep it for a time at least. So little Dulce, newly equipped even to a name, took her place among them and slowly began to thrive. But she did not grow pretty and never was a gay, attractive child, for she seemed to have been born in sorrow and brought up in misery. A pale, pensive little creature, always creeping into corners and looking timidly out, as if asking leave to live, and, when offered playthings, taking them with a meek surprise that was very touching.

Rose soon won her heart, and then almost wished she had not, for baby clung to her with inconvenient fondness, changing her former wail of "Marmar" into a lament for "Aunty Wose" if separated long. Nevertheless, there was great satisfaction in cherishing the little waif, for she learned more than she could teach and felt a sense of responsibility which was excellent ballast for her enthusiastic nature.

Kitty Van, who made Rose her model in all things, was immediately inspired to go and do likewise, to the great amusement as well as annoyance of her family. Selecting the prettiest, liveliest child in the Asylum, she took it home on trial for a week. "A perfect cherub" she pronounced it the first day, but an "enfant terrible" before the week was over, for the young hero rioted by day, howled by night, ravaged the house from top to bottom, and kept his guardians in a series of panics by his hairbreadth escapes. So early on Saturday, poor exhausted Kitty restored the "cherub" with many thanks, and decided to wait until her views of education were rather more advanced.

As the warm weather came on, Rose announced that Dulce needed mountain air, for she dutifully repeated as many of Dr. Alec's prescriptions as possible and, remembering how much good Cozy Corner did her long ago, resolved to try it on her baby. Aunt Jessie and Jamie went with her, and Mother Atkinson received them as cordially as ever. The pretty daughters were all married and gone, but a stout damsel took their place, and nothing seemed changed except that the old heads were grayer and the young ones a good deal taller than six years ago.

Jamie immediately fraternized with neighboring boys and devoted himself to fishing with an ardor which deserved greater success. Aunt Jessie reveled in reading, for which she had no time at home, and lay in her hammock a happy woman, with no socks to darn, buttons to sew, or housekeeping cares to vex her soul. Rose went about with Dulce like a very devoted hen with one rather feeble chicken, for she was anxious to have this treatment work well and tended her little patient with daily increasing satisfaction. Dr. Alec came up to pass a few days and pronounced the child in a most promising condition. But the grand event of the season was the unexpected arrival of Phebe.

Two of her pupils had invited her to join them in a trip to the mountains, and she ran away from the great hotel to surprise her little mistress with a sight of her, so well and happy that Rose had no anxiety left on her account.

Three delightful days they spent, roaming about together, talking as only girls can talk after a long separation, and enjoying one another like a pair of lovers. As if to make it quite perfect, by one of those remarkable coincidences which sometimes occur, Archie happened to run up for the Sunday, so Phebe had her surprise, and Aunt Jessie and the telegraph kept their secret so well, no one ever knew what maternal machinations brought the happy accident to pass.

Then Rose saw a very pretty, pastoral bit of lovemaking, and long after it was over, and Phebe gone one way, Archie another, the echo of sweet words seemed to linger in the air, tender ghosts to haunt the pine grove, and even the big coffeepot had a halo of romance about it, for its burnished sides reflected the soft glances the lovers interchanged as one filled the other's cup at that last breakfast.

Rose found these reminiscences more interesting than any novel she had read, and often beguiled her long leisure by planning a splendid future for her Phebe as she trotted about after her baby in the lovely July weather.

On one of the most perfect days she sat under an old apple tree on the slope behind the house where they used to play. Before her opened the wide intervale, dotted with haymakers at their picturesque work. On the left flowed the swift river fringed with graceful elms in their bravest greenery; on the right rose the purple hills serene and grand; and overhead glowed the midsummer sky, which glorified it all.

Little Dulce, tired of play, lay fast asleep in the nest she had made in one of the haycocks close by, and Rose leaned against the gnarled old tree, dreaming daydreams with her work at her feet. Happy and absorbing fancies they seemed to be, for her face was beautifully tranquil, and she took no heed of the train which suddenly went speeding down the valley, leaving a white cloud behind. Its rumble concealed the sound of approaching steps, and her eyes never turned from the distant hills till the abrupt appearance of a very sunburned but smiling young man made her jump up, exclaiming joyfully: "Why, Mac! Where did you drop from?"

"The top of Mount Washington. How do you do?"

"Never better. Won't you go in? You must be tired after such a fall."

"No, thank you. I've seen the old lady. She told me Aunt Jessie and the boy had gone to town and that you were 'settin' round' in the old place. I came on at once and will take a lounge here if you don't mind," answered Mac, unstrapping his knapsack and taking a haycock as if it were a chair.

Rose subsided into her former seat, surveying her cousin with much satisfaction as she said: "This is the third surprise I've had since I came. Uncle popped in upon us first, then Phebe, and now you. Have you had a pleasant tramp? Uncle said you were off."

"Delightful! I feel as if I'd been in heaven, or near it, for about three weeks, and thought I'd break the shock of coming down to the earth by calling here on my way home."

"You look as if heaven suited you. Brown as a berry, but so fresh and happy I should never guess you had been scrambling down a mountain," said Rose, trying to discover why he looked so well in spite of the blue flannel suit and dusty shoes, for there was a certain sylvan freshness about him as he sat there full of reposeful strength the hills seemed to have given, the wholesome cheerful days of air and sunshine put into a man, and the clear, bright look of one who had caught glimpses of a new world from the mountaintop.

"Tramping agrees with me. I took a dip in the river as I came along and made my toilet in a place where Milton's Sabrina might have lived," he said, shaking back his damp hair and settling the knot of scarlet bunchberries stuck in his buttonhole.

"You look as if you found the nymph at home," said Rose, knowing how much he liked the "Comus."

"I found her here," and he made a little bow.

"That's very pretty, and I'll give you one in return. You grow more like Uncle Alec every day, and I think I'll call you Alec, Jr."

"Alexander the Great wouldn't thank you for that," and Mac did not look as grateful as she had expected.

"Very like, indeed, except the forehead. His is broad and benevolent, yours high and arched. Do you know if you had no beard, and wore your hair long, I really think you'd look like Milton," added Rose, sure that would please him.

It certainly did amuse him, for he lay back on the hay and laughed so heartily that his merriment scared the squirrel on the wall and woke Dulce.

"You ungrateful boy! Will nothing suit you? When I say you look like the best man I know, you gave a shrug, and when I liken you to a great poet, you shout. I'm afraid you are very conceited, Mac." And Rose laughed, too, glad to see him so gay.

"If I am, it is your fault. Nothing I can do will ever make a Milton of me, unless I go blind someday," he said, sobering at the thought.

"You once said a man could be what he liked if he tried hard enough, so why shouldn't you be a poet?" asked Rose, liking to trip him up with his own words, as he often did her.

"I thought I was to be an M.D."

"You might be both. There have been poetical doctors, you know."

"Would you like me to be such a one?" asked Mac, looking at her as seriously as if he really thought of trying it.

"No. I'd rather have you one or the other. I don't care which, only you must be famous in either you choose. I'm very ambitious for you, because, I insist upon it, you are a genius of some sort. I think it is beginning to simmer already, and I've got a great curiosity to know what it will turn out to be."

Mac's eyes shone as she said that, but before he could speak a little voice said, "Aunty Wose!" and he turned to find Dulce sitting up in her nest staring at the broad blue back before her with round eyes.

"Do you know your Don?" he asked, offering his hand with respectful gentleness, for she seemed a little doubtful whether he was a friend or stranger.

"It is 'Mat,'" said Rose, and that familiar word seemed to reassure the child at once, for, leaning forward, she kissed him as if quite used to doing it.

"I picked up some toys for her, by the way, and she shall have them at once to pay for that. I didn't expect to be so graciously received by this shy mouse," said Mac, much gratified, for Dulce was very chary of her favors.

"She knew you, for I always carry my home album with me, and when she comes to your picture she always kisses it, because I never want her to forget her first friend," explained Rose, pleased with her pupil.

"First, but not best," answered Mac, rummaging in his knapsack for the promised toys, which he set forth upon the hay before delighted Dulce.

Neither picture books nor sweeties, but berries strung on long stems of grass, acorns, and pretty cones, bits of rock shining with mica, several bluebirds' feathers, and a nest of moss with white pebbles for eggs.

"Dearest Nature, strong and kind" knows what children love, and has plenty of such playthings ready for them all, if one only knows how to find them. These were received with rapture. And leaving the little creature to enjoy them in her own quiet way, Mac began to tumble the things back into his knapsack again. Two or three books lay near Rose, and she took up one which opened at a place marked by a scribbled paper.

"Keats? I didn't know you condescended to read anything so modern," she said, moving the paper to see the page beneath.

Mac looked up, snatched the book out of her hand, and shook down several more scraps, then returned it with a curiously shamefaced expression, saying, as he crammed the papers into his pocket, "I beg pardon, but it was full of rubbish. Oh, yes! I'm fond of Keats. Don't you know him?"

"I used to read him a good deal, but Uncle found me crying over the 'Pot of Basil' and advised me to read less poetry for a while or I should get too sentimental," answered Rose, turning the pages without seeing them, for a new idea had just popped into her head.

"'The Eve of St. Agnes' is the most perfect love story in the world, I think," said Mac, enthusiastically.

"Read it to me. I feel just like hearing poetry, and you will do it justice if you are fond of it," said Rose, handing him the book with an innocent air.

"Nothing I'd like better, but it is rather long."

"I'll tell you to stop if I get tired. Baby won't interrupt; she will be contented for an hour with those pretty things."

As if well pleased with his task, Mac laid himself comfortably on the grass and, leaning his head on his hand, read the lovely story as only one could who entered fully into the spirit of it. Rose watched him closely and saw how his face brightened over some quaint fancy, delicate description, or delicious word; heard how smoothly the melodious measures fell from his lips, and read something more than admiration in his eyes as he looked up now and then to mark if she enjoyed it as much as he.

She could not help enjoying it, for the poet's pen painted as well as wrote, and the little romance lived before her, but she was not thinking of John Keats as she listened; she was wondering if this cousin was a kindred spirit, born to make such music and leave as sweet an echo behind him. It seemed as if it might be; and, after going through the rough caterpillar and the pent-up chrysalis changes, the beautiful butterfly would appear to astonish and delight them all. So full of this fancy was she that she never thanked him when the story ended but, leaning forward, asked in a tone that made him start and look as if he had fallen from the clouds: "Mac, do you ever write poetry?"

"Never."

"What do you call the song Phebe sang with her bird chorus?"

"That was nothing till she put the music to it. But she promised not to tell."

"She didn't. I suspected, and now I know," laughed Rose, delighted to have caught him.

Much discomfited, Mac gave poor Keats a fling and, leaning on both elbows, tried to hide his face for it had reddened like that of a modest girl when teased about her lover.

"You needn't look so guilty; it is no sin to write poetry," said Rose, amused at his confession.

"It's a sin to call that rubbish poetry," muttered Mac with great scorn.

"It is a greater sin to tell a fib and say you never write it."

"Reading so much sets one thinking about such things, and every fellow scribbles a little jingle when he is lazy or in love, you know," explained Mac, looking very guilty.

Rose could not quite understand the change she saw in him till his last words suggested a cause which she knew by experience was apt to inspire young men. Leaning forward again, she asked solemnly, though her eyes danced with fun, "Mac, are you in love?"

"Do I look like it?" And he sat up with such an injured and indignant face that she apologized at once, for he certainly did not look loverlike with hayseed in his hair, several lively crickets playing leapfrog over his back, and a pair of long legs stretching from tree to haycock.

"No, you don't, and I humbly beg your pardon for making such an unwarrantable insinuation. It merely occurred to me that the general upliftedness I observe in you might be owing to that, since it wasn't poetry."

"It is the good company I've been keeping, if anything. A fellow can't spend 'A Week' with Thoreau and not be the better for it. I'm glad I show it, because in the scramble life is to most of us, even an hour with such a sane, simple, and sagacious soul as his must help one," said Mac, taking a much worn book out of his pocket with the air of introducing a dear and honored friend.

"I've read bits, and like them they are so original and fresh and sometimes droll," said Rose, smiling to see what natural and appropriate marks of approbation the elements seemed to set upon the pages Mac was turning eagerly, for one had evidently been rained on, a crushed berry stained another, some appreciative field-mouse or squirrel had nibbled one corner, and the cover was faded with the sunshine, which seemed to have filtered through to the thoughts within.

"Here's a characteristic bit for you: 'I would rather sit on a pumpkin, and have it all to myself, than be crowded on a velvet cushion. I would rather ride on earth in an oxcart, with free circulation, than go to heaven in the fancy car of an excursion train, and breathe malaria all the way.'

250

"I've tried both and quite agree with him," laughed Mac, and skimming down another page, gave her a paragraph here and there.

"'Read the best books first, or you may not have a chance to read them at all.'

"'We do not learn much from learned books, but from sincere human books: frank, honest biographies.'

"'At least let us have healthy books. Let the poet be as vigorous as the sugar maple, with sap enough to maintain his own verdure, besides what runs into the trough; and not like a vine which, being cut in the spring, bears no fruit, but bleeds to death in the endeavor to heal its wounds.'"

"That will do for you," said Rose, still thinking of the new suspicion which pleased her by its very improbability.

Mac flashed a quick look at her and shut the book, saying quietly, although his eyes shone, and a conscious smile lurked about his mouth: "We shall see, and no one need meddle, for, as my Thoreau says,

"Whate'er we leave to God, God does
And blesses us: The work we choose should be our own
God lets alone."

Rose sat silent, as if conscious that she deserved his poetical reproof.

"Come, you have catechized me pretty well; now I'll take my turn and ask you why you look 'uplifted,' as you call it. What have you been doing to make yourself more like your namesake than ever?" asked Mac, carrying war into the enemy's camp with the sudden question.

"Nothing but live, and enjoy doing it. I actually sit here, day after day, as happy and contented with little things as Dulce is and feel as if I wasn't much older than she," answered the girl, feeling as if some change was going on in that pleasant sort of pause but unable to describe it.

"As if a rose should shut and be a bud again," murmured Mac, borrowing from his beloved Keats.

"Ah, but I can't do that! I must go on blooming whether I like it or not, and the only trouble I have is to know what leaf I ought to unfold next," said Rose, playfully smoothing out the white gown, in which she looked very like a daisy among the green.

"How far have you got?" asked Mac, continuing his catechism as if the fancy suited him.

"Let me see. Since I came home last year, I've been gay, then sad, then busy, and now I am simply happy. I don't know why, but seem to be waiting for what is to come next and getting ready for it, perhaps unconsciously," she said, looking dreamily away to the hills again, is if the new experience was coming to her from afar.

Mac watched her thoughtfully for a minute, wondering how many more leaves must unfold before the golden heart of this human flower would lie open to the sun. He felt a curious desire to help in some way, and could think of none better than to offer her what he had found most helpful to himself. Picking up another book, he opened it at a place where an oak leaf lay and, handing it to her, said, as if presenting something very excellent and precious: "If you want to be ready to take whatever comes in a brave and noble way, read that, and the one where the page is turned down."

Rose took it, saw the words "Self-Reliance," and turning the leaves, read here and there a passage which was marked: "'My life is for itself, and not for a spectacle.'

"'Insist on yourself: never imitate. That which each can do best, none but his Maker can teach him.'

"'Do that which is assigned to you, and you cannot hope or dare too much.'"

Then, coming to the folded page, whose title was "Heroism," she read, and brightened as she read:

"'Let the maiden, with erect soul, walk serenely on her way; accept the hint of each new experience; search in turn all the objects that solicit her eye, that she may learn the power and the charm of her newborn being.'

"'The fair girl who repels interference by a decided and proud choice of influences inspires every beholder with something of her own nobleness; and the silent heart encourages her. O friend, never strike sail to a fear! Come into port greatly, or sail with God the seas.'"

"You understand that, don't you?" asked Mac as she glanced up with the look of one who had found something suited to her taste and need.

"Yes, but I never dared to read these Essays, because I thought they were too wise for me."

"The wisest things are sometimes the simplest, I think. Everyone welcomes light and air, and cannot do without them, yet very few could explain them truly. I don't ask you to read or understand all of that don't myself but I do recommend the two essays I've marked, as well as 'Love' and 'Friendship.' Try them, and let me know how they suit. I'll leave you the book."

"Thanks. I wanted something fine to read up here and, judging by what I see, I fancy this will suit. Only Aunt Jessie may think I'm putting on airs if I try Emerson."

"Why should she? He has done more to set young men and women thinking than any man in this century at least. Don't you be afraid if it is what you want, take it, and go ahead as he tells you

> "Without halting, without rest,
> Lifting Better up to Best."

"I'll try," said Rose meekly, feeling that Mac had been going ahead himself much faster than she had any suspicion.

Here a voice exclaimed "Hallo!" and, looking around, Jamie was discovered surveying them critically as he stood in an independent attitude, like a small Colossus of Rhodes in brown linen, with a bundle of molasses candy in one hand, several new fishhooks cherished carefully in the other, and his hat well on the back of his head, displaying as many freckles as one somewhat limited nose could reasonably accommodate.

"How are you, young one?" said Mac, nodding.

"Tip-top. Glad it's you. Thought Archie might have turned up again, and he's no fun. Where did you come from? What did you come for? How long are you going to stay? Want a bit? It's jolly good."

With which varied remarks Jamie approached, shook hands in a manly way, and, sitting down beside his long cousin, hospitably offered sticks of candy all around.

"Did you get any letters?" asked Rose, declining the sticky treat.

"Lots, but Mama forgot to give 'em to me, and I was rather in a hurry, for Mrs. Atkinson said somebody had come and I couldn't wait," explained Jamie, reposing luxuriously with his head on Mac's legs and his mouth full.

"I'll step and get them. Aunty must be tired, and we should enjoy reading the news together."

"She is the most convenient girl that ever was," observed Jamie as Rose departed, thinking Mac might like some more substantial refreshment than sweetmeats.

"I should think so, if you let her run your errands, you lazy little scamp," answered Mac, looking after her as she went up the green slope, for there was something very attractive to him about the slender figure in a plain white gown with a black sash about the waist and all the wavy hair gathered to the top of the head with a little black bow.

"Sort of pre-Raphaelite, and quite refreshing after the furbelowed creatures at the hotels," he said to himself as she vanished under the arch of scarlet runners over the garden gate.

"Oh, well! She likes it. Rose is fond of me, and I'm very good to her when I have time," continued Jamie, calmly explaining. "I let her cut out a fishhook, when it caught in my leg, with a sharp penknife, and you'd better believe it hurt, but I never squirmed a bit, and she said I was a brave boy. And then, one day I got left on my desert island out in the pond, you know the boat floated off, and there I was for as much as an hour before I could make anyone hear. But Rose thought I might be there, and down she came, and told me to swim ashore. It wasn't far, but the water was horrid cold, and I didn't like it. I started though, just as she said, and got on all right, till about halfway, then cramp or something made me shut up and howl, and she came after me slapdash, and pulled me ashore. Yes, sir, as wet as a turtle, and looked so funny, I laughed, and that cured the cramp. Wasn't I good to mind when she said, 'Come on'?"

"She was, to dive after such a scapegrace. I guess you lead her a life of it, and I'd better take you home with me in the morning," suggested Mac, rolling the boy over and giving him a good-natured pummeling on the haycock while Dulce applauded from her nest.

When Rose returned with ice-cold milk, gingerbread, and letters, she found the reader of Emerson up in the tree, pelting and being pelted with green apples as Jamie vainly endeavored to get at him. The siege ended when Aunt Jessie appeared, and the rest of the afternoon was spent in chat about home affairs.

Early the next morning Mac was off, and Rose went as far as the old church with him.

"Shall you walk all the way?" she asked as he strode along beside her in the dewy freshness of the young day.

"Only about twenty miles, then take car and whisk back to my work," he answered, breaking a delicate fern for her.

"Are you never lonely?"

"Never. I take my best friends along, you know," and he gave a slap to the pocket from which peeped the volume of Thoreau.

"I'm afraid you leave your very best behind you," said Rose, alluding to the book he had lent her yesterday.

"I'm glad to share it with you. I have much of it here, and a little goes a great way, as you will soon discover," he answered, tapping his head.

"I hope the reading will do as much for me as it seems to have done for you. I'm happy, but you are wise and good I want to be also."

"Read away, and digest it well, then write and tell me what you think of it. Will you?" he asked as they paused where the four roads met.

"If you will answer. Shall you have time with all your other work? Poetry I beg pardon medicine is very absorbing, you know," answered Rose mischievously, for just then, as he stood bareheaded in the shadows of the leaves playing over his fine forehead, she remembered the chat among the haycocks, and he did not look at all like an M.D.

"I'll make time."

"Good-bye, Milton."

"Good-bye, Sabrina."

Chapter 18 WHICH WAS IT?

Rose did read and digest, and found her days much richer for the good company she kept, for an introduction to so much that was wise, beautiful, and true could not but make that month a memorable one. It is not strange that while the young man most admired "Heroism" and "Self-Reliance," the girl preferred "Love" and "Friendship," reading them over and over like prose poems, as they are, to the fitting accompaniment of sunshine, solitude, and sympathy, for letters went to and fro with praiseworthy regularity.

Rose much enjoyed this correspondence, and found herself regretting that it was at an end when she went home in September, for Mac wrote better than he talked, though he could do that remarkably well when he chose. But she had no chance to express either pleasure or regret, for the first time she saw him after her return the great change in his appearance made her forget everything else. Some whim had seized him to be shaven and shorn, and when he presented himself to welcome Rose, she hardly knew him. The shaggy hair was nicely trimmed and brushed, the cherished brown beard entirely gone, showing a well-cut mouth and handsome chin and giving a new expression to the whole face.

"Are you trying to look like Keats?" she asked, after a critical glance, which left her undecided whether the change was an improvement or not.

"I am trying not to look like Uncle," answered Mac coolly.

"And why, if you please?" demanded Rose in great surprise.

"Because I prefer to look like myself, and not resemble any other man, no matter how good or great he may be."

"You haven't succeeded then, for you look now very much like the young Augustus," returned Rose, rather pleased on the whole to see what a finely shaped head appeared after the rough thatch was off.

"Trust a woman to find a comparison for everything under the sun!" laughed Mac, not at all flattered by the one just made. "What do you think of me, on the whole?" he asked a minute later, as he found Rose still scrutinizing him with a meditative air.

"Haven't made up my mind. It is such an entire change, I don't know you, and feel as if I ought to be introduced. You certainly look much more tidy, and I fancy I shall like it when I'm used to seeing a somewhat distinguished-looking man about the house instead of my old friend Orson," answered Rose, with her head on one side to get a profile view.

"Don't tell Uncle why I did it, please he thinks it was for the sake of coolness and likes it, so take no notice. They are all used to me now, and don't mind," said Mac, roving about the room as if rather ashamed of his whim after all.

"No, I won't, but you mustn't mind if I'm not as sociable as usual for a while. I never can be with strangers, and you really do seem like one. That will be a punishment for your want of taste and love of originality," returned Rose, resolved to punish him for the slight put upon her beloved uncle.

"As you like. I won't trouble you much anyway, for I'm going to be very busy. May go to L this winter, if Uncle thinks best, and then my 'originality' can't annoy you."

"I hope you won't go. Why, Mac, I'm just getting to know and enjoy you, and thought we'd have a nice time this winter reading something together. Must you go?" And Rose seemed to forget his strangeness, as she held him still by one button while she talked.

"That would be nice. But I feel as if I must go my plans are all made, and I've set my heart on it," answered Mac, looking so eager that Rose released him, saying sadly: "I suppose it is natural for you all to get restless and push off, but it is hard for me to let you go one after the other and stay here alone. Charlie is gone, Archie and Steve are wrapped up in their sweethearts, the boys away, and only Jamie left to 'play with Rose.'?

"But I'll come back, and you'll be glad I went if I bring you my—" began Mac with sudden animation, then stopped abruptly to bite his lips, as if he had nearly said too much.

"Your what?" asked Rose curiously, for he neither looked nor acted like himself.

"I forgot how long it takes to get a diploma," he said, walking away again.

"There will be one comfort if you go you'll see Phebe and can tell me all about her, for she is so modest, she doesn't half do it. I shall want to know how she gets on, if she is engaged to sing ballads in the concerts they talk of for next winter. You will write, won't you?"

"Oh, yes! No doubt of that," and Mac laughed low to himself as he stooped to look at the little Psyche on the mantelpiece. "What a pretty thing it is!" he added soberly as he took it up.

"Be careful. Uncle gave it to me last New Year, and I'm very fond of it. She is just lifting her lamp to see what Cupid is like, for she hasn't seen him yet," said Rose, busy putting her worktable in order.

"You ought to have a Cupid for her to look at. She has been waiting patiently a whole year, with nothing but a bronze lizard in sight," said Mac with the half-shy, half-daring look which was so new and puzzling.

"Cupid fled away as soon as she woke him, you know, and she had a bad time of it. She must wait longer till she can find and keep him."

"Do you know she looks like you? Hair tied up in a knot, and a spiritual sort of face. Don't you see it?" asked Mac, turning the graceful little figure toward her.

"Not a bit of it. I wonder whom I shall resemble next! I've been compared to a Fra Angelico angel, Saint Agnes, and now 'Syke,' as Annabel once called her."

"You'd see what I mean, if you'd ever watched your own face when you were listening to music, talking earnestly, or much moved, then your soul gets into your eyes and you are like Psyche."

"Tell me the next time you see me in a 'soulful' state, and I'll look in the glass, for I'd like to see if it is becoming," said Rose merrily as she sorted her gay worsteds.

"Your feet in the full-grown grasses,
Moved soft as a soft wind blows;
You passed me as April passes,
With a face made out of a rose,"

murmured Mac under his breath, thinking of the white figure going up a green slope one summer day; then, as if chiding himself for sentimentality, he set Psyche down with great care and began to talk about a course of solid reading for the winter.

After that, Rose saw very little of him for several weeks, as he seemed to be making up for lost time and was more odd and absent than ever when he did appear.

As she became accustomed to the change in his external appearance, she discovered that he was altering fast in other ways and watched the "distinguished-looking gentleman" with much interest, saying to herself, when she saw a new sort of dignity about him alternating with an unusual restlessness of manner, and now and then a touch of sentiment, "Genius is simmering, just as I predicted."

As the family were in mourning, there were no festivities on Rose's twenty-first birthday, though the boys had planned all sorts of rejoicings. Everyone felt particularly tender toward their girl on that day, remembering how "poor Charlie" had loved her, and they tried to show it in the gifts and good wishes they sent her. She found her sanctum all aglow with autumn leaves, and on her table so many rare and pretty things, she quite forgot she was an heiress and only felt how rich she was in loving friends.

One gift greatly pleased her, though she could not help smiling at the source from whence it came, for Mac sent her a Cupid not the chubby child with a face of naughty merriment, but a slender, winged youth leaning on his unstrung bow, with a broken arrow at his feet. A poem, "To Psyche," came with it, and Rose was much surprised at the beauty of the lines, for, instead of being witty, complimentary, or gay, there was something nobler than mere sentiment in them, and the sweet old fable lived again in language which fitly painted the maiden Soul looking for a Love worthy to possess it.

Rose read them over and over as she sat among the gold and scarlet leaves which glorified her little room, and each time found new depth and beauty in them, looking from the words that made music in her ear to the lovely shapes that spoke with their mute grace to her eye. The whole thing suited her exactly, it was so delicate and perfect in its way, for she was tired of costly gifts and valued very much this proof of her cousin's taste and talent, seeing nothing in it but an affectionate desire to please her.

All the rest dropped in at intervals through the day to say a loving word, and last of all came Mac. Rose happened to be alone with Dulce, enjoying a splendid sunset from her western window, for October gave her child a beautiful good night.

Rose turned around as he entered and, putting down the little girl, went to him with the evening red shining on her happy face as she said gratefully: "Dear Mac, it was so lovely! I don't know how to thank you for it in any way but this." And, drawing down his tall head, she gave him the birthday kiss she had given all the others.

But this time it produced a singular effect, for Mac turned scarlet, then grew pale, and when Rose added playfully, thinking to relieve the shyness of so young a poet, "Never again say you don't write poetry, or call your verses rubbish I knew you were a genius, and now I'm sure of it," he broke out, as if against his will: "No. It isn't genius, it is love!" Then, as she shrank a little, startled at his energy, he added, with an effort at self-control which made his voice sound strange: "I didn't mean to speak, but I can't suffer you to deceive yourself so. I must tell the truth, and not let you kiss me like a cousin when I love you with all my heart and soul!"

"Oh, Mac, don't joke!" cried Rose, bewildered by this sudden glimpse into a heart she thought she knew so well.

"I'm in solemn earnest," he answered steadily, in such a quiet tone that, but for the pale excitement of his face, she might have doubted his words. "Be angry, if you will. I expect it, for I know it is too soon to speak. I ought to wait for years, perhaps, but you seemed so happy I dared to hope you had forgotten."

"Forgotten what?" asked Rose sharply.

"Charlie."

"Ah! You all will insist on believing that I loved him better than I did!" she cried, with both pain and impatience in her voice, for the family delusion tried her very much at times.

"How could we help it, when he was everything women most admire?" said Mac, not bitterly, but as if he sometimes wondered at their want of insight.

"I do not admire weakness of any sort I could never love without either confidence or respect. Do me the justice to believe that, for I'm tired of being pitied."

She spoke almost passionately, being more excited by Mac's repressed emotion than she had ever been by Charlie's most touching demonstration, though she did not know why.

"But he loved you so!" began Mac, feeling as if a barrier had suddenly gone down but not daring to venture in as yet.

"That was the hard part of it! That was why I tried to love him, why I hoped he would stand fast for my sake, if not for his own, and why I found it so sad sometimes not to be able to help despising him for his want of courage. I don't know how others feel, but, to me, love isn't all. I must look up, not down, trust and honor with my whole heart, and find strength and integrity to lean on. I have had it so far, and I know I could not live without it."

"Your ideal is a high one. Do you hope to find it, Rose?" Mac asked, feeling, with the humility of a genuine love, that he could not give her all she desired.

"Yes," she answered, with a face full of the beautiful confidence in virtue, the instinctive desire for the best which so many of us lose too soon, to find again after life's great lessons are well learned. "I do hope to find it, because I try not to be unreasonable and expect perfection. Smile if you will, but I won't give up my hero yet," and she tried to speak lightly, hoping to lead him away from a more dangerous topic.

"You'll have to look a long while, I'm afraid," and all the glow was gone out of Mac's face, for he understood her wish and knew his answer had been given.

"I have Uncle to help me, and I think my ideal grew out of my knowledge of him. How can I fail to believe in goodness, when he shows me what it can be and do?"

"It's no use for me to say any more, for I have very little to offer. I did not mean to say a word till I earned a right to hope for something in return. I cannot take it back, but I can wish you success, and I do, because you deserve the very best." And Mac moved as if he was going away without more words, accepting the inevitable as manfully as he could.

"Thank you that makes me feel very ungrateful and unkind. I wish I could answer you as you want me to for, indeed, dear Mac, I'm very fond of you in my own way," and Rose looked up with such tender pity and frank affection in her face, it was no wonder the poor fellow caught at a ray of hope and, brightening suddenly, said in his own odd way: "Couldn't you take me on trial while you are waiting for a true hero? It may be years before you find him; meantime, you could be practicing on me in ways that would be useful when you get him."

"Oh, Mac! What shall I do with you?" exclaimed Rose, so curiously affected by this very characteristic wooing that she did not know whether to laugh or cry, for he was looking at her with his heart in his eyes, though his proposition was the queerest ever made at such a time.

"Just go on being fond of me in your own way, and let me love you as much as I like in mine. I'll try to be satisfied with that." And he took both her hands so beseechingly that she felt more ungrateful than ever.

"No, it would not be fair, for you would love the most and, if the hero did appear, what would become of you?"

"I should resemble Uncle Alec in one thing at least fidelity, for my first love would be my last."

That went straight to Rose's heart, and for a minute she stood silent, looking down at the two strong hands that held hers so firmly yet so gently, and the thought went through her mind, "Must he, too, be solitary all his life? I have no dear lover as my mother had, why cannot I make him happy and forget myself?"

It did not seem very hard, and she owned that, even while she told herself that compassion was no equivalent for love. She wanted to give all she could, and keep as much of Mac's affection as she honestly might, because it seemed to grow more sweet and precious when she thought of putting it away.

"You will be like Uncle in happier ways than that, I hope, for you, too, must have a high ideal and find her and be happy," she said, resolving to be true to the voice of conscience, not be swayed by the impulse of the moment.

"I have found her, but I don't see any prospect of happiness, do you?" he asked wistfully.

"Dear Mac, I cannot give you the love you want, but I do trust and respect you from the bottom of my heart, if that is any comfort," began Rose, looking up with eyes full of contrition for the pain her reply must give.

She got no further, however, for those last words wrought a marvelous change in Mac. Dropping her hands, he stood erect, as if inspired with sudden energy and hope, while over his face there came a brave, bright look, which for the moment made him a nobler and comelier man than ever handsome Prince had been. "It is a comfort!" he said, in a tone of gratitude that touched her very much. "You said your love must be founded on respect, and that you have given me why can I not earn the rest? I'm nothing now, but everything is possible when one loves with all his heart and soul and strength. Rose, I will be your hero if a mortal man can, even though I have to work and wait for years. I'll make you love me, and be glad to do it. Don't be frightened. I've not lost my wits I've just found them. I don't ask anything I'll never speak of my hope, but it is no use to stop me. I must try it, and I will succeed!"

With the last words, uttered in a ringing voice while his face glowed, his eyes shone, and he looked as if carried out of himself by the passion that possessed him, Mac abruptly left the room, like one eager to change words to deeds and begin his task at once.

Rose was so amazed by all this that she sat down trembling a little, not with fear or anger, but a feeling half pleasure, half pain, and a sense of some new power subtle, strong, and sweet that had come into her life. It seemed as if another Mac had taken the place of the one she had known so long an ardent, ambitious man, ready for any work now that the magical moment had come when everything seems possible to love. If hope could work such a marvelous change for a moment, could not happiness do it for a lifetime? It would be an exciting experiment to try, she thought, remembering the sudden illumination which made that familiar face both beautiful and strange.

She could not help wondering how long this unsuspected sentiment had been growing in his heart and felt perplexed by its peculiar demonstration, for she had never had a lover like this before. It touched and flattered her, nevertheless and she could not but feel honored by a love so genuine and generous, for it seemed to make a man of Mac all at once, and a manly man, too, who was not daunted by disappointment but could "hope against hope" and resolve to make her love him if it took years to do it.

There was the charm of novelty about this sort of wooing, and she tried to guess how he would set about it, felt curious to see how he would behave when next they met, and was half angry with herself for not being able to decide how she ought to act. The more she thought, the more bewildered she grew, for having made up her mind that Mac was a genius, it disturbed all her plans to find him a lover, and such an ardent one. As it was impossible to predict what would come next, she gave up trying to prepare for it and, tired with vain speculations, carried Dulce off to bed, wishing she could tuck away her love troubles as quietly and comfortably as she did her sleepy little charge.

Simple and sincere in all things, Mac gave Rose a new surprise by keeping his promise to the letter asked nothing of her, said nothing of his hope, and went on as if nothing had happened, quite in the old friendly way. No, not quite, for now and then, when she least expected it, she saw again the indescribable expression on his face, a look that seemed to shed a sudden sunshine over her, making her eyes fall involuntarily, her color rise, and her heart beat quicker for a moment. Not a word did he say, but she felt that a new atmosphere surrounded her when he was by, and although he used none of the little devices most lovers employ to keep the flame alight, it was impossible to forget that underneath his quietude there was a hidden world of fire and force ready to appear at a touch, a word from her.

This was rather dangerous knowledge for Rose, and she soon began to feel that there were more subtle temptations than she had expected, for it was impossible to be unconscious of her power, or always to resist the trials of it which daily came unsought. She had never felt this desire before, for Charlie was the only one who had touched her heart, and he was constantly asking as well as giving, and wearied her by demanding too much or oppressed her by offering more than she could accept.

Mac did neither; he only loved her, silently, patiently, hopefully, and this generous sort of fidelity was very eloquent to a nature like hers. She could not refuse or chide, since nothing was asked or urged; there was no need of coldness, for he never presumed; no call for pity, since he never complained. All that could be done was to try and be as just and true as he was, and to wait as trustfully for the end, whatever it was to be.

For a time she liked the new interest it put into her life, yet did nothing to encourage it and thought that if she gave this love no food it would soon starve to death. But it seemed to thrive on air, and presently she began to feel as if a very strong will was slowly but steadily influencing her in many ways. If Mac had never told her that he meant to "make her love him," she might have yielded unconsciously, but now she mistook the impulse to obey this undercurrent for compassion and resisted stoutly, not comprehending yet the reason for the unrest which took possession of her about this time.

She had as many moods as an April day, and would have much surprised Dr. Alec by her vagaries had he known them all. He saw enough, however, to guess what was the matter, but took no notice, for he knew this fever must run its course, and much medicine only does harm. The others were busy about their own affairs, and Aunt Plenty was too much absorbed in her rheumatism to think of love, for the cold weather set in early, and the poor lady kept her room for days at a time with Rose as nurse.

Mac had spoken of going away in November, and Rose began to hope he would, for she decided that this silent sort of adoration was bad for her, as it prevented her from steadily pursuing the employments she had marked out for that year. What was the use of trying to read useful books when her thoughts continually wandered to those charming essays on "Love" and "Friendship"? To copy antique casts, when all the masculine heads looked like Cupid and the feminine ones like the Psyche on her mantelpiece? To practice the best music if it ended in singing over and over the pretty spring song without Phebe's bird chorus? Dulce's company was pleasantest now, for Dulce seldom talked, so much meditation was possible. Even Aunt Plenty's red flannel, camphor, and Pond's Extract were preferable to general society, and long solitary rides on Rosa seemed the only thing to put her in tune after one of her attempts to find out what she ought to do or leave undone.

She made up her mind at last, and arming herself with an unmade pen, like Fanny Squeers, she boldly went into the study to confer with Dr. Alec at an hour when Mac was usually absent. "I want a pen for marking can you make me one, Uncle?" she asked, popping her head in to be sure he was alone.

"Yes, my dear," answered a voice so like the doctor's that she entered without delay.

But before she had taken three steps she stopped, looking rather annoyed, for the head that rose from behind the tall desk was not rough and gray, but brown and smooth, and Mac, not Uncle Alec, sat there writing. Late experience had taught her that she had nothing to fear from a tete-a-tete and, having with difficulty taken a resolution, she did not like to fail of carrying it out.

"Don't get up, I won't trouble you if you are busy, there is no hurry," she said, not quite sure whether it were wiser to stay or run away.

Mac settled the point by taking the pen out of her hand and beginning to cut it, as quietly as Nicholas did on that "thrilling" occasion. Perhaps he was thinking of that, for he smiled as he asked, "Hard or soft?"

Rose evidently had forgotten that the family of Squeers ever existed, for she answered: "Hard, please," in a voice to match. "I'm glad to see you doing that," she added, taking courage from his composure and going as straight to her point as could be expected of a woman.

"And I am very glad to do it."

"I don't mean making pens, but the romance I advised," and she touched the closely written page before him, looking as if she would like to read it.

"That is my abstract on a lecture on the circulation of the blood," he answered, kindly turning it so that she could see. "I don't write romances I'm living one," and he glanced up with the happy, hopeful expression which always made her feel as if he was heaping coals of fire on her head.

"I wish you wouldn't look at me in that way it fidgets me," she said a little petulantly, for she had been out riding, and knew that she did not present a "spiritual" appearance after the frosty air had reddened nose as well as cheeks.

"I'll try to remember. It does itself before I know it. Perhaps this may mend matters." And, taking out the blue glasses he sometimes wore in the wind, he gravely put them on.

Rose could not help laughing, but his obedience only aggravated her, for she knew he could observe her all the better behind his ugly screen.

"No, it won't they are not becoming, and I don't want to look blue when I do not feel so," she said, finding it impossible to guess what he would do next or to help enjoying his peculiarities.

"But you don't to me, for in spite of the goggles everything is rose-colored now." And he pocketed the glasses without a murmur at the charming inconsistency of his idol.

"Really, Mac, I'm tired of this nonsense, it worries me and wastes your time."

"Never worked harder. But does it really trouble you to know I love you?" he asked anxiously.

"Don't you see how cross it makes me?" And she walked away, feeling that things were not going as she intended to have them at all.

"I don't mind the thorns if I get the rose at last, and I still hope I may, some ten years hence," said this persistent suitor, quite undaunted by the prospect of a "long wait."

"I think it is rather hard to be loved whether I like it or not," objected Rose, at a loss how to make any headway against such indomitable hopefulness.

"But you can't help it, nor can I so I must go on doing it with all my heart till you marry, and then well, then I'm afraid I may hate somebody instead," and Mac spoilt the pen by an involuntary slash of his knife.

"Please don't, Mac!"

"Do which, love or hate?"

"Don't do either go and care for someone else; there are plenty of nice girls who will be glad to make you happy," said Rose, intent upon ending her disquiet in some way.

"That is too easy. I enjoy working for my blessings, and the harder I have to work, the more I value them when they come."

"Then if I suddenly grew very kind, would you stop caring about me?" asked Rose, wondering if that treatment would free her from a passion which both touched and tormented her.

"Try and see." But there was a traitorous glimmer in Mac's eyes which plainly showed what a failure it would be.

"No, I'll get something to do, so absorbing I shall forget all about you."

"Don't think about me if it troubles you," he said tenderly.

"I can't help it." Rose tried to catch back the words, but it was too late, and she added hastily, "That is, I cannot help wishing you would forget me. It is a great disappointment to find I was mistaken when I hoped such fine things of you."

"Yes, you were very sure that it was love when it was poetry, and now you want poetry when I've nothing on hand but love. Will both together please you?"

"Try and see."

"I'll do my best. Anything else?" he asked, forgetting the small task she had given him in his eagerness to attempt the greater.

"Tell me one thing. I've often wanted to know, and now you speak of it I'll venture to ask. Did you care about me when you read Keats to me last summer?"

"No."

"When did you begin?" asked Rose, smiling in spite of herself at his unflattering honesty.

"How can I tell? Perhaps it did begin up there, though, for that talk set us writing, and the letters showed me what a beautiful soul you had. I loved that first it was so quick to recognize good things, to use them when they came, and give them out again as unconsciously as a flower does its breath. I longed for you to come home, and wanted you to find me altered for the better in some way as I had found you. And when you came it was very easy to see why I needed you to love you entirely, and to tell you so. That's all, Rose."

A short story, but it was enough the voice that told it with such simple truth made the few words so eloquent, Rose felt strongly tempted to add the sequel Mac desired. But her eyes had fallen as he spoke, for she knew his were fixed upon her, dark and dilated, with the same repressed emotion that put such fervor into his quiet tones, and just as she was about to look up, they fell on a shabby little footstool. Trifles affect women curiously, and often most irresistibly when some agitation sways them. The sight of the old hassock vividly recalled Charlie, for he had kicked it on the night she never liked to remember. Like a spark it fired a long train of recollections, and the thought went through her mind: "I fancied I loved him, and let him see it, but I deceived myself, and he reproached me for a single look that said too much. This feeling is very different, but too new and

262

sudden to be trusted. I'll neither look nor speak till I am quite sure, for Mac's love is far deeper than poor Charlie's, and I must be very true."

Not in words did the resolve shape itself, but in a quick impulse, which she obeyed certain that it was right, since it was hard to yield to it. Only an instant's silence followed Mac's answer as she stood looking down with fingers intertwined and color varying in her cheeks. A foolish attitude, but Mac thought it a sweet picture of maiden hesitation and began to hope that a month's wooing was about to end in winning for a lifetime. He deceived himself, however, and cold water fell upon his flame, subduing but by no means quenching it, when Rose looked up with an air of determination which could not escape eyes that were growing wonderfully farsighted lately.

"I came in here to beg Uncle to advise you to go away soon. You are very patient and forbearing, and I feel it more than I can tell. But it is not good for you to depend on anyone so much for your happiness, I think, and I know it is bad for me to feel that I have so much power over a fellow creature. Go away, Mac, and see if this isn't all a mistake. Don't let a fancy for me change or delay your work, because it may end as suddenly as it began, and then we should both reproach ourselves and each other. Please do! I respect and care for you so much, I can't be happy to take all and give nothing. I try to, but I'm not sure I want to think it is too soon to know yet."

Rose began bravely, but ended in a fluttered sort of way as she moved toward the door, for Mac's face though it fell at first, brightened as she went on, and at the last word, uttered almost involuntarily, he actually laughed low to himself, as if this order into exile pleased him much.

"Don't say that you give nothing, when you've just shown me that I'm getting on. I'll go; I'll go at once, and see if absence won't help you 'to think, to know, and to be sure' as it did me. I wish I could do something more for you. As I can't, good-bye."

"Are you going now?" And Rose paused in her retreat to look back with a startled face as he offered her a badly made pen and opened the door for her just as Dr. Alec always did; for, in spite of himself, Mac did resemble the best of uncles.

"Not yet, but you seem to be."

Rose turned as red as a poppy, snatched the pen, and flew upstairs, to call herself hard names as she industriously spoiled all Aunt Plenty's new pocket handkerchiefs by marking them "A.M.C."

Three days later Mac said "good-bye" in earnest, and no one was surprised that he left somewhat abruptly, such being his way, and a course of lectures by a famous physician the ostensible reason for a trip to L——. Uncle Alec deserted most shamefully at the last moment by sending word that he would be at the station to see the traveler off, Aunt Plenty was still in her room, so when Mac came down from his farewell to her, Rose met him in the hall, as if anxious not to delay him. She was a little afraid of another tete-a-tete, as she fared so badly at the last, and had assumed a calm and cousinly air which she flattered herself would plainly show on what terms she wished to part.

Mac apparently understood, and not only took the hint, but surpassed her in cheerful composure, for, merely saying "Good-bye, Cousin; write when you feel like it," he shook hands and walked out of the house as tranquilly as if only a day instead of three months were to pass before they met again. Rose felt as if a sudden shower bath had chilled her and was about to retire, saying to herself with disdainful decision: "There's no love about it after all, only one of the eccentricities of genius," when a rush of cold air made her turn to find herself in what appeared to be the embrace of an impetuous overcoat, which wrapped her close for an instant, then vanished as suddenly as it had come, leaving her to hide in the sanctum and confide to Psyche with a tender sort of triumph in her breathless voice: "No, no, it isn't genius that must be love!"

## Chapter 19 BEHIND THE FOUNTAIN

Two days after Christmas a young man of serious aspect might have been seen entering one of the large churches at L——. Being shown to a seat, he joined in the services with praiseworthy devotion, especially the music, to which he listened with such evident pleasure that a gentleman who sat nearby felt moved to address this appreciative stranger after church.

"Fine sermon today. Ever heard our minister before, sir?" he began, as they went down the aisle together among the last, for the young man had lingered as if admiring the ancient building.

"Very fine. No, sir, I have never had that pleasure. I've often wished to see this old place, and am not at all disappointed. Your choir, too, is unusually good," answered the stranger, glancing up at several bonnets bobbing about behind the half-drawn curtains above.

"Finest in the city, sir. We pride ourselves on our music, and always have the best. People often come for that alone." And the old gentleman looked as satisfied as if a choir of cherubim and seraphim "continually did cry" in his organ loft.

"Who is the contralto? That solo was beautifully sung," observed the younger man, pausing to read a tablet on the wall.

"That is Miss Moore. Been here about a year, and is universally admired. Excellent young lady couldn't do without her. Sings superbly in oratorios. Ever heard her?"

"Never. She came from X, I believe?

"Yes, highly recommended. She was brought up by one of the first families there. Campbell is the name. If you come from X, you doubtless know them."

"I have met them. Good morning." And with bows the gentlemen parted, for at that instant the young man caught sight of a tall lady going down the church steps with a devout expression in her fine eyes and a prayer-book in her hand.

Hastening after her, the serious-minded young man accosted her just as she turned into a quiet street.

"Phebe!"

Only a word, but it wrought a marvelous change, for the devout expression vanished in the drawing of a breath, and the quiet face blossomed suddenly with color, warmth, and "the light that never was on sea or land" as she turned to meet her lover with an answering word as eloquent as his.

"Archie!"

"The year is out today. I told you I should come. Have you forgotten?"

"No I knew you'd come."

"And are you glad?"

"How can I help it?"

"You can't don't try. Come into this little park and let us talk." And drawing her hand through his arm, Archie led her into what to other eyes was a very dismal square, with a boarded-up fountain in the middle, sodden grass plots, and dead leaves dancing in the wintry wind.

But to them it was a summery Paradise, and they walked to and fro in the pale sunshine, quite unconscious they were objects of interest to several ladies and gentlemen waiting anxiously for their dinner or yawning over the dull books kept for Sunday reading. "Are you ready to come home now, Phebe?" asked Archie tenderly as he looked at the downcast face beside him and wondered why all women did not wear delightful little black velvet bonnets with one deep red flower against their hair.

"Not yet. I haven't done enough," began Phebe, finding it very hard to keep the resolution made a year ago.

"You have proved that you can support yourself, make friends, and earn a name, if you choose. No one can deny that, and we are all getting proud of you. What more can you ask, my dearest?"

"I don't quite know, but I am very ambitious. I want to be famous, to do something for you all, to make some sacrifice for Rose, and, if I can, to have something to give up for your sake. Let me wait and work longer I know I haven't earned my welcome yet," pleaded Phebe so earnestly that her lover knew it would be in vain to try and turn her, so wisely contented himself with half, since he could not have the whole.

"Such a proud woman! Yet I love you all the better for it, and understand your feeling. Rose made me see how it seems to you, and I don't wonder that you cannot forget the unkind things that were looked, if not said, by some of my amiable aunts. I'll try to be patient on one condition, Phebe."

"And what is that?"

"You are to let me come sometimes while I wait, and wear this lest you should forget me," he said, pulling a ring from his pocket and gently drawing a warm, bare hand out of the muff where it lay hidden.

"Yes, Archie, but not here not now!" cried Phebe, glancing about her as if suddenly aware that they were not alone.

"No one can see us here I thought of that. Give me one happy minute, after this long, long year of waiting," answered Archie, pausing just where the fountain hid them from all eyes, for there were houses only on one side.

Phebe submitted and never did a plain gold ring slip more easily to its place than the one he put on in such a hurry that cold December day. Then one hand went back into the muff red with the grasp he gave it, and the other to its old place on his arm with a confiding gesture, as if it had a right there.

"Now I feel sure of you," said Archie as they went on again, and no one the wiser for that tender transaction behind the ugly pyramid of boards. "Mac wrote me that you were much admired by your church people, and that certain wealthy bachelors evidently had designs on the retiring Miss Moore. I was horribly jealous, but now I defy every man of them."

Phebe smiled with the air of proud humility that was so becoming and answered briefly: "There was no danger kings could not change me, whether you ever came or not. But Mac should not have told you."

"You shall be revenged on him, then, for, as he told secrets about you, I'll tell you one about him. Phebe, he loves Rose!" And Archie looked as if he expected to make a great sensation with his news.

"I know it." And Phebe laughed at his sudden change of countenance as he added inquiringly, "She told you, then?"

"Not a word. I guessed it from her letters, for lately she says nothing about Mac, and before there was a good deal, so I suspected what the silence meant and asked no questions."

"Wise girl! Then you think she does care for the dear old fellow?"

"Of course she does. Didn't he tell you so?"

"No, he only said when he went away, 'Take care of my Rose, and I'll take care of your Phebe,' and not another thing could I get out of him, for I did ask questions. He stood by me like a hero, and kept Aunt Jane from driving me stark mad with her 'advice.' I don't forget that, and burned to lend him a hand somewhere, but he begged me to let him manage his wooing in his own way. And from what I see, I should say he knew how to do it," added Archie, finding it very delightful to gossip about love affairs with his sweetheart.

"Dear little mistress! How does she behave?" asked Phebe, longing for news, but too grateful to ask at headquarters, remembering how generously Rose had tried to help her, even by silence, the greatest sacrifice a woman can make at such interesting periods.

"Very sweet and shy and charming. I try not to watch but upon my word I cannot help it sometimes, she is so 'cunning,' as you girls say. When I carry her a letter from Mac she tries so hard not to show how glad she is that I want to laugh and tell her I know all about it. But I look as sober as a judge and as stupid as an owl by daylight, and she enjoys her letters in peace and thinks I'm so absorbed in my own passion that I'm blind to hers."

"But why did Mac come away? He says lectures brought him, and he goes, but I am sure something else is in his mind, he looks so happy at times. I don't see him very often, but when I do I'm conscious that he isn't the Mac I left a year ago," said Phebe, leading Archie away, for inexorable propriety forbade a longer stay, even if prudence and duty had not given her a reminding nudge, as it was very cold, and afternoon church came in an hour.

"Well, you see Mac was always peculiar, and he cannot even grow up like other fellows. I don't understand him yet, and am sure he's got some plan in his head that no one suspects, unless it is Uncle Alec. Love makes us all cut queer capers, and I've an idea that the Don will distinguish himself in some uncommon way. So be prepared to applaud whatever it is. We owe him that, you know."

"Indeed we do! If Rose ever speaks of him to you, tell her I shall see that he comes to no harm, and she must do the same for my Archie."

That unusual demonstration of tenderness from reserved Phebe very naturally turned the conversation into a more personal channel, and Archie devoted himself to building castles in the air so successfully that they passed the material mansion without either being aware of it.

"Will you come in?" asked Phebe when the mistake was rectified and she stood on her own steps looking down at her escort, who had discreetly released her before a pull at the bell caused five heads to pop up at five different windows.

"No, thanks. I shall be at church this afternoon, and the oratorio this evening. I must be off early in the morning, so let me make the most of precious time and come home with you tonight as I did before," answered Archie, making his best bow, and quite sure of consent.

"You may." And Phebe vanished, closing the door softly, as if she found it hard to shut out so much love and happiness as that in the heart of the sedate young gentleman who went briskly down the street humming a verse of old "Clyde" like a tuneful bass viol:

"Oh, let our mingling voices rise
In grateful rapture to the skies,
Where love has had its birth.

Let songs of joy this day declare
That spirits come their bliss to share
With all the sons of earth."

That afternoon Miss Moore sang remarkably well, and that evening quite electrified even her best friends by the skill and power with which she rendered "Inflammatus" in the oratorio.

"If that is not genius, I should like to know what it is?" said one young man to another as they went out just before the general crush at the end.

"Some genius and a great deal of love. They are a grand team, and, when well driven, astonish the world by the time they make in the great race," answered the second young man with the look of one inclined to try his hand at driving that immortal span.

"Daresay you are right. Can't stop now she's waiting for me. Don't sit up, Mac."

"The gods go with you, Archie."

And the cousins separated one to write till midnight, the other to bid his Phebe good-bye, little dreaming how unexpectedly and successfully she was to earn her welcome home.

Chapter 20 WHAT MAC DID
Rose, meantime, was trying to find out what the sentiment was with which she regarded her cousin Mac. She could not seem to reconcile the character she had known so long with the new one lately shown her, and the idea of loving the droll, bookish, absentminded Mac of former times appeared quite impossible and absurd, but the new Mac, wide awake, full of talent, ardent and high-handed, was such a surprise to her, she felt as if her heart was being won by a stranger, and it became her to study him well before yielding to a charm which she could not deny.

Affection came naturally, and had always been strong for the boy; regard for the studious youth easily deepened to respect for the integrity of the young man, and now something warmer was growing up within her; but at first she could not decide whether it was admiration for the rapid unfolding of talent of some sort or love answering to love.

As if to settle that point, Mac sent her on New Year's Day a little book plainly bound and modestly entitled Songs and Sonnets. After reading this with ever-growing surprise and delight, Rose never had another doubt about the writer's being a poet, for though she was no critic, she had read the best authors and knew what was good. Unpretentious as it was, this had the true ring, and its very simplicity showed conscious power for, unlike so many first attempts, the book was not full of "My Lady," neither did it indulge in Swinburnian convulsions about

> "The lilies and languors of peace,
> The roses and raptures of love.";

or contain any of the highly colored medieval word pictures so much in vogue. "My book should smell of pines, and resound with the hum of insects," might have been its motto, so sweet and wholesome was it with a springlike sort of freshness which plainly betrayed that the author had learned some of Nature's deepest secrets and possessed the skill to tell them in tuneful words. The songs went ringing through one's memory long after they were read, and the sonnets were full of the subtle beauty, insight, and half-unconscious wisdom, which seem to prove that "genius is divine when young."

Many faults it had, but was so full of promise that it was evident Mac had not "kept good company, read good books, loved good things, and cultivated soul and body as faithfully as he could" in vain. It all told now, for truth and virtue had blossomed into character and had a language of their own more eloquent than the poetry to which they were what the fragrance is to the flower. Wiser critics than Rose felt and admired this; less partial ones could not deny their praise to a first effort, which seemed as spontaneous and aspiring as a lark's song; and, when one or two of these Jupiters had given a nod of approval, Mac found himself, not exactly famous, but much talked about. One set abused, the other set praised, and the little book was sadly mauled among them, for it was too original to be ignored, and too robust to be killed by hard usage, so it came out of the fray none the worse but rather brighter, if anything, for the friction which proved the gold genuine.

This took time, however, and Rose could only sit at home reading all the notices she could get, as well as the literary gossip Phebe sent her, for Mac seldom wrote, and never a word about himself, so Phebe skillfully extracted from him in their occasional meetings all the personal news her feminine wit could collect and faithfully reported it.

It was a little singular that without a word of inquiry on either side, the letters of the girls were principally filled with tidings of their respective lovers. Phebe wrote about Mac; Rose answered with minute particulars about Archie; and both added hasty items concerning their own affairs, as if these were of little consequence.

Phebe got the most satisfaction out of the correspondence, for soon after the book appeared Rose began to want Mac home again and to be rather jealous of the new duties and delights that kept him. She was immensely proud of her poet, and had little jubilees over the beautiful fulfillment of her prophecies, for even Aunt Plenty owned now with contrition that "the boy was not a fool." Every word of praise was read aloud on the housetops, so to speak, by happy Rose; every adverse criticism was hotly disputed; and the whole family was in a great state of pleasant excitement over this unexpectedly successful first flight of the Ugly Duckling, now generally considered by his relatives as the most promising young swan of the flock.

Aunt Jane was particularly funny in her new position of mother to a callow poet and conducted herself like a proud but bewildered hen when one of her brood takes to the water. She pored over the poems, trying to appreciate them but quite failing to do so, for life was all prose to her, and she vainly tried to discover where Mac got his talent from. It was pretty to see the new respect with which she treated his possessions now; the old books were dusted with a sort of reverence; scraps of paper were laid carefully by lest some immortal verse be lost; and a certain shabby velvet jacket fondly smoothed when no one was by to smile at the maternal pride with filled her heart and caused her once severe countenance to shine with unwonted benignity.

Uncle Mac talked about "my son" with ill-concealed satisfaction, and evidently began to feel as if his boy was going to confer distinction upon the whole race of Campbell, which had already possessed one poet. Steve exulted with irrepressible delight and went about quoting Songs and Sonnets till he bored his friends dreadfully by his fraternal raptures.

Archie took it more quietly, and even suggested that it was too soon to crow yet, for the dear old fellow's first burst might be his last, since it was impossible to predict what he would do next. Having proved that he could write poetry, he might drop it for some new world to conquer, quoting his favorite Thoreau, who, having made a perfect pencil, gave up the business and took to writing books with the sort of indelible ink which grows clearer with time.

The aunts of course had their "views," and enjoyed much prophetic gossip as they wagged their caps over many social cups of tea. The younger boys thought it "very jolly," and hoped the Don would "go ahead and come to glory as soon as possible," which was all that could by expected of "Young America," with whom poetry is not usually a passion.

But Dr. Alec was a sight for "sair een," so full of concentrated contentment was he. No one but Rose, perhaps, knew how proud and pleased the good man felt at this first small success of his godson, for he had always had high hopes of the boy, because in spite of his oddities he had such an upright nature, and promising little, did much, with the quiet persistence which foretells a manly character. All the romance of the doctor's heart was stirred by this poetic bud of promise and the love that made it bloom so early, for Mac had confided his hopes to Uncle, finding great consolation and support in his sympathy and advice. Like a wise man, Dr. Alec left the young people to learn the great lesson in their own way, counseling Mac to work and Rose to wait till both were quite certain that their love was built on a surer foundation than admiration or youthful romance.

Meantime he went about with a well-worn little book in his pocket, humming bits from a new set of songs and repeating with great fervor certain sonnets which seemed to him quite equal, if not superior, to any that Shakespeare ever wrote. As Rose was doing the same thing, they often met for a private "read and warble," as they called it, and while discussing the safe subject of Mac's poetry, both arrived at a pretty clear idea of what Mac's reward was to be when he came home.

He seemed in no hurry to do this, however, and continued to astonish his family by going into society and coming out brilliantly in that line. It takes very little to make a lion, as everyone knows who has seen what poor specimens are patted and petted every year, in spite of their bad manners, foolish vagaries, and very feeble roaring. Mac did not want to be lionized and took it rather scornfully, which only added to the charm that people suddenly discovered about the nineteenth cousin of Thomas Campbell, the poet. He desired to be distinguished in the best sense of the word, as well as to look so, and thought a little of the polish society gives would not be amiss, remembering Rose's efforts in that line. For her sake he came out of his shell and went about seeing and testing all sorts of people with those observing eyes of his, which saw so much in spite of their nearsightedness. What use he meant to make of these new experiences no one knew, for he wrote short letters and, when questioned, answered with imperturbable patience: "Wait till I get through; then I'll come home and talk about it."

So everyone waited for the poet, till something happened which produced a greater sensation in the family than if all the boys had simultaneously taken to rhyming.

Dr. Alec got very impatient and suddenly announced that he was going to L to see after those young people, for Phebe was rapidly singing herself into public favor with the sweet old ballads which she rendered so beautifully that hearers were touched as well as ears delighted, and her prospects brightened every month.

"Will you come with me, Rose, and surprise this ambitious pair who are getting famous so fast they'll forget their homekeeping friends if we don't remind them of us now and then?" he said when he proposed the trip one wild March morning.

"No, thank you, sir I'll stay with Aunty; that is all I'm fit for and I should only be in the way among those fine people," answered Rose, snipping away at the plants blooming in the study window.

There was a slight bitterness in her voice and a cloud on her face, which her uncle heard and saw at once, half guessed the meaning of, and could not rest till he had found out.

"Do you think Phebe and Mac would not care to see you?" he asked, putting down a letter in which Mac gave a glowing account of a concert at which Phebe surpassed herself.

"No, but they must be very busy," began Rose, wishing she had held her tongue.

"Then what is the matter?" persisted Dr. Alec.

Rose did not speak for a moment, and decapitated two fine geraniums with a reckless slash of her scissors, as if pent-up vexation of some kind must find a vent. It did in words also, for, as if quite against her will, she exclaimed impetuously: "The truth is, I'm jealous of them both!"

"Bless my soul! What now?" ejaculated the doctor in great surprise.

Rose put down her water pot and shears, came and stood before him with her hands nervously twisted together, and said, just as she used to do when she was a little girl confessing some misdeed: "Uncle, I must tell you, for I've been getting very envious, discontented, and bad lately. No, don't be good to me yet, for you don't know how little I deserve it. Scold me well, and make me see how wicked I am."

"I will as soon as I know what I am to scold about. Unburden yourself, child, and let me see all your iniquity, for if you begin by being jealous of Mac and Phebe, I'm prepared for anything," said Dr. Alec, leaning back as if nothing could surprise him now.

"But I am not jealous in that way, sir. I mean I want to be or do something splendid as well as they. I can't write poetry or sing like a bird, but I should think I might have my share of glory in some way. I thought perhaps I could paint, and I've tried, but I can only copy I've no power to invent lovely things, and I'm so discouraged, for that is my one accomplishment. Do you think I have any gift that could be cultivated and do me credit like theirs?" she asked so wistfully that her uncle felt for a moment as if he never could forgive the fairies who endow babies in their cradles for being so niggardly to his girl. But one look into the sweet, open face before him reminded him that the good elves had been very generous and he answered cheerfully: "Yes, I do, for you have one of the best and noblest gifts a woman can possess. Music and poetry are fine things, and I don't wonder you want them, or that you envy the pleasant fame they bring. I've felt just so, and been ready to ask why it didn't please heaven to be more generous to some people, so you needn't be ashamed to tell me all about it."

"I know I ought to be contented, but I'm not. My life is very comfortable, but so quiet and uneventful, I get tired of it and want to launch out as the others have, and do something, or at least try. I'm glad you think it isn't very bad of me, and I'd like to know what my gift is," said Rose, looking less despondent already.

"The art of living for others so patiently and sweetly that we enjoy it as we do the sunshine, and are not half grateful enough for the great blessing."

"It is very kind of you to say so, but I think I'd like a little fun and fame nevertheless." And Rose did not look as thankful as she ought.

"Very natural, dear, but the fun and the fame do not last, while the memory of a real helper is kept green long after poetry is forgotten and music silent. Can't you believe that, and be happy?"

"But I do so little, nobody sees or cares, and I don't feel as if I was really of any use," sighed Rose, thinking of the long, dull winter, full of efforts that seemed fruitless.

"Sit here, and let us see if you really do very little and if no one cares." And, drawing her to his knee, Dr. Alec went on, telling off each item on one of the fingers of the soft hand he held.

"First, an infirm old aunt is kept very happy by the patient, cheerful care of this good-for-nothing niece. Secondly, a crotchety uncle, for whom she reads, runs, writes, and sews so willingly that he cannot get on without her. Thirdly, various relations who are helped in various ways. Fourthly, one dear friend never forgotten, and a certain cousin cheered by praise which is more to him than the loudest blast Fame could blow. Fifthly, several young girls find her an example of many good works and ways. Sixthly, a motherless baby is cared for as tenderly as if she were a little sister. Seventhly, half a dozen poor ladies made comfortable; and, lastly, some struggling boys and girls with artistic longings are put into a pleasant room furnished with casts, studies, easels, and all manner of helpful things, not to mention free lessons given by this same idle girl, who now sits upon my knee owning to herself that her gift is worth having after all."

"Indeed, I am! Uncle, I'd no idea I had done so many things to please you, or that anyone guessed how hard I try to fill my place usefully. I've learned to do without gratitude now I'll learn not to care for praise, but to be contented to do my best, and have only God know."

"He knows, and He rewards in His own good time. I think a quiet life like this often makes itself felt in better ways than one that the world sees and applauds, and some of the noblest are never known till they end, leaving a void in many hearts. Yours may be one of these if you choose to make it so, and no one will be prouder of this success than I, unless it be Mac."

The clouds were quite gone now, and Rose was looking straight into her uncle's face with a much happier expression when that last word made it color brightly and the eyes glance away for a second. Then they came back full of a tender sort of resolution as she said: "That will be the reward I work for," and rose, as if ready to be up and doing with renewed courage.

But her uncle held her long enough to ask quite soberly, though his eyes laughed: "Shall I tell him that?"

"No, sir, please don't! When he is tired of other people's praise, he will come home, and then I'll see what I can do for him," answered Rose, slipping away to her work with the shy, happy look that sometimes came to give to her face the charm it needed.

"He is such a thorough fellow, he never is in a hurry to go from one thing to another. An excellent habit, but a trifle trying to impatient people like me," said the doctor and, picking up Dulce, who sat upon the rug with her dolly, he composed his feelings by tossing her till she crowed with delight.

Rose heartily echoed that last remark, but said nothing aloud, only helped her uncle off with dutiful alacrity and, when he was gone, began to count the days till his return, wishing she had decided to go too.

He wrote often, giving excellent accounts of the "great creatures," as Steve called Phebe and Mac, and seemed to find so much to do in various ways that the second week of absence was nearly over before he set a day for his return, promising to astonish them with the account of his adventures.

Rose felt as if something splendid was going to happen and set her affairs in order so that the approaching crisis might find her fully prepared. She had "found out" now, was quite sure, and put away all doubts and fears to be ready to welcome home the cousin whom she was sure Uncle would bring as her reward. She was thinking of this one day as she got out her paper to write a long letter to poor Aunt Clara, who pined for news far away there in Calcutta.

Something in the task reminded her of that other lover whose wooing ended so tragically, and opening a little drawer of keepsakes, she took out the blue bracelet, feeling that she owed Charlie a tender thought in the midst of her new happiness, for of late she had forgotten him.

She had worn the trinket hidden under her black sleeve for a long time after his death, with the regretful constancy one sometimes shows in doing some little kindness all too late. But her arm had grown too round to hide the ornament, the forget-me-nots had fallen one by one, the clasp had broken, and that autumn she laid the bracelet away, acknowledging that she had outgrown the souvenir as well as the sentiment that gave it.

She looked at it in silence for a moment, then put it softly back and, shutting the drawer, took up the little gray book which was her pride, thinking as she contrasted the two men and their influence on her life the one sad and disturbing, the other sweet and inspiring "Charlie's was passion Mac's is love."

"Rose! Rose!" called a shrill voice, rudely breaking the pensive reverie, and with a start, she shut the desk, exclaiming as she ran to the door: "They have come! They have come!"


Chapter 21 HOW PHEBE EARNED HER WELCOME

Dr. Alec had not arrived, but bad tidings had, as Rose guessed the instant her eyes fell upon Aunt Plenty, hobbling downstairs with her cap awry, her face pale, and a letter flapping wildly in her hand as she cried distractedly: "Oh, my boy! My boy! Sick, and I not there to nurse him! Malignant fever, so far away. What can those children do? Why did I let Alec go?"

Rose got her into the parlor, and while the poor old lady lamented, she read the letter which Phebe had sent to her that she might "break the news carefully to Rose."

DEAR MISS PLENTY, Please read this to yourself first, and tell my little mistress as you think best. The dear doctor is very ill, but I am with him, and shall not leave him day or night till he is safe. So trust me, and do not be anxious, for everything shall be done that care and skill and entire devotion can do. He would not let us tell you before, fearing you would try to come at the risk of your health. Indeed it would be useless, for only one nurse is needed, and I came first, so do not let Rose or anybody else rob me of my right to the danger and the duty. Mac has written to his father, for Dr. Alec is now too ill to know what we do, and we both felt that you ought to be told without further delay. He has a bad malignant fever, caught no one can tell how, unless among some poor emigrants whom he met wandering about quite forlorn in a strange city. He understood Portuguese and sent them to a proper place when they had told their story. But I fear he has suffered for his kindness, for this fever came on rapidly, and before he knew what it was I was there, and it was too late to send me away.

Now I can show you how grateful I am, and if need be give my life so gladly for this friend who has been a father to me. Tell Rose his last conscious word and thought were for her. "Don't let her come; keep my darling safe." Oh, do obey him! Stay safely at home and, God helping me, I'll bring Uncle Alec back in time. Mac does all I will let him. We have the best physicians, and everything is going as well as can be hoped till the fever turns.

Dear Miss Plenty, pray for him and for me, that I may do this one happy thing for those who have done so much for Your ever dutiful and loving

PHEBE

As Rose looked up from the letter, half stunned by the sudden news and the great danger, she found that the old lady had already stopped useless bewailing and was praying heartily, like one who knew well where help was to be found. Rose went and knelt down at her knee, laying her face on the clasped hands in her lap, and for a few minutes neither wept nor spoke. Then a stifled sob broke from the girl, and Aunt Plenty gathered the young head in her arms, saying, with the slow tears of age trickling down her own withered cheeks: "Bear up, my lamb, bear up. The good Lord won't take him from us I am sure and that brave child will be allowed to pay her debt to him. I feel she will."

"But I want to help. I must go, Aunty, I must no matter what the danger is," cried Rose, full of a tender jealousy of Phebe for being first to brave peril for the sake of him who had been a father to them both.

"You can't go, dear, it's no use now, and she is right to say, 'Keep away.' I know those fevers, and the ones who nurse often take it, and fare worse for the strain they've been through. Good girl to stand by so bravely, to be so sensible, and not let Mac go too near! She's a grand nurse Alec couldn't have a better, and she'll never leave him till he's safe," said Miss Plenty excitedly.

"Ah, you begin to know her now, and value her as you ought. I think few would have done as she has, and if she does get ill and die, it will be our fault partly, because she'd go through fire and water to make us do her justice and receive her as we ought," cried Rose, proud of an example which she longed to follow.

"If she brings my boy home, I'll never say another word. She may marry every nephew I've got, if she likes, and I'll give her my blessing," exclaimed Aunt Plenty, feeling that no price would be too much to pay for such a deed.

Rose was going to clap her hands, but wrung them instead, remembering with a sudden pang that the battle was not over yet, and it was much too soon to award the honors.

Before she could speak Uncle Mac and Aunt Jane hurried in, for Mac's letter had come with the other, and dismay fell upon the family at the thought of danger to the well-beloved Uncle Alec. His brother decided to go at once, and Aunt Jane insisted on accompanying him, though all agreed that nothing could be done but wait, and leave Phebe at her post as long as she held out, since it was too late to save her from danger now and Mac reported her quite equal to the task.

Great was the hurry and confusion till the relief party was off. Aunt Plenty was heartbroken that she could not go with them, but felt that she was too infirm to be useful and, like a sensible old soul, tried to content herself with preparing all sorts of comforts for the invalid. Rose was less patient, and at first had wild ideas of setting off alone and forcing her way to the spot where all her thoughts now centered. But before she could carry out any rash project, Aunt Myra's palpitations set in so alarmingly that they did good service for once and kept Rose busy taking her last directions and trying to soothe her dying bed, for each attack was declared fatal till the patient demanded toast and tea, when hope was again allowable and the rally began.

The news flew fast, as such tidings always do, and Aunt Plenty was constantly employed in answering inquiries, for her knocker kept up a steady tattoo for several days. All sorts of people came: gentlefolk and paupers, children with anxious little faces, old people full of sympathy, pretty girls sobbing as they went away, and young men who relieved their feelings by swearing at all emigrants in general and Portuguese in particular. It was touching and comforting to see how many loved the good man who was known only by his benefactions and now lay suffering far away, quite unconscious how many unsuspected charities were brought to light by this grateful solicitude as hidden flowers spring up when warm rains fall.

If Rose had ever felt that the gift of living for others was a poor one, she saw now how beautiful and blessed it was how rich the returns, how wide the influence, how much more precious the tender tie which knit so many hearts together than any breath of fame or brilliant talent that dazzled but did not win and warm. In after years she found how true her uncle's words had been and, listening to eulogies of great men, felt less moved and inspired by praises of their splendid gifts than by the sight of some good man's patient labor for the poorest of his kind. Her heroes ceased to be the world's favorites and became such as Garrison fighting for his chosen people; Howe restoring lost senses to the deaf, the dumb, and blind; Sumner unbribable, when other men were bought and sold and many a large-hearted woman working as quietly as Abby Gibbons, who for thirty years had made Christmas merry for two hundred little paupers in a city almshouse, besides saving Magdalens and teaching convicts.

The lesson came to Rose when she was ready for it, and showed her what a noble profession philanthropy is, made her glad of her choice, and helped fit her for a long life full of the loving labor and sweet satisfaction unostentatious charity brings to those who ask no reward and are content if "only God knows."

Several anxious weeks went by with wearing fluctuations of hope and fear, for Life and Death fought over the prize each wanted, and more than once Death seemed to have won. But Phebe stood at her post, defying both danger and Death with the courage and devotion women often show. All her soul and strength were in her work, and when it seemed most hopeless, she cried out with the passionate energy which seems to send such appeals straight up to heaven: "Grant me this one boon, dear Lord, and I will never ask another for myself!"

Such prayers avail much, and such entire devotion often seems to work miracles when other aids are in vain. Phebe's cry was answered, her self-forgetful task accomplished, and her long vigil rewarded with a happy dawn. Dr. Alec always said that she kept him alive by the force of her will, and that, during the hours when he seemed to lie unconscious, he felt a strong, warm hand holding his, as if keeping him away from the swift current trying to sweep him away. The happiest hour of all her life was that in which he knew her, looked up with the shadow of a smile in his hollow eyes, and tried to say in his old cheery way: "Tell Rose I've turned the corner, thanks to you, my child."

She answered very quietly, smoothed the pillow, and saw him drop asleep again before she stole away into the other room, meaning to write the good news, but could only throw herself down and find relief for a full heart in the first tears she had shed for weeks. Mac found her there, and took such care of her that she was ready to go back to her place now indeed a post of honor while he ran off to send home a telegram which made many hearts sing for joy and caused Jamie, in his first burst of delight, to propose to ring all the city bells and order out the cannon: "Saved thanks to God and Phebe."

That was all, but everyone was satisfied, and everyone fell a-crying, as if hope needed much salty water to strengthen it. That was soon over, however, and then people went about smiling and saying to one another, with handshakes or embraces, "He is better no doubt of it now!" A general desire to rush away and assure themselves of the truth pervaded the family for some days, and nothing but awful threats from Mac, stern mandates from the doctor, and entreaties from Phebe not to undo her work kept Miss Plenty, Rose, and Aunt Jessie at home.

As the only way in which they could ease their minds and bear the delay, they set about spring cleaning with an energy which scared the spiders and drove charwomen distracted. If the old house had been infected with smallpox, it could not have been more vigorously scrubbed, aired, and refreshed. Early as it was, every carpet was routed up, curtains pulled down, cushions banged, and glory holes turned out till not a speck of dust, a last year's fly, or stray straw could be found. Then they all sat down and rested in such an immaculate mansion that one hardly dared to move for fear of destroying the shining order everywhere visible.

It was late in April before this was accomplished, and the necessary quarantine of the absentees well over. The first mild days seemed to come early, so that Dr. Alec might return with safety from the journey which had so nearly been his last. It was perfectly impossible to keep any member of the family away on that great occasion. They came from all quarters in spite of express directions to the contrary, for the invalid was still very feeble and no excitement must be allowed. As if the wind carried the glad news, Uncle Jem came into port the night before; Will and Geordie got a leave on their own responsibility; Steve would have defied the entire faculty, had it been necessary; and Uncle Mac and Archie said simultaneously, "Business be hanged today."

Of course the aunts arrived in all their best, all cautioning everybody else to keep quiet and all gabbling excitedly at the least provocation. Jamie suffered the most during that day, so divided was he between the desire to behave well and the frantic impulse to shout at the top of his voice, turn somersaults, and race all over the house. Occasional bolts into the barn, where he let off steam by roaring and dancing jigs, to the great dismay of the fat old horses and two sedate cows, helped him to get through that trying period.

But the heart that was fullest beat and fluttered in Rose's bosom as she went about putting spring flowers everywhere; very silent, but so radiant with happiness that the aunts watched her, saying softly to one another, "Could an angel look sweeter?"

If angels ever wore pale green gowns and snowdrops in their hair, had countenances full of serenest joy, and large eyes shining with an inward light that made them very lovely, then Rose did look like one. But she felt like a woman and well she might, for was not life very rich that day, when Uncle, friend, and lover were coming back to her together? Could she ask anything more, except the power to be to all of them the creature they believed her, and to return the love they gave her with one as faithful, pure, and deep? Among the portraits in the hall hung one of Dr. Alec, done soon after his return by Charlie in one of his brief fits of inspiration. Only a crayon, but wonderfully lifelike and carefully finished, as few of the others were. This had been handsomely framed and now held the place of honor, garlanded with green wreaths, while the great Indian jar below blazed with a pyramid of hothouse flowers sent by Kitty. Rose was giving these a last touch, with Dulce close by, cooing over a handful of sweet "daffydowndillies," when the sound of wheels sent her flying to the door. She meant to have spoken the first welcome and had the first embrace, but when she saw the altered face in the carriage, the feeble figure being borne up the steps by all the boys, she stood motionless till Phebe caught her in her arms, whispering with a laugh and a cry struggling in her voice: "I did it for you, my darling, all for you!"

"Oh, Phebe, never say again you owe me anything! I never can repay you for this," was all Rose had time to answer as they stood one instant cheek to cheek, heart to heart, both too full of happiness for many words.

Aunt Plenty had heard the wheels also and, as everybody rose en masse, had said as impressively as extreme agitation would allow, while she put her glasses on upside down and seized a lace tidy instead of her handkerchief: "Stop! All stay here, and let me receive Alec. Remember his weak state, and be calm, quite calm, as I am.'

"Yes, Aunt, certainly," was the general murmur of assent, but it was as impossible to obey as it would have been to keep feathers still in a gale, and one irresistible impulse carried the whole roomful into the hall to behold Aunt Plenty beautifully illustrating her own theory of composure by waving the tidy wildly, rushing into Dr. Alec's arms, and laughing and crying with a hysterical abandonment which even Aunt Myra could not have surpassed.

The tearful jubilee was soon over, however, and no one seemed the worse for it, for the instant his arms were at liberty, Dr. Alec forgot himself and began to make other people happy by saying seriously, though his thin face beamed paternally, as he drew Phebe forward: "Aunt Plenty, but for this good daughter I never should have come back to be so welcomed. Love her for my sake."

Then the old lady came out splendidly and showed her mettle, for, turning to Phebe, she bowed her gray head as if saluting an equal and, offering her hand, answered with repentance, admiration, and tenderness trembling in her voice: "I'm proud to do it for her own sake. I ask pardon for my silly prejudices, and I'll prove that I'm sincere by where's that boy?"

There were six boys present, but the right one was in exactly the right place at the right moment, and, seizing Archie's hand, Aunt Plenty put Phebe's into it, trying to say something appropriately solemn, but could not, so hugged them both and sobbed out: "If I had a dozen nephews, I'd give them all to you, my dear, and dance at the wedding, though I had rheumatism in every limb."

That was better than any oration, for it set them all to laughing, and Dr. Alec was floated to the sofa on a gentle wave of merriment. Once there, everyone but Rose and Aunt Plenty was ordered off by Mac, who was in command now and seemed to have sunk the poet in the physician.

"The house must be perfectly quiet, and he must go to sleep as soon as possible after the journey, so all say 'good-bye' now and call again tomorrow," he said, watching his uncle anxiously as he leaned in the sofa corner, with four women taking off his wraps, three boys contending for his overshoes, two brothers shaking hands at short intervals, and Aunt Myra holding a bottle of strong salts under his devoted nose every time there was an opening anywhere.

With difficulty the house was partially cleared, and then, while Aunt Plenty mounted guard over her boy, Rose stole away to see if Mac had gone with the rest, for as yet they had hardly spoken in the joyful flurry, though eyes and hands had met.

Chapter 22 SHORT AND SWEET
In the hall she found Steve and Kitty, for he had hidden his little sweetheart behind the big couch, feeling that she had a right there, having supported his spirits during the late anxiety with great constancy and courage. They seemed so cozy, billing and cooing in the shadow of the gay vase,

that Rose would have slipped silently away if they had not seen and called to her. "He's not gone I guess you'll find him in the parlor," said Steve, divining with a lover's instinct the meaning of the quick look she had cast at the hat rack as she shut the study door behind her.

"Mercy, no! Archie and Phebe are there, so he'd have the sense to pop into the sanctum and wait, unless you'd like me to go and bring him out?" added Kitty, smoothing Rose's ruffled hair and settling the flowers on the bosom where Uncle Alec's head had lain until he fell asleep.

"No, thank you, I'll go to him when I've seen my Phebe. She won't mind me," answered Rose, moving on to the parlor.

"Look here," called Steve, "do advise them to hurry up and all be married at once. We were just ready when Uncle fell ill, and now we cannot wait a day later than the first of May."

"Rather short notice," laughed Rose, looking back with the doorknob in her hand.

"We'll give up all our splendor, and do it as simply as you like, if you will only come too. Think how lovely! Three weddings at once! Do fly round and settle things there's a dear," implored Kitty, whose imagination was fired with this romantic idea.

"How can I, when I have no bridegroom yet?" began Rose, with conscious color in her telltale face.

"Sly creature! You know you've only got to say a word and have a famous one. Una and her lion will be nothing to it," cried Steve, bent on hastening his brother's affair, which was much too dilatory and peculiar for his taste.

"He has been in no haste to come home, and I am in no haste to leave it. Don't wait for me, 'Mr. and Mrs. Harry Walmers, Jr.,' I shall be a year at least making up my mind, so you may lead off as splendidly as you like and I'll profit by your experience." And Rose vanished into the parlor, leaving Steve to groan over the perversity of superior women and Kitty to comfort him by promising to marry him on May Day "all alone."

A very different couple occupied the drawing room, but a happier one, for they had known the pain of separation and were now enjoying the bliss of a reunion which was to last unbroken for their lives. Phebe sat in an easy chair, resting from her labors, pale and thin and worn, but lovelier in Archie's eyes than ever before. It was very evident that he was adoring his divinity, for, after placing a footstool at her feet, he had forgotten to get up and knelt there with his elbow on the arm of her chair, looking like a thirsty man drinking long drafts of the purest water.

"Shall I disturb you if I pass through?" asked Rose, loath to spoil the pretty tableau.

"Not if you stop a minute on the way and congratulate me, Cousin, for she says 'yes' at last!" cried Archie, springing up to go and bring her to the arms Phebe opened as she appeared.

"I knew she would reward your patience and put away her pride when both had been duly tried," said Rose, laying the tired head on her bosom with such tender admiration in her eyes that Phebe had to shake some bright drops from her own before she could reply in a tone of grateful humility that showed how much her heart was touched: "How can I help it, when they are all so kind to me? Any pride would melt away under such praise and thanks and loving wishes as I've had today, for every member of the family has taken pains to welcome me, to express far too much gratitude, and to beg me to be one of you. I needed very little urging, but when Archie's father and mother came and called me 'daughter,' I would have promised anything to show my love for them."

"And him," added Rose, but Archie seemed quite satisfied and kissed the hand he held as if it had been that of a beloved princess while he said with all the pride Phebe seemed to have lost: "Think what she gives up for me fame and fortune and the admiration of many a better man. You don't know what a splendid prospect she has of becoming one of the sweet singers who are loved and honored everywhere, and all this she puts away for my sake, content to sing for me alone, with no reward but love."

"I am so glad to make a little sacrifice for a great happiness I never shall regret it or think my music lost if it makes home cheerful for my mate. Birds sing sweetest in their own nests, you know." And Phebe bent toward him with a look and gesture which plainly showed how willingly she offered up all ambitious hopes upon the altar of a woman's happy love.

Both seemed to forget that they were not alone, and in a moment they were, for a sudden impulse carried Rose to the door of her sanctum, as if the south wind which seemed to have set in was wafting this little ship also toward the Islands of the Blessed, where the others were safely anchored now.

The room was a blaze of sunshine and a bower of spring freshness and fragrance, for here Rose had let her fancy have free play, and each garland, fern, and flower had its meaning. Mac seemed to have been reading this sweet language of symbols, to have guessed why Charlie's little picture was framed in white roses, why pansies hung about his own, why Psyche was half hidden among feathery sprays of maidenhair, and a purple passion flower lay at Cupid's feet. The last fancy evidently pleased him, for he was smiling over it, and humming to himself as if to beguile his patient waiting, the burden of the air Rose had so often sung to him:

"Bonny lassie, will ye gang, will ye gang To the birks of Aberfeldie?"

"Yes, Mac, anywhere!"

He had not heard her enter, and wheeling around, looked at her with a radiant face as he said, drawing a long breath, "At last! You were so busy over the dear man, I got no word. But I can wait I'm used to it."

Rose stood quite still, surveying him with a new sort of reverence in her eyes, as she answered with a sweet solemnity that made him laugh and redden with the sensitive joy of one to whom praise from her lips was very precious: "You forget that you are not the Mac who went away. I should have run to meet my cousin, but I did not dare to be familiar with the poet whom all begin to honor."

"You like the mixture, then? You know I said I'd try to give you love and poetry together."

"Like it! I'm so glad, so proud, I haven't any words strong and beautiful enough to half express my wonder and my admiration. How could you do it, Mac?" And a whole face full of smiles broke loose as Rose clapped her hands, looking as if she could dance with sheer delight.

"It did itself, up there among the hills, and here with you, or out alone upon the sea. I could write a heavenly poem this very minute, and put you in as Spring you look like her in that green gown with snowdrops in your bonny hair. Rose, am I getting on a little? Does a hint of fame help me nearer to the prize I'm working for? Is your heart more willing to be won?"

He did not stir a step, but looked at her with such intense longing that his glance seemed to draw her nearer like an irresistible appeal, for she went and stood before him, holding out both hands, as if she offered all her little store, as she said with simplest sincerity: "It is not worth so much beautiful endeavor, but if you still want so poor a thing, it is yours."

278

He caught her hands in his and seemed about to take the rest of her, but hesitated for an instant, unable to believe that so much happiness was true.

"Are you sure, Rose very sure? Don't let a momentary admiration blind you I'm not a poet yet, and the best are but mortal men, you know."

"It is not admiration, Mac."

"Nor gratitude for the small share I've taken in saving Uncle? I had my debt to pay, as well as Phebe, and was as glad to risk my life."

"No it is not gratitude."

"Nor pity for my patience? I've only done a little yet, and I am as far as ever from being like your hero. I can work and wait still longer if you are not sure, for I must have all or nothing."

"Oh, Mac! Why will you be so doubtful? You said you'd make me love you, and you've done it. Will you believe me now?" And, with a sort of desperation, she threw herself into his arms, clinging there in eloquent silence while he held her close; feeling, with a thrill of tender triumph, that this was no longer little Rose, but a loving woman, ready to live and die for him.

"Now I'm satisfied!" he said presently, when she lifted up her face, full of maidenly shame at the sudden passion which had carried her out of herself for a moment. "No don't slip away so soon. Let me keep you for one blessed minute and feel that I have really found my Psyche."

"And I my Cupid," answered Rose, laughing, in spite of her emotion, at the idea of Mac in that sentimental character.

He laughed, too, as only a happy lover could, then said, with sudden seriousness: "Sweet soul! Lift up your lamp and look well before it is too late, for I'm no god, only a very faulty man."

"Dear love! I will. But I have no fear, except that you will fly too high for me to follow, because I have no wings."

"You shall live the poetry, and I will write it, so my little gift will celebrate your greater one."

"No you shall have all the fame, and I'll be content to be known only as the poet's wife."

"And I'll be proud to own that my best inspiration comes from the beneficent life of a sweet and noble woman."

"Oh, Mac! We'll work together and try to make the world better by the music and the love we leave behind us when we go."

"Please God, we will!" he answered fervently and, looking at her as she stood there in the spring sunshine, glowing with the tender happiness, high hopes, and earnest purposes that make life beautiful and sacred, he felt that now the last leaf had folded back, the golden heart lay open to the light, and his Rose had bloomed.

Note from the Editor

Odin's Library Classics strives to bring you unedited and unabridged works of classical literature. As such, this is the complete and unabridged version of the original English text unless noted. In some instances, obvious typographical errors have been corrected. This is done to preserve the original text as much as possible. The English language has evolved since the writing and some of the words appear in their original form, or at least the most commonly used form at the time. This is done to protect the original intent of the author, and it is important to preserve the history of the English language.

Taylor Anderson